The
Munch Murders

A Megan Crespi Mystery Novel

Poorly edited!

The MUNCH MURDERS

A Megan Crespi Mystery Novel

Alessandra Comini

SUNSTONE
PRESS

SANTA FE

This book is a work of fiction. Names, characters, places, and incidents are either the product of the author's imagination or used fictionally. Any resemblance to actual events or locales or most persons, living or dead, is entirely coincidental. In the case of some easily recognizable living persons, their pseudonyms have been approved by them.

Sunstone books may be purchased for educational, business, or sales promotional use. For information please write: Special Markets Department, Sunstone Press, P.O. Box 2321, Santa Fe, New Mexico 87504-2321.

Book and cover design › Vicki Ahl
Body typeface › WTC Our Bodini
Printed on acid-free paper
∞
eBook 978-1-61139-448-1

Library of Congress Cataloging-in-Publication Data

Names: Comini, Alessandra, author.
Title: The munch murders : a Megan Crespi mystery novel / by Alessandra
    Comini.
Description: Santa Fe : Sunstone Press, [2016] | Series: Megan Crespi ; 4
Identifiers: LCCN 2015044705 (print) | LCCN 2015047157 (ebook) | ISBN
    9781632931030 (softcover : acid-free paper) | ISBN 9781611394481 ()
Subjects: LCSH: Women art historians--Fiction. | Art
    thefts--Investigation--Fiction. | Murder--Investigation--Fiction. | GSAFD:
    Mystery fiction.
Classification: LCC PS3603.O477 M86 2016 (print) | LCC PS3603.O477 (ebook) |
    DDC 813/.6--dc23
LC record available at http://lccn.loc.gov/2015044705

SUNSTONE PRESS IS COMMITTED TO MINIMIZING OUR ENVIRONMENTAL IMPACT ON THE PLANET.
THE PAPER USED IN THIS BOOK IS FROM RESPONSIBLY MANAGED FORESTS. OUR PRINTER HAS RECEIVED CHAIN OF CUSTODY
(COC) CERTIFICATION FROM: THE FOREST STEWARDSHIP COUNCIL™ (FSC®), PROGRAMME FOR THE ENDORSEMENT OF FOREST
CERTIFICATION™ (PEFC™), AND THE SUSTAINABLE FORESTRY INITIATIVE® (SFI®).
THE FSC® COUNCIL IS A NON-PROFIT ORGANIZATION, PROMOTING THE ENVIRONMENTALLY APPROPRIATE, SOCIALLY BENEFICIAL
AND ECONOMICALLY VIABLE MANAGEMENT OF THE WORLD'S FORESTS. FSC® CERTIFICATION IS RECOGNIZED INTERNATIONALLY
AS A RIGOROUS ENVIRONMENTAL AND SOCIAL STANDARD FOR RESPONSIBLE FOREST MANAGEMENT.

WWW.SUNSTONEPRESS.COM
SUNSTONE PRESS / POST OFFICE BOX 2321 / SANTA FE, NM 87504-2321 /USA
(505) 988-4418 / ORDERS ONLY (800) 243-5644 / FAX (505) 988-1025

To Lili,
who introduced her Scandinavia to me over the decades.

On May 2, 2012 a version of Edvard Munch's iconic painting, *The Scream*, sold in twelve minutes for $119.9 million to an unidentified buyer at a Sotheby's auction in New York.

1

The piercing cry echoed throughout the museum.

Edvard Munch's world-famous icon of angst, *The Scream*, was gone.

"Not again!" moaned the night guard who had discovered the theft and yelled out in disbelief.

In the sudden blackout that had overtaken the museum just seconds before, the guard stared with unbelieving eyes through the darkness at the white wall where the painting had hung in Norway's National Gallery. Where the screaming humanoid on a path enveloped by threatening undulations of strident color had been, the wall was now glaringly bare.

This particular 1893 Munch painting had been stolen from the venerable Oslo museum once before, in 1994. Ten years later another version of *The Scream* had been taken from Oslo's famous Munch Museum. Both stolen paintings had eventually been recovered and security had been substantially upgraded in the two museums. As with the 1911 theft of Leonardo's *Mona Lisa* from the Louvre, *The Scream*'s newfound fame had circled the globe.

And now the daring crime at the National Gallery had been repeated. How could this have happened? It was two o'clock in the morning, but within ten minutes of the guard's reporting the crime and electrical blackout on her cellphone, police with powerful flashlights were fanning out in all directions searching the grounds, gallery rooms, offices, closets, and restrooms. But nothing seemed out of order. Investigation of the basement also yielded nothing.

When the police got to the roof of the building, however, it was a different matter. There they found plentiful evidence of break and entry. A small, incapacitated drone crouching on the roof like a huge mechanical insect explained the electrical jamming that had taken place. All manner of feed lines had been severed and a large glass pane of the skylight had been cut out and laid alongside it. Next to the skylight was a large drop of what looked like oil. A helicopter had obviously hovered just above the roof. The intruders had vanished and with them, still in its frame, *The Scream*.

2

Megan Crespi, retired professor of art history turned detective, was vacationing in Scandinavia at the time of the Munch theft. She was a short, vivacious woman, with dyed brown hair to "match" her eyebrows, and brown eyes friends described as sparkling. Previously, with her expert knowledge of European art at the turn of the last century, she had helped to solve art crimes in Vienna concerning the city's famous trio of painters: Gustav Klimt, Egon Schiele, and Oskar Kokoschka.

This time in Europe, Megan's Danish friend of six decades, Lili Holm, was with her. Tall, slender, with blue eyes, and short blonde hair mixed with white, Lili was only a few months older than Megan. After a brief stay in Copenhagen they intended to drive up to the artists' colony town of Skagen in Jutland at the northern tip of Denmark. Lili had a time-share apartment there and over the years the two friends had made a number of visits to Skagen and its peripatetic sand dunes. After a week there they planned to cross over by ferry to Sweden and drive down to Stockholm where they would once again visit author August Strindberg's final residence.

With them this time was Megan's beloved Maltese, Button. The little white dog had been left at home in Dallas on Megan's previous trips to Europe these past few years, but she had promised herself not to leave him again. The two were well suited to each other. Megan, just turned eighty, had a daily Pilates, treadmill, and weight-lifting routine; twelve-year-old Button took his human for daily walks in search of interesting odors. Odors, not sights, because for the past two years Button had been completely blind: a sudden acquired retina degeneration syndrome referred to as SARDS by his veterinarian Geoff Bratton. This had made it doubly painful for Megan to leave Button behind on her previous art investigation trips.

Lili, who lived in Palo Alto, had flown to Dallas where Megan and Button met with her for a direct flight to Copenhagen. Business class in their SAS flight had been graciously receptive of and regally accepted by the small dog with the angel face and short haircut—purposefully short, unlike the ridiculous long hair of Maltese show dogs.

The Copenhagen Admiral Hotel where they had begun their Scandinavian travels was a pet-friendly one, and since the hotel was right on the water and faced a historic warehouse, plenty of beckoning sites demanded Button's thorough sniffing attention.

While they were still in their hotel room getting dressed for breakfast that sunny June morning, the television news broke the story of a bold theft at Oslo's National Gallery. Edvard Munch's *The Scream* had been stolen. The audacious heist, made with the help of an abandoned drone and a getaway helicopter, had been discovered in the early morning hours. Speaking on behalf of his museum, the agitated director was shown gesticulating in front of the blank wall where the painting had hung.

"Look, Megan!" cried Lili. "Isn't that your friend Erik Jensen?"

Megan, who had been doing Pilates planks on the floor, sat up and stared at the television.

"Oh, yes! That is Erik. Poor man. What a blow to him and to his museum. Terrible about history repeating itself. The same painting was stolen from them in nineteen ninety-four. I think I'll send him a condolence message right now," Megan decided, standing up and going over to her laptop.

"Who do you think would want to steal Munch's *Scream*?" Lili asked after Megan had sent her e-mail.

"Yes, who would want to steal it? It's such a famous painting it could never be offered for sale on the international market. And if it were stolen on behalf of a private collector, he or she could never, ever allow anyone to view it. I just don't think that's very likely."

"Why steal it then?"

"Well one motive would be for a ransom. A very large ransom."

"Oh, was that what the robbers did when they stole the Munch Museum's version of *The Scream* a few years ago?"

"No, oddly enough. In that case no ransom was asked. The thieves were probably trying to sell it to a shady private collector. Did you know that they also took another famous painting during that break-in at the Munch Museum?"

"Oh, I do remember something about that. Wasn't it his *Madonna* they took?"

"Yes," said Megan, "the beautiful dreaming woman with bare torso, long black hair and red halo all set in a swirling background. You know, it was painted seven years before Klimt portrayed his naked Judith of nineteen hundred and one, and I've often wondered if it might have influenced Klimt."

"What happened to Munch's two paintings? Were they found?"

"Yes, but it took two years. Six men were ultimately arrested as having a connection with the crime. Three of them were convicted and sent to prison. Did you know that a witness to the robbery managed to photograph two of the thieves as they ran outdoors with the paintings to their waiting station wagon? You can see the photo on the Internet. Amazing, this modern world we live in."

"So where were the two works found?"

"That has remained very mysterious. Two years after the paintings were stolen it was announced that a 'police operation' had resulted in the recovery of the two works. But no specific details were given."

"Were the paintings damaged?"

"The damage wasn't as bad as had been feared. If I remember correctly, the *Madonna* had two holes in her arm and *The Scream* had some moisture damage, but that's all."

"The Munch Museum must have been relieved by that, at least."

"Oh, yes. One plus was that after the two paintings were stolen, the museum closed for a number of months while a total security upgrade was instituted."

Megan took a sip of her coffee, then continued enthusiastically. "People have been stealing Munch works for a long time. In nineteen-eighty-eight a young soccer player turned crook named Pål Enger stole the artist's famous *Vampire* painting from Oslo's Munch Museum. For that he spent four years in prison. And he was suspected of having been in on the nineteen-ninety-four theft of the National Gallery's version of *The Scream*, but the police couldn't prove it. Now picture this: the two men who broke into the museum left a sarcastic note saying: 'Thanks for the poor security.'"

"Oh, dear, how embarrassing for the museum."

"It certainly was. Now in that case a ransom of one million dollars was demanded. But the Norwegian government refused to pay it. The painting was finally recovered with a sting operation set up by three players: the Norwegian police, Scotland Yard, and the Getty Museum in Los Angeles. A British under-cover man presented himself as an art agent for the Getty Museum which was offering to pay hundreds of thousands of dollars to buy *The Scream* and return it to Oslo. Crazy, of course, but it worked."

"All this is fascinating, but how about going downstairs for breakfast now?" Lili asked gently.

Button was also ready for breakfast so the trio made their way to the sinfully huge buffet offered on the ground floor. All ate to the bursting point and Button had his own little drinking bowl as provided by the hotel.

Their day began with a long visit to Megan's favorite museum in Copenhagen, the Bertel Thorvaldsen Museum, devoted to sculptures by the genial nineteenth-century Danish sculptor who had spent four enriching decades in Rome. After a late lunch, and for Button's benefit, they took a prolonged stroll around the Tivoli Gardens, attended an outdoor concert there, and ended with dinner under a leafy canopy of trees at one of Tivoli's outdoor restaurants—the Nimb Terrasse—just as the sun began to set.

When they returned to their hotel Megan turned her laptop on and checked her e-mails. One caught her eye—it was from Erik Jensen at the Oslo National Gallery. She read its brief text aloud to Lili: "Call me tomorrow, please. Important."

"Well, I guess we know what he wants to talk to you about," said Lili.

"Probably. But you never know with Erik. He has so many irons in the fire, always trying to increase the museum's collections."

Megan had once worked with the exceedingly helpful man when she was doing research for a 1990 book titled *World Impressionism*. The chapter she contributed, "Nordic Luminism and the Scandinavian Recasting of Impressionism," had taken her all over Denmark, Norway, Sweden, and Finland looking at art of the late nineteenth and early twentieth centuries. She was intrigued and gratified by how many of the major artists working then were women.

Although Megan and Lili had been visiting Skagen since the early 1980s, it was only later that they had begun methodically hunting out works and haunts of the various artists. And this was their plan for their latest visit as well.

Before they went to bed—Button had already taken over the foot of Megan's—the two friends found themselves discussing the Munch theft again. Who and why? Questions that seemed to have no answers.

3

Billionaire home appliances manufacturer Axel Blomqvist, Sweden's foremost private collector of the graphic works of Edvard Munch, was incensed. The damned robbery at Oslo's National Gallery was going to make security even tighter at any museum owning Munch paintings now. Not what the short man in his mid-sixties with his grandfather's wavy blond hair and wiry moustache needed. Certainly not now.

After years of canny collecting he had assembled all 748 prints by Munch in various media and editions, signed and unsigned. And just last evening he had met with and commissioned an extraordinary man by the name of Pål Enger to procure for him, by any means possible, Munch's haunting 1892 oil portrait of August Strindberg in Stockholm's Museum of Modern Art.

In exchange Blomqvist would pay Enger the hefty amount of 500,000 Euros. What an addition the painting would make to his Strindberg print collection! This included the one so hated by the Swedish playwright: the 1896 lithograph showing Strindberg's face against a black background. The background merges with an undulating, then zigzagging black frame containing a standing nude female on the right, and on the lower left, the sitter's name prominently misspelled: "A. Stindberg." This was Munch's famous Freudian slip, as "stind" in Norwegian slang of those days could mean "fatso." Strindberg was infuriated by the misspelling and the gratuitous nude and threatened Munch with a revolver. The two men had an intense on-again off-again relationship during their bohemian years in the 1890s, first in Berlin then in Paris.

From his first of three marriages Strindberg had fathered with the actress Siri von Essen two daughters and a son. The boy, Hans. had become irrevocably estranged from his mercurial father quite early, and after Strindberg's death, in 1912 at the age of sixty-three, he changed his surname to that of his wife's—Blomqvist. And it was this Hans Blomqvist—unreconciled son of Strindberg—who was Axel Blomqvist's father.

But unlike his father, Axel harbored no hatred for his famous ancestor, of whom people said he was the spitting image. On the contrary, consumed with curiosity about him, Axel had begun to collect images and photographs of Strindberg. This led him to Edvard Munch. After acquiring the Norwegian artist's lithographic portrayals of Strindberg, Axel became obsessed with Munch himself, amassing over the years the largest collection of his prints and drawings in private hands. It was then, for reasons of privacy, that he began denying his relationship to the author.

But the star Strindberg portrayal was neither a drawing nor a woodcut nor a lithograph nor an etching. It was the large oil painting Axel Blomqvist had contracted with Pål Enger to remove from Stockholm's Museum of Modern Art. *How* that would be accomplished was left to Enger, who, years earlier, had made a notorious name for himself by stealing Munch's *Vampire* from Norway's National Gallery. Enger agreed with Blomqvist that Munch's haunting portrait of the volatile Swede was a prize beyond measure.

Commanding the center of the canvas, Strindberg, seated and dressed in blue, was shown frontally amid a flurry of blue brushstrokes. His right arm was bent at the elbow and rested on a table, the fingers turned inward in a loose fist, while his left hand disappeared onto his hip. The unwavering stare of Strindberg's eyes locked with those of the viewer and a curly crown of bluish-black hair topped the unusually high forehead. Here was a force to be reckoned with.

Axel had coveted this stunning portrayal of his genius grandfather for years. And now within days it would be his.

4

Megan telephoned Erik Jensen as soon as she had finished sipping her coffee in the hotel room. Lili and Button had gone downstairs for the buffet breakfast where she would join them as soon as she got off the phone with Erik.

"Oh, Megan, good, good. Thank you for calling," Erik said, his voice echoing anxiety.

"You know what's happened at our museum of course. But there is something you do not know, that the public does not know, and also something you just might be able to help us with. Where are you now? Your e-mail mentioned that you were in Copenhagen. Are you still there? Could you possibly come to Oslo?"

"I suppose so," said Megan somewhat reluctantly. She and Lili had a full schedule of reunions with Lili's younger sister Rita and other relatives in the Danish capital before flying up to north Jutland and driving from the Aalborg airport in a rental car to Skagen.

"That would be super. Thank you. And, of course, at the museum's expense. What hotel do you usually stay at here?"

"Oh, the Bristol. And it's so conveniently close to your museum."

"The Hotel Bristol it will be. Any idea how soon you might be able to fly over?"

"Well, not until tomorrow. I have things going on here. How about my taking a noon flight? I could check into the hotel, take a brief rest—remember I'm eighty now—and then walk over to the museum around two o'clock."

"That sounds perfect, Megan. Just have the reception desk call up to my office when you get to the museum. And by the way, I too am a few years older than when you saw me last."

Megan laughed and hung up wondering what it was that she and the public did not know about the stolen Munch. And also how she could possibly help her treasured friend Erik Jensen?

But now she needed to join Lili and Button downstairs for breakfast. She was going to have to break the news that she would be temporarily abandoning them tomorrow for a quick business trip to Oslo. Like her dear friend Claire Chandler back in Dallas, Lili was a good sport and she was also extremely fond of Button. So perhaps she would take the sudden change of plans in stride and their canine companion would still have one interesting human with whom to explore Copenhagen.

5

While still in his twenties Olaf Petersen had made countless millions when, in the late 1960s, oil and gas deposits were discovered in the Norwegian sector of the North Sea. Shipping vessels would be needed for these resources and Olaf's fledgling shipbuilding business—originally named Petersens Skipsbygging—took off. While the nation's citizens benefited greatly under a socialist government from the fortuitous North Sea find, Olaf's privately owned shipping fleet grew ever larger. Soon oil and gas represented nearly one third of Norway's annual export earnings, while Olaf's personal wealth was estimated to be well over fourteen billion US dollars.

Now, at sixty-eight, Olaf was able to turn to his true passion, establishing once and for all the superiority of the Norse ancestors of modern Norway over those of more ancient ancestry, the Proto-Germanic peoples who had settled in the general area of modern Scandinavia a thousand years before Christ. In this respect his beliefs paralleled those of Norway's Minister-President Vidkun Quisling, who, despite his infamous collaboration with the Nazis during World War II, rejected the idea of German racial supremacy, seeing instead the Norwegian race as progenitor of all northern Europe.

As a child, Olaf had been enchanted by the seven enormous Viking burial mounds in the woods at Norway's famed seaside village of Borre. And was it not a Viking who discovered Iceland? As an adult, Olaf became an avid scholar of Norse mythology with its gods Thor, Freya, and Odin. He identified particularly with Odin because like the "all father" of the gods, Olaf had only one eye. The other had been irrevocably damaged in a childhood accident.

A tall, taciturn man of seventy with white hair, trim moustache, and a black patch over his left eye, Olaf had never married nor had he fathered any children. He took his role as one of the country's most powerful men very seriously. He was proud of being a Norwegian, some would say inordinately proud. He had renamed his shipbuilding company Norselands Skipsbygging—Norse Lands Shipbuilding—and his sprawling villa just outside Bergen was called Norsehjem—Norse home.

There was another house in Bergen with a name invoking something particularly Norwegian, and that was the home of the composer Edvard Grieg. Believing that trolls and elves could be good as well as bad, Grieg had named his atmospheric home *Troldhaugen*—troll hillock—and his music, especially *Peer Gynt*, invoked such supernatural images.

For Olaf Petersen, Grieg was one of several great Norwegians whom he worshipped. Two others were the playwright Henrik Ibsen and Edvard Munch, painter of the allegorical *The Frieze of Life*. The frieze, in a number of scenes and in several versions—one with twenty-two scenes—presented a person's course through life: adolescence, love, betrayal, sickness, and death. Through decades of astute collecting—occasionally with the help of shady dealers—Olaf had been able to assemble some seven of the individual scenarios from the frieze. This was due to Munch's penchant for painting a duplicate image whenever he had, reluctantly, to let one of his "children" go. The artist's home in Ekely overlooking Oslo's Filipstad harbor, where he spent the last twenty-seven years of his life, contained more than one thousand of his paintings, many of them replicas of key canvases in museums and private collections. Munch further "retained" his searing images in lithographs, woodcuts, and etchings, examples of which his admirer Olaf Petersen had passionately collected.

As for Henrik Ibsen, author of such major theatrical works as *Peer Gynt*, *A Doll's House*, *Hedda Gabler*, and *Ghosts*, Olaf had enshrined the sage's words over the entrance to his palatial home: "Anyone who wishes to understand me fully must know Norway." So true, Olaf would vigorously nod to himself when passing beneath it. The large living room at Norsehjem was stunning. It contained a continuous mural covering all four walls and extending above the doors. The subject addressed was ancient Norse mythology with its array of gods and goddesses of the sort that had so infatuated Richard Wagner.

Olaf's living room led to his spacious private den and there, in addition to the seven panels from Munch's *Frieze of Life*, the pictorial offerings gave way to portraits. Gracing the far wall were five Norwegian greats: Edvard Grieg, the celebrated violinist Ole Bull, Edvard Munch, Henrik Ibsen, and Bjørnstjerne Bjørnsen, the country's "other" famous author. It was he who, at the turn of the twentieth century, had urged artists to create a national art, to free themselves from the seduction of a frivolous Paris. The mere mention of Bjørnsen's name, according to the Danish cultural critic Georg Brandes, was like hoisting the Norwegian national flag. In fact Bjørnsen wrote the words to what became the unofficial Norwegian national anthem, *Ja, vi elsker dette landet—Yes, we love this country*.

Olaf often found himself exhorting his countrymen to practice the ancient Norwegian characteristics of seriousness and introspection championed by Bjørnsen.

Beyond the den was a smaller study and a short corridor with a permanent exhibition of photographs and portraits of what Olaf had titled "Lest We Forget: Modern Norwegian Traitors." They included mostly politicians but there were several images of writers, the most infamous of whom, for Olaf, was the 1920 Nobel Prize laureate Knut Hamsun, author of the epic *Growth of the Soil* and *Hunger*. During World War II Hamsun maintained that the Germans were fighting for Norwegians against British imperialism. He sent his Nobel Prize medal to Goebbels and later secured a meeting with Hitler at Berchtesgaden. After Hitler's death he published an article praising him as preaching the gospel of justice for all nations. Olaf had the obituary text written by Hamsun on display in his Traitors hall as well.

But it was in the great living room with its narrow stained-glass window band and inspiring Nordic gods mural that Olaf held his monthly Norseliga— Norse League—meetings. Here he hosted five of the country's wealthiest individuals. The select group shared Olaf's convictions concerning the superiority of their Viking roots over present day Germanic peoples. Yes, Olaf thought, the members of my Norseliga not only share my unswerving conviction of Viking supremacy but also my awe of the gods of Norse mythology. In fact, each of the league members had selected the name of a Norse deity as a pseudonym and they often referred to one another by these names. Olaf, as founder of the league, had, appropriately, assumed the name of the legendary father of the gods, Odin, who gave one of his eyes in exchange for wisdom.

The oldest in the group after Olaf was fifty-five-year-old Petter Norgaard, founder of Norway's hospital equipment company, Sykehusutstyr Norgaard. Of middle height, stout, and balding, he had chosen for his pseudonym the name Thor, the Norse god who wielded a giant hammer and from whom the day of the week Thursday came. Less known was the fact that he also represented healing. In Norse mythology Thor was the son of Odin and indeed the younger Petter/Thor did consider Olaf/Odin as his father figure.

The youngest, at forty-one, of the Norseliga group was green-eyed, chestnut-haired Myrtl Kildahl, fabled founder of Myrtl Cosmetics. Her choice of pseudonym—Hel, queen of Helheim, the Norse underworld—had amused the entire group.

A fourth member of the league, the shopping-mall tycoon Haakon Sando, had selected the name Magni, god of strength. And he looked it: tall, muscular, and blond. He had an impetuous nature and tended to act on impulse.

The remaining two members, the twin brothers Gunnar and Gustav Tufte of the computer design company Kontakt, had chosen the pseudonyms Týr, god of war, and Váli, god of revenge. And they looked rather like menacing powerful figures, short but athletic, with pointed blond beards and long curly hair. Together the group of six wielded enormous power and financial wealth.

The bold theft of Munch's *Scream* from Norway's National Gallery was the subject of today's hastily called meeting of the Norseliga. All but one of the members had been stunned by the news.

6

Megan was thinking about past Munch family history on her flight from Copenhagen to Oslo. Inger Marie Munch, the artist's youngest sister and the last of Edvard's four siblings, died in 1952. Although 506 letters to her from Munch were found among her effects, it was known that she had destroyed three years of his correspondence with her. Was this really so? And if so, why?

What was not generally known, or remembered perhaps, was that shortly before her death, the eighty-four-year-old Inger had asked for the assistance of Rita Stjele, a young librarian neighbor who had been exceedingly helpful to her over the years. Rita, an early feminist, was only too happy to help a sister of the famous artist Munch preserve her own legacy. Together they made an inventory of her and her brother's belongings, all of which were being left to the city of Oslo. Inger had taught piano students over the years, but her true passion was photography. In this endeavor Edvard had encouraged her, and in 1932 she had published a book with photographs of the winding Aker River and the picturesque Bjørvike harbor in Oslo. Some 200 negatives, mostly Aker River shots, constituted her own bequest to the city of Oslo.

But what did not number among the negatives were some dozen showing a dazed Edvard of November 1889, when he briefly returned from Paris to Oslo following the death of his domineering, religious fanatic father. Inger had taken the photographs but never developed the negatives and now, to Rita Stjele's shock, she had wanted to destroy them. Secretly, Rita removed them from the "Throw Away" box Inger was vigorously filling. She never did anything with them, but she felt they were important to preserve, witnessing how Edvard Munch's fame had continued to spread after the end of World War II. Photographs of the artist in the crucial year of 1889 might be of interest to the world of scholarship.

Finally, close to the age of eighty-four herself, Rita took action. She had read a chapter in a book on the world-wide phenomenon of Impressionism that addressed the movement in Scandinavia. What she read pleased her greatly since the author—Megan Crespi—had gone out of her way to cover the women artists of the movement as well as the better-known males. Rita decided that her Munch trove of negatives should ultimately, after so much time had gone by, be handed over to the world of scholarship. Crespi was one scholar she knew about and her distance from the inner world of continuous intrigue concerning Munch works she had witnessed in Oslo made entrusting the negatives to her attractive. Plus, she could rid herself of the gnawing guilt that had plagued her ever since her purloining of the negatives. And so, one day in May of 1992, Megan Crespi of Dallas, Texas, had been the surprised recipient of a large envelope from Norway that contained twelve negatives. When held up to the light they offered close-up, angstful images of Edvard Munch. An accompanying lawyer's note in English explained that the bequest was from one Rita Stjele of Oslo who had died earlier that year and whose directive asked simply that Professor Crespi do with the negatives what she thought was "right."

What Megan had thought was right was to send them immediately to the director of Oslo's National Gallery, Erik Jensen, and this constituted the basis of their cordial friendship over the years. If only she had another packet of Munch negatives to hand over to Erik to make up for the terrible Munch loss!

7

The sight of Oslo's elegant Hotel Bristol always cheered Megan. She loved its proximity to the National Gallery and the National Theater with its life-size statues of Ibsen and Bjørnsen. And running from the royal palace to the parliament was the famous Karl Johans Gate, its ominous, zombielike pedestrian traffic so hauntingly memorialized by Munch. And, of course, right on the Karl Johan's street was the Grand Hotel's famous Café, once the center of the city's active Bohemia. That is where the impressionable young Munch, son of a religious zealot turned physician, had first been initiated into the world of spiritual alienation and erotic angst.

Megan hoped to have late afternoon tea at the Grand Café following her two o'clock appointment with Erik Jensen. After checking in at the Bristol and unpacking her few belongings, she walked briskly over to the National Gallery and had herself announced to Erik. He came downstairs himself, a wide welcoming smile animating his face.

"Welcome to Oslo, *kjære* Megan!"

"It's wonderful to be back, if a bit of a surprise."

"You can imagine how 'surprise' seems to be the name of the game right now, with the theft of our *Scream*—again!"

"Who, in this day and age, given your museum's history, would have the nerve and the smarts to do such a thing?"

"Exactly, Megan. It was a real act of ingenuity and on a very high professional scale, considering that a helicopter and a drone were involved. The drone knocked out all electrical feeds and the copter provided access and exit. The whole thing couldn't have taken over seven minutes, the police say."

"Do they have any leads?"

"Not yet, at least not so far as they tell me. What we're all trying to do is establish a motive for the robbery."

"Indeed. As with the previous thefts of your and the Munch Museum's *Screams*, it just couldn't be for placement on the world market. The image is just too well known. And a private collector could never let anyone know he or she had it."

"Unless they lived in a cave with it or something."

"I suppose it's too early for a ransom note? After all, it only happened two days, or should I say two nights, ago."

"Getting a ransom demand at this stage of the game would almost be a relief," Erik said wanly, a curious smile on his face.

Megan wondered about the smile but her attention was drawn to the pile of local and foreign newspapers on Erik's desk, all of them with headlines bleating about the audacious robbery.

Erik observed Megan's glance. "Oh, yes, the news has hit the world press. One offshoot of the theft is that attendance is up at the museum and the gift shop has sold out of *Scream* images."

Megan laughed ruefully. "Small benefit. Now, Erik, I'm all ears to hear what you have to tell me concerning the robbery. Why you wanted me to come to Oslo."

"Of course." Erik buzzed his secretary and asked for all incoming calls to be held until further notice. Then he turned to Megan who had taken a seat opposite him.

"What I am going to tell you is in the strictest confidence, Megan. Not even the police know. And you must agree to tell no one, absolutely no one. At least not until I can give you the go ahead."

"Of course, Erik."

"All right. The thing is..." Erik hesitated. "The thing is Munch's *Scream* has not been stolen from the museum. It has not been on public view for over twelve years. What was stolen was a copy of the original. An exact copy and on an identical piece of cardboard, both in age and weight."

"What? I can't believe it! But why? Why has the museum exhibited a copy all these years? And isn't that deceiving the public?"

"Don't think this hasn't bothered me greatly, Megan. But the danger, the threat level has simply been too high. What only the museum knows is that there was a botched attempt to steal *The Scream* thirteen years ago. It happened right after the evening shift closed down at seven in the morning, and two of the daytime guards were involved. If I hadn't arrived at work early that day and needed to pick up something from the basement, they might have gotten away with the painting. As it was, they handed over the picture when I confronted them and apologized profusely, saying it was just a joke and please not to call the police. For me it certainly was not a joke and as soon as I supervised their rehanging the work I gave them their walking papers on condition that they never enter the premises again nor speak to anyone about what had transpired."

"And you didn't call the police?"

Erik looked shamefaced. "No. I didn't want to publicize the event in any way and possibly give ideas to a new generation of would-be thieves. I simply wanted to contain the mess, considering that *The Scream* had been successfully stolen from us once before."

"So how was the switch effected and where did you find the convincing copy?"

"I took our extraordinary restorer into my confidence and she agreed that creating an exact copy of the Munch would constitute an extraordinary safety measure even if displaying it would be misleading the public, in a sense."

"In a sense? It certainly was misleading the public! I am nonplussed that no one noticed over a period of, you said, twelve years. Surely if not one of your curators, then a Munch expert on visit to your institution."

"Well, we did a *Mona Lisa* with the work. That is, roped it off so that no one could get really close to it. This made sense because of the theft in nineteen ninety-four. And the increasing threat of a museum terrorist attack was also beginning to be taken in earnest."

Erik paused. "And the substitution worked. Well, at least until now."

"I'm still recovering from what you've just told me, Erik. Am I correct in thinking the situation you have right now is that the public and the police think Munch's *Scream* has been stolen—for a second time—from the National Gallery.

"Yes." Erik squirmed in his chair.

"When are you going to reveal the truth?"

"Not until a massive effort has been made to recover the stolen *Scream*. I want, I need, to give it a week or so. And that's where you come in, Megan."

"How so?" Megan was feeling most uncomfortable with Erik's revelation. On the one hand she was relieved that the original Munch was safe and secure, but on the other hand she felt that the museum had deceived its visitors. It was a conundrum that seemed to have no resolution.

"I understand your discomfort," Erik suddenly said, seeing the frown crossing Megan's face. "Believe me I have had nightmares about my decision, wondering time and again if I had done the right thing. And, of course, as director of the National Gallery, I take full responsibility. But in the light of this terrible theft, perhaps I did do the right thing."

"Well, let's say it was a moral question to which your answer was a practical one and, fortunately, with a happy ending."

A look of relief flushed her friend's face.

"But now tell me, Erik, how do you think I could be of any possible help?"

"Yes. Good. Well, you see, Megan, because of your greatly respected work on Nordic artists I believe you are in a unique outsider position to contact some of Scandinavia's best known private collectors and request a meeting to visit with them and see their artwork. It is entirely possible one of these avid collectors—and you of all persons know how fanatical they can be—that one of them is responsible for the theft. Not that they would tell you so, of course, but my thinking, my hope is that you might discern something suspicious in their attitude or conduct or collection, should you meet with them. Maybe something as simple as a recent rehanging of their artworks. Perhaps you could divine something that seems out of kilter."

"That is really a very, very long shot, Erik. And I'd have to dream up some valid reason for asking to meet with these collectors."

"I've been thinking about that. What if you said you were doing research for a monograph on one of the women artists in their collection, seeing as how you were one of the first in modern times to give them scholarly publicity and inspire exhibitions of their work."

"Hm. That might possibly work. Do you have any particular collectors in mind?"

"Yes. Three as a matter of fact. All of them with the financial means to back a helicopter raid on the museum."

"Oh?"

"One possibility would be that weird, obsessive champion of all things Norse, Olaf Petersen in Bergen."

"The big shipping magnate, right?"

"Yes. He is known to have a four-wall mural of Nordic deities in his living room and, more interestingly, he collects portraits of Norwegian cultural figures like Grieg and Ibsen and Munch."

"Oh, yes! I actually did contact him when I was working on Harriet Backer and Kitty Kielland because he owns paintings by both of them. He was most forthcoming, I remember, and he not only sent me color photographs of some of the works he owns by them but also one of a second version of Asta Nørregaard's eighteen-eighty-five portrait of the twenty-three year-old Munch."

"A second version? I know only the large pastel portrait over at the Munch Museum right here in Oslo."

"That's the only one I knew as well until Petersen sent me the photo. Like the one you know, it shows a very young-looking Edvard seated in three-quarter profile in front of an easel with his chalk drawing study of a nude boy. Munch's eyes are dreamy, he has soft, smooth cheeks, and a bulging Adam's apple. Very appealing. In fact I think it's a better portrait than the Munch Museum's."

"I am amazed that I don't know about this second portrait."

"I'm not surprised you don't. Remember, Olaf Petersen has never allowed any part of his extensive collection to be shown to the public. Based on what he told me in the letter accompanying his photos, I think he may possibly own an unknown early Munch self-portrait as well."

"What on earth makes you think that?"

"Well, he wrote that Munch so liked Asta Nørregaard's portrayal of him that he gave her a just-completed small self-portrait and offered to paint her as well."

"This is all new to me."

"And I never followed it through because at the time I was more interested in Nørregaard than I was in Munch."

"Well, I will pass on, if you permit, your intriguing information to my counterpart at the Munch Museum."

"Of course, you are welcome to do so. I should have thought of doing that myself."

"Since you have had personal contact with Olaf Petersen, do you think you might be able to set up a meeting in person?"

"I can certainly try. I've always loved visiting Bergen. Its harbor is so picturesque. And of course, Grieg's house and composing hut are just five miles out of town. In fact I am just finishing up an essay on Grieg's 'lost lady loves' for a Festschrift in honor of the Grieg scholar Knut Mostrom. That might afford an opening ploy, since Olaf is such a fan of the composer."

"Oh! That's a perfect connection!"

"But now tell me, Erik, who are the other two collectors you would like me to try to contact?"

"One would take you to Sweden, I'm afraid. He is Axel Blomqvist, owner of the world's largest private collection of Munch graphics. Blomqvist became interested in Munch because, although he tries to keep it secret, he's actually the grandson of Strindberg. I'm thinking he might want to own more than just etchings and woodcuts and lithographs by the artist. He might covet a major painting like *The Scream*."

"Hm. Axel Blomqvist. Oddly enough, Erik, I was planning to visit Stockholm on this trip. I wanted to see Strindberg's last apartment again. If you provide me with Blomqvist's contact information, preferably his e-mail address, I could give it a try."

"Great! We do have his e-mail address and as of now he and I are on good terms. So I could, in fact, recommend you. Ask him on your behalf."

"Okay, we'll handle it that way and you can set up a meeting."

"I'll tell him you will be in Stockholm in—when might that be?—in a few days?"

"Let's wait until we see if I can get an invite from Petersen up in Bergen."

"Oh, good thinking."

"And so who is the third individual you'd like me to check out, so to speak?"

"Someone right here in Oslo. Myrtl Kildahl, the cosmetics queen."

"I vaguely know of the cosmetic company, but I didn't know it was founded by a woman."

"Indeed. And she, like Petersen, is known to be interested in Norwegian history and culture. Some of her products carry the names of different Norse gods and goddesses."

"Do you know if she has an art collection?"

"Yes, I know so. She recently consulted me in person concerning an auction that was coming up. Two late works by Munch were being offered—both landscapes without figures."

"So you are thinking she might be tempted to aim for a figural scene, as with *The Frieze of Life* or, more to the point, *The Scream*?"

"Exactly. She is known as being a hard-nosed business woman—she's worth several billions, I'm told—but also capricious and unpredictable. I found her sudden interest in Munch to be a bit curious. I have to say that when I met her in person she struck me as a life-size version of Munch's luscious, dark-haired *Madonna*."

"Might have been all that makeup. Something I've never used since I read Desmond Morris's book *The Naked Ape* back in the nineteen-sixties and learned that bright red lips are a sign of being in heat."

"Oh, my! I never knew that."

"Well it's true. All right, now. Where were we? We have three candidates, two of them, Olaf Petersen and Myrtl Kildahl in Norway, and Axel Blomqvist in Sweden. I'll contact Petersen immediately if I can borrow your computer."

"Help yourself, by all means."

After Megan had sent what she hoped would be an irresistible suggestion that she visit Petersen while on "vacation" in Bergen, Erik proposed Megan's visit in an e-mail to Axel Blomqvist in Stockholm. Then, with Megan listening, Erik called, Myrtl Kildahl. Yes. She would be pleased to meet Professor Megan Crespi, expert on Scandinavian women artists and on Edvard Munch. Tomorrow morning would be fine. Could it be at her office, as her home had just finished undergoing expansion?

"Undergoing expansion?" Erik repeated after hanging up.

The two friends looked at each other conspiratorially, then shook their heads. No. It couldn't be as simple as that. But still, it set one ruminating.

8

Megan and Erik had been right to ruminate. Myrtl Kildahl's expansion of her country house in the hills of exclusive Holmenkollen to the north of Oslo, with its view of the islands in the Oslo fjord, did indeed have something to do with Munch. But not with *The Scream* or its disappearance.

As a young girl growing up in Lillehammer, tall, green-eyed Myrtl, with her rich cascades of chestnut hair, had felt painfully different from her classmates, who were almost uniformly blonde, and blue-eyed. Her olive complexion and stiff, outsider ways had inspired one popular schoolmate to refer to her as an imperious gypsy queen. A few days later that same schoolmate's books were found immersed in one of the bathroom toilets.

As an adult, when Myrtl first heard herself jokingly compared to Munch's *Madonna*, she had no idea who Munch was. But the amorous young man she had just made love to was insistent upon the similarity between her and the painter's seductive, bare-breasted *Madonna*, with red-haloed head, long black hair, and eyes closed in private ecstasy. Myrtl hastened to inform herself about Munch and almost immediately fell under the spell of the lonely, alienated man whose inexplicable buoyancy and energy alternating with periods of deep depression so paralleled her own ups and downs.

Munch's dark-complexioned 1895 *Madonna*—the same oil version once famously stolen from the Munch Museum—became the revered object of Myrtl's many pilgrimages to that institution. As her cosmetics business flourished Myrtl made it a point to donate generous sums of money to Oslo's two museums containing important works by Munch. Recently, and against stiff competition, she had introduced a new lipstick, rouge, and nail polish called Madonna Red. Its subsequent blockbuster sales had taken the market by surprise and more than doubled her already considerable fortune.

And now Myrtl had applied some of that fortune to the construction of a private gallery that adjoined her study. It was a temple to Munch's *Madonna* figures as well as an homage to Myrtl's phenomenal achievement in the business world. That success had grown just as her competitors in the cosmetics business began to suffer a series of mysterious warehouse fires.

The pinnacle of Myrtl's collection was an exact replica of the Munch Museum's 1885 *Madonna*. The copy had been created in secret at Myrtl's request by a retired restorer who had worked at that museum for some thirty-five years. He was well acquainted with the artist's wrangled application of oil pigment and casein on cardboard or board or canvas. No one was to know of the copy, and the restorer had been paid sufficient enough funds to accompany him to the grave with his secret. In fact he did die in an unexplained home accident shortly after completion of his work for Myrtl. Soon after that event Myrtl had carefully added Munch's signature and the date 1895 to the canvas.

The gold-framed *Madonna* copy was hung behind a black velvet curtain. On the wall to the right of it were four hand-colored lithographic versions of the theme by Munch in different shades of sinuous black and bleeding red. In these variations a crimson compositional frame within the print consisted of squiggling threads of spermatozoa on their way to a dead fetus—a pathetic tiny white skull atop cradled, crushed arms.

For Myrtl, who had ultimately given up love with men for the thrill of business, the symbolism spoke volumes; she would never be tied down with motherhood. The devoted friendship of the woman she had hired eighteen years ago as her private secretary was enough for her. And Sophia Grimm was an elfin, red-haired, freckled, friendlier version of herself. Her amber eyes radiated warmth and empathy. Unlike the male friends with whom Myrtl had been intimate, Sophia never expected her, after putting in a ten-hour workday, to prepare dinner when they arrived home. They shared the tasks of domesticity and reveled in the fact that they were very much kindred spirits. Eventually, as business took more and more time, they hired a housekeeper to manage the spacious home Myrtl bought to accommodate her growing art collection and Sophia's grand piano. For Sophia's mother, who had died when she was born, had been a concert pianist.

Another Munch image cherished by Myrtl commanded an exalted place in her gallery. This was the artist's lovesick depiction of the stunning, dark-haired English beauty and violin virtuoso Eva Mudocci. Munch met her in Munich in 1903 while she was on concert tour with her pianist partner Bella Edwards—a partnership that lasted fifty years. Although Munch's friendship with Eva seemed to have remained platonic, his tribute to her resulted in several lithographs during the tumultuous year following their meeting, the most commanding of which he titled *Madonna (The Brooch)*. In it the young woman's heavy-lidded eyes gaze past the viewer while the thick ringlets of her long dark hair fall past her breasts to either side of a large white brooch fastening her black garment.

Two more lithographic images of Eva Mudocci by Munch existed and Myrtl had secured them both. One showed her in a white dress standing and facing outward with her violin next to the black-clad Bella who was seated in profile at an upright black piano. Myrtl loved this image of artistic partnership as much as she detested Munch's third depiction of Eva—an image Eva herself had hated. It was a sensuous looking bust view of the beautiful woman, her long white neck stretched against the "severed" head of Munch. His pale, lifeless face was positioned at the exact spot where she would have held her violin, and the artist's despair at not being able to replace that treasured object in her life was conveyed by his title: *Salome*. Eva's career came first, and in Paris in 1915 she was portrayed in graphite by no less an artist than Matisse. It was a drawing Myrtl had tried in vain to purchase from the Metropolitan Museum in New York.

There was no doubt that Myrtl Kildahl considered herself the living reincarnation of Eva Mudocci. She had assembled a collection of photographs of the exotic woman with whom Edvard had been besotted. Photographs of her as a young woman and also, from 1950, as a white-haired old lady in an English nursing home, her face still beautiful and commanding.

Many of the always eye-catching advertisements for Myrtl Cosmetics featured a Mudocci-like young woman with shoulder-length dark hair and sleeveless dresses. Fashion analysts had credited the sudden penchant for long hair and bare arms among professional women, and especially contemporary television anchors, to the ubiquitous Myrtl images. "A force to be reckoned with," wrote one of the interviewers of Myrtl Kildahl.

And now she had agreed to meet a visiting American art historian recommended to her as "fascinating" by her friend Erik Jensen at the National Gallery. Perhaps, if the woman was interesting and informed, she would show her the two Munch landscapes she had recently bought at auction which hung in her inner office. She wondered what this Megan Crespi was doing in Oslo and so soon after the theft of Munch's *Scream*. Could there be a connection? Tomorrow would tell.

9

"So that's why it would probably be best if you and Button joined me here in Oslo," Megan urged Lili over the phone.

Her Norwegian schedule was beginning to fill up. Olaf Petersen had answered her e-mail with surprising speed, asking if she might visit him in Bergen three days hence. Megan figured that her car trip with Lili and Button could just as easily begin in Norway rather than in Denmark as originally planned. After Oslo and Bergen they could swing over to Sweden, drive down and across to Stockholm and, after saying hello to Strindberg there, take the three-hour ferry trip from Gothenburg to Frederikshavn. From there it was only a half-hour drive up to Skagen and Lili's time-share apartment. Everything would work out just fine and, after all, neither one of them had been to Bergen in a long time. And who knows? Megan might chance upon more data in the city's Grieg Archives for the Festschrift essay she was writing about Grieg's "lost lady loves."

Lili quickly adjusted to the new itinerary and, after checking flight times, called Megan back with her Oslo arrival time, which would be at one o'clock the next afternoon. That would give Megan plenty of time to make her morning office visit to the cosmetic queen, Myrtl Kildahl.

Megan's visit with Erik Jensen had come to an amicable end just before "tea o'clock," as Munch used to say, and after leaving the museum Megan walked over to Karl Johan's street and the Grand Hotel Café. She was able to get a table opposite the long wall mural showing the café's clientele at the beginning of the last century. The black-clad figure of Ibsen entering on his cane with his white whiskers and famous top hat greeted her and she smiled, thinking of the energetic conversations that took place here when the bohemians of Kristiania, as Oslo was called then, met to drink and discuss the great issues of the day.

Megan reviewed the strange events that had brought her so unexpectedly from Copenhagen to Oslo. She pictured to herself Munch's famous *Scream—Skrik* in Norwegian—with its shrieking figure, elongated hands clasped to the side of its skull-like face, set within a streaking bridge of brushstrokes that rushed right out to encompass the viewer. In the distance behind Munch's screaming alter ego, two top-hatted figures followed on the overlook path with its guardrail and all around in the sky above and water below there churned a color bedlam of sinuous sound waves. The view of the water looked down over Oslo and the Kristiania Fjord as seen from the south on Ekeberg Hill, a favorite site for painters. Below Ekeberg Hill was Gaustad, the city lunatic asylum. It was there that the artist's beloved sister Laura, who suffered from mental illness, was confined. Within hearing distance stood the city slaughterhouse. Reports refer to the horrendous sound of the screams of the insane accompanied by the screams of the animals being killed. A very personal picture but one that could strike resonance in others across two centuries, not just in 1893.

And now Norway's national treasure had been stolen. Or, rather, it had not been stolen, thanks to Erik Jensen's ingenious switching of the original for an exact copy. Had his action been wise or foolish? Megan still was not sure how she felt about Erik's decision, but she was glad the original was safe even if that fact had to be kept secret for a time. If Interpol knew, their search for the culprits might possibly be suspended, and if the public knew, indignation at the museum's deception could be deafening.

And then there was the courteous but mysterious e-mail from Olaf Petersen in Bergen setting up a meeting for noon three days hence. He had proposed showing her recently acquired, unknown works by Norwegian women artists. Well, that could prove interesting, Megan thought. But now it was time to take an afternoon lie-down before dinner. Later, over at the National Theater, there was a seven-o'clock performance of Ibsen's *A Doll's House* which was being presented in English for tourists. As Megan's Norwegian was next to nil, except for words that were akin to German words, she was only too happy to take advantage of the English-language performance.

The next morning, a few minutes before ten o'clock, saw her sitting in the luxurious waiting room of Myrtl Cosmetics. It was all in white, trimmed in beige with darker brown leather furniture. Lighted wall cabinets displayed a variety of elegant cosmetic products. Oh dear, Megan thought. I hope the fact that I don't bother with makeup doesn't put off Myrtl Cosmetics' CEO. She looked around her. The name plate on the glass and metal desk of the welcoming secretary read "Sophia Grimm." Might she be related to the German folktale collectors, the Grimm brothers, Megan wondered but did not ask.

At exactly ten o'clock Megan was shown into a surprisingly small office with no windows and all black walls. On one of the walls hung Munch's red-drenched *Madonna/Brooch* lithograph, framed in gold. Standing up from her long glass desk to greet Megan was a tall woman dressed in crimson with wavy dark hair reaching to her bare shoulders. Thick false eyelashes graced penetrating green eyes.

"Welcome to Oslo, Professor Crespi," Myrtl said evenly without a smile.

"Thank you, and thank you for seeing me."

"I hear from our mutual friend Erik Jensen that you are an expert on Scandinavian art, and especially women Scandinavian artists."

"Well, yes, I've had the lucky opportunity of coming into contact with much of their work, an opportunity that has taken me all over Scandinavia."

"And why did you want to do that in particular?" Myrtl asked as they both sat down, Megan in a comfortable brown leather chair facing the desk.

"To redress the balance."

Myrtl Kildahl's dark eyebrows rose enquiringly and she examined her guest with interest.

"What exactly do you mean?"

"I mean exactly that: to redress the uneven balance. When I first studied art history as an undergraduate and then graduate student, our textbooks and lectures contained no references to women artists. Except perhaps for Mary Cassatt and Georgia O'Keeffe. My studies in New York exactly coincided with the feminist movement of the nineteen-sixties, and I was only one of many who were determined to research and highlight the accomplishments of women artists and women sculptors. As my own field dealt with European art of the late nineteenth and early twentieth centuries, I began to look for women artists wherever I traveled and to publish and lecture on them. And, when I became a professor, I made sure to include women artists in my lectures."

"Give me an example." Myrtl was beginning to take a genuine interest in her American guest.

"Well, take nineteenth-century realism in France. It used to be that only

Gustave Courbet was taught. But we feminist art historians began including Rosa Bonheur as well and that began to change things—for students and for teachers. For myself personally, and in a neglected art market, I was able to acquire a signed and dated Bonheur oil painting of a ewe in a fenced meadow. It is in my Dallas living room and two generations of students have come to visit the appealing little creature."

Myrtl was beginning to like this energetic scholar from Texas who spoke English without a Texas accent. But still she was guarded.

"And have you also acquired works by Scandinavian women artists?"

Megan gave a broad smile. "Oh, I could only wish! No such luck...yet."

"I hear you have written on Scandinavian male artists as well."

"But of course! They are legion and some are marvelous."

Myrtl decided she did like her interlocutor.

"So would you be interested in seeing two Munch landscapes we have here?

"Oh, yes! How exciting!"

"Let us go into my inner office then," Myrtl said, rising from her desk and pushing a button on the wall that caused a sliding black door Megan had not noticed before to open up behind the desk.

The two women entered an enormous room with sunlight streaming in from a bank of windows on one side. Like the waiting room, the walls were painted white with beige trim and the furniture was in brown leather. On the far side of the room facing the windows hung two resplendent Munch landscapes framed in gold. One was of Oslo's harbor as seen from the artist's home high up at Ekely. The other showed a thick forest with sinuous shoreline gleaming through the trees.

"Both are late works, I see," observed Megan quietly. "And both equally wonderful."

A small smile of pride flitted across Myrtl's features. "Yes, I was able to buy them at auction recently. I feel I have a special affinity for Munch."

"Perhaps you identify with the *Brooch* portrait of Eva Mudocci you have in your office," Megan dared to suggest.

Myrtl looked directly into Megan's eyes. "She is my idol."

"What a pity there are no recordings of her violin playing."

"Ah, so you know about her!"

"I do know a bit, yes. As much as is possible some sixty-plus years after her death. I do know that her partner was with her when she died in a British retirement home."

"Are you, have you ever been married?" Myrtl asked suddenly.

"I've been married, as they say, to my work."

"I too," said Myrtl, holding Megan's eyes with her own. Then abruptly she changed the subject.

"What do you think about the terrible National Gallery theft of our Munch treasure, Professor Crespi?"

"It is awful, simply awful."

"And do you think the painting will be retrieved?"

"I think there is every likelihood," Megan said diplomatically.

"Why steal it? A person could not possibly let anyone know he had it, or show it to anyone."

"My question exactly."

There was a brief silence. Megan looked admiringly at the two Munch landscapes again.

"Something about this forest painting reminds me of the trees around Grieg's *Troldhaugen*."

"Oh, you've been to his home in Bergen then?"

"Yes, indeed. Several times. I've been an admirer of his music for decades. And right now I'm writing an essay for a Festschrift on him and a young English pianist named Bella Edwards."

"Bella Edwards?"

"Yes. She gave concert recitals around Europe with the Danish singer Margrethe Petersen. And then later..."

"...with Eva Mudocci," they both said at the same time.

Myrtl stared at Megan, then came to a momentous decision.

"How long are you in Oslo, Professor Crespi?"

"Only until tomorrow afternoon"

"Are you busy this evening?"

"Um, no. I saw *A Doll's House* last night but I don't have anything planned for tonight. My friend Lili Holm and my dog Button are flying in from Copenhagen this afternoon and I thought we'd just take it easy as we'll be renting a car tomorrow and heading up to Bergen."

"Oh, you are traveling with a dog?"

"It's a small one, a Maltese named Button."

There was a silence. Then Myrtl spoke.

"I tell you what. I propose that you, your friend, and your dog come out to my home for dinner this evening. I will show you Eva Mudocci as you've never seen her. No women artists, I'm afraid, but Munch's depictions of a woman artist. And in a special placement. One that has never been envisioned before."

Megan was astonished by the unexpected invitation. What an opportunity to get an insight into the workings of the woman's mind and her motivation for collecting Munch. Had she feigned indignation over *The Scream*'s heist? But if she had anything to do with the theft why would she invite a stranger, especially an art historian, into her inner sanctum? Quickly she accepted the invitation.

Myrtl touched a bell on the desk and her secretary entered.

"Sophia, we will be having guests for dinner. Three of them, one a dog."

Sophia looked at Megan, smiled, and raised her hands. "How delightful!"

"We shall see each other at seven o'clock, if that is agreeable with you, Professor Crespi," Myrtl instructed. "Fru Grimm here will give you the directions."

A few minutes later Megan exited the handsome Myrtl Cosmetics building with a printout of the directions to Oslo's elite suburb of Frogner and Myrtl Kildahl's home. She was sure Lili would be intrigued by the invitation. And Button would be excited to be included—a new home to sniff-vestigate.

10

Five members of the Norseliga had been shocked by the theft of Munch's *Scream* from the National Gallery. The sixth member was not. He had master-minded the successful heist.

And now Olaf Petersen sat in his newly constructed underground bunker contemplating with his single eye Edvard Munch's riveting incarnation of angst.

Only I have the moral right to possess this treasure, Olaf told himself. The Norseliga members, committed as they are to filtering Nordic pride into the veins of our insipid school system, they simply do not yet comprehend the unique genius of Munch. The courageous philosopher who all his many days confronted the great mysteries of life, love, loss, and death. No, this masterpiece must be protected, removed from the public eye until Norwegians are strong enough to emulate their national hero's quest for answers to the meaning of life and death. The explanations of religion were weak and misleading. Munch had rightly rejected his father's extreme religious views. He had been brave enough to demand and pursue his own answers. And he had found them, even if they were not always comforting.

How similar had Olaf's life been to Munch's. He too, as a young man had had tumultuous, short-lived love affairs with women who deceived or mocked him. He too had lost mother and favorite sister to tuberculosis. He too had never come to terms with a domineering father nor had he been there when his father died. He too had not married. He too had been through periods of deep depression and debilitating, extended alcoholic binges. But he too, like Munch, had ultimately succeeded brilliantly in his chosen profession.

And now he must prepare for a visit by the scholar from America whom he had once helped with her research on two female artists in his collection. He had admired the published results of Professor Megan Crespi's study, and thought that, should they ever meet, he would show her Asta Nørregaard's "other" portrait of Munch at the age of twenty-three. He had sent her a photo of the charming work and her response had been enthusiastic. And he might even show her young Munch's self-portrait gift to Nørregaard. Yes, showing her the fascinating artworks might take the focus off what was bound to come up in their conversation: the inexplicable theft at the National Gallery.

11

As he lay dying in April of 1940, the respected ophthalmologist Dr. Maximilian Linde of Lübeck could feel only bitter irony. Irony that many of the works once in his prestigious collection of modern art, ranging from Auguste Rodin to Edvard Munch, had been declared "degenerate" by a Nazi regime. Eighty-two of Munch's paintings had been so classified in 1937 and removed from museums. Linde's own collection, already partially sold off because of hyperinflation after World War I, was further scattered by Hitler's henchmen. One of those henchmen was his own son.

Linde had recognized the twenty-nine-year-old Munch's talent as early as 1903, the year he commissioned the little-known Norwegian artist to paint his four young sons. Munch had produced an endearing group portrait of the boys standing in front of closed double doors in various attitudes of waiting and watching the artist at work. Thirty years later the oldest Linde boy, Hermann, succumbed to Hitler's seductive siren call and served the Third Reich with loyalty, dying on the Russian Front and leaving a widow with one son to care for. That son became a successful architect and raised a son of his own whom he named Max.

And now, well into the twenty-first century, Maximilian Linde's fifty-two-year-old great-grandson, blond, hazel-eyed Max, obsessed with Hitler's old idea of a master race, was a neo-Nazi. A neo-Nazi with a cause. From the seductive neo-Nazi website *Deutschland Erst—Germany First*, he had learned of an unusual sect, in Norway of all places, that was hell-bent on teaching and establishing the primacy of its Viking ancestors over modern-day Germans. This despite the fact that Germanic tribes had appeared as early as 500 BC, the Nordic Bronze Age, whereas the Viking Age did not even commence until about 700 AD. What utter nonsense! And anyway, the term Viking referred to an activity—raiding—and not to a particular ethnicity.

Pale, lean of build, with shaved head and tattoos on his arms and neck, Max eked out a living as a software programmer for a large German armaments firm in Lübeck. Hacking into the accounts of competitors was also part of his job and he enjoyed it. With no social skills, Max's all-consuming hobby was browsing the Internet. He was always on the lookout for neo-Nazi developments in Germany, across Europe, and around the world.

Closer to home, his searches had pulled up the names of two Norwegian brothers, Gunnar and Gustav Tufte, owners of Kontakt, a computer-design company. Online photographs of the brothers revealed they were twins—and spitting images of one another. Their business had a vast mailing list and when Max hacked Kontakt's e-mail he found that recipients were inundated with messages urging pride in all things Norwegian and gratitude for Norway's Viking past as opposed to any "Germanic" heritage. Wrong again, thought Max. We Germans and our language were first; Norwegian, Danish, and Swedish are all derivations of our North Germanic language tree. Only Finnish is not Germanic or even Indo-European. And what have the Finns ever done?

Obviously, Max thought, he should keep an eye on the Tufte brothers, as their e-mail propaganda—regularly sent to all Norwegian institutions of learning—could easily crystalize into anti-neo-Nazi activities. What the two brothers referred to as their Norseliga might become dangerous. He could malware their website or simply continue to monitor its e-mail exchanges. From his hacking Max had gleaned that once a month the Norseliga met in Bergen. Now to find out who the members were and exactly where in the city they met. Just the sort of cyber searching he loved.

Two hours later and despite his sizeable cyber knowhow, Max had come up with precious little information. He was only able to identify six individuals as having any connection with the Norseliga. Surely there had to be more. As for the league's activities, as listed on its website, there were numerous references to educational goals but that was all. All right then, he would focus on the six individuals. They were Gunnar and Gustav Tufte, Petter Norgaard, Haakon Sando, Olaf Petersen, and Myrtl Kildahl.

He would begin with the woman.

12

As their Uber taxi looped higher and higher up toward Holmenkollen, Lili declared: "This must be the most elegant suburb of Oslo."

She and Megan had been admiring the mostly old mansions with their spacious grounds and remarking on the select views the houses had of Oslo's harbor down below. Regardless of the fact that he was now blind, Button, his ears cocked, was on his hind feet at the car window sniffing the view and relishing the scent of a new neighborhood. The plane flight from Copenhagen had been without incident and he had been allowed out of his roller carrier and onto Lili's welcoming lap. When they joined Megan at the Hotel Bristol the clerk discreetly looked the other way as they checked in.

And now they had passed through an open gate and were pulling up to a handsome Art Deco house—rather a surprise in this old neighborhood. Megan glanced at her watch. It was exactly seven o'clock.

As they were confirming with the Uber driver the time to pick them up, Sophia Grimm appeared at the front door, smiling and beckoning them to come inside. Behind her, barking excitedly, was a large black poodle. Megan instantly scooped up Button. They had been in this sort of large dog/small dog situation before and, because of his blindness, Button was likely to be unpredictable in his reaction. For the moment he was unanimated and silent.

The trio entered the large living room where Myrtl was waiting to greet them. She waved them to a long leather couch and took a chair opposite them, as did Sophia. Megan noted appreciatively that the luxurious furnishings were consistently Art Deco in style, matching the exterior of the house. And there was a concert grand, probably from the 1930s, standing in isolated splendor on one side of the room. It was unusual in that the wood was blond maple and had a swirly grain.

"Down, Magnus!" commanded Myrtl as the black poodle suddenly tried to get to Button who was standing on Megan's lap. Both dogs began to growl menacingly. Sophia pulled the poodle back by his collar and Button, although unseeing, bravely stood his ground. Not a very good beginning, Megan thought.

"I'll put Magnus in the game room, not to worry," Sophia said, drawing the dog to her.

"That would be best," Myrtl said, the disappointment in her voice audible.

They could hear the sound of a distant door being firmly closed and then Sophia reappeared. Megan felt obliged to explain about Button's blindness again but Sophia interrupted her with apologies for Magnus.

"We had so hoped the dogs would get along."

"That's enough, Sophia," Myrtl commanded. "It's time we offered our visitors a drink."

At first, conversation seemed stilted after the canine event but soon, due to Megan's animated appreciation of the beautiful house, the mood improved.

"And what an unusual blond-wood piano you have in here," Megan gushed purposefully. "Who plays it?"

"I don't but Sophia does," said Myrtl, looking appreciatively at her friend.

"Won't you play something?" Lili requested.

"What would you like?"

"Something by Grieg?"

"Do you like his *Peer Gynt* music?"

"Oh, I adore it!" Lili nodded her head in affirmation.

Sophia went over to the piano and played a keyboard arrangement of the composer's incidental music for Ibsen's eponymous play.

"Oh, that was lovely!" Lili and Megan both exclaimed when Sophia had finished.

"I believe I know the opening lines of Solveig's song," Megan offered.

"Oh, very good! Can you sing it in this key?" Sophia articulated a chord in E minor.

"Yes, I think so. Let's give it a try."

Sophia began the plaintive introduction and on the last chord of the ninth measure Megan started to sing:

Kanske vil der gå
både Vinter og Vår
både Vinter og Vår.
Og næste Sommer med
og det hele År
og det hele År
Men engang vil du komme,
det ved jeg visst
det ved jeg visst
Her skal jeg nok vente,
for det lovte jeg sidst.
det lovte jeg sidst.

"And that's all the Norwegian, or should I say Dano-Norwegian, I know," Megan broke off laughing.

"Yes, Dano-Norwegian," said Lili emphatically, keenly aware of the fact that written Norwegian had been in Danish for centuries.

"Sing it in English then," Myrtl enjoined, looking at her American guest with new appreciation.

Sophia began the introduction again and Megan sang:

Perhaps there will pass
both winter and spring,
both winter and spring.
And next summer too
and the whole year,
and the whole year.
But one day you will come,
I know this for sure,
I know this for sure.
And I shall surely wait
for I promised that last,
I promised that last.

"Brava! Very nice," said Sophia, sounding a concluding chord.

A maid came into the room. "Dinner is served."

The four women rose and Megan began to loop Button's leash around the arm of a chair.

"Oh, no need to do that," Myrtl said. "You can bring him to the dinner table if you like."

"It's probably better if he stays here. I don't let him beg for food."

"Good training. We should do that with Magnus," Myrtl said, looking pointedly at Sophia who good-naturedly fended off Myrtl's look with raised hands.

The dinner was a typical Norwegian one, ample and quite delicious. It featured small cakes of ground beef and onion served with a brown tomato sauce along with carrots, stewed peas, and potatoes. As a relish, a jam of lingonberries was served on the side.

Conversation during the meal touched again on the daring theft of Munch's *Scream*, but Megan could sense nothing other than indignation in Myrtl's attitude toward the crime. Sophia seemed equally outraged. They then talked about Grieg and Megan asked if they knew he was quite a ladies' man in spite of his enduring marriage to the lyric soprano Nina. She was his favorite performer of the countless songs he composed. But nevertheless he had a "wandering eye."

"How do you mean 'wandering eye'?" Myrtl asked.

"Well, for example, once in Copenhagen Grieg met Bella Edwards who, as you probably know, later became Eva Mudocci's musical and life partner. Well, Grieg fell for Bella completely. He wrote several passionate letters to her but her answers were polite and noncommittal, nothing more. The rumor grew afterward that Bella Edwards was gay, and that would explain her indifferent response to Grieg's display of passion."

Sophia and Myrtl exchanged the briefest of glances.

"Ah! Here comes dessert," Sophia exclaimed, quickly changing the subject.

After a paper-thin rolled cake filled with whipped cream, some strong coffee, and a bit of chitchat about the merits of poodles and Malteses, Myrtl announced: "And now let me take you ladies to our just-completed gallery. Professor Crespi, I promised to show you Eva Mudocci exhibited as never before."

Megan and Lili followed their hostess back into the living room, where Button was quietly sleeping, and on through a spacious study studded with overflowing cabinets and shelves. A heavy door—obviously quite new—was on the far side of the study between two bookcases. Myrtl opened it and beckoned the women to step through into a short, dimly lit hall with black walls. She walked quickly ahead of her guests.

"The Stygian darkness is to prepare us for this," announced Myrtl, pushing open a door at the end of the hall. It opened onto an enormous, black-walled room shaped most peculiarly. It was an earthbound isosceles triangle. From where the women stood at the base, two long walls slanted toward the peak. Across the peak a black velvet curtain was drawn. A series of ceiling spot lights revealed the triangular configuration of the room as well as the artworks on the walls.

Megan and Lili gasped. On the left wall were seven different editions of Munch's depiction of Eva Mudocci and Bella Edwards, *The Violin Concert*. They were all framed in gold. While Bella's hands were poised over the piano keys, Eva was not yet playing. Instead she was holding up her violin so that it faced the audience. It was an extremely valuable Stradivarius, the "Emiliano d'Oro." Quite a prize for a young British girl whose birth name, Evangeline Hope Muddock, had been changed to the Italian-sounding Eva Mudocci.

On the opposite wall were three slightly varying editions of the famous *Salome* lithograph, with Munch showing himself symbolically decapitated by Mudocci. Then came four blood-drenched lithographic versions of Munch's oil painting *Madonna* of 1895, with their framing additions of dead fetuses and swimming spermatozoa. The gold-framed prints led the viewer directly to the black curtain in the room's pinnacle. Megan and Lili expressed their appreciation of the lithographs, then looked questioningly at their hostess. What would drawing the curtain away reveal, they wondered.

"First," said Myrtl, "let me ask you what you think could be the climax for such an assemblage of Munch and Mudocci."

"Perhaps enlarged photographs of her?" Lili asked.

Myrtl slowly shook her head, no.

Megan took a shot. "A reproduction of Munch's *Madonna* to demonstrate how closely the Eva Mudocci he met eight years after the painting's completion resembled her?"

"Close, close indeed. But instead of a reproduction, how about *the real thing*?" Dramatically, Myrtl drew open the curtain. Her guests gasped. There in front of them hung Munch's *Madonna*. It was signed and dated 1895 and it was the living incarnation of the artist's other two *Madonnas* of 1895, the one in Oslo and the other, paler one, at the Hamburg Kunsthalle.

"But this is extraordinary," exclaimed Lili. Megan was incredulous.

"I knew he painted several *Madonna* versions," she said at last, "but I thought they were all accounted for—there were four of them, weren't there?"

"And this is the fifth," Myrtl confirmed.

"What a climax to your collection," murmured Lili.

"But does the art world know of this version?" Megan asked, wishing she could get closer to the artwork without antagonizing her hostess.

"They will know in due course. But right now not even Erik Jensen knows. And I mean to keep it that way for the present. Therefore I must ask you to keep this to yourselves."

The two women nodded in silent agreement and continued to gaze at the legendary icon of female ecstasy.

Myrtl broke the silence. "Is it not remarkable how much the woman in this painting looks like Eva Mudocci, even though Munch did not meet Mudocci until eight years after *Madonna* was finished?"

"I was actually thinking the same thing," confessed Megan. "In a sense he painted his ideal woman before he met her in the flesh."

"Yes, yes! I like that."

"And then of course later, after Edvard and Eva had met and he was trying to dislodge her from the older Bella, there was that letter from Eva to him in, I think it was nineteen-six, declaring that her two biggest aims in life were to be a great violinist and to have children by a great artist. And now she had met him."

"*What?*" Myrtl looked at Megan incredulously.

"But surely you've seen the recent news stories about Janet Weber? The seventy-something-year-old British-born nun who claims she is the *grandchild* of Mudocci and Munch?"

Myrtl's face went ashen.

"Please explain yourself," she commanded in a steely voice.

"If I remember correctly, the nun maintains that in nineteen-eight—the year Munch had his prolonged nervous breakdown— Mudocci checked into a private clinic in Denmark and gave birth to twins, a girl, Isobel, and a boy, Kai. Supposedly their natural father was Munch."

"But Munch died childless!" protested Sophia.

"Well, that's what we've all always thought. But apparently Mudocci kept the news about her children from Munch who, at the time, was dangerously besotted with her. Kai died in infancy and Mudocci's daughter, Isobel, never knew who her father was. Not until Bella Edwards, who outlived her life partner Mudocci by a year, told Isobel. Told her that Munch was her father."

"This is pure nonsense!" Myrtl exploded, looking at Sophia.

"Nevertheless, the nun is willing to have her DNA tested. So time will tell, I suppose."

Just then the maid appeared to say that there was an Uber cab waiting outside to pick up the two guests.

Hastily and in sudden silence the four women returned to the living room where Megan gathered up Button and his leash. Thanks for the evening were expressed and a few minutes later Megan, Lili, and Button were in the back seat of the comfortable Uber taxi as it made its way down the winding Holmenkollen neighborhood back to Oslo.

Back in the house Myrtl released Magnus from his banishment. Then she turned to Sophia, green eyes blazing with rage.

"Megan Crespi has ruined Eva Mudocci for me. Now I shall ruin Megan Crespi."

13

Although Stockholm's weather outside was sunny and mild, there was only gloom in Axel Blomqvist's mansion in Östermalm. It had been so ever since Erik Jensen's call concerning the pending visit to the city by an American scholar who was passionately interested in seeing his collection of Munch graphics. Since then he had been trying to contact Pål Enger. He wanted to tell the man not to go through with the Strindberg portrait job until after his visitor had left the city, preferably the country. All hell could break loose if Enger were to deliver the stolen Strindberg to him just as he was entertaining a Munch expert. The theft must be put off for at least a week. But he had been unable to get hold of Enger. Where the devil was he? Why didn't he answer his urgent messages to call him back?

Axel tried to ease his frustration by seeing whether Google would turn up anything on his American visitor. They had not yet set a precise date but she had informed him that she was driving to Sweden within the next few days. His Internet search turned up a number of photographs and a noteworthy enough biography for a scholar. A vita full of research, teaching, publishing, lecturing, and travel. Under hobbies, however, which one of the URLs saw fit to address, Axel saw listed several musical instruments that the Crespi woman enjoyed playing "when she had time": flute, guitar, and piano. Interesting combination, he thought. They had been Axel's instruments too as a boy.

The landline phone rang. It was Pål Enger at long last.

"Where the hell have you been?" Axel demanded.

"Busy. Busy lining up what is going to happen in your precious Museum of Modern Art tomorrow."

"Tomorrow? No, by god, it can't be tomorrow. That's what I've been telling you in my phone messages. We have to delay a week."

"Sorry. It's too late. The horses are out of the gate, so to speak."

"What the hell do you mean?"

"I mean that tomorrow morning there is going to be a tour conducted in Serbo-Croatian at the museum. And tomorrow morning, ten minutes after the tour begins, there is going to be an armed attack on them by Albanian nationalists. I've flown three of them in from Kosovo. While that major distraction is going on, Munch's portrait of Strindberg will be removed."

"An armed attack? People killed? Surely there must be another way? And think of the number of police who will be responding to the outbreak!"

"I am. And my own 'police' van will be first on scene. The artwork will be carried out of the museum 'for protection' and loaded into the van by two of my agents dressed as policemen."

"But it's too daring a plan, too much shooting, and too much bedlam!"

"Bedlam is what I am counting on. There will be a lot of loud shooting, but only to scare people into lying down. No lives will be taken if possible."

"And you can't postpone this for a week?"

Enger's answer was one word.

"No."

14

"Well, if that wasn't an absolutely bizarre ending to our evening," said Lili after she, Megan, and Button had returned to the Hotel Bristol.

"It certainly took me by surprise," Megan laughed. "I guess I shouldn't have mentioned Mudocci's letter to Munch about wanting to have children by a great artist. Myrtl acted as though that were somehow sacrilegious."

"And both Myrtl and Sophia were outraged by the idea of that English nun's claiming to be Munch's granddaughter via Mudocci."

"Well, it's their problem, not ours. The case still hasn't been resolved, so far as I could find out when I looked on the Internet last time. At least we got to see a remarkable collection of Mudocci images in a most unusual setting. Whether or not Myrtl Kildahl will be able to keep secret her ownership of yet another version of *Madonna* remains to be seen. It's amazing she showed it to us, virtual strangers."

"Something persuaded her."

"Yes. And so suddenly."

"I think it was your rendition of Solveig's song..."

"Ha! Of course. That's it."

The two friends continued to joust verbally until they went to bed. Tomorrow would be a driving day, taking them from Oslo across the high mountains to Bergen.

The next morning after an energizing breakfast of salmon omelet and mixed berries, the trio picked up a blue Volvo station wagon from a Hertz rental agency not far from the National Theater and headed northwest out of the city toward Bergen. Lili was driving and Button was peacefully snoozing in Megan's lap.

About an hour out Megan suddenly cried: "Wow! There is a Munch picture if I ever saw one! Slow down. Pull into that turnout, please, Lili."

Lili obliged and they parked facing the border of a dense, very green forest. Sticking out from the even tree line was one very large felled log, the yellow tip of its hacked trunk pointing straight at them.

"Don't you see? It's just like Munch's painting!"

"You're absolutely right. What fun!"

Button also thought the stop was fun and as the women tentatively entered the forest he trotted ahead of them to do his business, then returned obediently to Megan.

Just then they heard the loud sound of a crash and crunching metal. When they turned toward the sound they saw that a large black pickup truck had crashed into the back of their Volvo.

With protesting shouts the women ran to the turnout but the Arctic truck—a Toyota Hilux AT38—had backed away and was already on the highway, speeding off in the direction of Oslo. Megan grabbed her iPhone to take a photo but the truck was too far away. She looked at the damage. It was serious. The rear compartment was crunched inward and the back left tire had been turned in on itself. Lili took a look at the glove compartment papers provided by Hertz and dialed the number given for roadside assistance, giving the auto club KNA their approximate location.

"They say they'll be here within the hour," she reported with relief, pulling Button close to her.

Megan hardly heard her. She was sputtering with anger. "What the hell was that truck doing? This was no accident. The driver purposefully turned off the highway and rammed into our car." She began taking photos of the damage with her iPhone.

By the time the KNA tow truck arrived, some forty-five minutes later, Megan had calmed down enough to give an exact account of what had happened. They hitched a ride back to the Hertz office with the sympathetic driver, and once they established that the wreck was not their fault they were given another Volvo wagon to drive. This time it was a green one.

Underway again on highway E16, and looking forward to driving through the longest tunnel in the world, they were discussing the fortunate fact that Megan's appointment with Olaf Petersen was not until the next day. When they passed the turnout with "Munch's yellow log" they could not help looking around apprehensively for the black pickup truck that had so delayed their seven-hour drive to Bergen.

"We were just lucky they didn't ram into us on the highway," Lili said.

"What I still can't understand is why anybody would want to do such a mean thing."

"And what's really weird is that I keep thinking I see black trucks behind us or in front of us."

"Me too," agreed Megan, who was driving now. "I thought for sure I saw one following us just a while ago and I actually slowed down to see, but then it passed us at quite a speed. All the same, I tried to grab sight of the license plate to memorize it, but the truck was going too fast and then it was out of sight."

"Tell me. Which hotel did you reserve for us in Bergen?" asked Lili, eager to change the subject.

"I chose Steen's Hotel, about fifteen minutes from the harbor. Its website shows it's actually an old Victorian house with several floors, but the dining room looks straight out onto a small park and pond, so I thought it would be perfect for Button as well as for us."

"Sounds quite nice. But I hope we don't have to climb any stairs."

"That was my thought exactly, so I asked for a large room on the ground floor. And they do take pets, without extra charge even, so no problem there."

Seven and a half hours later, with two short rest stops on the way, they pulled up in front of Steen's Hotel and checked into a nice ground-floor room near the reception desk. Parking was on the street, but that was no trouble as both women traveled lightly. They decided to drive down to the old harbor for a dog walk along Bryggen, the harbor where many colorful Hanseatic League buildings still stood. Grilled salmon and boiled potatoes was their choice in a small restaurant right on the old wharf. The menu proudly stated that the establishment went back to 1910. After devouring some almond macaroon rings for dessert Megan and Lili drove back up to the hotel.

They did not notice that a black truck was following them at a discreet distance. Now more cars were parked on the street outside and they had to leave their car almost at the end of the street. Tired from their all-day drive with its false start, the trio went to bed and fell asleep almost immediately. They knew a delicious breakfast would be waiting for them in the morning.

Outside Steen's Hotel a black pickup truck had pulled up behind Megan's green Volvo. A thin, middle-aged man with a limp got out of the truck and walked to the car. He bent down suddenly and placed a GPS tracking device with a motion sensor underneath the vehicle. Then he returned to his truck, placed a call to his employer in Oslo, and drove away. He would spend the night in his truck by a park not far away from Steen's Hotel. He shivered a bit as the cool Norwegian night enveloped him.

15

The results of Max Linde's cyber snooping had turned up some thought-provoking information about the sole woman on his list of Norseliga members, Myrtl Kildahl. From photos he had beamed up on the web Max discovered that, in looks at least, Kildahl was certainly no Norseliga poster child. He wondered what attracted the green-eyed brunette to an organization that touted Nordic, specifically Norwegian, superiority but ostentatiously celebrated on its website the stereotypical "Nordic" makeup of blonde hair, blue eyes—*blondt hår, blå øyne.*

Similarly, Kildahl's extremely successful company, Myrtl Cosmetics, was focused upon looks. She herself was frequently featured in the company's eye-catching advertisements. Was this perhaps the key? Was she trying to change the stereotypical norm? And a supposed one at that. In his travels Max had encountered plenty of "dark" Norwegians, especially on the country's west coast where interaction with outsiders had taken place for centuries.

Searching the web, Max began methodically to collect and classify Myrtl Cosmetics advertisements over the past ten years. They fell into two main groups that were significantly unequal. Out of 100 ads, some eighty-one featured brunettes of all shades or women with jet-black hair. Only twelve ads presented blondes; the remaining ones pictured redheads. The same figures held true for eye coloring. Green eyes were the norm; blue eyes were the exception.

Equally interesting was the pitch of the ads. Contrary to the prevalent advertising mode of presenting women as something to be looked at, and men as involved in some sort of action, Myrtl Cosmetics ads featured beautiful women on the go, driving luxury cars, carpentering bookcases, coaching sports, building houses, sculpting art, chairing board meetings. The men, on the other hand, were shown without exception as auxiliary, either admiring their female companions or engaging in excesses of self-admiration. An interesting if blatant turnaround, Max thought, frowning. In other ads red-lipped, black-haired women displayed almost vampiric qualities, staring down the viewer while ostentatiously licking Madonna Red lips or fingertips.

"That's it!" Max declared out loud to his empty computer room. All these Myrtl ads engage in what could be called *the gaze.* A self-possessed, consuming stare that left the hapless beholder/victim in its thrall. And yet the riveting gaze was not a sexual invitation. It was, rather, an evaluation. Are you worthy of my gaze?

So this was the secret of the company's success. It championed a different sort of female, in personality as well as in looks. Independent, self-sufficient, and capable. And beautiful but with a hint of danger. Was this possibly the persona of Myrtl Kildahl herself?

Max began to write down his tumbling questions. Why would being a member of the Norseliga appeal to Kildahl? She was the only female member. Did she hope to redefine the Nordic woman in her own image? What about the Norseliga website, replete with photographs of invariably blond, blue-eyed people of both sexes engaged in various healthy activities? Was Kildahl's mission simply to persuade fellow League members to break and broaden the stereotypical scope of their images? Perhaps she thought that in doing so Myrtl Cosmetics—with its profitable emphasis on dark Norwegians—would be the grand beneficiary. Yes, that must be what this scheming, obviously feminist woman wanted. Female Nordic superiority, in fifty shades of brunette.

why ?
50 shades of grey

16

That enterprising art historian from America, Professor Megan Crespi, would be arriving in the morning at ten. Olaf Petersen had thoroughly prepared for her visit. It would be gratifying to show her those newly acquired works in his collection by the two Norwegian women artists they had corresponded about several years ago. And he would enjoy watching her admire Asta Nørregaard's handsome portrait of the young Munch. This, one of the gems in his collection, had never been on exhibit. Allowing Crespi to see Munch's self-portrait gift to Nørregaard was certainly not an option, as only a few trusted confidants—the members of his Norseliga—were even aware of its existence. And that was how Olaf intended to keep it.

He looked at his watch. Eight-forty-five. He still had time to say good morning to the priceless Munch treasure glimmering in his bunker. He had greeted the painting every day since it had come into his possession. It was amazing how fickle the news coverage concerning its theft from the National Gallery had been. All blaring headlines the first day, now just five days later, hardly a mention either in the papers or on television. Fine. The less publicity the better. Perhaps he would not even have to go through practiced mock shock should his visitor bring it up.

Down in the handsomely outfitted bunker, its temperature regulated at an even 18° Celsius, Olaf drew the curtains back from across *The Scream*. Once again he gasped involuntarily at the sight of it with its sweeping vermilion, shrieking cadmium yellow, blue-green viridian, and deep ultramarines. And that churning, blood-red sky! Olaf knew one of the theories explaining the volcanic sky was exactly that: Munch's remembrance of the cataclysmic 1883 eruption on the Indonesian island of Krakatoa which had colored world sunsets crimson as far north as Norway for months afterward. The shock waves from the violent explosion were recorded on barographs around the world. Whether or not this actually applied to *The Scream* did not matter to Olaf. He was simply enthralled by the idea. And, feeling as close to the painter as he did, he felt that the palpable pressure radiating outward in the painting could indeed have been triggered in part by the lingering Krakatoa phenomenon.

Not that this was the whole story by any means. Munch had written in his diary about the inspiration for *The Scream* and Olaf had printed it out, placing it in a small red frame to the right of the painting. It read:

> I was walking down the road with two friends when the sun set; suddenly, the sky turned as red as blood. I stopped and leaned against the fence, feeling unspeakably tired. Tongues of fire and blood stretched over the bluish black fjord. My friends went on walking, while I lagged behind, shivering with fear. Then I heard the enormous infinite scream of nature.

And that, of course, was what Munch had originally titled the picture, *The Scream of Nature*. But Olaf knew from personal reconnoitering that there were other cries to be heard. Below the high pathway that looked down over Oslo from the east had stood the city insane asylum, Gaustad, and within hearing distance had been the city slaughterhouse. Reports referred to the horrendous sound of the screams of the insane accompanied by the screeches of the animals being killed. Olaf shivered when he thought of the terrible trio of screams—shrieks—Munch could have experienced as he poured his agonized soul into the painting.

Olaf knew that all his life Munch had been haunted by the specter of going insane like his sister. In his mid-forties the artist did, in fact, suffer an extreme anxiety attack, exacerbated by manic depression and heavy drinking. He recovered but only after spending eight months in a Copenhagen clinic in 1908 where he was given electric shock treatment. Again, what a parallel, Olaf thought. He too suffered from bipolarity, all under control with modern medications, of course. His astute and caring physician, Michael Rosenthal, had found an effective combination of drugs that kept him steady and motivated.

Olaf looked again at the inscription Munch had placed on the top of this particular version of *The Scream*: "Can only have been painted by a madman."

Yes, Olaf nodded, but by a madman who worked himself out from under the siege of near insanity and created pictures of light and love for his great *Frieze of Life*.

The day after the removal of Munch's *Scream* from Oslo's National Gallery, Olaf had called a special meeting of the Norseliga. He wanted to observe how each member reacted to the news. He needed to test each one of them, to be sure they would all keep his dangerous secret, should he share it with them. He was encouraged by their uniform reaction of dismay. And by their instant agreement that the world-famous painting was a uniquely Norwegian treasure and must be recovered, whatever the price. Pleased with his Norseliga members' response, Olaf decided that he could and would reveal his treasure to them at their next monthly meeting. A convening that was on the calendar for day after tomorrow.

But now it was time to go back to the big house and greet his visitor from America.

17

Axel Blomqvist's television was blaring the shocking news. Bedlam had broken out at Stockholm's Museum of Modern Art. During an early morning tour held in Serbo-Croatian at the museum, a trio of Albanian nationalists wielding revolvers had suddenly attacked the tour members. A guard who tried to intervene had been knocked to the floor. Amid commands to lie down and a bevy of loud shots, police had entered the museum, arresting the wild Albanians and shouting to people to continue lying on the floor. For safety reasons they then removed Edvard Munch's famous portrait of Strindberg. It and the Albanians were loaded into a police van, which drove off before anyone realized what was happening. No one was hurt, the newscaster reassured viewers, but officials had so far not been able to make contact with the policemen who had arrested the Albanians and carted off the Strindberg portrait. How did the two events connect?

The answer came soon enough as television cameras focused on the city's harangued captain of police while she held a hastily called press conference. Captain Långsam admitted that no police had been dispatched to the museum until after the Albanians and the painting had disappeared. The whole attack had been a ruse to get to and remove the Munch. A disaster for the city and for Sweden. And just a few days after the theft of Munch's *Scream* in Norway! What was happening in the art world?

Pål Enger and Axel Blomqvist knew the answer. That evening, after Enger had delivered the Strindberg portrait to his client and had been paid off handsomely as promised, Blomqvist triumphantly carried the painting up to a specially outfitted attic room to which he alone had the key. It ran the length of the house. The staff—a housekeeper and a butler—had been given the day off and no one would be in the house until the next day.

Now, trembling with excitement, the grandson confronted his grandfather. The resemblance was extraordinary. Same wavy blond hair and wiry moustache. Axel looked from the portrait to the many photographs of Strindberg he had framed and mounted on three walls of the room. The fourth wall was now dedicated to the Munch portrait of his grandfather. Next to it was a full-length mirror so that Axel could look from it to the painting and back. A mirror image if ever there was one.

For years Axel had tried to buy the apartment building at Drottninggatan 85 where his illustrious grandfather had spent the last four years of his life. Strindberg's three rooms, as well as a large room on a higher floor containing his vast library, had long been a museum, but Axel saw no reason why the government should not allow him to purchase the building in which it was housed. However, all attempts to acquire the *Blå Tornet*—Blue Tower—as Strindberg had nicknamed it, had failed. All right! Now he had a Strindberg Museum of his own. A very private museum of immense value not only to the world but, more importantly, to himself. The deed was done. The miracle had been accomplished. No more gawking by crowds of unworthy tourists at the man to whom Sweden owed so much. Only one thing was missing—someone with whom Axel could share his triumph.

18

"That's fine you've now got a tracking device under Crespi's car but you should have gotten her while she was still on the highway and not in the city," Myrtl Kildahl said, irritation raising her usually deep voice to a high pitch.

"What I asked for was a major car accident, not a minor car ramming."

"I didn't know she was not in the car," whined Snorre Uflaks, intimidated by his employer's tone of voice.

"At least you've managed to trace Crespi and her damn dog and friend to their Bergen hotel."

"Yes. I'm sitting one block away from Steen's Hotel right now. The motion sensor in my tracking monitor will let me know when Crespi drives off for the day and I'll follow far behind her until I get a chance to crash my truck into her broadside without any witnesses around."

"See that you do. Report back to me immediately. And remember, I do not want her dead, just incapacitated, preferably for life."

Kildahl hung up before Uflaks could answer.

19

True to his word, Snorre Uflaks was in his truck and waiting for the GPS motion-sensor to activate when Megan and her crew exited their hotel at nine-thirty the next morning and started up the green Volvo. Snorre had studied a map of Bergen, surrounded as it was by a range of majestic mountains, and he felt familiar with the orientation of the town and its suburbs. What he was not prepared for was the route the Crespi car took. It cut right through the city center and headed off in the direction of Mount Fløyen, the funicular destination of generations of tourists eager to take in the breathtaking views of snow-capped mountains and a city straddling two immense blue fjords. So that's where they are going, Uflaks concluded.

But just as both vehicles began the steep climb toward the cable car station, the Crespi car made a sudden right turn and started down a heavily forested private road. Well, that was unexpected! Should he follow at a discreet distance or pull up to the side of the main road and wait? The lane into the forest was narrow, certainly not wide enough for two cars to pass each other. He decided to park on the side of the road and backed up a number of car lengths so as not to be noticeable when the Crespi car reemerged. He wondered when that might be as he looked up the weather forecast on his smart phone. The patter of raindrops had begun to sound on the roof and hood of his truck. Oh yes, Bergen. Where it rained some 275 days of the year. And traffic accidents are more likely to happen in the rain, he smiled to himself.

It was just a brief sprinkle, however, and had already stopped when Megan pulled up in front of the enormous log mansion hidden away in the Fløyen forest. Over the wooden entranceway was an imposing inscription carved in large letters painted black. Lili translated: "Anyone who wishes to understand me fully must know Norway."

"Oh, that's Ibsen, isn't it?"

"Correct."

"Well, that is just what we're trying to do. Our first Norwegian, Myrtl Kildahl, turned out to be rather unfathomable, however."

A tall, white-haired man with a black-and-white Norwegian Elkhound at his side opened the thick wooden door and gave a tight-lipped smile of welcome. The black patch over his left eye could not be missed. Petersen's smile faded as he saw not only Megan but another woman and a small dog emerge from the car.

"Professor Crespi?" He recognized the brown-haired woman from her website.

"Yes. Herr Petersen?"

The man nodded in silent, expressionless affirmation. His dog looked disapprovingly at Button, then turned and reentered the house.

"This is my friend Lili Holm and this is my dog Button, but they will be continuing on up to the Mount Fløyen cable car. What time do you recommend they come back to pick me up?"

A look of relief crossed Petersen's features. "Two hours should be sufficient, I think. It is ten o'clock now, so noon would be fine."

Megan placed Button, who had taken advantage of being outdoors to do his business, back inside the car and Lili, after a polite, wordless handshake with Petersen, got into the driver's seat. With a cheerful wave and a questioning bark they turned and disappeared back down the rural lane to the main road. Lili did not notice the black pickup that began to follow them up the mountain.

"I am sorry not to be able to entertain your friend as well, but I had expected only one person. As you know from our correspondence, my collection is not open to the public."

"Oh, no, I quite understand and so does my travel companion." Megan hesitated, wondering whether a little humor might brighten the morose mood. She decided to try. "But my little Maltese was really hoping to meet your Elkhound."

It worked. To a point.

"She may have that pleasure when your friend returns with her,"

"It's a he," Megan could not help correcting her lugubrious host.

"We go inside now," Petersen said, without acknowledging Megan's comment.

He led the way through a dark foyer with antlers on the walls into an enormous room illuminated by narrow stained-glass window panels running horizontally just beneath the ceiling. Below them, and extending along all four walls of the room was a mural of what looked like a crowded convention of Nordic gods and goddesses, most of them glowering.

"Oh!" gasped Megan looking around in astonishment at the animated figures. "I feel as though I'm in Valhöll!" She was proud of knowing the old Norse form of Walhalla.

Olaf Petersen looked at her with approval through his one eye.

"You know about the old Norse gods?"

"Um, well, mostly from Wagner's Ring cycle."

"Oh, yes, of course." No reaction registered on Petersen's face. But he was thinking with disapproval about the liberties that insufferable German composer had taken with Norse material for his librettos.

"We go now through my den and into the study where I have placed works from my collection for you to see. Some of them you already know from the photographs I sent you, but some others you do not yet know."

Along with her glum host's silent hound dog, Megan followed Petersen into a spacious den. She gasped again. On three of the walls were several scenes from Munch's *The Frieze of Life*—that massive undertaking which ultimately produced twenty-two different images in multiple renditions. On either side of the door through which they had come were portraits of famous Norwegians, all of whom Megan recognized immediately: Munch, Ibsen, Grieg, Bull, and Bjørnsen.

"What a marvelous collection!" Megan could not help but exclaim, looking around at the walls. Petersen received the compliment in silence, paused to let his guest take in the sight, then led Megan through the den and into an adjacent study. The hound followed possessively. The room was a smaller one and stacked three-high on the walls were small paintings by the two Norwegian artists Megan had focused upon in her work. There were six nostalgic landscapes by Kitty Kielland and several Vermeer-like interiors by Harriet Backer, three of them showing a woman playing an upright piano. In addition there were two portraits by Asta Nørregaard of her fellow artists Kielland and Backer.

"You were correct, Herr Petersen. Several of these painting are completely unknown to me."

"As they are to the outside world. In general, I do not like to share my collection. These three piano pictures by Backer are not known, for example. I've often wondered why she featured the piano so."

"Oh, I can tell you why. Backer's sister Agathe became a noted concert pianist. She was a colleague of Grieg and, in fact, her brilliant interpretation of his piano concerto was his favorite."

"I wonder why I have never heard this before. Are you sure?"

"Yes, I am sure," Megan smiled. "She was quite famous in her day. George Bernard Shaw heard her perform Grieg's concerto in London and pronounced her one of the century's greatest pianists."

"But I am delighted to learn this!" Petersen looked at his visitor with new appreciation. He walked over to his desk and dramatically opened up the wings protecting an artwork hanging on the wall above it.

"Now I show you Asta Nørregaard's second version of her pastel portrait of Munch. Just think! He was only twenty-three years old here."

Megan was thrilled by what she saw. As in the Munch Museum version, the dreamy youthfulness of the artist was emphasized and convincingly conveyed. It was a sensitive rendition by the observant, older Nørregaard of an extremely sensitive soul.

After a long pause, Megan said quietly and truthfully, "Certainly this version is the more profound one."

Petersen beamed with pride. And he wondered how a woman with an Italian name could be so taken with Norwegian artists in general and Munch in particular. He decided to explore her background.

"Tell me, Professor Crespi, are you Italian yourself, or is that your married name?"

"I'm half Italian. My father was from Bologna. But my mother was Scotch-Irish—her maiden name was Laird."

"Ah, then you have some Viking blood in you, thanks to their eighth-century invasions of Scotland and Ireland," Petersen said with approval.

"Well, I hadn't thought of it that way, but now that I think of it, my mother's father did treasure an old horn drinking cup passed on to him by his father. I suppose that counts for something."

"Interesting, very interesting." Olaf Petersen made a spontaneous decision, something very rare for him.

"Professor Crespi, I have something further to show you. But only if you give me your word not to share knowledge of its existence with others, especially people in the museum world."

Megan paused. She hated making bargains like this. But her curiosity got the better of her. "I give you my word."

"If you will be so kind as to stay here, I shall fetch it and bring it down to you."

"I'm only too happy to stay here with all these interesting works by women artists."

Petersen and his faithful hound left the study for his bedroom on the second floor and Megan continued to regard the pictures on display. In fact, after checking for any surveillance cameras that might be overhead, she whipped out her iPhone and took some photos of the artworks, including the portrait of Munch. This was a long ingrained habit with her and hardly one that she was going to give up now. She photographed with lightning speed and replaced her iPhone in her jacket pocket.

A single happy bark from his hound heralded her host's return. He held a small, gold-framed picture in his hands, its back turned to Megan.

"And now just see what young Edvard gave to Asta Nørregaard," he commanded, turning the painting to face his guest.

It was the third gasp of her visit, Megan realized, but the sight in front of her merited that sharp, involuntary intake of breath. What she beheld was a youthful self-portrait by the artist, painted in oil and so at such close distance that only his face, neck, and hair showed. His prominent Adam's apple was lightly indicated, as was the faraway gaze of the eyes. The hint of a smile danced across his slightly parted lips—so out of character for Munch, thought Megan, recalling not only his self-portrayals over the decades but also the many photographs of the serious, unsmiling man. It had been the same way with "her" Egon Schiele of Vienna. Artists who attempt to paint the soul of others or of themselves rarely see smiles before them. Finally Megan began to speak.

"This is just amazing! An unknown early self-portrait! And what a wonderful, winning one. How lucky you are, Herr Petersen."

"Yes, I am that. I was successful in tracking down the Nørregaard heirs and it turned out they had no idea of whom the portrait was. I recognized it immediately but why should I identify it for them? Instead I offered to buy the portraits by Kitty Kielland and Harriet Backer that you have seen here, and I asked that they throw in the unknown work as well. They did, and voilà."

Megan tried not to show the revulsion she felt at her host's words. But Petersen sensed it.

"You have to understand, I am not encumbered by other people's ignorance."

Megan understood. She also wished she could figure out how to take a quick iPhone shot of the rare Munch painting in front of her. Then she realized that she too was unencumbered when it came to obtaining documentation of artworks. But it was, in her opinion, an uneven draw. She decided to try her second line of defense.

"Would you have any objections to my making a quick aide-mémoire sketch of this fabulous self-portrait?"

"Indeed I would."

Megan's cheeks flushed.

"Oh! Do forgive me, Herr Petersen. It's just my art history training speaking up. We were taught to make a quick sketch of every artwork we encountered."

"And why was that?"

"Mainly to acquire a feeling for the particular style of the artist, you know, for any specific characteristic of drawing or painting. That is how Bernard Berenson became such an authority on Renaissance artists and was able to make positive attributions."

"Are you saying you wish to authenticate my Munch?"

"Heavens, no! You couldn't get anything more genuine than what you have here." Boy, oh, boy, Megan thought to herself, I can't say anything right to this one-eyed, querulous old man. She recalled the depiction of one-eyed Odin she had seen in the mythological mural suffocating the living room walls. Maybe he believes he is Odin.

"I think perhaps we return now to the living room," Petersen said petulantly, gesturing in its direction. As they turned to leave the study Megan saw a picture-lined corridor leading off from the den.

"Isn't that Sonja Henie?" Megan asked.

Petersen looked pleased and his mood changed abruptly. "Indeed it is. Come. I show you my Traitors Hall."

"Your Traitors Hall?"

Megan followed her bewildering host into the narrow corridor. It was lined with photographs. A sign above them on the right wall read: "Lest We Forget: Modern Norwegian Traitors." The sign over a mass of photographs on the left wall read simply "Vidkun Quisling, 1887-1945." Megan pointed to the shot of Sonja Henie that had caught her eye.

"I understand why Quisling is here but why on earth is one of the world's greatest ice skaters here? I know she was Norwegian, but..."

"She was a Nazi," Petersen interrupted Megan.

"I never, ever heard that!"

"Not only did she greet Hitler with a Nazi salute in Berlin, but right after the nineteen-thirty-six Winter Olympics she had lunch with him at Berchtesgaden. And Joseph Goebbels personally arranged the release of her first film in Germany."

"Goodness, I never knew about any of this. That she was a Nazi sympathizer. Was she put on trial after the war the way Knut Hamsun was?" Megan pointed to the author's photograph on the wall right next to that of Sonja Henie.

"No. She got out of Europe during the war and went to Hollywood to pursue her acting career, so she was never brought to trial."

Megan looked at the other photographs on the wall. She did not recognize any of the faces or names, so she turned to the Quisling wall. She thought he looked a little bit like Hitler without a moustache. She held up her forefinger to furnish it, explaining what she was doing to Petersen.

"Good god! You are right! With moustache he looks like a blond Hitler."

Megan was amazed she had managed to score a point with her unpredictable host.

As they left the Traitors Hall to return to the living room, she decided the time had come to assess Petersen's take on the theft of Munch's *Scream*. After all this was the true reason for her visit.

"How lucky you are here in Bergen, with your extraordinary collection, to be removed from that terrible Munch theft in Oslo. But you must be so shocked by it."

"Shocked by it? The whole nation is shocked by it."

"Do you have any theories as to why the robbery was committed and by whom?"

Petersen looked at Megan in silence. Damn the woman, he thought. She just had to bring it up.

"Theories? Oh, not I. Why, I only know what the newspapers and television have reported."

"But surely your museum director friends must have commented to you?"

"The only traffic I have with museum directors is when they want to borrow one of the works known to be in my collection, even though they know my answer will be no. This is why I have asked you to promise that you will not discuss having seen the Munch self-portrait here."

"And I will keep my promise," Megan said sincerely, if with a bit of regret. Then before she could stop herself, she found herself saying to Petersen: "The Munch loss may not be as big a catastrophe as might be thought."

"What on earth do you mean by that?" Petersen looked at her with his one eye, now opened wide in surprise.

The sound of an approaching car was heard. It was exactly noon.

"Oh that must be Lili!" Megan hoped the relief in her voice did not register with Petersen who was already striding to the front door. As was his barking hound. The open door revealed not only Lili but also Button who, blind as he was, suddenly lunged directly at the hound. A moment later a chase was in progress as Petersen's hound fled from an enthusiastically chasing Maltese, hot on the scent of the fleeing animal. Lili ran after them as Megan yelled for Button to stop.

The dogs raced around to the back of the mansion, their humans in hot pursuit. Abruptly the race stopped. They all pulled up in front of the entry to a large cylindrical structure built into a densely wooded hill. Three-quarters of it was buried underground. Four cement steps led down to a heavy steel door before which the two dogs had called a panting truce.

"Bad, Button, bad," chided Megan insincerely.

"Your dog is a bully. Let us go back to the front of the house," Petersen commanded, livid that the visitors had seen his bunker.

A few minutes later, after an awkward farewell, Lili was driving the reunited group back down through the Mount Fløyen forest toward Bergen.

Suddenly she exploded. "What does that horrible man need a bunker for? World War II has been long gone for well over half a century!"

Megan agreed and began a hilarious recounting of her visit to the eccentric Norwegian.

At a discreet distance behind them a black pickup truck pulled out from the side of the road and began following their car as they wound down the mountain road.

20

What about the other five members of the Norseliga? Max Linde asked himself. He now had the lowdown on the first Norseliga member he had researched online. She was Myrtl Kildahl and her quirky feminism was embodied in the many dark-haired femmes fatales gazing out so brazenly from her ubiquitous cosmetic ads. It would be amusing to figure out how to sabotage Kildahl's Myrtl Cosmetics business and thus bring her down, no longer a threat to his neo-Nazi brothers. Their growing numbers populated cities across Germany and there were even some comrades in Norway, nostalgic for Quisling days. Their aim was to assimilate modern-day Norwegians into Teutonic solidarity.

Max's best cyber buddy in Norway was a neo-Nazi named Christian Drapsmann. The man's all-too-suitable-surname meant "killer" in Norwegian and he carried out assignments mostly in Oslo. He would regale Max with the weird, always successful tasks he accepted from the city's underworld chiefs. His specialty was trailing individuals and putting them out of commission, either temporarily or permanently as the job required.

The bête noir of Drapsmann and the other Norwegian neo-Nazis, Max knew, was the exponentially growing Muslim presence in Norway. Their hero was mass murderer Anders Behring Breivik, who in a manifesto accused the ruling Labor Party of colluding with Arab nations to swamp Europe with Muslim immigrants. In July of 2011 Breivik attacked Oslo government buildings with a fertilizer bomb, killing eight people. Then, dressed as a policeman, he went to the lake island of Utøya where the Labor Party's Youth League members were at summer camp. He walked calmly around the island shooting groups of teenagers with a Ruger rifle and a Glock pistol. By the time he was apprehended he had executed sixty-nine people. Their average age was nineteen and Breivik demanded to be treated as a hero for his preemptive attack against potential traitors whose aim, by encouraging Muslim immigration, was the deconstruction of Norwegian culture and the Norwegian ethnic group. Yes, Breivik was truly a hero.

But now it was time to research the male members of the Norseliga with their hatred of Germans. With whom should he begin? The twin brothers Gunnar and Gustav Tufte immediately came to mind. Max had already hacked into their computer-design company Kontakt. He discovered that, under the guise of advertising, Kontakt regularly inundated the country's learning institutions with pro-Norse exhortations.

Max decided to take a look at the Tuftes' personal e-mail correspondence. It took a bit longer than he had thought it would to break through the firewall, but on the fifth attempt he was successful. And he quickly discovered something interesting, if mystifying. Often the brothers did not address each other by first names. Their salutation, like their signature, was "Týr" and "Váli." What the hell was that all about?

Max looked up the first of the two odd names online—Týr. Seemed that Týr was the Norse god of war. Interesting, but was there any direct connection with the brothers' computer design company? None that Max could find or think of. Gunnar's choosing the pseudonym of a god of war, however, certainly conveyed a fighting spirit. A warrior god fighting on behalf of the Norseliga most probably. The Nordic god of war against the "inferior" Germans. Yes, that made sense.

So, this is Gunnar, who signs "Tyr" in private e-mails to his brother Gustav, whose code name is "Váli." Okay, so who is Váli? Max looked up the Norse name. Wikipedia told him it was the god of revenge. Oh, nifty, the pieces were beginning to fit. Revenge for Germany's invasion of Norway in World War II. And there was more.

Going through the previous week's worth of private correspondence between the Tufte brothers, Max ascertained that a special meeting of the Norseliga had been called on the day after that much publicized Munch theft in Oslo. Amazing how that writhing, wormlike *Scream* image was so prized in Norway. An irrefutable manifestation of the country's phobic character. Back in the good old days, Hitler had tried to assimilate the neurotic nation for its own good, but instead it was happy to be "liberated" at the end of World War II.

So what went on at that special meeting called in such haste? Perhaps Max could find out as he zeroed in on other members of the League. And it would be interesting to see what quirky pseudonyms they had chosen. He decided to explore Haakon Sando next simply because he liked the name Haakon. It sounded strong. A few cyber passes and he was in. This was Haakon's personal e-mail. There were several messages from the Tufte brothers hailing him as Magni. Okay, who the hell was Magni? Aha! The god of strength. My instinct was right, Max congratulated himself. A shopping mall tycoon who identifies with power. Makes sense. But there was nothing in any of the e-mails the last few days surrounding the Munch robbery about why that special meeting was called.

So how about Petter Norgaard? What did he bring to the group? As Norway's only supplier he had made multimillions in the manufacture of hospital equipment. Would his Viking pseudonym also conjure up antagonism or power of some sort? Max read through Norgaard's personal e-mails for the past week. There it was, his signoff to Norseliga members: "Thor." Wow! Max didn't even have to look up that brawny, red-bearded god of thunder. He knew what his attribute was. A giant hammer. Good choice for an anti-German group. And perhaps some resentment that Germany's great Richard Wagner had dared to borrow Thor from Scandinavian mythology in his *Ring of the Nibelung*.

And now for the most fun of all. Researching the leader of this crazy cult, Olaf Petersen. Max had saved looking him up last as a reward for his labors. Hacking the grand master's personal e-mail should provide the reason for the hastily called meeting of the clan. But, frustratingly, he was not able to get access, even though he successfully broke through three separate firewalls. Damn!

21

August Strindberg's painted eyes seemed to follow Axel as he moved around the spacious attic room he had transformed into a museum honoring his celebrated grandfather. Axel could not resist posing at a small table in front of the full-length mirror he had installed next to the Strindberg portrait. The result was a doubling of identical semblances—one painted, the other live. Yes, Axel assured himself as he compared the two likenesses, I truly am the mirror image of my grandfather. He echoed these thoughts aloud to the vocal little companion he had brought upstairs with him, Maya, his short-haired Persian kitty. Then he put her down and took a selfie of himself with his grandfather's portrait.

Despairing newspaper accounts of the daring robbery of Munch's Strindberg portrait by what appeared to be several policemen could offer no further information. There were no suspects and the identity of the faux police remained unknown. Not even the number of thieves could be substantiated. Some witnesses attested to there being three "police," while others swore there were at least five. Perfect, Axel thought to himself as he carefully clipped relevant newspaper articles for his album. Pål Enger_had certainly lived up to his nefarious reputation.

As Axel regarded his vast photograph collection of Strindberg and his colleagues, his thoughts turned once more to the turbulent, on again, off again relationship between painter and sitter. Munch's infamous slip of misspelling the playwright's name as "Stindberg" on the lithographic portrait of him was infuriating, if revelatory. Each had been considered mad by the general public. And, at times, each considered himself mad as well. Flirting with insanity was seductive as well as necessary to creativity. Was he, Axel, mad as well? Was it mad, was it unnatural to crave ownership of his grandfather's portrait?

Would it not be grand also to own the Stockholm building in which Strindberg had lived the last four years of his life and where he had died? The apartment complex in central Stockholm the writer had christened the Blue Tower? All Axel's attempts to purchase it had failed. But now, with the fabulous Munch portrait of his grandfather in his possession, Axel realized he longed more than ever to be able to see it in the perfect surround. Not in his attic museum, no matter how private and safe it was, but at the Drottninggatan apartment. There, where the actress Fanny Falkner, his grandfather's last great love, had lived. There, where, when the terminally ill Strindberg read eye-witness reports of the sinking of the *Titanic* in April of 1912, he had staggered to his upright piano and played the hymn "Nearer My God to Thee." That, just a month before his death from stomach cancer.

Yes, somehow, if only for a few hours, Axel must hang Munch's portrait of his extraordinary grandfather in the Blue Tower apartment where it belonged. He began to formulate a bold, if dangerous plan. One that might include an art historian from America who was scheduled to visit him soon.

22

"So what's the delay?" Myrtl Kildahl found herself yelling into the phone at Snorre Uflaks. He had picked up the call while following the Crespi car down Mount Fløyen in his truck.

"There has been a complication," he tried to explain to his demanding employer. "She has not been alone this morning. Another woman and a dog have been with her all the time. I followed their car across Bergen and up Mount Fløyen. Before they got very far up they turned down a private lane. Then the car appeared a few minutes later but Crespi wasn't in it, so I sat tight. Waited a discreet distance behind the turnoff for a good two hours before the car reappeared coming down the mountain and turned back into the private drive. I thought I was in for another long wait but about five minutes later the car exited, with Crespi back inside. Right now, at this very moment, I am following them back down Mount Fløyen. But as long as Crespi has company it's going to be tough."

"Damn! I didn't say this was going to be easy. Just keep at it and phone me when it's done." Partly mollified, Myrtl hung up.

Snorre followed the car back to Bergen's city center, keeping back as far as possible. When the trio in the car stopped and parked in a square, so did he. He watched as the women and dog climbed out of the car and walked over to gape at a life-size bronze statue of a man playing the violin. What the devil?

After they had paid their respects to the virtuoso violinist who had encouraged a fifteen-year-old Edvard Grieg to pursue a musical career, Megan, Lili, and Button returned to their car.

"I remember now, Ole Bull became a millionaire through concertizing and bought land in Pennsylvania," said Megan.

"Yes, and he called it 'New Norway'," added Lili happily as they strolled back to the car.

Are they not ever going to stop for lunch? Snorre asked himself as he resumed following the trio. As if in answer to his question the car pulled into a parking spot. He did as well, on the opposite side of the street. What now? There's no restaurant here. He watched as the two women, their dog on a leash, climbed out of the car. Crespi picked up the dog and stood looking at the wall of a building. She kept urging the dog to look at it. What the hell? They were looking at the image of a large dog stenciled on the wall. Then Snorre understood. They had stopped to look at Bergen's famous graffiti artist Dolk. After the live dog had thoroughly examined the stencil dog, the women got back into the car and headed away from the city.

Snorre was really getting hungry now. Surely they must be hungry too? His quarry turned south onto highway E39. Now where were they headed? In about fifteen minutes he had the answer. Edvard Grieg's home, *Troldhaugen*. Groups of tourists were milling around the entrance to the small two-story, Swiss-style house with its large veranda and a tower. Below the house was the panorama of Lake Nordaas. If Snorre could get a chance to push Crespi down off the promontory he might inflict some significant physical damage, just as Kildahl had specified. But not with all these people around.

Hurrying in spite of his limp, he followed the trio—the damn dog was trotting right along—inside a modern building near the house identified as the Edvard Grieg Museum. He watched as they and their mutt entered the museum's little café. So that's where they'd planned to have lunch! The need to remain inconspicuous meant that he would have to go without.

The women took their time. After lunch they entered the museum's store and invested in a few items, including T-shirts. Finally they walked over to the Grieg house and entered. Snorre remained outside, sitting on a bench outside the museum. He had a perfect view of the entryway and, despite a growling stomach, patience. This rural setting might be just what he needed if he could get the Crespi woman alone for a few moments.

Some twenty minutes passed. Suddenly from around the back of the house Snorre saw the trio walking briskly toward the parking lot. How had they avoided leaving from the front door? A man was with them, talking animatedly to Crespi and pointing down a path. Snorre clearly heard Crespi say to the other woman: "Are you sure you don't want to see the composing hut again?" The woman shook her head, no. Then she and the dog returned to their car while Crespi strode off alone. Snorre immediately jumped up and followed her down the narrow path overlooking Lake Nordaas on the right. Ahead of them was a small, single-room structure that constituted Grieg's modest composing hut.

Golly, Megan was saying to herself, both Grieg and Mahler, to say nothing of Strindberg, maintained isolated little composing huts. She had been to Grieg's once many years ago with Lili, and she had been to two of Mahler's three: the one at Maiernigg on the Wörthersee, and the one in Toblach, then part of Austria, now part of Italy and called Dobbiaco. In the summers she had several times visited her dear friend, the Mahler expert, Henri-Claude de La Granger, at Toblach. And now she was about to enter Grieg's inner sanctum. Perhaps he had composed his jubilant piano piece, *Wedding Day at Troldhaugen*, right here! She entered the tiny room. No other tourists were in sight. There against the wall was the piano opposite the window that gave the room its light.

Megan's reverence suddenly gave way to exasperation. In the big house she had admired Grieg's concert grand but she had neglected to make a mental note of the piano maker. Was it a Bösendorfer or a Steinway or a Bechstein? Her guess was a Steinway. But she couldn't stand not knowing for sure. Impetuously she flung open the door of the hut to rush back to the big house and was startled to discover it had hit an approaching tourist right in the face, almost knocking him to the ground. Tossing him an apology but not stopping, she ran back to Grieg's house, entered, and ascertained that the piano was indeed a Steinway, just as she had thought. That was all she needed. She wheeled around and exited the house. Worrying that Button might be getting hot in the car, she ran toward it and within seconds Lili was driving them back to Bergen.

Rubbing his painful forehead, a limping Snorre Uflaks looked with disbelief at the museum parking lot. The green Volvo he had been following was gone. Thank god for the tracking device he had installed under the car.

23

Max Linde was a stubborn man. One hardware and two software firewalls had prevented him from hacking into Olaf Petersen's personal e-mail. The German-hating Norseliga leader was well protected. But Max did not give up. After an hour's work and some online consultation with computer security experts of dubious reputation, he was finally able to hack into Petersen's private account. Then, just out of pique for the extra trouble involved, he created a malicious worm which he attached to all of the man's business computers, instantly infecting them. He did the same for those twin brothers Gunnar and Gustav Tufte and their computer design company Kontakt. Teach them to assume Viking god pseudonyms!

Now, after calming down, he scrutinized Petersen's personal e-mail of the past few days to see what reactions had been produced by his summons ordering the five Norseliga members to gather the day after the Munch *Scream* heist. But he could find absolutely no follow-up discussion of what had taken place at the meeting. The only online Norseliga reference Max found at all was a reminder to members of the next monthly meeting. They were to gather two days hence at ten in the morning in Bergen. But where in Bergen? Certainly not at Petersen's ship-building offices. Possibly at his own private residence?

In the comfort of his Lübeck home computer den Max zoomed in on Bergen from above. The satellite view of Petersen's private address showed it was situated within a dense forest slope at the base of Bergen's Mount Fløyen. And seen from overhead, the house looked huge. Good place for a conference.

There seemed to be another, quite small building in back of the main house, but Max couldn't be sure what it was from the satellite photo. What he was sure of was that day after tomorrow all six German-hating members of the Norseliga would be in one place.

Max decided he would be there too.

24

"The Munch loss may not be as big a catastrophe as might be thought."

Megan Crespi's startling words were still resounding in Olaf Petersen's head. What the hell did that woman mean? Olaf had not been able to forget what came across as a throwaway comment but which carried so much meaning for him personally. Of course the theft was a catastrophe for Norway. How could she think otherwise? Never mind that the treasure was safe in his bunker. What his American visitor should have been was distressed. Distressed for Norway. Distressed over the loss of a national treasure.

Olaf looked at his watch. His business for the day was concluded and it was nearing the green hour. He walked into his den, sat down before the flat screen of his television set, turned it on for the latest news, and rang for his butler, and sometime bodyguard, Sven. A few minutes later, laid out on the coffee table in front of him, were a tall beveled glass and a perforated, trowel-like silver spoon, along with a supply of sugar cubes, cracked ice, and water. A bottle of Vieux Pontarlier absinthe stood to one side. Olaf took the bottle and slowly poured an ounce and a half of the green liquid into the glass. Then he laid the notched spoon across the rim of the tulip glass and set three sugar cubes on top. Pouring a small amount of water on the cubes, Olaf allowed them to soften. As they began to dissolve, he slowly drizzled a narrow stream of water onto the sugar cubes, coordinating the speed of the pour with the mingling of sugar and water with the absinthe. As water diluted the spirit, those components with poor water solubility— anise and fennel—began to cloud the drink. Soon the absinthe emulsified, creating an opalescent and translucent emerald green louche.

Yes, it was Olaf's diurnal green hour. And it pleased him to think he shared the soothing ritual with Edvard Munch. During his Paris drinking days, along with his colorful cohorts, the young painter was addicted to the "Green Fairy," reveling in the super sensibility it gave him as his body seemed to float and his senses were heightened. Unlike Olaf, who knew when to stop, the artist had become addicted, suffering sleeplessness and hallucinations as well as long periods of depression. All this charged his art, however, and made it unique. No one had ever painted like Munch. And no one had ever written plays like his Swedish cohort Strindberg, who had been addicted to absinthe for nine years. Paradoxically, it amused Olaf to think of Sarah Bernhardt's dismissal of all Scandinavian creativity: *"c'est de la Norderie."*

Now that Olaf was relaxed and no longer thinking of business, his thoughts returned to Megan Crespi and her bizarre comment on the theft of *The Scream* from Oslo's National Gallery. He began to feel an intense hatred for the woman. Her knowledge and ardent interest in Scandinavian art were laudable, of course, but her attitude concerning the lost Munch was incomprehensible. In fact it was outrageous. He would like to teach her a lesson.

A bold, no, insane plan began to form in his mind. What if he were to show Crespi the actual *Scream*? Confront her with the real thing. Then she might not be so flippant. Instead she would be floored, absolutely in awe. Not only of being in the presence of the genuine Munch but also in awe of him, Olaf, that he could have engineered such a bold and stellar acquisition.

And afterward? And afterward she would have to be put out of the way. A convenient, lethal "accident." But before she perished, this upstart from America would have been exposed to what real Norwegian art was and what true ingenuity had been involved in the procurement of it.

Yes. This could be a reality. At the imminent meeting of the Norseliga day after tomorrow, he was planning to reveal the Munch to the five loyal members. He had not said a word about knowing the painting's whereabouts when he called that special session right after the theft. He wanted to witness the members' reactions at first hand. Without exception they had expressed stupefied envy. Why had not one of them thought to "organize" this icon of Norway? This was exactly what Olaf wanted to hear. He vowed to himself that at the next meeting he would share his acquisition with them, now that they had demonstrated not only loyalty but also the same procurement mode of mind. Special art should be seen only by special people. What a treasure for the Norseliga his Munch masterpiece was.

If he wanted to show it to Crespi, he would have to do it before the monthly meeting. It would have to be tomorrow. Was she still in Bergen? He had her contact information and quickly texted her: "Can you return tomorrow? Have something extraordinary to show you IN ALL CONFIDENCE. Come alone."

The green hour had had its effect.

25

Museum director Erik Jensen had come to a major decision. In a few days, during the nation's joyous summer solstice, he would make an evening statement to the press concerning the shocking theft at the Oslo National Gallery. He would reveal that twelve years ago, for safety's sake, an exact copy had been created and placed on exhibition as Munch's *The* Scream. The substitution had been known only to him and the restorer involved. Yes, it was deceiving the public, but the difficult decision to do so had also resulted in the real *Scream's* remaining at the museum.

Earlier in the day Erik had informed the Norwegian prime minister of the situation, and as leader of the Conservative Party, she had sanctioned the wisdom of the substitution. Sophisticated new security measures were now being put into place and within a week or so the public would be able to visit and admire the original *Scream*. From Erik's point of view, and he hoped the press would agree, all was well that ended well.

26

After repeated negotiations the Stockholm city council had at last succumbed to Axel Blomqvist's latest and extraordinary financial offer. They had adamantly refused to sell the Blue Tower apartment building with its popular Strindberg museum to a private individual. But the council did agree to allow

Strindberg's grandson private visits to the author's apartment during which, on Monday evenings, no one else would be present. There, entering with his own private punch key combination, Blomqvist would be able to commune with his august relative's spirit. That was all he asked for.

For now.

27

In preparation for his reconnoitering visit to Olaf Petersen's forest mansion outside Bergen, Max Linde had created succinct dossiers on the six members of the Norseliga, along with their Internet photographs. He had blown up the images to poster size and printed them out in multiple copies with matching pseudonyms and a large text line below each one. His Lübeck Lufthansa flight to Bergen via Frankfurt and Oslo left at one the next afternoon. He would overnight at the Scandic Bergen Airport, rent a car the next morning and be at the turnoff to Petersen's large estate by nine. It was not his intention to monitor or interfere with the ten o'clock meeting in any way. His work would begin as soon as the full membership had convened.

28

Megan glanced at her iPhone and scoffed out loud as she read the message Olaf Petersen had texted her.

"Does the man think I am at his beck and call?"

"What man?"

"Oh, that zany Olaf Petersen. Who else? He wants me to come back to his place tomorrow. Says he has something 'extraordinary' to show me."

They were back at Steen's Hotel and had just taken Button for an after-dinner stroll. Before driving back to Oslo they had decided to stay one more night at the hotel so they could make an all-day visit to the just reopened 1924 mansion that housed Bergen's famous Munch Museum. The collection contained some fifty paintings and more than a hundred works on paper, all assembled by one of the artist's most devoted patrons, Rasmus Meyer.

One of the works on paper was known as "the Bergen *Scream*," a horrific close-up version of the painting's screaming figure drawn in pen and shrieking black ink by the artist. Megan had never seen it in the original, nor had Lili. Because the artwork was so fragile it had not been on display for the past twenty years, but for the occasion of the museum's reopening it was on exhibit.

"So, are you going to skip going to the Munch Museum tomorrow morning?" Lili asked, disappointment sounding in her voice.

"Are you kidding? Of course not. I can't miss a chance like this."

"What will you tell Petersen?"

"Nothing. I simply won't answer his text. After all it's rather infrequently that I notice getting texts at all. I vastly prefer e-mail."

"Well, aren't you the old-fashioned one, Megan. Texting is fun and you don't have to write; you can simply dictate your message."

"Don't think I haven't tried doing that, Lili. You should see the misspellings that produces."

"Okay, I give up. And I'm awfully glad you're putting the Munch Museum ahead of that Olaf Petersen character."

"Oh, yes, well I do have my priorities. And anyway, Rasmus Meyer was such a methodical, discerning collector. He assembled paradigms, acquiring major works from each period of Munch's artistic career. From *The Frieze of Life* alone, which you know he considered his major oeuvre, the museum has *Melancholy*, *Jealousy*, *Women in Three Stages*, *Evening on the Karl Johan*, and *By the Death Bed*. You can't get any more Munchian than that!"

"Unless you are a Munchkin from *The Wizard of Oz*," Lili punned.

"I will ignore that."

"And remember, we also want to admire the earlier works that belonged to Rasmus Meyer there. All artists from Scandinavia's golden period of art. It's going to be a full day, Megan."

"That's why I'm happy not to return to Olaf Petersen's."

"You know, Megan, I really think you ought to text him back. You might need to count on his continued friendship in the future."

"Oh, all right, that's a good point. I'll tell him sorry, but I have to spend the day at the Munch Museum—curator appointments and so on—and we have a dinner engagement. And that we're leaving Bergen early the next morning."

Megan typed out the text on her iPhone and sent it. Almost immediately she received an answering text, announced to her by the dulcet tones of a Sherwood Forest French horn.

It read: "UNACCEPTABLE. Call." With appropriate emphasis Megan read it out loud to Lili.

"Okay, now he's done it," Megan pronounced angrily. "No more communicating with that demanding man for a while. We really ought to go to bed," she added, realizing their museum visit would be rewarding but taxing, and that they would have to take intermissions to drive back to the hotel and give Button a chance to do his outdoor routine. As for the next day, they needed to check out of their hotel very early in the morning since the drive back to Oslo would be a long one.

The two friends retired almost immediately. The last thing either of them heard was Button's gentle, regular snoring at the foot of Megan's bed.

29

Norseliga members Gunnar and Gustav Tufte were talking animatedly on a secure line. Gustav, or Váli, was shouting: "Not possible, it's not possible!" Gunnar, or, Tyr, shouted right back: "But it is true! We have been hacked. All of Kontakt's computers have been compromised."

"What do you mean by 'all'?"

"I mean all of them—our business computers at the home office and also at our warehouse offices. Our chief computer engineer has shown me the proof. And if you go to our homepage site there is now a warning in blue font that reads: 'This site may be hacked.'"

"Damn it! Do you think this means our Norseliga membership and activities are compromised?" Gunnar was speaking from Oslo, home of the brothers' computer-design company. Gustav was on the phone from Skien, the birthplace of Ibsen, where their extensive warehouses were located.

"Only if our private e-mail has also been hacked. I'm having Olly check on that right now."

"Damn! They'll have our phones tapped next."

"Now don't get paranoid, Gustav," said Gunnar, forgetting in the stress of the situation to use Gustav's Norseliga pseudonym. "This sort of thing happens all the time, Olly assures me."

"How long will it take to fix it?"

"He's working on it now. Says it shouldn't take too long. A couple of hours maybe."

"Okay," said Gustav, slightly relieved.

"On another subject, shall we synchronize our arrival times in Bergen for this evening?"

"Yeah, good idea. I'll be coming in at five o'clock; how about you?"

Gunnar looked up his arrival time. "Won't be getting there till seven-thirty. Still on for dinner?"

"Sure. At our usual hotel?"

"Right. See you at Steen's."

30

The blonde woman, Isabell Farlig, was petite, athletic, and utterly reliable. Olaf Petersen had used her for delicate missions before and she had always come through. Now, in spite of the short notice, she had accepted Petersen's new assignment. It was to waylay the Crespi woman at the Munch Museum tomorrow and bring her, forcibly if necessary, out to his Norsehjem at the foot of Mount Fløyen. Petersen would take it from there.

31

"I pay you to get results, not to procrastinate," Myrtl Kildahl was shouting at the other end of Snorre Uflaks's phone line.

"Yes, but you don't understand. There are always other people around. I thought I had a chance when there were no tourists in the vicinity and she went inside Grieg's isolated composing hut. But just as I got there she suddenly pushed the entry door open and ran back out toward the main house. The door slammed smack into my face and it hurt!"

If Snorre was hoping for a little sympathy he did not get it. Myrtl was still livid. "If I don't get results by tomorrow evening you're off my payroll, permanently, understand?"

"Yes, ma'am," sniffed Snorre. Once again he was hung up on by his testy, terrifying employer.

It was 9:30 am and he had followed the Crespi car from Steen's Hotel to a parking lot outside Bergen's Munch Museum. The two occupants, the brunette Crespi and her blonde companion, had disappeared into the museum. There was no sign of the dog that had previously been with them. Snorre was prepared for what he knew could very likely be a long wait. To his surprise, just after a couple of hours, he saw the blonde woman walk back to the Crespi car. She was alone. A minute later she had driven off in the direction from which they had come. Snorre smiled. This meant that Crespi was also alone. And no dog. He opened the glove compartment and fished out one of his pair of brass knuckles. All he had to do was simply locate his prey and wait for his chance.

Snorre left his truck and entered the museum lobby. So many rooms. But not many people. He entered the first room on his right and looked around. Some horrible pictures on the wall. Two more rooms and then he spotted Crespi. She was in the next room, standing in front of one of the awful artworks. She had a smart phone—was it an iPhone?—in her hand. She seemed to be waiting for something. Then Snorre understood what she was waiting for. Two other people who had been looking at nearby paintings left the room and the second they did Crespi immediately raised her iPhone to photograph the painting she had been staring at. This was Snorre's moment. His instructions were to disable, not eliminate. A really hard blow between the shoulder blades with his brass knuckles should fracture some bone and do the job.

Looking around quickly to confirm they were still alone, Snorre charged at Crespi, his right fist striking out in front of him. But just as he lunged forward she moved to the edge of the painting to take a detail shot. Snorre's brass knuckles smashed into the painting, loosening it from the wall. It fell on Snorre who found himself flat on the floor and encased by a canvas. Crespi's left shoulder was nicked by the painting's heavy frame. She shouted in alarm and two guards ran to the room. Seeing the brass knuckles on the fallen man's fingers, they held him down while the police were called. Within minutes they had escorted the man with the brass knuckles to a police van.

Megan Crespi's account to the police was brief, vivid, and entailed more questions than answers She had more heard than seen a man dive straight into the Munch painting. No, she did not know him; she had never seen him before. Why had he wanted to destroy the artwork? And why in front of a witness? Was this a terrorist attack? And if so, why a non-controversial Munch at that—a snow landscape?

A number of museum visitors attracted by the hubbub had gathered in the room where the art attack had taken place and where an elderly woman who had witnessed the event was being interviewed. The crowd thinned and began to disburse after the police left. One person did not leave, however. She was a blonde in blue jeans, petite and athletic. Her name was Isabell Farlig.

32

The airport lobby was jam-packed and noisy but Max Linde had found a good seat, isolated and away from the distracting crowd. He was using the time before his departure to Bergen to delve further into the personal data of the Norseliga members.

He had already found out a lot about Myrtl Kildahl—pseudonym, "Hel"— and her cosmetics business and brunette Viking mania, and more than enough on ship builder and founder of the Norseliga, Olaf Petersen, alias "Odin." Also he had zoomed in on the Tufte brothers, "Tyr" and "Váli," noting that Gunnar worked out of Oslo and Gustav supervised the Kontakt warehouses in Skien. Both were married and had children. Nothing unusual there.

But Gustav had made a local name for himself by snapping up auction items that had anything to do with Ibsen. To the disappointment of Skien, he did not donate the objects to the city's Ibsen House Museum; he kept them for his private collection. For example, in addition to bidding on original photographs of the playwright, and a signed letter written in German, Gustav had made a successful bid for Ibsen's *Peer Gynt* with illustrations by the English artist Arthur Rackham. It looked as if Gustav had a friendly rivalry with Olaf Petersen in that regard, for Petersen too was known for his collection of Ibsen images and first edition books. Gustav could have admired these Ibsen likenesses and volumes in Petersen's home during the monthly meetings there of the Norseliga. And surely both men owned editions of Munch's 1902 lithographic portrait of Ibsen at the Grand Hotel Café.

Max was beginning to get a picture of the Norseliga members' priorities. Images and items referring to great Norwegians seemed to be the norm. A newspaper photograph of the hospital equipment man Petter Norgaard—"Thor"—at his desk showed photographs of Ibsen, Grieg, and Munch behind him on the wall.

When he hacked into the creditcard charges for "Magni" Haakon Sando, Max found some unexpected and rather interesting repeat charges. Over the past few months a number of "tools" had been bought from Oslo's largest purveyor of erotic toys. Also a subscription to *S & M* magazine had been renewed.

Max smiled to himself as the first boarding announcement for his flight sounded. He had a jolt in store for these "superior" Norseliga people.

33

Olaf Petersen's gardener had been given an urgent assignment that morning. He was to dig a ditch, six by six by two feet, directly behind the bunker. And he was to do so immediately.

Every now and then Olaf went out to view the progress but he only stayed a short while as he was expecting two visitors. They would be coming together: Megan Crespi and Isabell Farlig.

While he waited he began to plan the next day's event. Once the Norseliga associates had assembled in his living room, with its inspiring continuous mural of Viking gods, he would pass out cards and ask each member to write down what he or she thought would be the greatest treasure one could wish to donate to their permanent meeting room at Norsehjem. The answers would be anonymous. He would then collect them, adding his own, and place them in a glass bowl. Then he would ask Myrtl Kildahl—"Hel"—to draw out the answers one by one and read them aloud. Then, depending on the tone and content, Olaf would or would not show them the fabulous icon he had acquired for the League. The members had proven their loyalty. Now did they have the imagination and the vision to comprehend what would be best, indeed essential for them to hold in trust for the nation?

Olaf looked at his watch. It was two in the afternoon. The gardener had completed his task. His guests should be arriving any minute now. He was ready.

34

"Are you going to be all right, do you think?" Isabell Farlig concernedly asked a still slightly dazed Megan Crespi. She had been listening in on the woman's account to the police of what had happened to the Munch landscape, and Crespi's features matched the photographs she had downloaded from the Internet. The vain woman actually had a website that read megancrespi.com.

"Oh, thank you. Yes. I think I just need to freshen up and pull myself together in the ladies room."

"Do let me help you there," Farlig offered.

The two women walked slowly to the front of the museum where the restrooms were. Crespi headed straight for a toilet booth. When Farlig heard the door lock she immediately opened her purse and pulled out a cloth and a small vial of morphine. She squirted a generous amount onto the cloth and waited by the door of the booth. She heard the toilet flush. Any second now...

"Megan! Are you in here?" The entry door swung open and a frustrated Lili entered and looked around for Megan. A small white dog also trotted in.

What the hell is this? Farlig screamed inwardly.

"Yes, yes, I'm here," Megan said, emerging from the booth.

"We've searched all over the museum for you. And look! They let Button in!"

Button ran to Megan and stood on his hind legs, sniffing, licking, and barking in excitement.

"Good boy, good boy," Megan crooned.

Button turned from Megan to the stranger and stopped dead in his tracks. Suddenly he began to growl at the woman. He began sniffing her scent noisily. Then he began barking.

"No, no, Button, this is a nice lady. She helped me to the ladies room."

Obviously Button did not believe Megan. He approached the stranger and mounted a barking campaign.

"*Åh*, I just turn me *ut*," Farlig said, her command of English not exactly substantial. She practically ran to the exit door and had already disappeared when Megan, Lili, and Button came out of the restroom.

"Who was she? And why were there police outside the museum?" Lili asked.

"I have no idea who she was, just a solicitous stranger. But clearly Button did not care for her."

Megan told Lili about the strange event that had just occurred in the museum and the strange man who attacked a Munch painting with brass knuckles, even though there was a witness present, namely, herself.

"And when the painting fell to the floor the frame nicked me on my left shoulder, but it's just a black and blue trophy, no flesh cut or anything."

"Good lord! I can't leave you alone for even half an hour, can I?"

Megan lifted Button up in her arms. "How come you brought him back with you?"

"When I left the museum to give him a bathroom break, I asked at the ticket desk if dogs were allowed in the museum and the answer was yes, if on a leash, and so of course I brought him back with me."

"Let's see if he likes Munch." The two friends linked arms momentarily. Button, on his leash, hurried to catch up with them. After Munch, the "golden age of Scandinavian painting" waited for them upstairs. The visit would be long and rewarding. Neither woman would ever know how rewarding their visit had already been.

35

Monday evening had arrived at last. The silent white Audi station wagon pulled up in front of Drottninggatan 85. Gingerly holding a canvas encased in bubble wrap, Axel Blomqvist exited his car and entered the code to the Blue Tower apartment house that, in the year of its construction, 1907, had offered all the modern conveniences, including an elevator. He took the elevator up to the third floor and, using his own personal combination on the key punch panel by the door, reverently entered Strindberg's last apartment. He walked through the small foyer, decorated by the playwright with inexpensive printed wallpaper, and into the narrow bedroom, with its single bed, side table, and chair. Should he place Munch's portrait of his grandfather over the bed? Axel removed the bubble wrap and held the canvas up high over the bedstead. Certainly an option. But possibly the study, small as it was.

Axel walked to the study, which was separated from visitors by a room-high panel of glass. Things had been left just as they had been meticulously laid out by the great man himself. His letter to a young woman he had recently met lay ready for mailing. No, Munch's magnificent painting was too large for the study; one couldn't stand back far enough from it.

Now Axel did what he had deliciously put off till last. He had known all along where the portrait should be placed. He entered the dining room, largest room in the three-room apartment. It was in bright colors—yellow, red, and green. Two small busts of Goethe and Schiller greeted him, as did the life mask of Beethoven, which, like so many people, Strindberg had mistaken for his death mask. It hung over the upright piano. Axel lifted up and removed the Beethoven mask from its single nail. Yes. The wall is ideal. Axel sucked in his breath and held the portrait up over the piano. The placement was perfect.

He gently rested the painting on top of the piano and stepped back to gaze at the mesmerizing image. The portrait literally seemed to glow.

This is where it belongs, this is where it has belonged for over a century.

36

Button let Megan and Lili know it was time to leave the Munch Museum and have dinner. His two humans obliged and decided to return to the old wharf restaurant where they had eaten so well the night of their arrival in Bergen. And then they wanted to go back to the hotel, pack, and get to bed early to be fresh for the exciting detour they had decided to take on the way back to Oslo.

Lili had been the one to suggest it, since their planned stay at Skagen had become victim to Megan's unexpected busy schedule in Norway and forthcoming trip to Stockholm. And unfortunately the Skagen condo was fully booked for the next few weeks. So Lili asked if, on their way back to Oslo, they could drive down south to the little waterfront town of Åsgårdstrand, so beloved by Munch and where he had finally bought a cottage. The town was now an artists' haven, with workshops, studios, and galleries. They could spend part of their week there. Perhaps make a side trip to Ibsen's birthplace, Skien. And since they'd be arriving in Åsgårdstrand on June twenty-third, they could attend the town's famous solstice celebration, *Sankthansaften*—St. John's Eve. Every year, during the evening of one of the longest days of summer, a huge bonfire was built on the beach and busloads of tourists joined in with the local music and dancing. And then came the burning of the witch, a doll made of cloth and straw. It was quite a spectacle.

Megan had agreed to the idea immediately. She sent an e-mail to the Swedish collector of Munch, Axel Blomqvist, asking to defer their meeting for some four days or so. Then a brief Internet search brought her to the Thon Hotel, a very cheerful, very modern conference lodging right on the waterfront with its small boat docks, nearby beach, and splendid views of the Oslo fjord. And, even more importantly, the hotel accommodated pets. Within minutes they had made their reservations. It would be at least a seven-hour drive without scenic and bathroom stops, but they felt up to it and would indeed take short breaks not only for their benefit but also for the little critter with them.

"I think I'll tell them at the front desk to be sure and wake us up at six tomorrow morning," Megan said, walking to the door.

"Why don't you just call them?"

"Because I also want to give Button one last chance to do his business. He hasn't done anything in hours and I don't want him waking us up during the night."

When Megan reentered the hotel after Button's little night music out-doors, there were two men checking in at the front desk. She waited to one side and listened to their conversation with the night clerk. The men were middle-aged, had short blond beards, and looked just alike. They must be twins. Even without Lili's translation help Megan was still able to pick up that they were going to have dinner in the hotel restaurant. Button, the gourmet, must have heard the word "restaurant" because his tail began wagging and he gave a joyous bark. The two men turned to see what was going on, then smiled at the sight of the happy little dog. One of them bent down to pat Button while the other asked Megan what breed the dog was.

"Maltese," Megan said, understanding his question right away. Her slight command of Norwegian and Danish, thanks to having traveled around Scandinavia with Lili for decades, helped her in understanding the many similar words in both languages. And when trying to read either language, her knowledge of German was often a huge help. So she took the leap.

"*Zwillinge?*" she asked in German, pointing to both men.

"*Ja, Tvillinger,*" Gunnar and Gustav answered in concert, confirming that they were twins. Nodding and smiling broadly at her and the dog, they turned and headed for the hotel restaurant. Megan made her request with the front desk clerk to call her at six in the morning for the long drive to Åsgårdstrand.

"Åsgårdstrand? You go for the summer solstice then?"

"Yes, indeed. I hope it won't be too crowded."

" That depends. But you can get good view of main bonfire from Hotel Thon—is that where you go?"

"Yes, and that's good to know. Thank you."

She and Button returned to their room and finished packing. Lili was already through and was writing in her diary. They would both dress in blue jeans for the long drive tomorrow. All were in bed and asleep by ten o'clock.

37

Max's third lap on his flight from Lübeck to Bergen had brought him to the Norwegian city a little before seven in the evening. He checked into the airport hotel and waited until the sun had finally set to see if he could catch a glimpse of the famous northern lights. But it was too late in the season. He found it difficult to fall asleep as thoughts of what he would be doing the next day kept him awake.

After a very early breakfast the next morning Max went to the airport car rental where he was talked into renting Norway's new favorite, the Nissan Leaf. It was the first electric vehicle he had ever driven and, after being assured that it was at full charge, he drove into Bergen's old town and parked by the Hanseatic buildings. It was 8:00 in the morning and no tourists were around. Taking twelve flyers with Olaf Petersen's photograph on them, he quickly entered the public restrooms, both men's and women's, and posted them on the mirrors. That would certainly puzzle people and soon the police, then the newspapers, would hear about it.

Returning to his car unobserved, he then drove to the base of Mount Fløyen where, with the help of the satellite image on his iPad, he located the turnoff for Olaf Petersen's forest home. He backed his Nissan Leaf into a lane in the woods opposite and was able to have a clear view of Petersen's private drive without being seen from the road. It was now 8:45 in the morning. Members of the Norseliga would be arriving within the hour or so. Max fitted his telephoto zoom lens onto his Canon PowerShot and waited, a satisfied smile on his lips.

38

It had been well after 10:30 the preceding evening that Isabell Farlig had finally gotten up the courage to phone her employer with the bad news that her efforts to bring the Crespi woman to him had failed. After she absorbed the sputtering shock waves of Petersen's wrath, she managed to tell him that she did have some ameliorating news. By checking with different hotels in town she had ascertained not only where Crespi was staying but the fact that she and her companion were leaving by car in the early morning for Åsgårdstrand. Did Herr Petersen still desire her to intercept Crespi and bring her to him?

"Absolutely not. I explained to you that your commission was a time-sensitive one. There is no longer a reason to have her in my home. You have failed. I shall never do business with you again."

Olaf Petersen slammed down the phone. He was irate. Now the pleasure of seeing the shock on Crespi's face at sight of *The Scream* was denied him. She would live to scoff at Norway's national loss another day. Or?

He picked his phone up and dialed Farlig. She answered instantly when she saw the caller ID.

"Herr Petersen?" she asked tremulously.

"Yes. Now look here, Farlig. I am going to give you another chance. But this time you *must not fail*. I want Crespi brought to me within the week. Either persuade or coerce her. Not tomorrow, mind you, but any day afterward up to a week from now. Do you think you can accomplish this?"

"I will give it my very best effort, Herr Petersen, and I thank you for giving me another chance."

"See that you make the best of it."

Isabell sat still in thought after Petersen hung up. To isolate Crespi from the other woman and especially from her horrid dog was going to be challenging. And harder now. Because of the bathroom incident in the Munch Museum, the two women knew what she looked like. She was going to have to alter her appearance. She would begin with her hair color. A short, brunette wig was in her closet for just this type of challenge. Isabell would fill up her Beetle's gas tank right now, although it was late in the evening. And the next morning early she would be on site, watching for the Crespi menagerie to leave Steen's Hotel.

39

From the main police station in Bergen, Snorre Uflaks had desperately called Myrtl Kildahl for help. He had been arrested in a "misunderstanding" and had spent the night in jail. Would she please, please stand bail for him? Unfortunately it was very high and he had been cautioned not to leave the country. With tremendous misgivings Myrtl had done so, but not before she took out her anger on him with nouns he had only heard in the army.

Now, at eight o'clock in the morning, he was free and had made it back to his truck, left in the Munch Museum parking lot. He checked his tracking device. The Crespi car was in motion. Nuts! It was on highway E16 heading southeast, about two hours out from Bergen. She was obviously driving back to Oslo. He had better get cracking. Filling up at the nearest gas station, he took off, driving as fast as he dared. All he needed now was to be harassed by the police again.

how many times
This phrase is used

40

It was not until 9:50 in the morning that, from his secluded observation point in the woods, Max Linde saw the first of the Norseliga members arrive at the turnoff for Petersen's forest house. There were two male occupants in the car. Probably the Tufte brothers. He snapped photos of them with his telescopic lens.

Almost immediately another car appeared, a white limo with darkly tinted windows and the emblem "MC" on the doors. Max guessed it must stand for Myrtl Cosmetics and that, in addition to the Kildahl woman, the occupants might also include the shopping-mall tycoon, Haakon Sando, as well as Petter Norgaard of the hospital equipment company. All three lived in Oslo and they had probably all flown into town the evening before. Most likely these German-hating billionaires stayed at Bergen's swank Hanseatiske Hotel if they overnighted. Max knew from hacking her e-mail that Kildahl kept a white limousine, with the Myrtl Cosmetics crest, at all the major airports in Scandinavia. Time passed. No more cars turning into the Petersen driveway. He must have been correct about his identification of the occupants of Kildahl's limo. At twenty past ten o'clock no more cars had entered the Petersen grounds. It was time for him to go into action.

Gathering up tools and a supply of his large flyers, Max went by foot up the long, winding lane that led to Petersen's house. From the satellite photos he had studied, he had a good idea of the distance to it and he stopped in plenty of time not to be visible from the house. He began affixing the posters to large trees on either side of the lane, skipping a few trunks each time, and working his way slowly back to the main road. The photographic images of the six Norseliga members all ran the same banner underneath: "WANTED IN GERMANY."

Within twelve minutes Max's work was done: some eighteen startling flyers now lined the verdant lane down which Petersen's visitors would be driving when the meeting was over. It was Max's bet that after they had seen them, they would be turning around and heading right back to the forest mansion. Outrage, incomprehension, fear, and recrimination would be the order of the day. The proclaimers of Nordic superiority were nothing more than wanted criminals.

41

Their second rest stop on the way to Åsgårdstrand was by a cascading waterfall. Megan, who could not keep up with Lili's long stride, released Button from his leash and watched him trot with interest toward the sound of the falling water.

"No, no! Stay with us, Button," admonished Lili, grabbing his collar. Megan reattached his leash when she reached them.

"Let's sit on this bench and have some of our smoked salmon, cream cheese, and bagels," said Megan, slipping off her blue jacket and spreading it out on the bench.

` "Are you hungry again?" Lili laughed.

"No, but Button is."

They all three partook of the delicious little banquet, supplemented by fresh cherry tomatoes for Button's two humans. They were talking about a war movie they had both seen recently in which every third word, it seemed, had been "fuck."

"I just hate it," Lili declared. The word has no meaning any more. Not that I ever cared for the meaning to begin with. But what's happening to society when you hear the word 'fuck' come out of children's mouths?"

"Couldn't agree with you more. What's wrong with the good old-fashioned 'damn'? Conveys a lot more punch, seems to me. Or even 'heck'?"

Her eye was caught by the sight of a colorful butterfly hovering over Button's head.

"Oh, look! That's a Red Admiral!" she cried, cupping her hands to catch it. It just eluded her grasp.

"How do you know what it is?" asked Lili, surprised by her friend's knowledge. "Or are you just making it up?"

"No, no, those butterflies are common in Texas too. I used to chase after them as a girl. Easy to recognize with that orange-red marking."

Suddenly Megan's iPhone played the Méditation theme from Massenet's *Thaïs*.

"Hello?"

"Ah, Megan! I'm so glad you answered." It was Erik Jensen from the National Gallery.

"Oh, wonderful to hear your voice, dear. What's up?"

"I wanted you to know something that must remain confidential until seven o'clock this evening."

"Until seven? What could that be?"

"At seven this evening I am going on national TV to hold a press conference concerning the Munch *Scream* we have here at the museum. I am going to announce that the stolen painting was merely an exact copy and that the real one is safe and sound and will be put on exhibit in a few days, once our new, enhanced security is installed."

"Why, Erik, that's wonderful. The whole nation will rejoice at the news. And I don't think anyone will fault you for having had that exact copy made."

"Ah, I'm very glad to hear you say that. I do hope this is the case. I did inform the prime minister and she also did not fault me for having kept the original under wraps."

"Well, I shall certainly look for your broadcast when we arrive at our hotel in Åsgårdstrand this evening."

"I just wanted you to know in advance, Megan."

"Thank you, thank you. So now there need be no more search for the copy?"

"On the contrary! The police and museum are still absolutely interested in finding out who the thieves are. In that regard, did Myrtl Kildahl and Olaf Petersen strike you as possible robbery culprits?"

Megan had to laugh. "They are both so zany, each in their own way, that I wouldn't be surprised if either one of them, or perhaps both of them were responsible for the theft. If so, serves them right."

"Oh, Megan, be serious."

"All right. I do think Petersen might be in possession of something important, although whether or not it is the Munch copy I couldn't say."

"What do you mean?"

"I mean that yesterday I received a text from him urging me to come back to his house: he had something 'important' to show me."

"Oh? Did he say what?"

"No. And since I've had it up to here with him and his Viking palace, and hadn't yet been to Bergen's Munch museum, I texted him that I couldn't come."

"Yes?"

"Well, I immediately received the most outlandish text. It read: 'IMPOSSIBLE. Call.' That's all. But it was enough to make me *not* call him."

"But this is most interesting. I think it is a lead the police may want to follow. May I pass this on to them?"

"Why don't you wait until I get back to Oslo? We could go together then, and I could show them the text, since I haven't erased it."

"Whatever you think best, Megan."

"Good luck with your press conference this evening then. And I really think you are doing the right thing by going public."

"Thank you. I hope so too."

After they hung up, Megan elaborated for Lili the other side of the two-way conversation. Then they turned their attention to the mouth-watering apple slices they had been far-sighted enough to bring with them. Button was enjoying being outdoors and the sound of the cascading waterfall clearly intrigued him.

"You know what?" asked Megan suddenly. "I just remembered that the Munch *Scream* stolen in nineteen-ninety-four was recovered in a hotel room in Åsgårdstrand!"

"Wow, that sends shivers down my spine. Do you know which hotel?"

"No, but you can bet it wasn't our hotel. The Thon is too classy. Three thugs and a canvas would certainly have been noticed. It was probably a small dump of a place and off the beaten track."

"Still, there is something poetic about *The Scream*'s finding its way back to a Munch town. A place he loved so much."

"Well, poetic and ironic."

About ten minutes later, their picnic finished, they were back in the green Volvo station wagon heading for an Åsgårdstrand that had suddenly taken on a new dimension.

Two vehicles had flashed past the waterfall stop. One was a black pickup truck and the other, far to the rear, was a light blue Volkswagen Beetle. At one interval both of them had come to halts by the side of the highway. They did not get back on the highway until a green Volvo station wagon with two passengers and a small dog passed them.

42

It was with great gratification that Olaf Petersen looked at the five people in the great living room of his forest mansion. Here, sitting around the rough-hewn wooden banquet table in the center of the room, were five of the most important people in Norway. They were all so different, yet all of one mind. The privilege of having been born Norwegian, of sharing a proud Viking past, all this animated their thoughts and actions. They each agreed how important it was to educate their countrymen and the nation concerning their noble heritage and to take pride in it. They had all worked hard to instill Norse self-esteem in their various professions. And witness the success of Norwegian studies in schools around the country—something they had fought hard for through surrogates in the teaching field. Yes, the Norseliga members deserved the extraordinary experience Olaf was about to provide them.

On the table in front of each member was a watercolor set, a brush, and a small bowl of water. The Norseliga members began the ancient Viking routine of painting their cheeks with the Web of Wyrd—the matrix of fate. It consisted of nine bars arranged in an angular grid that contained all the shapes of the runes. The interlocking red and green bars symbolized past, present, and future as all inextricably interconnected.

Myrtl Kildahl, as might be expected of a cosmetics queen, was especially adept at applying the rectangular grid on her cheeks. On her forehead she added the black Valknut: an interconnected knot of three Borromean triangles. Not only was the Valknut associated with Odin's power to blind and unblind, it was also associated with maternity, representing rebirth, pregnancy and the cycles of reincarnation. This was why Myrtl had chosen to add it. A powerful female symbol. Viking women's rights had lapsed with the introduction of Christianity. In defiance, Myrtl always kept an S-shaped shiny brass key—Viking symbol of the exalted status of woman—on a chain around her neck.

When the Norseliga's temporary tattooing was completed, Petersen rose to his feet and in a rich baritone voice addressed the members.

"This morning, my dear colleagues, is not a routine monthly meeting of our League. It is, to put it succinctly, a celebration of our success. It is a tribute, I can say, to your great efforts on behalf of our common cause."

The group looked at Petersen with curiosity. He was not known as one who made formal speeches. But here he was doing just that. He continued.

"I, Odin, say to you, Thor, Magni, Tyr, Váli, and Hel, you have done well.

You have pumped life blood back into our beloved Norway. I am so proud of you. And you shall be rewarded. It gives me the greatest pleasure to tell you that our Norseliga has acquired a treasure of unspeakable worth. A treasure that you have earned."

The Norseliga members looked at Petersen/Odin with surprised interest. This was certainly different from the usual monthly meeting. Ordinarily each member gave a report of various successes, with Odin going last. It was most unusual that Odin had broken the pattern. The last time that had happened was at the emergency meeting on the day after the theft of Munch's *Scream* from the National Gallery. Then they had discussed the brilliance of the maneuver and the boldness of the idea. Since that time some of them had wondered why there had been no ransom demands or any progress in the police investigations.

"If you will please follow me," Petersen said, his hand indicating the front door. He began to walk in that direction and the mystified Norseliga members followed. Why were they being led outside? Only their cars were there.

They were led past Kildahl's dozing chauffeur and around to the back of the great house and toward a large bunker—perhaps a leftover from World War II, but newer looking. Petersen unlocked the heavy entry door and motioned the others to enter. He brought up the rear, closed, and locked the door. Then he turned on a CD player primed the evening before. The sound of a brass Viking lur filled the room with the haunting call of a hunting horn. Then there followed a rendition by mixed choir of the unofficial Norwegian national anthem, penned by Bjørnson and set to music by his cousin Rikard Nordraak. Stirred but mystified, the members sat down on folding chairs that had been set up facing the opposite wall which was covered by drawn, crimson velvet curtains. A large magnifying glass hung to one side on the wall. What was behind the curtains?

"Behold and be in awe," said Petersen as he drew them open.

There was an audible gasp. *The Scream* was before them. Hanging on the wall, the framed painting seemed to flood the room with its sinuous waves of orange and red.

Haakon Sando, was the first to speak, and he echoed the question of the other members. "But how is this possible?"

Peterson savored the moment. Then he spoke. "All things are possible for Norseliga."

Silence prevailed as the members continued to stare in disbelief at the pulsating gem in front of them. It was as though Munch himself stood before them. The angst emanated by the screaming figure with its hands to its ears was palpable. The silence continued. Then Petersen spoke.

"No other image in modern Western history is so well known. Munch, the supreme painter, Munch, the great Norwegian, Munch, through whose veins ran Norse blood. We have long discussed the idea of having an altar where we can honor the ancient Norse gods. Here we have it."

Sounds of approval and affirmation followed. Almost as though in a trance Gustav Tufte got up from his seat and walked slowly toward the painting. The others soon followed his lead. Being this close to the masterpiece—far closer than was possible in a museum—was hypnotizing. Gunnar Tufte dared to pick up the hanging magnifying glass and reverently scrutinized details of the masterpiece through it. No one spoke. The icon inspired worship. Haakon Sando found himself not only worshiping but feeling envious. Envious of Petersen's brilliant idea and wishing he had thought of it, had been the one to bring it to Norsehjem. But for now he shared in the group's veneration and awe.

"And now, although reticence and trust are components of our Norseliga, I must ask each of you to swear an oath of silence and sign the document I hand you."

One by one the members read aloud the oath printed on the paper handed them, then signed it with both their true names and their pseudonyms. Afterward, they respectfully read the Munch diary quotation Petersen had installed to the right of the picture with its harrowing conclusion: "I heard the enormous infinite scream of nature."

"We can all be uplifted by the fact that our great countryman dealt with and mastered the dread inspired in him by experiencing that scream," mused Petter Norgaard quietly.

"And now it is our sacred task to keep secret the location of the Norseliga Scream," Petersen reminded them.

He continued: "Let us sit here in silence now, blissful in the presence of our prize, and absorb our noble countryman's message of victory over all adversaries. Let us be reminded of the work we still have ahead. Then let us go forth and disseminate the message of Norse greatness. May we double our efforts! And double our successes."

Petersen filled five small brass drinking horns with Norwegian akevitt from an oak bowl and passed them around, pouring a final one for himself.

The silence was broken by the word *skaal*—the Norwegian toast word derived from the old Norse *skål*. Reverently, the group raised their drinking vessels and let the anise-flavored liquid slowly slip down their throats. They were inspired by their leader's brilliant act of acquisition. Commitment to their collective mission was revitalized. All was well with the Norseliga.

43

"What colossal nerve!" In his Stockholm office Axel Blomqvist was reading the morning paper. His eyes were fixed on an illustrated article about "the new career" of Norway's notorious Pål Enger, former art thief who was now exhibiting fourteen of his own works at an Oslo gallery. The public response had been astonishing. All of the paintings—portraits in the style of Munch, each with a sly quotation of The Scream in the background—had been sold to enthusiastic buyers on the first day of the show.

Why that scoundrel! He's gone legit. No one can arrest him for Munch quotations in his own works. And his portraits aren't half bad. An idea began to form in Axel's mind. What if he were to commission Enger to paint a portrait of him holding Munch's portrait of his grandfather? Then he could have Munch's image openly in his own home, in addition to the real thing hidden up in the attic he had turned into a Strindberg gallery. A wonderful little museum, but a museum that could only ever be visited by one person. Although, of course, he always took his little feline companion Maya upstairs with him.

He typed out an e-mail proposal to Enger and clicked the Send key.

44

Ever since she pulled off the highway because the Crespi car stopped by a waterfall, Isabell Farlig had had to stay behind an annoying black pickup that often slowed down but refused to pass the green Volvo in front of it. She wanted to be closer to the Crespi car but she also did not want to be close enough to attract the occupants' attention. So, frustrating as it was, she continued following the truck. In a way she should be grateful, as it provided useful cover for tailing the Volvo.

When the three vehicles reached the outskirts of Åsgårdstrand the pickup finally turned off. Good riddance! Isabell held back, allowing another car to be ahead of her, but keeping the target in her sights.

Snorre Uflaks knew that his tracker would inform him exactly where in

Åsgårdstrand Megan Crespi's car would park. Probably at a hotel. Most likely the town's best hotel, the Thon. He parked by the pier in front of it and kept an eye on the hotel. Sure enough the green Volvo pulled to a stop at the side of the hotel and its occupants clambered out. One barking dog and two scolding women. A smiling porter carried their bags inside. Then Crespi drove the car to one of the parking places in front of the hotel annex on the Havengate, the Harbor Street. Snorre could see from his truck the spot she chose. It was in the shade and very close to the pier and beach. A place that in a couple of hours would be thronging with people making their way to the huge bonfire in front of the hotel. Snorre abandoned his truck and ran up the hotel's front porch stairs. He sat down in a rocker and had an unencumbered view of whoever came in or out to watch the fireworks. All he had to do was follow Crespi into the crowd of noisy, drunken celebrants. His brass knuckles had been appropriated by the police. But the short-handled claw hammer he had up the arm of his jacket would be enough to inflict injury.

Isabell was not surprised to see Crespi turn into the Hotel Thon parking area. She drove past the hotel, then turned and found a parking place the next street over. She walked over to the hotel, entered the front lobby that faced the enclosed pier and took a seat out of sight, watching and waiting for Crespi and her inconvenient friend to appear. Certainly they would be exiting from the hotel porch to watch the summer solstice bonfire spectacle. Dozens of people were already beginning to gather around the pier and on the rocky strip of beach. There was no danger of Isabell's being recognized as she was wearing her brown wig. Her blue parka helped her blend into the crowd.

Isabell's plan was flexible. All she needed was to catch Crespi in a noisy, tipsy crowd so dense that no one would notice when she gave her a quick jab in the upper arm with a dose of fentanyl. That would knock her out almost instantly. It was eight o'clock. The long midnight sun should be setting by ten, chilling the already cool Norwegian summer night.

45

At Olaf Petersen's forest mansion a late lunch was being served to the Norseliga members. The atmosphere was that of a jubilant celebration. Everyone appreciated the great privilege that had been awarded them and each member was uplifted by the direct contact with one of Norway's greatest treasures.

Around two o'clock in the afternoon the group began to disperse. The Tufte brothers were the first to leave. Myrtl and Haakon were still talking with Olaf in the living room while Petter had wandered into Olaf's den to admire once again his host's inspiring portraits of the five great Norwegians—Munch, Grieg, Ibsen, Bull, and Bjørnson.

Suddenly there was the sound of an approaching car coming to a sudden stop just outside the front door. A moment later the door was yanked open and Gunnar and Gustav ran into the living room.

"We've been exposed! We've been exposed!" they shouted. Both were extremely agitated and kept pointing to the door.

"Whatever do you mean?" Olaf barked, not hiding his irritation at the brothers' dramatic demeanor.

"Outside!" Gustav yelled. "You haven't seen what's outside! Lining your driveway right after the first curve and all the way to the main road! *Large flyers with our photos.* Attached to trees on both sides of your drive!"

"And the posters say 'WANTED IN GERMANY,'" Gunnar added grimly.

"What the hell?" Olaf looked at the brothers in disbelief. They all ran outside to see for themselves.

Sprinting down the driveway they rounded the first curve, then came to a stop. There, as far down the drive as they could see, were blown-up photographs of themselves affixed to every other tree on both sides of the lane. Each one said the same thing underneath: "WANTED IN GERMANY."

"But this is horrible!" Myrtl turned to the others. Who could have done such a thing?"

"And why?" Petter asked.

"My god! Do you think they continue out onto the highway?" Haakon voiced a new fear.

"One of you go and see," commanded Olaf, regaining his composure. "I'll have my gardener take down the driveway ones right now. We'll examine them in the house. Perhaps there will be some hint as to who the perpetrator of such a vile act could be."

The Tufte brothers both broke into a run along the driveway to the highway while the others regrouped around the banquet table in Olaf's living room. Olaf sent his butler out to get the gardener to help him take down the outrageous posters.

Within minutes the brothers returned with their report. It was negative, thankfully. No flyers outside the grounds. Both sides of the highway were clear.

"What I can't understand is why they say 'WANTED IN GERMANY.' Germany? Our various businesses have footholds in Germany, but not our Norseliga," Haakon voiced the question in all their minds.

"Well," Petter answered for the others, "I think the posters are aimed at the Norseliga members and not our businesses. It's the Norseliga that is the object of this outrageous attack."

"But why would they wish to do us harm? Look how we have heightened Norwegian awareness in schools around the country." Myrtl looked around at the others.

No one had an answer but suddenly each member was surreptitiously looking at the others, silently assessing his or her loyalty to the group. Could it have been someone within their tight group?

But there seemed to be no reason for what they now all referred to as the attack. Surely it could not be explained by anger, since existence of the Norseliga was a secret. Or was it? Someone obviously knew about its existence.

Suddenly Haakon looked accusingly at Myrtl. "What about your chauffeur? Could he know why you come here once a month?"

Myrtl's cheeks flushed with indignation. "Of course not! He knows you and Petter come with me for monthly conferences here, but he certainly has no idea as to the content of those conferences, or that we are members of an organization. Or whoever else is here."

"So you don't think he could have put the flyers up while we were having lunch here?"

Myrtl did not grace Haakon's question with a spoken answer. A vigorous shaking of her head sufficed.

Just then the gardener made a timid entrance. "Herr Petersen?" he asked, holding up a large batch of posters.

"Yes, yes, come in, just put them on the table here. And I want you to continue searching the grounds in case there are any more of the damned things about." Olaf was clearly perturbed.

Silently, intensely, the Norseliga studied the sheets of paper with their blown-up images of the six members.

"Well, I suppose we can be thankful that our real *names* are not on them," Gustav said finally, "Just our Norse pseudonyms." The others nodded agreement.

"So there is actually nothing that insinuates that we six belong to a secret organization," ventured Petter. Haakon picked up the thread.

"Considering the fact that the posters say we are wanted in Germany..."

Haakon was interrupted by Gunnar: "Yes, I've been pondering that. All of us probably have outreach in Germany. What we are going to have to do is think back to see if our actions there could have offended anyone or any organization."

"Considering that each and every one of us has been targeted," said Olaf, "that is a damn good idea."

"All right," Myrtl intervened. "And let's all of us assign our systems security engineers to check for any recent computer hacking."

"Oh, yes!" the Tufte brothers cried in unison. "We have had our business attacked; just yesterday!"

"Well, then, that's where we have to begin our investigation. We shall each check with our security personnel and report back. There is also the possibility that our private e-mail has been hacked," said Olaf. "I will keep these hateful flyers as evidence in case we have any need of them later on. It is truly a lamentable situation."

Slowly, and with heavy hearts, the group parted company, their earlier buoyant mood completely dissolved by the bizarre incident.

Olaf saw the last of them to the door then closed it, returned to the banquet table with its preposterous posters, sat down, and put his head in his hands.

Could whoever committed this sacrilege also know about the Munch Scream's being here?

46

Max Linde had not waited around to see what sort of reaction his 'WANTED IN GERMANY' posters had triggered. He drove straight to the airport, returned his electric rental car, and boarded the noon flight from Bergen to Oslo. There he waited for his connection to Frankfurt with an hour to spare before the final lap to Lübeck. Recharging his laptop at a convenient electrical outlet in the waiting room, Max began to sift through the most recent e-mails sent out by the Norseliga members. He smirked as he read a couple of frantic communications sent by the Tufte brothers to their security systems engineer. The same agitated tone characterized the personal and business e-mails of the other four members of the Norseliga. In other words, general confusion and anxiety reigned. Good. Exactly what Max wanted. And now just wait for phase two, when the members would have cause, legitimately, to suspect each other.

Tomorrow, after company engineers had delivered the breached security reports to their bosses, he would release his cyber missile. It would appear to be a personal e-mail from Olaf Petersen to a mythical recipient with "accidental" blind copies to the other five members of the Norseliga. Its subject line would read simply: "Our plan has succeeded." No ensuing message was needed.

47

In their spacious room overlooking the waterfront at the Thon Hotel Megan and Lili were having a much deserved lie-down in their comfortable beds as they awaited Erik Jensen's televised press conference. Button was sleeping at his human's feet, snoring ever so slightly.

Sure enough, at exactly seven o'clock the regular news was interrupted by a breaking news report. A beaming Erik Jensen had called a press conference to make his momentous announcement to the Norwegian people. He was standing in front of *The Scream* which had been placed on an easel. His announcement was brief and to the point. The Munch masterpiece reported purloined from the National Gallery last week had, in fact, not been stolen. What the thieves had taken in their daring heist from the air was an exact copy of *The Scream*, a copy put in place for security reasons some twelve years ago. The original painting was safe at the museum—as the TV audience could see behind him—and would be put on exhibition, along with the most modern of security systems, in a few days. He made no apologies. Erik hoped that the public would think just as he thought, that all was indeed well that ended well. In this case it was a fabulous piece of good news. Norway still had its national treasure.

After the broadcast was over, Megan and Lili discussed the event from every angle, agreeing that Erik had certainly done the right thing.

"Say, how about having a light supper sent up to the room so we don't miss the solstice spectacle?" Lili proposed.

"Super idea. I'm really exhausted. I don't want much. Maybe just some chicken soup, if they have it, and bread?" Button's ears lifted.

"Fine with me. And let's get some fruit for dessert." Lili picked up the phone and placed the order. Button gave a yelp of delight as he heard the word 'dessert.'

After room service delivered their meal, the friends carried the room's two bamboo armchairs and long coffee table over to the window so they could eat and watch the bonfire about to be lit below.

Megan yawned. "You know what, Lili? Do you think it would be all right if we didn't go down for the bonfire activities at all and just watched the whole thing from up here?"

"That's funny. I was just about to suggest the same to you. We've had a long day for two eighty-year olds and after all, we have a splendid view from right here."

"Yes, splendid and comfortable."

"And it would be even more comfortable if we got into our pajamas," Lili added.

"Great idea!"

The two women changed clothes, turned out the lights, and settled down by the large picture window. A busy scene unfolded before them. Although it was relatively chilly, girls and boys were skinny dipping. Other people were already joining hands and beginning to dance around the enormous blazing bonfire. They were singing Norwegian folk songs and a brass band could be heard from far away. It was ten o'clock and the summer sun was finally setting.

48

The first Norseliga member to hear the television news that evening was Myrtl Kildahl. The flight back to Oslo with her two comrades had arrived in the late afternoon and after a quick trip to the office she, with Sophia in tow, had gone home, chatting on the way about the Bergen visit and its astonishing Munch revelation. Myrtl had no qualms about breaking the oath of secrecy the Norseliga had taken. She had no secrets from her partner. They had just settled down in front of the TV with their nightly Saint Angel cheese, thin oatmeal crackers, and red wine when the seven o'clock evening news was interrupted. The breaking news was Erik Jensen's stunning press conference announcement that the National Gallery's *Scream* had not been lost. It was a *copy* that had been stolen.

No one could have been more dumbfounded than Myrtl. Incredulity was followed by outrage. She called Olaf Petersen on his private line immediately.

"Have you heard the news just now on TV?" she blurted out when he answered, not taking the time to identify herself.

"Hel?"

"Never mind the pseudonyms, Olaf. Have you heard the news?"

"I have no idea what in blazes you are talking about!" Olaf had not moved from the table with its bundle of poisonous leaflets since the Norseliga members had left. He had had a call from the Bergen police informing him of the curious posting in public restrooms of images of him with the legend, 'WANTED IN GERMANY.' Did he have any idea who might have wished to trash him? Olaf could feel the hairs on his neck rise. Who was persecuting him in this manner and why?

He told this to the police but a few minutes later his phone rang again. This time it was a damn reporter from the local newspaper, *Bergens Tidende*, asking for his explanation of the bizarre incident at the wharf's public restrooms. Why would Bergen's most illustrious citizen be attacked like that? And what did Germany have to do with it? Olaf had put him off, but he was still furious at the realization that the newspaper would be reporting the inexplicable event. He hoped the other members of the Norseliga would miss the local publicity. Never had he felt such worry and anxiety.

Puzzled by Olaf's silence, Myrtl repeated her question. *"Have you heard the news?"*

"No. What are you talking about?" Certainly *Bergens Tidende* couldn't have broken the story yet.

"It's the Munch! It's *The Scream*! Haven't you *heard*?"

"Calm down and tell me what you mean." Olaf could feel perspiration on his forehead and he felt a little dizzy.

"It was just on the news. The director of the National Gallery announced that the real Munch is still in the museum. *It was a copy that was stolen!*"

Olaf's vision clouded over, although his eye was wide open. He seemed to be seeing pinpoints of light. And his face felt numb. He tried to speak, but could only murmur a few words.

"Olaf? Listen to me. Turn the news on. The painting you showed us this morning is not by Munch. It is a copy. Do you understand?"

Olaf Petersen understood, but he could not speak. The phone dropped out of his hands and he fell onto the floor. He had just had an ischemic stroke.

49

"You know what?" Megan asked. "I think that before the witch is set on fire, I'll put on my blue jeans and jacket over my pajamas and just run downstairs with Button so he doesn't have to go during the night."

"Good idea."

Megan zipped up her blue denim jacket as she took Button down into the lobby and started to go through it out to the front porch overlooking the solstice celebrations. But then she thought the noisy crowds and exploding firecrackers might scare Button. She turned on her heels and headed for the side exit.

But not quickly enough. The petite woman with short brown hair who was sitting in the lobby had seen her. Instantly she sprang up and, hanging back at a discreet distance, followed Megan, who was already out the door.

"Okay, okay, we'll go see what's happening," Megan told a yapping Button, who was running ahead of her and straining at the leash in his eagerness to find out what all the noise was. She walked briskly after him toward the front of the hotel and he quieted down, content to be getting nearer to all the strange sounds. But Megan was in no mood to extend the walk; her feet began to hurt and it was too cool outside for her, used as she was to warm Texas summer evenings. So, spotting a service entrance door on the side of the hotel, she turned in abruptly, pulling an unwilling furry little companion in with her.

Isabell Farlig was mystified. Giving them a minute's head start, she had followed Crespi and the yapping dog outdoors, but there was no sign of them. Impossible! Attracted by the noise and lights, they must have walked down toward the bonfire. She did the same, slipping on her blue parka against the chill –it was fifty-five degrees out there—and hurrying her steps.

But she did not see her prey. All right, Crespi must have reentered the hotel from the front porch. Isabell climbed up the steps and looked around. Every one of the brown wicker armchairs was occupied by hotel guests watching the solstice events. There was no sign of Crespi. All right then, she must have joined the crowd outside. Isabell walked back outside and headed down toward the bonfire.

A thin, middle-aged man with a slight limp rose from one of the porch chairs. He followed the small brown-haired woman dressed in blue outdoors. Crespi was alone. No dog, no companion. His opportunity had come.

50

Olaf Petersen's butler Sven had come upon him on the living-room floor and an ambulance was on its way. By now Herr Petersen was talking, but his words could not be understood.

The incoherent employer was taken to the Haukeland University Hospital where he underwent a CT scan, was diagnosed, and given medication to dissolve the single blood clot in his brain. Fortunately, because he had been taken to the hospital quickly, Herr Petersen's chances for recovery were good to excellent. He would spend the night at the hospital but he could most likely return home the following day. Sven, ever loyal, spent the night in his employer's hospital room.

The next person Myrtl called after Olaf apparently hung up on her, was Haakon Sando. They were quite friendly given the fact that the shopping-mall tycoon had always allowed her to hold publicity events for her cosmetics on his premises.

She got right through to him. "Have you heard?" she blurted out.

"Yes, The TV's on right now. They're not talking about anything else. I was just about to call Olaf to hear what he had to say. He hadn't said anything to us about its being a copy. I could swear he thought it was the real thing. We certainly did."

"I think he did too. When I called him just now to ask if he'd heard, he got so upset he hung up on me!"

"How very unlike him. It must be as great a shock to him as it is to us."

"Or," Myrtl said, suddenly seeing the situation in a new light, "perhaps he did realize it was a copy when he saw it and simply decided to install it anyway, since he had gone to such trouble to acquire it. He didn't say a word to us about how the robbery was executed. All we heard on TV was that a helicopter and a drone had been involved."

"Well, certainly none of us was going to ask how it had been done."

"I suppose we should assume that he is as surprised about this as we are. I think I'll call the Tufte brothers, or do you want to do that, Haakon?"

"No, why don't you call them and I'll call Petter Norgaard."

"Fine. But do call me back and tell me what he has to say."

Myrtl decided to have some tea before calling the Tufte brothers. She needed to calm down. And she could not understand why Olaf had hung up on her. Maybe it was his hurry to turn on the TV and hear the news for himself. Still and all, hanging up on someone was not his style.

She and Sophia always had a ceremony with their tea. They both loved using tetsubin, the Japanese cast iron tea pots that came with matching small iron tumblers. Between the two of them they had several sets in different colors, shapes, and designs.

But Myrtl had hardly gotten through her first soothing cup of white tea when the phone rang. Sophia answered and handed the receiver over with a frown. It was Gustav Tufte, calling from Skien.

"Yes, Gustav, I've heard the news, and I was about to call you," Myrtl said, not giving the man time to speak.

"But isn't it terrible! Just terrible! Such a disappointment. Do you think Olaf knew?"

"No, I don't think so, Gustav. He seemed so genuinely thrilled about having acquired it and being able to share it with us."

"So you think we should call him?"

"I have already done so, but he had not yet heard the news, so he cut me short to see it on TV for himself."

"I've talked to Gunnar there in Oslo and he thinks we should all go back to Bergen and talk strategy."

"That's a little hasty for now. Why don't we wait and let Olaf contact us after he's had a chance to digest the news."

"Yes, right. But it'd better be by phone since our e-mail is being hacked. What is going on? Things like this just don't happen in Skien."

"Listen, Gustav, I have to go now, but I will call you whenever I hear something, all right?"

Myrtl needed some peace and some more tea. Still she was tempted to call Olaf back, now that he would have had time to absorb the news. She did call Haakon and reported on her conversation with Gustav. Then, after slowly sipping another cup of tea and discussing the course of events with Sophia, she decided to call Olaf again. By now he would be updated on the news and willing to talk.

It was the housekeeper who answered and her voice sounded agitated. "No, Herr Petersen is not here. An ambulance took him to the hospital! He fainted. Was on the floor! Sven is with him."

"Oh, my goodness! I am so sorry. Which hospital?"

"The big one."

"The University Hospital. Thank you."

Myrtl called Haakon Sando and Gustav Tufte back to report briefly on the astonishing turn of events. After that she and Sophia decided they had had enough of Norseliga drama for one night. Myrtl would call the hospital tomorrow morning and find out about Olaf's condition. Visit him there if necessary.

A comforting thought came to her as she lay down exhausted next to Sophia. With the original *Scream* safe at the National Gallery, the police would probably put searching for the stolen copy on a back burner. That should bring some solace to Olaf. His altarpiece would be safe. And after all, even if it were only a copy, it was still a magnificent work of art.

51

That damn woman Crespi was a fast walker! With his limp, Snorre Uflaks was almost panting trying to keep up with her. She was heading into the densest part of the throng of revelers as they watched the huge straw witch being slowly lowered from a crane above the flaming bonfire. A loud cheer went up and the crowd began shouting: *"Brenn heks, brenn!"*—"burn witch, burn!"

What a perfect moment to injure the Crespi woman. Snorre pushed his way through the noisy crowd and got right up to the woman's side. All eyes were on the witch. Just as it burst into flames, Snorre's hammer hit Crespi hard on the right ear. No one noticed as she silently fell to the ground. And no one saw the man who limped away from the crowd.

After the straw witch had burnt to a black crisp, someone spotted a woman collapsed on the ground, thick blood clotted around her head. The police and an ambulance were called and the woman was rushed to the nearest emergency facility. It was no use. Isabell Farlig was dangerous no more. She was dead on arrival.

52

Early the next morning Myrtl Kildahl received a call from Haakon Sando.

"Good morning. Have you looked at your e-mail yet this morning?"

"No," replied a sleepy Myrtl, putting the phone on loudspeaker for Sophia's sake.

"I thought you told me Olaf was in the hospital."

"Yes?"

"Well, he can't be too badly off because he's well enough to be sending out e-mails."

"What do you mean?"

"I have an e-mail from him on my laptop addressed to someone else, but somehow a copy also came to me. There is no message. Just an inexplicable and very troubling subject line."

"What do you mean? What is it?"

"Just listen to this. It reads: *'Our plan has succeeded.'*"

"What?"

"'Our plan has succeeded.'"

"Is that all?"

"Yes, that's all."

"But what plan?"

"That's why I'm calling you. I have no idea. I hoped you would. Check and see if you received the same e-mail, wouldn't you?"

"Immediately," said Myrtl, pulling her laptop toward her from her crowded bedside table. She logged in. Only five e-mails had come to her private account since last evening. Sure enough, there was one from Petersen. Sent on his personal e-mail account. The subject line went exactly as Haakon had read aloud to her: "Our plan has succeeded."

"What plan?" Myrtl could not help repeating.

"But that's why I'm calling you. It's addressed to 'adolfgermania@aol.de.' Do you see? We're apparently just blind copy recipients. So what do you think it means?"

"Could it refer to the Norseliga meeting yesterday and the unveiling of our treasure? A treasure that we now know is apparently a copy of the original?"

"Indeed, that's what I thought too. But why would Olaf be writing someone who is *not* a member of our Norseliga about that? Who is this Adolf? And what about our oath of secrecy? It should still hold, should it not?"

"Yes, of course the oath still holds," Myrtl assured Haakon. "I'm more interested in this Adolf person. Weird handle: 'adolfgermania@aol.de.' We may not know who Adolf is, unless it's Hitler, ha, ha, but with the 'de' we can presume that the recipient of Olaf's e-mail is German. The important thing is to find out whether all the Norseliga members received the same blind carbon copy. Shall I send them e-mails?"

"No, no. Better to call them in case all our e-mail is still being hacked. Let's do as we did last night, Myrtl: you speak with Gunnar and Gustav and I'll contact Petter."

"Right. But first I'll call the hospital and find out about Olaf's condition. Perhaps I can even talk to him on the phone since he seems to have been well enough this morning to send out that e-mail."

Myrtl got through to Olaf's room almost immediately. Although he certainly sounded weak, he was coherent.

"Olaf! How are you?"

"I am recovering. It seems that I had a transient ischemic attack last night, just as we were speaking on the phone. I suddenly felt dizzy, fell to the floor, and lost consciousness for a minute or two. Fortunately, my wonderful Sven got me to the ER in record time and they treated me there. Aside from a bit of a memory problem, I seem to be all right and will be released from the hospital this afternoon, they tell me."

"Wonderful. I'm so glad to hear that."

"I feel well enough to leave now, but the doctors want to check me one more time before I get out of here."

"Excellent. Um, I don't suppose you've had a chance to glance at your e-mail this morning?"

"Furthest thing from my mind. Anyway they took my smart phone away from me. Wait a minute, let me see," Olaf said, looking at the items laid out on his tray table at the foot of the bed. "Oh, there it is," he said straining to reach for it. "Why?"

"Oh, no, I don't want to bother you with anything right now, but when you get back home and are feeling better, do check it."

"All right. And thank you for your concern."

Myrtl gasped. The man doesn't even remember what I told him last night! He is unaware of Erik Jensen's sensational announcement on TV that the real Munch *Scream* is still at the museum. She wondered if she should send him an e-mail about it but decided not to. He would learn about things soon enough.

In fact, Olaf Petersen learned about the Munch switch just minutes after their phone conversation. A nurse entered the room to take his vitals and automatically turned on the overhead TV for the patient. A question-and-answer segment with National Gallery director Erik Jensen was in progress.

"Will you be conducting a search for those who took *The Scream* thinking it was the real thing?"

"Yes. The police have informed me they are still most interested in finding the people responsible. If for nothing else, the damage done to our museum roof. And we are thinking of posting a reward for any information that leads to the arrest of the person or persons involved in the heist."

"Do you think that will get any results?"

"The police think so. If we talk to the thieves we will learn the motive for their purloining the work. There may be a mastermind out there who had his own private reasons for wanting the painting."

Olaf sat up and watched in stupefaction, his one eye staring wildly. His *Scream*? A "copy"? Then he fell back on the bed sheets. He had suffered another TIA.

53

At last Snorre had something positive to report to his demanding boss, Myrtl Kildahl. Weaving his way back through the boisterous solstice crowds, he had gotten into his truck and driven to the small hotel on the outskirts of town where he was staying. It was eleven at night. Too late to call Kildahl. He would do so first thing tomorrow morning.

But he overslept. Three suspenseful days of tracking the elusive, peripatetic Crespi, plus having spent one night in jail, had taken its toll. He did not waken until half past twelve in the afternoon, and only then because the cleaning maid had knocked on his door. Snorre washed, dressed, and left his room. As he checked out he realized he was starving. But before he entered a small restaurant across the street he knew he should phone Kildahl. She must have been impatiently waiting for his call. He sat down on a bench outside the hotel and called her private number.

He was surprised when she answered the phone immediately.

"Yes, have you done it?" Kildahl asked crisply.

"The deed is done," Snorre answered with a bit of pride. "I took advantage of the solstice crowds last night and got right up close to her with my hammer. She literarily didn't know what hit her."

"And how debilitating was her wound, would you say?"

"I didn't stay around to see. But she sure fell to the ground fast."

"All right. Come round to my office tomorrow when you get back to Oslo and we'll finish up things."

She hung up before Snorre could answer. Just typical, he thought. Oslo was only about sixty miles north of Åsgårdstrand so he could take his time and enjoy a hearty lunch. Maybe he'd go back to town and replace his hammer before he left. Less crowded than in Oslo. He had passed a hardware store when trailing the woman's car into town yesterday. Just in case anyone stopped him last night, he had tossed his hammer into the consuming bonfire.

54

The second ischemic attack, although not as severe as the first, was enough to keep Olaf Petersen in the hospital for another day. A nurse had left a copy of that day's edition of *Bergens Tidende* with him. As he listlessly paged through it he suddenly saw a name he recognized. It was Isabell Farlig! She had been found bludgeoned and bleeding to death on the beach during Åsgård-strand's solstice celebrations. Papers in an abandoned Volkswagen nearby had produced her identity. What in hell's name? No wonder he had not heard from her. But why was she attacked and left to die? Had she been trying to take Crespi by force back to Bergen and his house? But surely the Crespi woman was not capable of turning with such force on her kidnapper. No, it couldn't have been Crespi. Someone else must have killed Isabell Farlig. Just bad luck to be out on the beach during that wild, drunken summer solstice they held every year down there in provincial Åsgårdstrand. What a colossal inconvenience for him.

Late that afternoon Olaf felt well enough to access e-mail on his smart phone. Good god! There it was! The e-mail Myrtl Kildahl had asked if he'd seen. The addressee was one adolfgermania@aol.de. But the addressor, the sender, was himself! How could that be? This was the third blow to hit him in two days.

He picked up the hospital phone and called his security systems engineer. "Get on this right away! My private e-mail is being hacked and now e-mails are being sent out in my name!"

What is happening to my world? Olaf asked himself desperately. The Munch *Scream* in his bunker, shown so proudly to the Norseliga just two days ago, was apparently only a copy. Isabell Farlig had been murdered. And now his outgoing e-mail was being used by a hacker pretending to be him. No wonder he was in the hospital!

What he could make no sense of was the subject line of the e-mail sent out in his name: "Our plan has succeeded." Who was the "our" that this sentence implied? And what had the Norseliga members thought when they received, by "accident," such a strange message from "him"? He would contact each member, tell them of his hospitalization, and assure them that he had not sent the e-mail. His private e-mail account had been hacked, just as some of their businesses had. And yes, he had seen the outrageous Erik Jensen announcement on TV.

Picking up his phone Olaf called the Norseliga members on their private lines and told them the same thing: one, he was not the sender of the "our plan has succeeded" e-mail, and two, the Norseliga's Munch was the original; it was a complete farce the National Gallery was staging. It was they who now had a copy. Trying to save face. Typical bureaucratic thinking. Pretend the real thing had not been on display for twelve years. Come on now, really? In his head he began composing a letter to the editor at Norway's important *Aftenposten*. The same for the leading tabloid, *Verdens Gang*. He was, after all, the nation's major private collector of Norwegian art. He should know!

▲ ▲ ▲

Over lunch in Stockholm under a cloudy sky Axel Blomqvist was going through the bouquet of Scandinavian newspapers he subscribed to. Two items caught his attention. One was a long, illustrated article on the front page of *Verdens Gang* concerning the director of Oslo's National Gallery, Erik Jensen. Seems the man had made a bombshell of a statement on national TV that the museum's recently stolen Munch was merely a copy. That the original had been kept out of sight for twelve years! Astonishing, to say the least.

The other article was a short one in *Bergens Tidene* concerning the strange fact that flyers printed with the face of Olaf Petersen, a prominent Bergen businessman, had been found posted in two public restrooms. Although Petersen had not been identified on the flyers, underneath his enlarged image ran the banner: "WANTED IN GERMANY." What was that all about? Were these police posters? If so, Norwegian or German?

Blomqvist had heard of Olaf Petersen of course. He knew that the secretive Norwegian had one of the largest private collections of Munch artworks in the country. And that some of them had been obtained from German dealers. In fact he and Petersen had actually been in competition over a preparatory sketch by the artist for his oil portrait of Strindberg. Petersen had won out through an anonymous intermediary who, Blomqvist heard, had then forfeited full payment after delivery of the work to Petersen had taken place. Foolish of the German gallery dealer.

The fact that Petersen had been declared on the flyers as now "wanted in Germany" must mean the gallery had lodged a formal complaint with the police and that, should the Norwegian step foot in Germany, arrest would be the consequence. Novel place to post a wanted flyer. Perhaps the purpose was to shame Petersen into giving up the artwork.

And perhaps Axel would have a chance after all to acquire the sketch of his grandfather.

55

Åsgårdstrand was beautiful in the morning. Lili called Megan, who was doing her interpretation of Pilates exercises on her bed, to come see the vast view out across the Oslo Fjord. It was clear as a bell and sail boats were already bobbing in the sapphire water.

"A perfect day to visit the Munch house," Megan declared happily. The cold she thought she might have come down with while walking Button last night had dissipated and she felt happy and ready to take on the day.

"Well," said Lili, who was still sad about their not being able to go to her Skagen condo, "they do say that Åsgårdstrand is the 'Skagen of Norway.'"

"There you go, Lili! Now doesn't that cheer you up? And just think, here we can repeat that photo we made long ago of the two of us on the pier with the huge tree and house beyond, just as Munch painted them." They had visited Åsgårdstrand together back in the 1960s and posed for the shot in honor of Munch's *Two Girls on a Bridge*, painted in the small town. It would be fun to do that again, now that they were "mature."

At breakfast, Lili laughed at Megan's taking so many vitamins in addition to her "senior" pills. What are they all, anyway?

"Well, this one is a multivitamin..."

Lili interrupted. "So why would you need anything more than a multi?"

"You don't understand. This particular soft gel over here, for instance, has in addition to vitamin E and C, lutein and zexanthin for age-related macular degeneration..."

"Have you got that?" Again Lili interrupted her friend.

"I do in my left eye. Things can look oddly distorted, say, like some Munch paintings."

"You do have an ability to bring things home, don't you? But truly, that's terrible. I'm so sorry!"

"Doesn't bother me really. I have what they call alternating strabismus, so that while one eye is looking, the other seems not to see directly, more like peripheral vision. And I favor my right eye, so all is okay. Sometimes for fun I switch to my left, or "crossed" eye just to see how distorted things can be."

"All right. I can see why you take that additional pill. But all the others?"

"Too tedious to tell you what they are. But the point is that I think they have all contributed, over the years, to my general good health."

"Well, that's what counts."

They were gorging themselves on rolled up Norwegian sweet pancakes and they took a piece of one back to the room for Button, as dogs were not allowed in the hotel restaurant. Then, although it was not far, they walked to the car and drove to the Munch house which was on a street aptly named for him. On the rise of a hill, the little summer house, formerly an eighteenth-century fisherman's cottage, had an unobstructed view of the water. Since Megan and Lili had been there last, a large bronze bust of the artist had been placed on a white marble pedestal near one side of the cottage. Inside, on one side there was a double bed, table, and chair, as well as a miniscule kitchen. The rest of the woodframe house consisted of a large studio area, the walls now hung with historic photographs of Munch and color reproductions of his Åsgårdstrand-related works. It was wonderful to be there again and both women left enthusiastic comments in the visitor book. Megan was especially tickled to see an unused roll of Kodak film on one of Munch's shelves. It had all of eight exposures.

Back outside the ochre-painted house, and after photographing Munch's view of the Oslo Fjord, they went in search of the pier that was the subject of some twenty versions of his *Girls on a Pier*. They soon found it. It looked onto a large rounded silhouette of a tree to the left and a distinctive, walled-in, two-story white house on the right. Behind the great tree with its dense leafage was a humbler house with a yellow orb low in the sky just above it.

Munch lovers had been mystified for decades as to why, although the small house cast its reflection onto the water, the low golden circle above it was not reflected. Recently, using topographic calculations, scientists had established that the orb was a rising moon and not a setting sun. They had also demonstrated that at the offset of approximately eleven feet above the water, the eye would not have seen a reflection of the moon in the water because it was blocked by the house in front. The painter's celestial accuracy was demonstrable and extraordinary. And, for once, not imbued with angst.

Several of the versions of *Girls on a Pier* had narrowed the number of girls at the railing down to just two, and that was the picture Megan and Lili wanted to take, with exactly the same background as in Munch's painting. They established the correct distance, then looked around for some passerby whom they could importune, graciously, into taking their photograph, leaning their elbows on the railing just as the painted girls did.

"But I've met that dog before!" exclaimed a man approaching them. "It's a Maltese, isn't it?"

Megan gave a start. This was one of the twin brothers she had come across at the front desk of Steen's Hotel in Bergen.

"Well, hello again," she said, recovering her composure. What brings you to Åsgårdstrand?"

"Oh, I live in Skien, but I came here with my wife and kids for the solstice celebration," answered Gustav Tufte in perfect English, shielding his eyes from the sun with his hand.

"So did we. And now we were hoping someone might come along whom we could ask to photograph us here at the pier guardrail, just as in Edvard Munch's paintings," smiled Megan.

"Oh, I would be happy to do so," Gustav said, reaching for Megan's extended iPhone. He took several shots, with and without the dog, and handed back the device.

"How is it that you are so knowledgeable about Munch's exact positioning of the girls in relationship to the background scene?"

"My friend is a Munch expert," Lili said proudly, while Megan waved away her comment.

"Do tell me your name. I may have heard of it in connection with our great national artist."

"I'm Megan Crespi," the so-called expert said quietly, with actual embarrassment—unusual for her.

"And I am Gustav, Gustav Tufte. I have indeed heard of you. I own your volumes on Klimt and Schiele and I have read your articles on Munch. Very interesting ones, I must say."

"Thank you. But how is it that you know of my books?

"Oh, I am, along with my brother—whom you also met at Steen's—a collector of Norwegian literary paraphernalia, modern and old. In my case I pursue items pertaining to Henrik Ibsen; in Gunnar's case it's Bjørnstjerne Bjørnson. We are the owners of a computer design company called Kontakt. You may have heard of it?"

"I have," said Lili, who was an avid reader of several Scandinavian newspapers online.

"How gratifying. Well, I see we are going in opposite directions, so I won't keep you ladies." He began to walk away, then turned abruptly toward them again.

"Oh! But wait a moment. Dr. Crespi, what did you think about the recent Munch news at our National Gallery?"

"I thought it was terrific! What a happy position the museum is in now. A truly good ending to a disastrous event."

"So you think it really was a copy that was stolen?"

"Yes indeed. I was advised of this before it became public knowledge."

"What! Oh. Do you have any theories as to who the thieves of the 'copy' might have been?" Like the other Norseliga members, Gustav had been telephoned and briefed by Olaf from his hospital bed.

"None whatsoever," Megan answered emphatically, realizing all of a sudden that she indeed did have some theories buzzing about her head, all of them having to do with Olaf Petersen and his strange two texts to her, the last of which she had not deigned to answer. She answered Gustav in greater length.

"I wouldn't be surprised if someone offers to buy the *copy* from the thieves. After all, it was certainly a fine forgery to have fooled hundreds of thousands of viewers, and I include myself, for some twelve years."

Gustav was finding Crespi increasingly interesting. He learned that the ladies were staying at Hotel Thon for a week. He acted on an impulse.

"What would you say, ladies, to making a drive down to Skien to see my Ibsen collection?"

Lili was the first to answer, after looking at Megan's immediate grin.

"The funny thing is that we had planned a side trip to Skien during our stay here."

"That's right," Megan confirmed. "We have both been to the Ibsen apothecary museum in Grimstad where he worked as a young boy, but not to his birthplace museum in Skien. That's what we were planning to do sometime this week."

"Well, I make a suggestion, ladies. You pick the day, and you drive down to visit the Skien museum and the Venstøp farm museum where Ibsen's family moved when he was seven, but then you visit me and see my collection. What do you say?"

"That sounds like a lovely idea," Megan responded with enthusiasm. What would you say to day after tomorrow?" she said, looking from Gustav to Lili. Both nodded in agreement.

"Shall we say two o'clock in the afternoon then?" Gustav asked. He pulled out a business card with his Skien home address on the back. "My house has a grand view of the Telemark Canal."

"Wonderful. We will see you then."

"I hope you enjoy your time here in Åsgårdstrand." Gustav smiled and turned toward the harbor.

When he was out of sight of the two women Gustav took out his smart phone and called Myrtl Kildahl. After getting an update on Petersen's condition, Gustav brought up the reason he had called.

"I've just met, by the most curious coincidence, one of the top Munch scholars in the field, the American Megan Crespi. Do you think Olaf might contact her and ask her opinion on the Munch *Scream* he showed us at Norsehjem?"

"Interesting idea. I will bring it up with him when we speak this evening. I have already heard from Petter and Haakon, both expressing their tremendous concern over the news statement that it was only a copy that was stolen from the National Gallery. Olaf told them, as he told us, that it was absolutely preposterous."

"Yes, Gunnar and I thought it was outrageous. After all, we five were in the actual presence of Olaf's extraordinary acquisition. And we all felt the power of that painting."

"It does seem impossible to think that we were not in the presence of Munch."

"I wonder how we can get the Crespi expert to render her opinion on the Norseliga's Munch without giving away the circumstances of its acquisition?"

"That is the problem, of course. But I will speak to Olaf."

"And I shall be speaking to Dr. Crespi again day after tomorrow. I have invited her to visit me in Skien."

"Oh, Gustav? I am not sure that is a good idea. Is there anything in your home that might betray your Norseliga membership?"

"What? With a nosey wife and two curious kids? No, of course not. Only testimonials to my interest in Ibsen."

"Still, I cannot emphasize too greatly how important it is to protect Norseliga, especially in these days of sensationalist art crime publicity."

After he hung up Gustav realized he was beginning to regret his invitation to the pleasant art historian.

56

"Well, here's an interesting item," Sophia said to Myrtl as she looked through the morning paper. You'll want to read this, Hildechen," Sophia urged, using the pet name she had for her partner. Their preferred language when in the bosom of their home was German.

"Read it to me, would you, *Liebling*? My eyes need a rest right now."

"The headline is 'Death at Åsgårdstrand Solstice Celebration.' And it goes on to say that as the twenty-four-hour St. John's Eve began to wind down late last night, the body of a woman was found on the beach. She had been hit on the side of the head by a blunt instrument. In her jacket pocket was a hypodermic needle with a dose of fentanyl. No identification was on the body but police think that an abandoned Volkswagen Beetle left on a street nearby may possibly be connected."

"Nothing more?"

"Nothing more. Sounds as if the celebrations got dangerously out of hand."

"Or perhaps someone used them as a cover for murdering the woman," Myrtl said, pouring them both more tea. "But on the other hand, if she was walking around the solstice celebrations carrying a lethal dose of fentanyl it sounds more as though *she* was thinking of murdering someone."

"You don't think your man could have blundered and that the body is Crespi's, do you?"

"Damn! I certainly *hope* not! Snorre's report was that he had knocked her to the ground with a hammer blow. That was all. He didn't stick around to see what happened next. And anyhow, what would an elderly woman scholar be doing with fentanyl on her person?"

"Right! Well, speaking of glum subjects, are you going to find out how Olaf is today?"

"Oh, yes! I'll call him right now."

Myrtl dialed Petersen's cellphone number and got through to a much better sounding Olaf.

"Yes, I'm back home now, Myrtl, thank goodness. Now listen. I had a talk with my security systems manager this morning. The cyber address of the person who was the recipient of the 'our plan has succeeded' e-mail is untraceable. And so far my man has not been able to ascertain who the real sender was. He says he may never be able to, as a fake account in my name could have been opened and closed within minutes, or the sender could simply have piggybacked on my account."

"Hm, that is far too complicated for me, but I am delighted to hear your voice sounding stronger today, Olaf."

"Thank you. I feel stronger. And I have two competing theories as to what might be behind our mystery e-mail."

"Oh, do tell me!"

"Here's the first theory. Since that outrageous poster attack on us as 'WANTED IN GERMANY' preceded the 'our plan has succeeded' e-mail, and since the named recipient of the e-mail was one 'adolfgermania,' then whoever nailed those flyers down my driveway could simply have been communicating his success to a German collaborator. Perhaps 'adolfgermania' is the person who commissioned the outrageous attack. And our names were included in the e-mail out of sheer spite."

"But 'adolfgermania' has been proven to be a fictitious cyber address," Myrtl protested.

"Fictitious address yes, but a very real person. It is now obvious that someone in Germany masterminded the heinous attack on our Norseliga."

"Yes, I see what you mean. Scary. And your second theory?"

"All right. You are probably going to think this too improbable. I can't explain the 'WANTED IN GERMANY' flyer incident except as an act of pure hatred, but I think the 'success' e-mail could have been sent by someone at the National Gallery. Very possibly the director himself, Erik Jensen. He was disgustingly upbeat and self-congratulatory on TV, didn't you think?"

"Yes, I see what you mean. He was that. But how could he possibly know about and have access to the Norseliga's personal e-mail accounts—all six of us—and why would he say 'our' plan had succeeded? Also, we don't know how many other people were sent blind copies of the message. Maybe dozens, or hundreds, for all we know."

"True, but I see it differently. I really wonder if it might not be this Erik Jensen man, gloating over his mistaken notion that the National Gallery still has the original Munch in its possession. After all, *we* have the original."

"Olaf, I think your first theory is the more credible: that the poster attack was commissioned by a 'germania' fanatic. One who has discovered Norseliga's mission is to establish the superiority of our Viking forebears over Germans. Hence the 'germania' in the cyber address."

"Perhaps both my theories are correct, Myrtl. It is not inconceivable that Erik Jensen could be of German extraction."

57

Coming out of Åsgårdstrand's hardware store with his new hammer and another tool the next afternoon Snorre Uflaks did a double take. A green Volvo had just driven by and the person in the blue jacket driving it was the woman he had knocked to the ground on the beach last night! But that was simply not possible. The crushing hammer blow he had given Crespi on the ear would have felled a man, much less a slight old lady. She should be in the hospital. How the hell could this be?

Up ahead of him the Volvo slowed down and pulled to a stop in front of a shoe store. Two women got out and one of them held a white mutt in her arms. Shit! It really was the Crespi dame, along with her damn dog and that constant companion.

Snorre parked his truck across the street so he could monitor the shop entrance. About fifteen minutes later the party of three emerged from the store and walked back to the car. The two women were wearing new blue and white sneakers. So that's what that was all about. He followed their car. It stopped in front of the Thon Hotel and pulled into the same spot where Snorre had first seen it park. The noisy trio emerged and entered the building's long front porch with its view of the pier and harbor.

How was he going to explain this to Myrtl Kildahl? Not two hours ago he had bragged to her about felling Crespi. If the woman he laid low last night wasn't Crespi, who the hell was she? Could Kildahl be reading about the accident in Åsgårdstrand right now? Would she learn that it was someone else he had attacked? Perhaps that the woman had died?

Snorre entered the hotel lobby, making sure he was out of Crespi's sight, and bought a copy of *Aftenposten* at the newsstand. Back in the safety of his truck he eagerly perused the paper. Yep! There it was. A short article mentioning the discovery of an unidentified woman's body on the beach last night. She had been hit on the head and left to bleed to death. A syringe of fentanyl had been discovered on her body.

Well, if Kildahl had read the newspaper account she certainly must have realized that an old dame like Crespi would hardly be carrying fentanyl around with her. This was just an odd coincidence that two women had been attacked on the beach during the solstice. Whew! Guess he was in the clear as far as having dealt Crespi a mortal blow was concerned.

And if he acted quickly enough he could still get to Crespi. Disable her, as Kildahl had specified, before appearing in his employer's office tomorrow. All he needed to do was put Crespi temporarily out of commission and fast.

He had an idea and it entailed returning to the hardware store.

58

In his gleaming white office overlooking Oslo's harbor Petter Norgaard—Thor—was going over the accounts of his hospital equipment company, *Sterling Sundhed*—Sterling Health. Its quarterly market report confirmed that *Sterling Sundhed's* value had risen once again. This was largely due to Norgaard's having underbid hospital equipment to German clients. No German rivals had been able to meet his artificially low prices, and now that more and more hospitals in Germany were relying on *Sterling Sundhed* products this was the time to jack up prices.

Things had not always been this good. Five years ago Germany had threatened to be in the lead due to breakthrough technology in monitoring dual-chamber pacemakers. But, working from their Oslo office, Norgaard's team of hackers had managed to infect the cardiac pace readout of the German continuous monitoring devices. This had resulted in inexplicable faulty readings across the country. A number of lawsuits against German hospitals and German hospital equipment makers had been the result and that is when Norgaard stepped in with his low prices and impeccable technology.

Now he was wondering if the recent attack on Norseliga—the "WANTED IN GERMANY" posters with his and the other members' faces plastered across them—was in retaliation. If a really good cyber hack had discovered German equipment had been infected with a foreign virus. If the virus had been traced back to his company. That would explain why his face was on the flyers. But how about the other Norseliga members? Certainly not all five of them had also, should he say, "transgressed" international boundaries in their business dealings enough to provoke the poster assault. Myrtl Cosmetics was as hugely popular in Germany as it was in Scandinavia. Enough to inspire animus? The Tufte brothers' computer design company had a strong foothold in Germany. So did Haakon Sando's trendy shopping malls. And how about Norseliga's leader?

His ship-building empire had only Germany as a rival. Could Petersen have antagonized someone in Germany?

Yes, it all came down to a resentful German company's attempt at revenge. Revenge through the amateur medium of leaflet tweaking of Norseliga members at their meeting place. That would explain the curious e-mail sent the following day to an unknown recipient confirming that "our" plan had succeeded.

It was also possible that this poster attack was initiated by someone who had fathomed Norseliga's secret aim. The establishment of Viking superiority over Germany. Perhaps the two motives had merged. Norgaard would ask Petersen to call a summit meeting. Damage control was an absolute necessity. And, of course, his own viral manipulation of the German hospital market would remain under wraps.

59

That evening back at his Skien home with its broad view of the Telemark Canal, Gustav Tufte was already preparing for the visitors who were due to arrive day after tomorrow. He had arranged for his wife and children to be out so that he would have the house to himself and the full attention of his visitors. Eight Ibsen holographs were preserved behind hinged Plexiglas along the top of a low wall cabinet in his study. Above them, arranged in three parallel rows, hung some thirty of the over 400 illustrations Munch had made of Ibsen's plays. The searing messages of those terse family dramas had held tremendous importance for the artist. He had supplied woodcut responses to *The Pretenders* and oil sketches for *Ghosts*. A few of Gustav Tufte's works by Munch were lyrical drawings for *Peer Gynt*. And then, too, Tufte owned a copy of the lithographic portrait Munch had done of Ibsen with his mighty white mutton chops seated before a window in the Grand Café, the busy life on Karl Johan's street going on behind him. Yes, Tufte thought to himself, my guests will certainly enjoy the Ibsen/Munch connection so evident in this room.

He looked with admiring eyes at his antique standing desk, one very much like those Danes Hans Christian Andersen and Søren Kierkegaard had used. There, on top of the desk, was one of Ibsen's own ink wells and feather quills. Thrilling, absolutely thrilling! Norway had every reason to be proud of its latter-day Shakespeare. No other playwright of modern times equaled Ibsen. How wrong of his brother Gunnar to place Bjørnstjerne Bjørnson above Ibsen, to waste time and money in collecting holographs and ancillary items related to the poet. Bjørnson, the nauseating idealist. No, give him Ibsen's stirring realities anytime! Ibsen. No wonder Norway was superior to other nations.

He hoped his American and Danish guests would appreciate the honor he was about to bestow upon them.

60

The Åsgårdstrand hardware store had exactly what Snorre needed. Returning to the Thon Hotel he found Crespi's car parked exactly where she had left it, nose in to the hotel front, back facing the pier, rocky beach, and harbor. Snorre approached the car. There was no one around. Quickly he slid under the right front wheel. With the pair of lineman pliers he had picked up at the hardware store he clipped both the right and left brake lines. Then he went to the back of the car, slid under the gas tank and cut the two back brake lines. The procedure took all of one minute. When Crespi tried to brake while in reverse, the car would continue to back. His job done, he made for his truck. Now all he had to do was wait and watch.

He did not have to wait long. The Crespi trio, obviously newly invigorated, emerged from the hotel porch and climbed into the Volvo. Crespi was at the wheel. She backed out carefully, then braked. Except that the car continued to back and with increasing speed. Seeing that she was about to go off the street and down the rocks toward the pier, Crespi desperately turned the steering wheel to her left, sending the car broadside into the single pine tree that lined the street. Instantly the car airbags were deployed.

That was all Snorre needed to see. The women would be black and blue at the least, suffer some rib or spinal fracture at the most. Just what his boss had ordered. He took one photo of the wreck with his smart phone, gunned up his truck and headed for Oslo. He would report in to Kildahl tomorrow.

61

Norseliga's founder, Olaf Petersen, immediately agreed with Petter Norgaard. They should call another meeting, a summit meeting. It was crucial to find out who had hacked their private e-mail—all servers and addresses now changed, of course. And why the poster attack at Norsehjem? Who could have been behind that bizarre incident? Most importantly, was Norseliga's very reason for existence compromised?

But unfortunately not all members were available. Gunnar Tufte was in France for the next five days and Haakon Sando was on his way to Istanbul. Skyping seemed too dangerous now as an online conversation might be subject to hacking. So a phone conference was set up instead. The alarmed members would be standing by for the following afternoon at three o'clock, Norway time.

▲ ▲ ▲

In his Lübeck computer den a frustrated Max Linde was rethinking his lines of cyber inquiry. Although he could still hack into their business e-mails, he was no longer in possession of the private e-mail addresses of the Norseliga members. The accounts he had ferreted out were, without exception, now closed. And so far, despite his best efforts, he was unable to determine which new service providers the members had turned to. It was obvious they were all now using far more complicated monikers. He tried their Norse-gods pseudonyms in various combinations. No luck. Well, sooner or later one of them would make a mistake, perhaps like communicating on Norway's number one social media outlet, Blip.no.

And perhaps he had wreaked enough havoc in Norway for a while. He had other important issues to address. A German anti-neo-Nazi group named *Hitlerscheiße*— Hitler Shit—and based in Munich had become a forceful presence on Facebook, Twitter, YouTube, Lokalisten, and other popular social media. He would turn his attention to it. Events in Germany were, after all, more important to him than some lunatic Norwegian fringe group.

He checked events in the neo-Nazi cyber world first. Were they fighting back against the *Hitlerscheiße*? The most active organization had always been *Deutschland Erst—Germany First*. Their website had a rolling homepage featuring the 1936 eleventh summer Olympiad in Berlin and beginning with the image of Hitler stiffly saluting the contestants. A few pages into the website Max glanced at comments logged by members. They were, of course, signed with pseudonyms. One was "Brunhilde." Hm, some gal trying to link herself with the *Nibelungenlied*. She probably plays Wagner nonstop, Max mused, thinking of the German epic of the 1200s from which the composer took characters for his *Ring of the Nibelung* cycle. I wonder if she's blonde or brunette?

He looked more closely at some of the neo-Nazi commentaries. Sure enough, lots of the contributors signed off with familiar mythological Teutonic names like Odin, Freya, and Sigurd. An enthusiastic commentary signed Wotan extolled what the neo-Nazis called "Western Imperium"—a call to major Aryan world powers to combine their nuclear arsenals and thus attain world domination. Yes, his fellow combatants were on their toes, no doubt about that.

Let's see if that Brunhilde subscribes to Western Imperium. Max went back to her commentary. No, it was a rant about not marrying an Aryan unless he could out-perform her in feats of strength and courage. Weird. How did that advance the cause of neo-Nazism? Oh, wait. He reread it. Now he understood. It was a declaration of renewing the Master Race. Mating with only the best.

62

A minute after the colossal bang, which sounded like an explosion, Lili was the first to speak. The instantly inflated airbags—front, knee, and side—had pinned her in place and stunned her momentarily. She saw the deflated nylon fabric bunched around her and looked over at Megan, who was stretching her neck and blinking her eyes.

"What happened?"

"I don't know! I don't know! The brakes didn't work. It was all I could do to stop the car from backing off the street into the pier. If I hadn't yanked the steering wheel I don't know where we'd be now. What's this terrible powder in the air? It's stinging my eyes." Megan began to cough. Lili started coughing as well, waving her hands to clear away the white smoke and powder.

"I wonder how bad the damage to the car is?" she asked after some moments.

"Wait a minute!" gasped Megan suddenly. "Where's Button?"

Hearing his name, Button gave a howl the likes of which Megan had never heard before. He had been sitting on the floor in the back behind Lili when the car came to its sudden halt. The jolt threw him against the door. Scared, he had instinctively crawled underneath the passenger seat. Now, in response to Megan's question, he tried to climb toward her voice. But he was dazed and could not orient himself.

"There he is!" Lili cried, turning around to look at him. It was then that she felt a pain across her right rib cage. She fumbled with her seat belt, unlocking it, and repositioned her body. But the pain was still there. "Ouch!" she moaned, "I think I might have a cracked rib."

"Yikes! I hope not," Megan said looking concernedly at her friend.

"Good god, is your face ever black and blue, Lili!" She glanced at her own face in the rear view mirror and saw it was also bruised. Her nose was bright red. She looked at her wrists. They were red as well.

"Don't you think we'd better get out and see what damage has been done to the car?" Lili urged weakly.

Megan started to open her door.

"Please don't move!" a man's voice suddenly commanded. "I've called for an ambulance. It's on the way."

Megan looked up and into the face of a tall, sunburned young man straddling a bike. He had barely missed being hit by the Volvo's exterior airbag, designed to protect pedestrians and cyclists in a crash. It was he who had immediately phoned 113 for help. Having heard the conversation between the two dazed women he addressed them in English.

"It would be best for you if you do not move."

"Yes, you're right. I understand what you mean," said Megan, looking over at her friend with concern. Lili had started to moan.

A siren was heard approaching and a minute later a yellow ambulance pulled up next to the green Volvo that had crashed sideways into a pine tree. Megan and Lili were examined by a sympathetic paramedic. Megan passed with only a seat belt bruise across her chest, and face and body bruises. But because of Lili's involuntary moaning the paramedic asked her first to exhale and then inhale as deeply as she could. She did so and screamed with pain.

"Yes, you may have some broken ribs, the paramedic told her. "It is best that we take you to the hospital for an X-ray. They will be able to tell for sure."

Megan and Button got into the ambulance with Lili and they were sped off to Kong Carl Johans Hospital where, after a brief wait, Lili was examined and given an X-ray. It showed two broken ribs on her right side. But no internal injuries. She was given a small plastic exhaler/inhaler device with a tube and a mouthpiece for respiratory training and the doctor urged her not to try to escape the pain by taking shallow breaths. Expanding the lungs would help keep the ribs where they belong. And deep breathing would prevent her developing pneumonia. If she needed to cough, she should do so; not try to suppress coughing. The worst time would be in the morning when she got up. Otherwise, aspirin and normal breathing would get her through the four-to-six weeks time that complete healing required. So, painful, but not serious. The ribs would heal on their own.

Meantime in the hospital waiting room Megan had called their Hertz car rental in Oslo, reporting the failed brakes and resulting accident. She was directed to the local Åsgårdstrand office where a helpful agent said he would send a tow truck to the accident site as well as a car to bring them to the office for a substitute rental car. After their release from the hospital a taxi brought them back to the Thon Hotel and to their banged up car where a tow truck was already on the scene. A woman in a light gray Volvo nearby called out to them and, painfully, they climbed into the car.

"I recognized you because of the dog," she said, smiling. "And this is your replacement rental car. I just need to take you to the office to fill out the paperwork. We apologize profusely for the brake failure."

Twenty minutes later, after stopping at a pharmacy to buy some cosmetics to cover up their bruises, Megan and Lili were back at the hotel and more than ready for the long lie-down they thankfully took. Button still seemed a bit dazed but he jumped right up onto Megan's bed as though nothing had happened.

see p.144

"Thank goodness we're not driving to Skien until day after tomorrow," Lili sighed after using her breathing device.

Megan and Button were already asleep.

▲ ▲ ▲

Myrtl Kildahl looked at Snorre Uflaks with contempt as he limped into her Oslo office the following morning.

"You told me you had hit Megan Crespi with a hammer on the Åsgård-strand beach during the evening solstice celebrations. Don't you find it somewhat curious that another woman, on the same evening, on the same beach, was found bleeding to death from a hammer blow?"

"Oh, well I meant to tell you about that. I misspoke. I had heard rumors about a woman getting murdered on the beach and I got mixed up when I reported to you on the phone yesterday about disabling Crespi."

Myrtl's eyebrows rose in disbelief.

"You got mixed up?"

"Yes, Ma'am. I got mixed up. What I meant to say was that I engineered an accident at the Thon Hotel to happen when Crespi and her companion got into their car to drive off. I fixed it so the car brakes wouldn't work. So when she backed out she just kept going and crashed into a tree. You should have seen those airbags pop! Crespi probably broke some ribs, that's for sure."

"And why should I believe this new, amazingly revised account?"

"'Cause that's what really happened, Ma'am. I just got confused before. But I can swear to you about the crash. Here, I took a photo of it." He handed Kildahl his cellphone. Sure enough, there was a disabled Volvo, its side embedded in a tree. Two women could be seen inside the car, clawing at their seatbelts.

"Just get out, Snorre, get out! I never want to see you again. And as for payment, forget about that." Kildahl flung the phone after Snorre's retreating figure.

63

Pål Enger had arrived in Strindberg's Stockholm. The proposal by Axel Blomqvist that he paint him holding Munch's portrait of his celebrated grandfather was too intriguing to turn down. What a lark! First, he had organized delivery of the original painting to Blomqvist after a brilliant theft from Stockholm's Museum of Modern Art. Second, capitalizing on his nefarious reputation as the man who stole Munch's *Vampire* in 1988, he was now creating a wildly successful career for himself with his portraits in Munch's style. And now, here he was back in the Swedish capital with his fanatic former employer who was about to pay him another fortune for creating an image of him holding Munch's Strindberg portrait. Crime does pay.

"I'll have to have a photograph of you to work from, of course," he said.

"Oh, no, definitely not!"

"Why not?"

"It's out of the question. I must protect my privacy and my identity as much as I can in relation to Strindberg."

"All right then. But I'll need to do a sketch of you while I'm here in your home."

"That is acceptable. Let us begin right now. I have suitable paper in my study if you will follow me."

Pål followed Axel, glancing at the dozens of framed Munch lithographs, etchings, and woodcuts lining the walls. The study did afford ideal lighting and the large sheets of paper Axel handed him would do quite nicely. They were obviously meant for drafting architectural designs.

The two men sat down, Axel in a chair facing the window, Pål with his back to the light, sketching his subject with swift, sure strokes. He did not like his first sketch, however, and began to draw another, ultimately more finished one. The result pleased both men.

"Now let me get this straight," Pål said in parting. They were both speaking in English. Pål found Swedish, with its hiccups as he called them, too dramatic and Axel had no love for the childish singsong, to his ears, inflection of Norwegian.

"So I fly back to Oslo, incorporate your figure and face into the background of *The Scream,* the same one lifted from the National Gallery. I have access to plenty of reproductions of it online. But I am to show you actually holding the picture, correct?"

"Correct. Both my hands will be on the frame, my right one on top and my left one on the side. You are to show nothing else. No environment that could be recognizable. No additions. Just the two of us: my grandfather and myself."

"Ah, but my 'signature' has become the inclusion of a quotation from *The Scream* in each of my paintings. I must do that."

"Then our deal is off! The picture can show only Strindberg and myself. Absolutely nothing else. Not a table, not a chair."

"All right, all right. But then I will sign it in capital letters."

"As long as they are small and do not distract from the two images," Axel agreed, envisioning how quickly he would blot them out.

The interview was over. Axel gave Pål half of the price they had agreed upon—500,000 Euros—the same as he had paid for the real Strindberg portrait's delivery. Grimly, the two men parted company. Neither one liked the other, but business was business.

64

It was ten minutes to three in Norway the following day. In Bergen, Olaf Petersen was sitting at his desk waiting to connect at the appointed hour with the first person of the preplanned conference call. In Oslo, Myrtl Kildahl had told Sophia to hold all calls as she waited for the one that would be coming in from Petersen on her personal line. Haakon Sando was also sitting by his phone in Oslo. In Skien Gustav Tufte was by his phone waiting for the call and in Paris, Gunnar Tufte was also awaiting Petersen's call. Petter Norgaard was doing the same thing in his hotel room in Istanbul.

At exactly three o'clock Olaf dialed Myrtl. They exchanged a few words, then Olaf put her on hold and hit the Add Call icon to dial Gustav. He did the same with the other three members. Then he tapped Merge Calls and watched as his ticker was replaced by Conference. They were all on board and talking in measured tones.

"I have asked each of you to check any competitive business outreach you may have in Germany, and it appears that we all do in some manner or another," Olaf began.

"Correct and not surprising," said Petter Norgaard, knowing in advance that he would never admit to having infected German-made cardiac pace read-outs on behalf of his Norwegian hospital equipment company.

"My cosmetic products do vie with German cosmetic companies, but I've never had any repercussions concerning that," volunteered Myrtl.

"Well, the same with our Kontakt: only friendly rivalry as far as we can see," Gustav said. "In fact we are thinking of merging with a small German company that..."

"Perhaps that's the problem," Haakon Sando interrupted.

"Hardly," Gunnar said quickly. "The company approached *us*, not the other way around."

"I wonder if we should consider this whole unlucky business as the work of some neo-Nazi group?" Petter Norgaard offered.

The group immediately took up the idea. Of course! This would explain things. Especially if Norseliga has been compromised and our aims discovered. Haakon Sando offered to have one of his computer geeks research neo-Nazi websites and social media comments. He also touched upon a topic that infuriated Olaf Petersen.

"We do have to take into account that *The Scream* we admired at

Norsehjem might, as the television and newspapers are maintaining, actually be a copy."

"How many times do I have to say that it is *not a copy*!"

"But if we could investigate this a little more deeply," inserted Gustav Tufte, "I am most concerned, as I know you are, Olaf, about the much-publicized claim by the National Gallery that *The Scream* they are about to put on display is the original. This would mean that what you showed us is the copy the museum claims was on exhibit for the past twelve years until it was delivered to your home."

"What the museum is claiming is utter and total nonsense," Olaf countered immediately. "Of course our Norseliga has the original. The museum is just trying to save face with its fabrication of having substituted a copy for the real thing."

"Oh, I am sure of that, Olaf. But I was just thinking. Perhaps we could bring in a Munch expert who would look at the painting and declare it to be genuine. Write out an authentication, so to speak."

"What? And expose me and the Norseliga to charges of theft? How can you even *think* such a thing?"

"It's just that, by utter chance, I happened to meet a renowned Munch expert in Åsgårdstrand yesterday and it occurred to me that if she were shown the painting she could concur with you that it is the original."

"She? You don't mean the American Megan Crespi, do you?"

"Yes, as a matter of fact I do. She was most agreeable. Asked me if I would photograph her friend and their dog with her standing on the pier Munch had painted so often."

"Even her dog? Damn that nosey dog! Yes, I do know Crespi. Actually allowed her to visit my collection recently. Her dog wandered all over my place."

"As a matter of fact, I have invited her to visit my Ibsen collection. She arrives in Skien tomorrow afternoon. Along with her Danish friend and the dog. They were coming south anyway to visit Venstøp."

"Tomorrow, you say?"

"Yes, tomorrow at two."

Olaf decided to let the topic go, but his mind was working overtime to see whether he could contact one of his underworld sources in time to get on Crespi's trail and bring her to Norsehjem by "enhanced" invitation. He needed to get her authentication of his Munch in writing. His thoughts were interrupted by Petter, who was still thinking about Haakon's offer to have his geek ferret out neo-Nazi websites and social-media outlets.

"I think we should all assign our various research assistants to find and pin down the main neo-Nazi players. When we do locate the most likely organization or individuals, then we can act."

"Yes," agreed Olaf, "and speed is of the essence. We absolutely have to identify this danger to us and to Norseliga."

"I am not so sure we can tie any neo-Nazi association to what happened," Myrtl spoke up. "I think it has to be one of our German business competitors. That is where we should look; not a neo-Nazi one."

After more animated discussion the conference call was coming to an end when suddenly Gustav asked a seemingly unrelated question.

"By the way, does anyone recognize the name Isabell Farlig?"

There was a general silence.

"Why do you ask?" Olaf finally said, cursing silently.

"Oh, I was just wondering. I know that Crespi is in Åsgårdstrand right now and staying at the Hotel Thon. And in today's papers there is an article mentioning that an Isabell Farlig was found murdered on the beach in front of Hotel Thon on solstice night."

"So?"

"I just wondered if there could somehow be a connection."

Laughter could be heard on the conference phone lines all the way to Paris and Istanbul. Petter asked: "So you're saying that an American art expert is going around murdering Norwegian women?"

"On the contrary," said Gustav in exasperation. "Someone might be trying to murder *her*. And she'll be in my home day after tomorrow!"

65

Lili was in tremendous pain. Just as the doctor had predicted, getting out of bed in the morning with two broken ribs was the hardest part of the day. Button simply could not understand why one of his humans was moaning so, but he tried to show sympathy by uttering groans of his own.

Megan had breakfast sent up to the room and they spent their morning sending and checking e-mails and reading online reviews of things to do in and around Åsgårdstrand.

"Please, nothing that requires any exertion," pleaded Lili.

"I couldn't agree more. I am pretty banged up myself. In fact I could rest in the hotel all day."

"Sounds like a lovely idea."

"Yes, well we're no longer in our twenties. Which reminds me. I think I'd better e-mail that Swedish collector who is expecting a visit from me. I'll tell him that I'll be delayed getting to Stockholm for a few days."

"Good idea."

"And what would you like to do now that I've sent the e-mail?" Megan asked a few minutes later.

"Why don't we just go downstairs with our laptops and sit on the screened front porch? We can let Button tend to business outdoors every now and then and we could order a nice pot of tea and stare out at the sea, rhyme intended."

"That's fine with me," Megan said, picking up her things. They were both dressed in slacks and T-shirts and were wearing their new blue and white sneakers, bought to give them better purchase on the uneven Åsgårdstrand streets and rocky beach.

Downstairs they settled in a cozy corner of the porch that had a spectacular view of the pier and harbor. The tea was refreshing and they began people watching. Two young girls in tight shorts and very brief halters sauntered by. They were both wearing what looked like six-inch heels and one of them stumbled and fell, emitting a loud scream. Several people rushed to help her up, including her companion who, while attempting to help, tripped and toppled over herself.

As other people were expressing their concern, Megan voiced her exasperation sotto voce to Lili, who was only too used to her friend's sermons on the health dangers of wearing high heels.

"It's stupid, just plain stupid! Do you remember the time we were in Harrods in London and I tried to explain to the young sales clerk who was wearing six-inch heels that if she kept on wearing them she would experience extreme pain in later life? And how she said: 'But it's the style'?"

"I certainly do. And I remember what happened next."

"Yes. I asked her whether she cared more for health or style and she instantly answered 'style.'"

"Megan, Megan, when are you going to learn that you can't convert the world?"

"You do have to admit that I'm getting better at not trying to do so."

"Yes, but there is always room for improvement."

"Okay, I'll tell you one thing I have actually refrained from doing."

"What's that?"

"Writing in to TV stations complaining about the way all female anchors wear sleeveless dresses and short skirts, forcing them to have their legs tightly crossed, while male anchors wear shirts, ties, and jackets. We know the temperature is kept low in those studios and I've even seen video bits of women who, when not in front of the TV cameras, are wearing shawls over their shoulders and legs. Now isn't that ridiculous?"

"Yes, it's ludicrous, I agree with you, but the TV producers would say that's what the public wants."

"I think I'll go walk Button for a bit," Megan said abruptly, rising slowly from her wicker armchair. Her whole body ached from the car crash the day before. Even more, she thought, than yesterday. And putting a cosmetic cream on her neck and face just to cover up the bruises had been an arduous morning task.

Lili continued to study online what local attractions were nearby which they could visit that afternoon. When Megan and Button returned she looked up with a suggestion.

"Remember when we visited the Borre Viking mounds years and years ago? Well, I've found there's an interesting museum there now. We might drive over, if we're brave enough to get into another car this soon. It's only about two and a half miles north of here if we take the forest road."

"What's the museum?"

"Appropriately enough, it's a Viking museum. The Midgard Historisk Senter. Internet photos show that it's quite modern, in four parts, with a little indoor café, and lots of Viking artifacts that have been found in mounds around there. They have the nails from a Viking ship that was found in one of the burial mounds back in 1852. And also a glass beaker."

"I guess we'd have to leave Button in the car?"

"Probably, but the grounds outside the museum look just fine for him. Plenty of grass. And there is even a Viking playground for children."

"You know what, Lili? Somehow I just don't feel like visiting another museum right now. But the idea of driving to Borre and just sitting in the high grass along the beach, that appeals to me."

"Well, hurrah, me too! I was just trying to be art historical for you."

"No need. I think we both need to rest today and what could be better than in the beautiful forest of Borre?"

Twenty minutes later the trio was happily encamped on a grassy mound under a tree at the edge of the Borre forest, looking out to sea and the large Bastøy peninsula.

"How absolutely peaceful" Lili sighed.

Button did not think so. He suddenly stood up sniffing loudly with great intakes of air. Then a series of growls. What did he smell? He trotted around to the other side of the mound and began barking nonstop. Reluctantly Megan stood up and followed. When she came upon Button she saw that he was facing several baby rabbits. Blind, like Button, and furless, they appeared to have been abandoned by their mother.

"Come on back, Button, let's not bother the bunnies." Megan packed some grass and leaves around them and Button obediently followed her back around to Lili.

"Did you two find a Viking ship or something?" Lili laughed.

"No, no. Just baby rabbits."

The long, restful day did a great deal to restore Button's humans and an early dinner at Åsgårdstrand's atmospheric, friendly Naustet Pub capped their activities.

Just as they were turning in for the night Megan's iPhone sounded its Massenet melody.

"Hello?"

"Megan, it's Erik. *The Munch Museum's Scream has been stolen!*"

66

It was a wise decision Haakon Sando had made. Wise and timely for the Norseliga. And he would carry it out by himself, just as a little over a century ago an Italian named Vincenzo Perugia, wishing to "return" the *Mona Lisa* to Italy, had single-handedly made off with her from the Louvre in Paris.

Knowing that Oslo's Munch Museum, home to over 28,000 prints and paintings by the artist, as well as his private library, opened late on Saturdays, Haakon gathered a couple of items and drove to the museum on Friday after-noon immediately after the Norseliga conference call. He parked near the staff parking lot, then went inside the museum through the main entrance. After familiarizing himself with the layout on both floors, he hid in a large basement storage closet just before the museum closed at five. He spent the night there, knowing that any movement on the exhibition floors of the museum during the night could set off alarms and also be visible to security video feed.

At six-thirty the next morning, dressed in a white smock very much like those worn by the museum's maintenance staff, and holding a broom, he headed straight for *The Scream*. Great god! There were two of them. Side by side. One, in bright tempera colors on board, was labeled 1910 with a question mark. The other, paler, in pastels on cardboard was dated 1893. There was no question. He could not handle the one on board. He would head for the earlier one on cardboard.

Haakon looked around. There was no one in sight. With the handle of his broom he pushed the room video camera lens up so that it faced the ceiling. Then he lifted the swirling work down from off its stabilizers and quickly returned to the storage closet. He had not been detected, no alarms had gone off, and the museum did not open until eleven.

Inside the closet Haakon sliced the 36-by 28.9-inch painted cardboard out of its narrow frame. Then, using a sponge and the water he had brought with him, he carefully dampened the back of the picture with little dabs of water. After that he gently curved it around his torso underneath his smock. He was ready. He reemerged from the storage closet and headed for the staff entrance. On his way, he nodded to a cleaning woman, then exited to the outdoors and walked quickly over to his car. Two minutes later he was headed back to his home in Oslo's wealthy west suburb Marienlyst.

Haakon was quite unaware that the sequence of his successful theft followed almost letter for letter the purloining progression of Vincenzo Perugia's abduction of the *Mona Lisa* back in 1911.

67

It was with extreme interest that Axel Blomqvist had read *Svenska Dagbladet's* account of the daring theft of *The Scream* from the Munch Museum in Oslo. It set him thinking. He already possessed the world's largest private collection of Munch graphic works, to which he had recently added the artist's oil portrait of his illustrious grandfather. But why should he not also have the benefit of being able to admire one or two of *Strindberg's* oil paintings in private?

The playwright had engaged in densely tactile painting and experimental photography in the 1890s and the results were extraordinary. His "celestograph" photographs were created with neither camera nor lens. Strindberg simply placed his photographic plates on the ground or on a window sill and allowed them to be exposed to the night sky and stars. With his small oil paintings he believed in chance and that he was imitating "nature's way of creating" in his layers of aggressive impasto, slashing with a loaded palette knife rather than with a brush. His extant paintings numbered well over a hundred and addressed motifs such as roiling sea storms, disturbed night skies, lonely beaches, enigmatic caves, single trees, or buffeted buoys. All symbols for how he viewed himself: anguished, standing alone while a fulminating society seethed around him. So like the situation of his friend/enemy Munch in the 1890s.

Axel's favorite work by his formidable grandfather was a painting showing Stockholm's miniscule bright skyline as seen from an immense distance across raging black water and under a thrashing night sky. This is the painting he would love to have! But it was in Stockholm's Nationalmuseum, and since the theft of Strindberg's portrait by Munch, which now graced his attic, security had been doubled.

No, not another daring heist. Instead, he would commission Pål Enger simply to paint him a copy, minus his damn signature. He would specify that it be ready, along with the painting of himself holding Munch's portrait of his grandfather, in time for the American art historian's visit to him, whenever that might be rescheduled.

68

Megan and Lili were eating a late breakfast the next morning in their Hotel Thon room when television news broke the story of the disappearance of Munch's *Scream* from the Munch Museum. They were all ears. After a search of the entire museum, an empty plastic water bottle and sponge had been found in one of the storage rooms—tools evidently belonging to the robber. There were no witnesses to the event and the video feed exhibited only the ceiling after 6:35 that morning. A cleaning woman had noticed a man heading toward the staff exit around seven, but as he was dressed in a white smock she simply presumed he was a staff member. He was not carrying anything in his hands so apparently he did not have the painting with him at that time.

"Wow, what a state the people at the Munch Museum must be in right now," Lili commiserated.

"I know, I know. But can you imagine: *two* of Munch's *Screams* stolen within one week?"

"Yes, and despite supposedly state-of-the-art security in both institutions."

"The success of the helicopter theft I can understand better than I can comprehend how a person could slip in and then out of a museum, a painting presumably in his hands at one point, without being observed."

"Assuming that it was only one person," Lili mused.

"And can you imagine what the condition of the Munch Museum's *Scream* must be, considering that it was executed on cardboard? Of course it was pastel on cardboard, not oil or tempera, at least," said Megan. "But still, there must be some crackle damage."

The two had finished breakfast and Megan took Button out briefly. They were not due in Skien for their visit to the Ibsen collector until two that afternoon. That meant they would not have to leave until around 12:30 since the drive on the E18 was only a little more than an hour. So again, they decided to take it easy and let bruises and wounds continue to heal. They returned to the corner on the hotel front porch they had staked out for themselves the morning before. Button was more than content to do so as well and eagerly led them to the wicker easy chair and couch. They began their *dolce far niente*, congratulating themselves on the mild temperature and gentle sea breeze.

An email for Megan came through on her laptop. It was from Eric Jensen.

"Well!" Megan looked at Lili. "They want to do an 'experts panel' on TV concerning the two stolen Munchs and that they would like me to participate."

"When would that be?"

"Say again?"

"I asked when would that be?"

"Tomorrow evening."

"Would you like to do it?"

"I suppose so. I'd be glad to help Erik."

"So we could go back to Oslo tomorrow then."

"You sound as if you're eager to do so."

"Frankly, I wouldn't mind a few spoiled days in our elegant Hotel Bristol there."

"Well, then let's do it. I'm certainly game. And Erik would be overjoyed."

Megan was watching a middle-aged woman in high heels walking purposefully toward the hotel lobby but, for Lili's sake, she imploded her bursting disapproval.

"I'll go tell the front desk that we'll be checking out after breakfast tomorrow," said Lili.

"Fine. And I'll go to that delicious bakery we spotted yesterday and pick up a few items for lunch. Come on Button, let's go for a walk."

Megan felt aches come and go through her whole body as she walked the two short blocks to the bakery and she was aware that ever since that cannon-shot deployment of the car airbags, her sense of hearing had been affected. Oh, well, let's hope it's just temporary. *(to readers) Sheeesh!*

An hour later, feeling well fed and with Button happily ensconced in the back of what they jokingly referred to their "daily" Volvo, the two friends headed inland for the scenic E18 highway and Skien.

An hour later they were turning onto Gustav Tufte's street. It had, just as he had boasted, a splendid view of the Telemark Canal. Since they were some fifteen minutes early they continued down the street and made a brief tour of the handsome houses in the neighboring streets. Then, at exactly two o'clock, they pulled up in front of Tufte's house—a log mansion with wooden balconies running around the front of the second and attic floors.

They rolled the car windows down to give Button plenty of the cool breeze that was gently blowing. As they started to get out of the car, the front door of the house opened and a beaming Gustav Tufte came out to greet them. Spotting the little white Maltese on his hind legs at one of the car windows he said "I have an enclosed back yard. Would you like to let your dog play there while we talk?"

This was the way to Megan's heart. "Oh yes, thank you so much, Herr Tufte."

With Button in tow they followed their host around to the back of the house and lifted an excited canine over the fencing.

"We can go in this way," Tufte said, beckoning to a side door.

The women followed and entered a beautiful sunroom. Its walls were white stucco as were those of the rooms beyond and they were all hung with what looked like Santa Fe Indian weavings. Megan remarked on this and Tufte beamed with pleasure.

"Yes, I have been to America's Santa Fe in New Mexico several times. My wife fell in love with the stucco interiors and I with Indian rugs. Only I wanted figural designs. So I commissioned a very fine Navajo weaver to create these shuttle-woven serapes featuring figures from Norway's Viking past. Thus we have a very different interior from the other houses in Skien and people are always surprised when they enter."

"It's a lovely surprise," Lili said, eyeing the bright weavings with appreciation. She and Megan had often met in Santa Fe for the summer opera season.

"And I suppose you and your wife took in the opera while you are there?" asked Megan.

"Only if it was an Italian one."

Megan was surprised her host narrowed down opera by nationality.

"Before we proceed to Ibsen, ladies, let me ask you what you think of the terrible robbery at the Munch Museum?"

"Outrageous!" exclaimed Lili.

"I cannot get over that two Munch *Screams* have been stolen within a week's time," Megan added.

"And do you think the first one stolen was merely a copy, as the National Gallery maintains, or could it have been the original after all?" Tufte was fishing and he was disappointed by the American Munch expert's answer.

"I believe it was indeed a copy. I have the story from the director himself, Erik Jensen. Seems he had it created twelve years ago after a bungled attempt to take the original. So, whoever stole the work is left with a copy on his hands. A very good copy, mind you, but just a copy."

Tufte tried to hide his disappointment and dropped the topic. Instead, he led them into his large study. It looked even more Santa Feish than the other rooms Not only were the walls in stucco, the wooden ceiling had mighty vigas running across it.

"May I offer you some *akevitt* before we look at my collection?"

Both women looked pleasantly surprised and nodded silent assent, although Lili was thinking "It's *akvavit, akvavit.*" Tufte poured the green liquid into three miniature metal goblets, then hoisted his and with an unsmiling face said "*Skål.*"

Megan remembered that Lili had often told her that Scandinavians don't smile when toasting until after they have taken a drink of what they have been served. So she did not smile but merely clinked Tufte's goblet with hers and said, seriously, "*Skoal,*" while Lili simultaneously said "*Skål.*"

"To good health," Megan smiled at Tufte.

"*Til god helse,*" he responded in Norwegian as Lili said in Danish, "*Til et godt helbred.*"

"Well, we may spell it differently, but our two languages have a lot in common," Tufte said, now smiling at Lili. Megan decided to skip the spelling bee and joined in the smiling.

"As you know," Tufte began, turning to his holograph cabinet, "Henrik Johan Ibsen was Europe's greatest playwright in modern times. *Strindberg,* thought Lili, her face a study. *Shaw, Wilde, Miller,* thought Megan.

"If you come closer you can see eight of his holographs along the top of this cabinet."

The women followed Tufte across the room to the low display cabinet. Yes, there under Plexiglas, were eight pen-written documents in the playwright's hand.

"What clear handwriting," Lili said. "It is so straight and almost without slant. I can read it easily, especially since he was writing in Danish."

"I don't understand why Norwegians still wrote in Danish at Ibsen's time," Megan addressed Tufte. "I mean I realize that Norwegians wrote in Danish during those four centuries of domination by Denmark, but after your country was forced into union with Sweden in eighteen-fourteen, why did they continue speaking and writing in Danish? To irritate the Swedes, perhaps?" she said, laughing at her own joke.

"Ibsen *did* write all his plays in Danish, didn't he?" she asked Tufte.

"Well, yes, in nineteenth-century Dano-Norwegian, or Bokmål.

"Ibsen lived only six years into the twentieth century," Lili supplied.

"Nevertheless many *Norwegian* idioms originate from Ibsen," Tufte added immediately.

Megan decided she would step into the breach and attempt to break up what was beginning to sound like a linguistic tussle.

"I've heard that Danes have an easier time understanding Norwegians who are drunk because their slurred speech more closely resembles Danish."

Both Lili and Tufte regarded Megan with surprise, then broke out laughing.

"On that note, let us return to Ibsen," Tufte said, indicating the documents on his showcase.

"Each one of these eight sheets here is part of a dialogue from a different Ibsen play: here on the left, the earliest one I have, *Brand,* then *Peer Gynt,* then *Pillars of Society,* and here, *A Doll's House,* followed by *Ghosts.* Next you see a page from *The Wild Duck,* here, *Hedda Gabler,* and here, his last play, *When We Dead Awaken.*"

"Extraordinary!" exclaimed Lili. She read each document slowly out loud, then asked: "How did you ever assemble such a collection?"

"Predominantly from auctions, occasionally from other collectors. Ibsen items are very, very hard to come by, as you can imagine."

Lili looked from the sheets of Ibsen autographs to the three rows of Munch images above—all illustrations to, or inspired by, Ibsen's dramas.

"The *Peer Gynt* drawings are quite wonderful. Oh, here is his mother Åse's death. And here, various moments from Anitra's dance. Fascinating."

Megan agreed, then found herself walking over to a compelling canvas on the wall over Tufte's desk. A half-length portrayal, it showed a man with unmanageable blond curls and moustache dressed in a capelike blue overcoat, his arms bent at the elbows.

"Isn't that portrait of Strindberg by Christian Krohg?"

"Yes, indeed it is. In all, he did seven different portraits of the playwright."

"But why would you have a portrait of Strindberg as part of your Ibsen collection?" pressed Lili.

"Oh, I know the answer to that," Megan said happily. In her teaching days she used to give a seminar on Munch and the Scandinavian North.

"Because, although they were diametrically opposed to each other and no love was lost between them, Ibsen kept an imposing portrait by Krohg of Strindberg in his study across from his desk, where the "mad" Swede's eyes could bore into him. Correct, Herr Tufte?"

"Correct."

"Ibsen used to say," continued Megan, her old professorial self taking over, "that he liked to gaze at the portrait of the younger man while he worked, and that it seemed as though Strindberg were looking straight at him, like a lunatic approaching him with demonic eyes. Ibsen once said: 'He is my mortal enemy; he must hang there and observe everything I write.'"

"Scary," commented Lili, looking at the portrait with new appreciation. "I do remember visiting Ibsen's apartment, now a museum, in Oslo decades ago with you, and seeing the Krohg portrait."

"Yes," Megan seconded her friend enthusiastically, "we went there to-gether and then we walked over to the National Theater which was nearby and photographed the two bronze statues of Ibsen and Bjørnsen in front of it."

"Ah, yes," Tufte said. "You know, my brother collects Bjørnsen holographs and personal knickknacks. Speaking of which, look over here at this standing desk. You know several of Ibsen's characters are described as 'standing' at their desks. Well, look at the top of this one. This is actually one of Ibsen's own inkwells and one of his quill pens. Exciting, isn't it?"

"It is marvelous that you have managed to gather all these Ibsen items," Lili complimented her host.

"Yes, this has been a wonderful visit," Megan said, glancing at her watch and calculating how much time they had left to visit Ibsen's birthplace.

"Oh, you have not been to Venstøp yet?"

"No, we came straight here."

"Well it's only five kilometers from here, so you have plenty of time. You know that Ibsen's family moved to the farm when he was only seven. And they stayed there until he was fifteen. So some very important adolescent years for his developing psyche. It was a period that, of course, meant a lot to his work later on."

Tufte walked his visitors out the side entrance where they had entered the house and toward the back yard where Button was fast asleep. When he heard voices he jumped up and began joyously barking.

A few minutes later, back in the car with their happy canine and on their way to Venstøp, Megan asked: *"Did you notice the word 'Norseliga' inscribed on the metal goblets we drank from?"*

69

Olaf Petersen walked around to the back of his bunker. The open grave prepared for the Crespi woman was still there—empty. The agent he had sent to bring her to him, Isabell Farlig, had failed him horribly. In fact she had gotten herself murdered. Totally inconvenient.

But his underworld contact had come up with the name of a man in Oslo who understood the circumstances required in bringing a person to Norsehjem by enhanced invitation. He would be interviewing him later that afternoon. His name was Drapsmann. Christian Drapsmann.

Olaf's private phone rang. He picked it up to hear the high, quavering voice of a very excited Haakon Sando.

"Hallo, Olaf! What do you think about a second Munch *Scream* being stolen in only one week?"

"I think it is a copycat operation."

"Oh." Haakon sounded disappointed.

"It is interesting," Olaf continued, "there are now only two *Screams* in the public domain. The later, nineteen-ten tempera version at the Munch Museum, and the eighteen-ninety-five pastel on cardboard version that was put up for auction at Sotheby's a few years ago."

"Isn't that the only one of the four that has one of the two figures at the back leaning over the railing?"

"Yes. An interesting variation, and one that makes so many people think the scene is taking place on a bridge, whereas those of us who know Oslo, know the setting is on the Ekeberg Hill path with its safety railing high above the city."

"And what about the 'original' that the National Gallery says it had on reserve when the so-called copy was stolen?"

"What about it?" Olaf snapped.

" Shouldn't an expert be called in to authenticate the one at Norsehjem?"

"It's the National Gallery that needs to have its Munch *Scream's* genuineness confirmed. Of course I will have ours authenticated by an authority. I have in mind a person who, I can guarantee, will be discreet, but all in due time. Now, what is the purpose of your call, or did you just want to chat about *Screams* all day, genuine and false?"

"As a matter of fact this is indeed the purpose of my call," Haakon replied, his courage and sense of purpose returning to him.

"Meaning what?"

"Meaning that the 'copycat' removal of *The Scream* from the Munch Museum has resulted in something beneficial for our Norseliga. By a fortuitous set of circumstances which I cannot go into, I am now in possession of the work. And I am ready to bring it to Bergen and Norsehjem to join the other one."

For once, Olaf was at a loss for words. Finally, with an audible tremor in his voice, he spoke. "Does our Norseliga mean so much to you that you would put yourself in such danger?"

"Indeed. Shall I bring it to you?"

"When can you come?"

"I would need to come by car, as it is entirely possible airline passengers with parcels that look even remotely as if they might contain artwork could be judged as suspicious and open to search by the police. God knows they are watching airports and seaports. Even the ferry stations. But I could leave tomorrow morning and be at Norsehjem in the late afternoon. It's only a seven-hour trip after all.

"That would be perfect. Especially as I have something going on this afternoon. Something, I may say, in connection with what we have been talking about. You will stay for dinner of course?"

"Yes, thank you. I'll book a room in my usual hotel and leave from here tomorrow around nine in the morning."

"Very good. Until tomorrow then." Olaf was beginning to comprehend the dimensions of Haakon's information and offer. Why, this meant that, in the remote chance the Norseliga *Scream* was a copy after all, *they would still have an original*. Impetuous Haakon Sando was indeed an invaluable member of the Norseliga.

70

The white one-and-a-half-story wood frame farmhouse, host to Ibsen's impressionable boyhood, had been somewhat of a disappointment to Megan and Lili. The simply furnished rooms contained mostly wall didactics and a detailed family tree on one wall. Only in the creepy attic to which they were allowed to climb was there any hint of future plays, such as *The Wild Duck*, with its deep garret where Hedvig shoots herself. There were other, red frame buildings on the grounds of the farm to which Ibsen's father moved the family after suffering bankruptcy, but they were not of particular interest except for one on stilts, enabling storage of firewood beneath. Button had thoroughly checked it out upon their arrival and left a little deposit.

That evening back in their hotel room for what would be their final night, Lili admitted she was more than ready to return to the big city. Megan did not hear her. She was sadly studying her figure in the full-length bathroom mirror.

"You know what, Lili?" she called through the door. I now have a *twenty-pound* stomach. I *hate* it. But I just can't get rid of it. And I try to eat so healthily. It's absolutely *frustrating*."

"It's not your fault," Lili said comfortingly and with conviction. "We just cannot fight the law of gravity."

Megan smiled. A great weight—some twenty pounds of it—had been taken off her mind. Bless Lili!

On their way back to Oslo the next afternoon they played The Song Game, one they had invented to amuse themselves on long car drives. The object was to hum only the first two notes of a popular song or opera aria and have the other one guess what it was. If it proved impossible then one more note was added, then another and another until the musical identification became obvious. Now and then Lili would stun Megan with a Danish popular song and Megan would strike back with a country Western. The time flew.

An hour and a half later, just a little after five o'clock, they were happily ensconced in the same room they had had before at the Hotel Bristol and munching on the supper they had had sent up.

Megan called Erik and they arranged for him to pick her up at seven for their eight o'clock live television panel on NTV. The interviewees had been asked to assemble a half hour before the show so they could meet each other before the live event. Megan took advantage of the show's makeup artist's ability to cover her car crash legacy of a red nose and wrist bruises with concealing cosmetics. A much better job than she had been able to achieve on her own with just Johnson's baby powder, the only "cosmetic" she ever had with her.

The other panelists, in addition to Megan and Erik, were Astrid Tandberg, director of the Munch Museum, Werd Goll, renowned author of the catalogues raisonnés of Munch's graphics as well as his paintings, Police Chief Inspector Finne Raske, and outspoken art critic Rolf Reiff, known for his work in bringing attention to Munch works stolen from Jewish owners during World War II. The moderator was Valdemar Spør, whose nightly show, "ASK," boasted an enormous viewership across Scandinavia, North Germany, and the Baltic countries. This evening, as with so many evenings, the event would take place in English.

At exactly five minutes to eight the six-person panel was seated around the moderator and the countdown commenced.

"Five, four, three, two, one!" The cameras began to pan.

"Welcome to NTV and to ASK ladies, gentlemen, and kids," Valdemar Spør began.

"This evening we are going to talk about two mysterious Munch robberies at two major museums here in Oslo. To discuss this, we have six distinguished guests with us. They are, starting on my right, Dr. Erik Jensen, director of Oslo's National Gallery, from which a version of Munch's *The Scream* was stolen late last week; Megan Crespi, American expert on Scandinavian artists; Dr. Werd Goll, producer of authoritative oeuvre catalogues on Munch's graphics and paintings;

Finne Raske, Oslo Police Chief Inspector for art crimes; Dr. Astrid Tandberg, director of the Munch Museum here in Oslo from which a second version of *The Scream* was stolen this week; and last but not least, Norway's most outspoken art critic, Rolf Reiff."

The unseen studio audience gave an enthusiastic round of applause as the screen behind the panelists showed the two paintings in question: on the left, the National Gallery's 1893 tempera on cardboard, with its radiant undulating scream waves; on the right, identical in composition, the Munch Museum's 1893 pastel on cardboard, its rays of anguish more muted in tone.

"Let me begin with you, Erik Jensen, as yours was the first museum to be robbed. All Norway heard your recent announcement on television when you assured the public that it was a copy that had been stolen, and not the original, which has yet to be hung in your galleries. Two questions: how did the thieves access the museum and why is it that you had a copy on display?

The cameras zoomed in on Erik. "Thank you for having us on your show, Valdemar. I am sure we all welcome the publicity and hope it will lead to the crimes being solved. But to answer your questions: the police have established that the break-in was accomplished by drone and helicopter during the wee hours of the morning. No alarms were tripped as the drone had cut all lines. It was a guard who discovered the theft, apparently just minutes after it had taken place. But it was already too late. The helicopter with its stolen artwork was gone."

There was a murmur in the audience and the camera panned the sympathetic faces of the other panelists.

"As for your second question. It was my executive decision to have a copy on display ever since another, thankfully aborted, attempt to steal *The Scream* took place twelve years ago. Our chief restorer, Katarina Kopi, made the amazingly exact duplicate for us and that is what the thieves took when they invaded the museum."

"And do you not think this was deceiving the public by exhibiting your so-called copy?"

"I see it as protecting the public and protecting Munch as well. *The Scream* is so well known that few museum visitors are unaware of it. Mostly, when they see it, they just confirm the vision they have of it in their heads. They spend only a minute or so in front of the actual picture."

"Interesting. Does anyone have a comment?"

Critic Rolf Reiff and Munch specialist Werd Goll spoke up simultaneously.

"You first, Werd Goll, if we may." Valdemar looked, to Werd smiling.

"Well, I only want to say that had the robbers consulted my oeuvre catalogues before their heist they might have come across a sentence about the National Gallery's *Scream* that should have given them pause for thought."

"And what is that?"

"In my paintings catalogue I recorded the fact that the National Gallery's version, like the two at the Munch Museum, shows the pointed steeple of Oslo Cathedral in the miniature view of the city painted beyond the fjord to the right. Now this close-up photo taken by me just out of habit a few weeks ago, shows a detail of what was on display then and *it does not show the steeple*. That mystified me and I'd been meaning to ask the museum staff about it but things just got too busy."

"So you're saying that the copy left out the pointed steeple of Oslo Cathedral?"

"Yes. And had the thieves researched what they were planning to take, they would have realized it was not the original."

"Can I intervene here?" asked Rolf.

"By all means."

"What gets me about all this is that, with one *Scream* gone from the National Gallery, the Munch Museum did nothing to double up its security, or at least that's what it looks like to an outsider."

Astrid Tandberg spoke up and the cameras pivoted to her.

"As director of the Munch Museum I can tell you that we did indeed increase security. We placed the two *Screams* side by side, and on the more popular one, the radiant one from probably nineteen-ten, we added a touch alarm to the frame."

"And not the other one?" Rolf asked in indignation. The studio audience gasped.

"We were waiting for our second sensor to come in. They are terrifically expensive and state funds were slow in coming," Astrid looked pleadingly over at Erik for confirmation. Erik nodded vigorously.

"Let's see what Police Chief Inspector Finne Raske has to say about this," said Valdemar, turning to him.

"Well, I think rather than getting into recriminations about what was done and not done, we should concentrate on pursuing the criminals—and they are criminals—who took the paintings, regardless of whether or not one of them was the original. We have in one case, the National Gallery's, the theft of a copy, but nevertheless a theft. And in the Munch Museum's case, we have the theft of an original Munch. What we need to ask is did the same person take both paintings? Did he later realize, after taking the first one, that it was only a copy? Perhaps he heard you, Dr. Jensen, announce that it was a copy on TV. That would have frustrated and emboldened the thief to strike again, and this time he had two Munch *Screams* to choose from, both with miniscule steeples in the background, if I am correct." Raske looked at Astrid Tandberg, who nodded vigorously in affirmation.

Valdemar Spør asked: "And of course you are in daily touch with Interpol?"

"Around the clock, you can be sure of that. Police in every country all over the world have been advised of the two thefts."

Megan, who had been silent so far, spoke up and the cameras pivoted to the American panelist.

"As an American art historian with a deep love of Munch, may I first say to all of you how shocked and concerned I am by the recent terrible events here in Norway. To say nothing of the recent Munch theft in Sweden. Might I ask, Chief Inspector, have there been any ransom demands?"

"So far not a one."

"So this could indicate that the paintings were stolen for, shall we call it politely, private consumption. A private collector might be involved, possibly through a middleman?"

"That is a distinct possibility. If so, the artworks in question will be that much more difficult to run down. The private collector could be in Japan, for all we know."

"One wonders why someone would steal two almost identical works," Megan pondered out loud.

"Perhaps, as I've said, the thief heard Dr. Jensen's television announcement a few evenings ago with the good news that only a copy had been taken from his museum."

"And what about rewards?" Megan pursued. "Has the Norwegian government offered a reward for return of one or even both of the items?"

"Yes. I am authorized to announce on this show that Norway is prepared to pay a five-million-Euro reward for information leading to the capture of the individual or individuals involved and for the return of the original painting. Or for both stolen items for that matter."

Rolf Reiff spoke up. "Wait a minute! Are you telling us that the government is willing to dole out five million Euros for a *copy* of The Scream?"

Police Inspector Raske's cheeks turned red. "If we retrieve the copy we are close on the heels of the thief, I believe. The two crimes are closely linked and the connection is obvious. I repeat: the most likely theory is, after Dr.

Jensen's announcement that a copy had been taken, that the thief, stuck with the copy, turned to one of the two originals in the Munch Museum."

"Do you think the paintings are still in Norway?" asked Erik Jensen.

"Every flight and dock departure has been monitored since day one. I would say yes, the artworks are still in Norway. Unless the thief drove over into Sweden, or even across to Finland, or Russia, for that matter." Finne Raske looked overwhelmed.

Moderator Valdemar Spør chose his moment well. "Right now, ladies and gentlemen, I should like to tell you and our television audience that we have a surprise guest."

The panel looked at Spør in surprise.

"Katarina Kopi, will you please come out and join us?"

The cameras rotated to the left side of the set and followed a tall, white-haired woman as she made her entrance. Spør rose to shake her hand and she took an empty chair to the far right.

"Ladies and gentlemen, this is Katarina Kopi, senior restorer for the National Gallery."

Applause was heard from the studio audience and Erik Jensen looked at his colleague in genuine surprise.

"We are hoping, Fru Kopi, that you can help the Munch investigation by affirming that it was indeed the copy you made that was stolen from your museum."

In Bergen where he was watching the television show, a breathless Olaf Petersen leaned forward to hear the answer, his one eye fixed on the image of the white-haired woman before him.

"Yes, I did, at Director Jensen's request, create an exact copy of our museum's version of Edvard Munch's *The Scream* as documented on your screen now, both in progress and in its finished state. We agreed to keep this a secret for the sake of the original when we made the substitution. And yes, I did purposefully omit Munch's minute detail of Oslo Cathedral's spire so that the two paintings could be told apart, should the need ever arise. In addition, I added in microscopic print my initials, K K, to the back of the canvas."

"No! No! No! It cannot be!" Olaf screamed. His picture at Norsehjem, not the original? This was all a lie. A lie to save the reputation of the museum. The whole show had been designed to convince the public that the Munch stolen from the National Gallery was not the original. Whoever heard of a museum exhibiting a forgery—and that's what it was, not a "copy"—as the legitimate work of an artist. And such a major artist. And for the past twelve years? Not possible.

Valdemar Spør was winding up the show, the screen behind him now showing the original *Scream* and the copy side by side.

"And there you have it, ladies and gentlemen. Absolute proof as provided by the talented creator of this copy on the right, that at least one of the two Munch *Screams* kidnapped these past few days was not lost to the world. It is safe and sound at the National Gallery and, Director Jensen assures me, will be on exhibit at the beginning of next week after final security precautions have been put in place. Isn't that right, Director Jensen?"

"Absolutely. And we hope that viewers of this show will visit the National Gallery to say hello to a magnificent masterpiece that has outwitted the world of crime."

Although it was nine o'clock at night Olaf Petersen ran from his house to the bunker behind it. Quickly he unlocked the heavy door, flipped on the interior lights, and entered, closing the door again. He drew the crimson curtains apart and gaped at the painting. *There was no cathedral spire.* No matter how hard he looked. He picked up the magnifying glass to the side of the painting and scrutinized the work again. Still no spire. Then he took the cardboard canvas down from the wall and turned it around. No visible initials at first glance. But then, on the extreme lower left, with the aid of the glass, he spotted what he hoped he would not: the very small initials "K K."

"May they all burn in hell!" he shrieked, lashing out at the smug panel members he had just been watching. With his hands raised to his face cupping his ears and his mouth open, he looked for all the world like the humanoid in *The Scream.*

71

Valdemar Spør's national television show ASK had been watched by over thirteen million viewers. Six of these viewers had particular interest in the show. In addition to Olaf Petersen in Bergen, there were Snorre Uflaks and Myrtl Kildahl in Oslo, Max Linde in Lübeck, Axel Blomqvist in Stockholm, and Benno Landau in northern Norway's harbor town of Trondheim.

Their individual reactions were vastly and incompatibly different. An astonished Snorre Uflaks, seeing that Crespi had apparently survived with no broken bones from the car crash he had engineered, had an inspiration. He would right things with his angry former employer, Myrtl Kildahl, by trying to disable Crespi in Oslo. He began making calls to various hotels around the city to ascertain where she might be staying.

Myrtl Kildahl, on the other hand, was merely interested to see that Crespi had apparently been able to walk away from the automobile accident despicable Uflaks had described to her as having been successful. Typical of his penchant for exaggeration, she told Sophia who was sitting next to her on the couch in front of their large flat screen television.

"We may yet have a use for an intact Megan Crespi," Myrtl mused out loud, thinking ahead to the master plan she had for Norseliga.

There was another person who was thinking there might be a use for Crespi. Sitting in front of his television in Lübeck, Max Linde was struck by the name, if not the persona, of Megan Crespi. That moniker rang a distant bell. Then he remembered: he had seen it as the recipient of a terse text sent by Olaf Petersen: "UNACCEPTABLE. Call." Now why would the Norseliga's leader be in contact with an American scholar of the painter Edvard Munch? The same artist highlighted in the ASK show as the subject of two recent robberies from Norwegian museums. Just for the fun of it Max decided he would hack into Crespi's e-mail when he had time. See what the connection was between her and the Norseliga.

In Sweden Axel Blomqvist had been pleasantly surprised to have a chance to see his future visitor from America on ASK's intriguing television episode. She looked younger than he thought she would look for a retired professor. Her passion for Munch was genuine, he felt, and he now looked forward even more to her visit. He should be hearing from her any day now with the dates of when she would be in Sweden. It would indeed be gratifying to show her his vast collection of Munch graphics. A pity that he could not show her an even greater jewel in his collection.

In Trondheim, in a mansion just one block from the city's historic synagogue, multimillionaire investment banker Benno Landau had watched that evening's ASK show with keen interest. The only Munch collector in the world who possessed the entire twenty-two panels of *The Frieze of Life*, he had made it his life's work to create two museums for his native city of Trondheim—Norway's third largest city, located just 200 miles below the Arctic Circle. One museum was devoted to Trondheim's Jewish history and was housed in the basement of the town's historic synagogue. On permanent exhibition there were poignant vintage photographs of the city's Jews from pre-Hitler times.

The second museum, a modern, one-story rectangular building built out over the Nid River as it joined the Trondheimsfjord, was devoted to Munch and had been built especially to house *The Frieze of Life* panels of the 1890s. Unlike the much later and larger twelve *Frieze of Life* canvases at the Freia chocolate factory cafeteria in Oslo, which were lightly suffused with sunlight, cheerful, and created during a settled time in the artist's life, Landau's twenty-two small panels ranged from birth and innocence to lust and jealousy to despair and death. Perhaps the most unusual thing about them was that the panels were uncharacteristically small. All of them measured exactly fifteen-inches high and twenty-inches wide.

Having heard Professor Crespi's comments and witnessing her genuine distress at the Munch robberies, Benno had a happy idea. Always a man to put his thoughts into immediate action, he telephoned NTV, got though to the producer of ASK, and was connected to the show's moderator, Valdemar Spør.

"I don't know where Professor Crespi is staying but I am sure Erik Jensen does," was Spør's response to Landau's eager question. "I'll see if I can reach him and call you back," he offered.

No sooner said than done. "She's staying at the Hotel Bristol," Erik told Valdemar after being told Benno Landau was trying to reach her.

"I'm not sure how much longer she will be staying in Oslo, however,," he continued. "We have an appointment with Chief Inspector Raske tomorrow morning, by the way. Here, I'd better give you Crespi's cellphone number."

After noting it down and thanking Erik, Valdemar called Benno Landau back with the contact information.

"May I ask why you want to reach her, Herr Landau?"

"Indeed you may. I wish to invite her to speak at our Munch Museum here in Trondheim."

"What a super idea. I do hope it works out. I imagine she would probably be most interested in seeing your Munch Museum. As far as I know it hadn't been built last time she was in Norway."

"Very good. And as long as we are speaking, let me invite you to hold an ASK interview at my museum sometime."

"Excellent! I shall speak to my producers about the idea. Given all the Munch publicity right now, this could be an ideal time."

No sooner had Benno Landau hung up from speaking to Spør than he dialed Crespi's cellphone number. Back at the Hotel Bristol, Megan answered immediately.

"Hello?"

"Professor Crespi?"

"Yes?"

"This is Benno Landau calling from Trondheim. I saw your panel on ASK this evening and, as a Munch collector, I appreciated your sentiments concerning the two recent thefts of Munch artworks."

"Thank you."

"You perhaps know that there is a new museum here in Trondheim in which all twenty-two of Munch's *The Frieze of Life* panels are displayed."

"Your museum is world-famous, Herr Landau. I am only sorry that it hadn't yet been built the last time I was in your country."

"This is why I am calling. We can rectify that. I should like to invite you to present a lecture—on any topic you desire concerning Munch—here at our museum, all expenses paid, of course. And with a stipend commensurate with your international reputation as a distinguished art historian."

"Oh, dear. I don't know about the timing. I am due in Stockholm soon, and am not sure how much longer I'll be in Norway."

"Could you give the lecture day after tomorrow?"

"Day after tomorrow?" Megan had an appointment with Chief Inspector Finne Raske in the morning tomorrow and she needed to spend the rest of the day in the music division of Oslo's Deichman Library researching its digital collection of Grieg's letters and diaries for her Festschrift essay. Time had run out to do this at the Grieg Archives in Bergen.

"Yes, would that be too soon?"

"Well, it's certainly sudden. I suppose I could pull together a PowerPoint talk between now and then. How about something like 'Munch's Impact on Vienna'?" There was nothing Megan liked better than composing with Power-Point images.

"Ah! I love it!"

"I'll have to consult my travel companion first. Could you hold on a minute?"

"Happily."

"Megan cupped her hand over her iPhone's mouthpiece and conveyed the sudden invitation to Lili.

"Shall we fly up to Trondheim?"

Lili's response was adamant. "*You* go. Button and I will be only too glad to stay here. My ribs are killing me and Button would only be in your way."

"Are you sure it would be all right with you if I go?"

"Absolutely. I need some peace and quiet and, to be frank, a break from Munch."

Megan took her hand off the phone's mouthpiece and spoke into it: "Herr Landau, I think I will be able to come. Can you make it an evening lecture?"

"Yes, that is when we always have our lectures here. I shall make the flight arrangements and book you into our nice riverfront hotel here, the Radisson Blu."

A few minutes later Megan hung up, her face flushed with excitement.

"I'm going to Trondheim!"

72

Before the shock of Valdemar Spør's rebarbative television show the previous evening, Olaf Petersen's day had started off nicely. The phone call from Haakon Sando with his encouraging news about bringing him a certain glorious item from the Munch Museum had lifted his spirits.

And then in the afternoon the interview with Christian Drapsmann had gone well. He liked the businesslike, short, muscular man with graying hair and trim moustache immediately. Drapsmann seemed to think it would not be difficult to bring Megan Crespi back to Bergen in a timely fashion and he was glad to know that he would be able to get a direct impression of her on NTV that very evening. One thing Drapsmann did not tell his new employer after looking around the man's living room devoted to Norwegian cultural heroes, was that he was a devoted neo-Nazi.

It had been child's play locating where Megan Crespi was staying in Oslo. The Hotel Bristol, his third hotel call, was only too helpful in answering his inquiry as to whether a Professor Megan Crespi was staying with them. Yes, indeed, should they put him through to her room? No need, Drapsmann had quickly answered, hanging up.

And now, leaning on his motorcycle and on the job watching the hotel entrance since early morning, Drapsmann saw what he was waiting to see. At precisely ten minutes to ten, Professor Crespi, along with another woman and a small white dog, exited the hotel in the company of one of the men he had seen on television last night, Erik Jensen, director the National Gallery. They entered a black Mercedes sedan and drove off, Drapsmann discreetly following. A few minutes later the Mercedes pulled up at the very modern, seven-story central police station at number twelve, Hammersborggt. Well, this was an unexpected surprise! Drapsmann watched the two enter the station, then took up a post across the street, leaning against his cycle and lighting a cigarette.

Inside the building Megan and Erik were greeted by Finne Raske, the Police Chief Inspector who had been on ASK with them the night before. He led them into his office and they sat around a small conference table. Megan broke the ice by saying that she thought Raske's surname was a most appropriate one for English speakers, because it implied that he got things done "fast."

The discussion turned serious.

"Professor Crespi, Dr. Jensen has told me that you have first-hand impressions of two persons connected with Munch who might be of possible interest to the law."

"Yes. I met the first, Myrtl Kildahl of Kildahl Cosmetics, a few days ago at her home here in Oslo. After we'd talked for a while she showed me into an annex she had just completed building for her house. It constituted a little art gallery and there were several hand-colored lithographs by Munch on the wall. But the highpoint, behind curtains, was what she assured me was a fifth version of the artist's famous painting *Madonna*. The fascinating thing was that Myrtl Kildahl seems to have modeled not only herself but the advertising images of her company on Munch's dark-haired femme fatale."

"So do you think she might be capable of wanting to own a version of *The Scream?*"

"I think it is possible. Another Munch iconic painting. Her interests may have moved from the *Madonna* to *The Scream* in concert with events in her personal life. Erik tells me of a recent setback in her business—an ongoing lawsuit from a British competitor."

"Let me see if I get this," said Raske, stroking his chin with his right hand. "You think that because of a business problem this Kildahl woman might have wanted to possess *The Scream?*"

"No, I didn't say that. Not at all. I just mean to convey that I was struck by Kildahl's abrupt mood changes. For example she suddenly became furious when I mentioned to her that a few years ago a British-born nun claimed she was the grandchild of Eva Mudocci and Munch. She seems to alternate between a certain jauntiness and a mysterious, um, *sulk*, is the only way I can characterize it."

"Interesting, but I don't see how we have an excuse to investigate her."

"I think what Professor Crespi is trying to articulate is that, in the rarified world of art fanatics, Myrtl Kildahl is a candidate. And one with the means to effect whatever end she might desire."

"All right. From that point of view I can see our putting her on a watch list of possible suspects."

"Yes, that is all I am trying to convey," said Megan, looking at Erik gratefully.

"And now please tell me your impression of the second Norwegian collector you visited, Olaf Petersen of Bergen."

"Gladly. I can say that the encounter was a bizarre one from the very beginning. I had previously been in touch with Petersen by mail back in the nineteen-nineties when writing an essay on Scandinavian artists, of whom he has a substantial collection. So when I contacted him saying I was here in Norway, he invited me to visit him at his home Norsehjem on the outskirts of Bergen, at the base of Mount Fløyen. Well, I happened to be in the company of my travel companion, Lili Holm, and my dog, Button, when we arrived by car. Petersen came out of his house as we pulled up and when we got out of the car he became visibly upset; had expected only me. We hastily assured him that Lili and the dog were going on up to the cable car station, but it took him a bit of time to settle down."

"And?"

"The interior walls of his sprawling living room are given over to huge murals depicting Nordic gods. He also has portraits of famous Norwegians like Ibsen and Munch. In contrast to these images, Petersen has a corridor of portraits and photographs of what he termed 'Modern Norwegian Traitors.' People like Quisling, Sonja Henie, and Knut Hamsun."

"Interesting," said Raske.

"From his images to the name of his house—Norsehjem—to the way he spoke, I received the strong impression that he considered Norwegians a superior race. I can tell you, but it absolutely must remain in confidence as I am breaking a promise I made to him, that he showed me a youthful self-portrait by Munch unknown to the art world."

"What?" Erik looked at his friend with surprise.

"Yes, it is a closeup, just his face and, surprisingly, with a slight smile, but it is absolutely genuine, not a copy."

"So in other words, your impression of this collector is that he's rather a fanatic?"

"Yes, absolutely. And I'll tell you something else. When my friend and my dog arrived to pick me up, the dog got loose and chased Petersen's Elkhound around to the back of the house where they ended up in front of a very new-looking bunker. A bunker like the ones built during World War II. Petersen was absolutely livid that we saw it. Bizarre, as I said, *bizarre*."

Chief Inspector Raske looked interested. "What would the man need a bunker for? You say his house was full of art. Would he have even more art, art that had to be stored in a bunker?"

"That's what I wondered as well. But now let me show you the strange text exchange we had after I left his home." Megan pulled out her iPhone and held up the text exchange between her and Petersen. "You see, he wanted me to return to Norsehjem. Look what he wrote here."

Megan read the text out loud: "Can you return tomorrow? Have something extraordinary to show you IN ALL CONFIDENCE. Come alone."

"Ah, now this is becoming very, very interesting," Raske said, sitting straight up and staring at the text message.

"It gets more interesting. See, here, I texted him that it was not possible for me to return. Now look at his answer: 'UNACCEPTABLE. Call.'"

"And did you?" Erik asked.

"No. I simply didn't answer his text."

"What is interesting to me is the timing," said Raske. "All this happened shortly after the first Munch *Scream* was stolen, correct?"

"Yes. And, by the way, when I asked him what he thought of the robbery at the National Gallery—the other theft hadn't happened yet—he claimed that it was a national disaster and that he had no theories on why or who had done it. Well, I decided to bait him, so I said that the robbery might not be as catastrophic as people might think. His reaction was a picture of surprise and indignation. And with that single eye of his it was quite a picture!"

"I would very much like to know what is in Petersen's bunker," said Raske very slowly and seriously, making notations on the pad in front of him.

"So would I!" exclaimed Erik.

"A search warrant is going to be extremely difficult to obtain, however."

"There is one more collector who might be of interest to your investigation," Erik added.

"Yes?"

"Axel Blomqvist of Stockholm. He has the world's largest and best private collection of Munch graphics. Megan is due to visit him in a few days, again, to size him up."

"Stockholm? Where Munch's portrait of Strindberg was stolen last week? Oh, yes, we are in constant contact with the Swedish police about that. My opposite number there, Berndt Hammar, is an art-crimes specialist. There just seems to be a spate of Munch thefts, even beyond Norway's borders."

"Yes, exactly. So perhaps Blomqvist is involved. I can see a graphics collector wanting to branch out into paintings," Erik added.

"Perhaps he was able to engineer the Strindberg theft, but could he also have been responsible for the two thefts in Norway? And all within a week of each other?" Megan looked at the two men quizzically.

"Good point," said Erik. "Oh, and Megan, before I forget. For when you're in Stockholm let me give you the name of my curator friend there at the Museum of Modern Art. She's Ingrid Konstrom and has, of course, been involved in the aftermath of the robbery there." Both Megan and Raske wrote down the name.

"Um, there is one more person I've met recently who might possibly be suspect," Megan volunteered. "He's Gustav Tufte and lives in Skien. I visited him in his home there a few days ago and he showed me his very impressive collection of Ibsenania. I noticed that woven wall decorations in his hall all featured Nordic gods and heroes. And I also noticed that, when he served me aquavit, or I guess I should say *akavitt*, the goblet had a word inscribed on its stem. The word was 'Norseliga.'"

Both Erik and Raske were taken by Megan's observations and the policeman made another note on his writing pad.

"Well, you have both been extremely helpful. Given me a lot to think about. I shall have my people scrutinize Olaf Petersen immediately—Myrtl Kildahl and Gustav Tufte as well—and I shall confer with the Stockholm police about Axel Blomqvist." Finne Raske looked at his watch, then rose to his feet, indicating that the interview was coming to an end.

When Megan and Erik pulled away from the central police office a motorcyclist started out after them, keeping a car's distance from the Mercedes. He followed the car past the Rockefeller Music Hall to the Deichman Library where the Crespi woman got out and waved farewell to her driver companion before disappearing into the new public library. Drapsmann pulled his cycle up across from the building entrance and pulled out his smartphone. He would spend most of the day waiting for Megan Crespi to reappear.

73

Myrtl was lecturing Sophia and the air around them on one of her favorite topics: the massacre of the German language by the influx of immigrants from the south and from Middle Eastern countries—much like the ruination of the Norwegian language by the growing immigrant population in Norway. The latter had been a major reason for her joining the Norseliga—to preserve the Norwegian language.

"They are right to call it 'pizza' German and 'pizza' Norwegian. And the same in Denmark. Why don't any of these countries fight back? Look at France and its long fight to prevent the spread of 'Franglais.' Remember the Toubon Law? The one requiring that forty percent of songs played on French radio should be in French? Well, that's what Norway and Germany should be doing."

Sophia was used to Myrtl's tirades on the subject. One of the reasons they spoke German at home was to preserve their fluency in the language. Another reason was their mutual German ancestry. Sophia Grimm was indeed, as Megan had wondered, related to the two nineteenth-century Grimm brothers of folktale collecting fame. Tales like "Cinderella," "Snow White," and "Hansel and Gretel." Sophia was descended from the older brother, Jacob, and like him, she had been born in Hanau. But her mother was Norwegian and when Sophia's father died prematurely, her mother took her to Norway where she was educated. At home, however, they conversed in German.

Myrtl had a similar story, but one she had managed to keep secret from everyone, especially from the Norseliga. Sophia of course knew; it was one of the things that linked them. Myrtl's father had been Norwegian, but her mother Gretchen, née Krupp, was of the famous Krupp armaments family, and had brought part of the enormous family fortune with her to Norway. Gretchen, as well as Myrtl, had kept their German roots a secret, especially as, after World War II, Norway had no love for Germans. But at home Gretchen made sure her daughter mastered and kept up her German.

In school Myrtl with her green eyes and long chestnut hair had stood out from her blonde, blue-eyed classmates and she was the butt of cruel jokes about her looks. This was the reason Munch's black-haired *Madonna* had become her favorite painting and why she had had it exactly copied for her Holmenkollen house's private art gallery. And of course this was the reason why so many of Myrtl Cosmetics advertisements featured dark-haired women—all second selves.

All representatives of the superior German Aryan race.

74

It was a little past five o'clock when Haakon Sando pulled up in front of Norsehjem. He had put a narrow frame around the dried cardboard bearing Munch's *The Scream* in his trunk, and as he was unloading it Olaf Petersen appeared at the front door.

"Welcome to Norsehjem, Haakon."

"Thank you, Olaf. Or, I want to say Odin, considering the importance of this mission to our Norseliga."

"You are right, Magni, you are right. If what you bring me is genuine, then the Norseliga is truly redeemed."

"It is genuine, I can assure you."

"Then let us not lose a moment. We shall go to the bunker immediately."

The two men—Olaf, tall and taciturn with white hair and moustache, the younger Haakon, equally tall and with long blond hair—walked around to the back of Norsehjem. Olaf unlocked the massive steel door while Haakon carefully held the linen-wrapped *Scream* in his raised hands. Once inside they went to a small table on one side of the room. Olaf laid the artwork down and removed the covering with a flourish.

Olaf gasped. It was truly *The Scream*. The 1893 one from the Munch

Museum. Exactly as all four versions had been described on the ASK show, with the miniscule spire of Oslo Cathedral just visible.

"This is indeed miraculous. You have made a fantastic contribution."

"Thank you. Thank you. I just had to do it to save the honor of Norseliga."

"And you have done so."

"But now we are going to have to discuss how we can repair the damage that occurred to the picture during its deaccession from the Munch Museum. You have to realize that, after I removed the picture's frame, it was necessary to dampen the back of the cardboard to make it pliable enough to wrap around my body underneath the smock I was wearing. That was the only way I could get the picture out of the museum."

"Ingenious, my Viking man, ingenious."

"Of course, this pastel version of *The Scream* is much paler than the other, the later tempera on board version the Munch Museum still has. But to its credit it may very well be the first version, the inspiration and model for the other three."

"That would give it tremendous historical significance as well. As for the damage, I think that I can quiz a restorer employee of mine who handles my house collection as how best to remove these few cracks in the pastel overlays."

"That is just what I hoped might be done. It's so good that you know a restorer. Of course you won't let him know why you are asking."

Olaf's one eye bore into Haakon, his indignation almost palpable.

A long silence ensued as the two men turned their attention back to the artwork on the table.

"Olaf. Might it be possible to show me again the other *Scream*, what the television panel concluded was a copy?"

"No."

"Oh, sorry. I didn't mean to trespass or anything."

"Let us go back to the house and have dinner. Sven should have it ready by now."

Olaf did not share with his boorish visitor the plan he had for authenticating the so-called copy of *The Scream*.

In Lübeck Max Linde finally had a moment to hack into Professor Crespi's e-mail. A few messages were directed to "lil' Sis," obviously her sister, and others were addressed to a Claire Chandler, apparently a good friend, as Crespi was continuously updating for her what she was doing in Norway. She included an attachment in the latest e-mail along with the news that she would be flying

up to Trondheim the next day. Max opened the attachment. It was an announcement of Crespi's lecture at the Munch Museum in Trondheim, scheduled for
seven o'clock tomorrow evening.

By coincidence, in his own incoming mail, there was something from
his Norwegian neo-Nazi buddy, Christian Drapsmann. The man's e-mail was
always hilarious, so Max opened it right away. Christian was detailing his latest
assignment for him and joked that all he had to do was follow a little old lady
from America currently in Oslo and deliver her to his employer in Bergen. A lot
simpler than his routine jobs which usually involved tasering and eliminating
an individual. At the end of the e-mail he signed off "Christian in pursuit of
Crespi."

What a hilarious man Christian was. But wait a minute. Crespi? That's the
person Max had been reading the e-mail correspondence of a moment ago!

Max wrote Christian back immediately with a bit of braggadocio. "Hey,
buddy, do you want to know a little something about your new assignee? I saw
her on TV last night, some sort of panel about stolen paintings and whether they
were genuine or fakes. I can give you a good description if you like. Plus, cyber
bro, for a case of good Norwegian salmon, I can tell you exactly where she's
going to be tomorrow evening, and it sure as hell ain't Bergen or Oslo."

His e-mail was answered almost immediately. "Hey! Awesome that you
know who my client is. I'm sitting on my mobike across from the building she
just entered. Yeah, I saw her on TV last night too. Short, brown hair, and kinda
lively. But now you've got my interest. Promise I'll send you some Norwegian
salmon if you tell me where she'll be tomorrow evening."

Max had been waiting for an answer and was not surprised when it came
so soon. He dragged Crespi's attachment over onto his answer to Drapsmann
and sent it off. Within a minute he received a text: "Million thanks, bro. Makes
my job a whiz. Salmon on way."

Snorre Uflaks was hanging out in the lobby of the Hotel Bristol. He too
had been lucky in locating where the American Megan Crespi was staying.
After seeing her on television last night he had called around to the major
Oslo hotels and found where she was booked. He spent the night in his truck
in an underground garage near the Hotel Bristol. Then this morning he had
parked his truck opposite the hotel and taken up his post by seven in the
morning. Sure enough, at ten to ten o'clock he saw Crespi stride past the
concierge's desk and greet a man. It was a man Snorre recognized from the
TV show last night. He followed them out the door and watched them enter a

black Mercedes sedan. He made a limping run to his truck and managed to fall in behind them.

The sedan pulled up in front of the Hammersborggt police station and parked. Snorre did likewise and sat watching the building's entrance. About an hour later Crespi and the man came out and headed to the Mercedes. They pulled out into the street and Snorre was a car's length behind them.

Some ten minutes later the sedan stopped in front of the National Library and Crespi got out and entered the building. The Mercedes drove off. Now I've gotta find a good vantage point, Snorre told himself. Across the street he saw a parking place that was almost free—some damned motorcyclist was leaning against his bike at the edge of it looking at his cellphone. In compensation for his limp, when Snorre was in his truck, he was an aggressive man. Gunning his motor, he took off. At the next intersection he made a U-turn and pulled up just beyond the desired parking place. Then slowly and deliberately, he backed into it, almost touching the motorcycle. Its owner, a short, muscular man with graying hair and moustache, shouted at him; a few curses were exchanged and both men held their ground. The result was a shared parking place for an untold number of hours. Ostentatiously shunning one another, both men passed the time on their smartphones.

In the music section of the Deichman Library Megan was having a grand time reading passages from Grieg's diaries. The librarian had been most helpful and even translated a few of the more obtuse words Megan came across. What she was looking for was any mention of his affairs, of any of the other women in his life, his "Lost Lady Loves," as she was titling her Festschrift essay on him. Of course his wife Nina had lived on after Grieg's death in 1907 for some thirty years, so she would have had plenty of time to remove or alter anything she did not like in her husband's diaries. Megan found nothing that related to other women who might qualify as lovers, but the diary entries were so fascinating that she kept reading.

Suddenly it was five o'clock. Megan ought to rejoin Lili and Button. And that evening she needed to assemble some PowerPoint images. Dashing off an e-mail to the Swedish collector Axel Blomqvist, she suggested a date for their meeting. Since she would be in Trondheim tomorrow and Oslo again the next day, and because she wanted to overnight during the 300 mile drive to Stockholm, she proposed that they consider meeting a day after she arrived. There were things she wanted to do in Stockholm before meeting with him. Closing her laptop and slipping it into her lightweight shoulder bag, she thanked the friendly librarian who directed her to the music library's side exit. "You'll have better luck with a taxi there," the helpful lady said in farewell.

It had been a game of who could ignore the other longer. Neither Snorre Uflaks nor Christian Drapsmann was about to give up his excellent vantage point vis-à-vis the large library opposite them. When the five o'clock traffic started to thicken, both men began wondering if it were worth their while to linger any longer. But they waited it out.

Six o'clock came and went. Drapsmann was the first to leave, throwing a look of hatred back at the driver of the black truck who had insisted on sharing his parking place. After all, Drapsmann knew where Crespi would be tomorrow evening. He stopped at a crowded café, parked his cycle, and ordered a meal inside. While he waited he went online and reserved a ticket on Norwegian Airlines leaving Oslo for Trondheim tomorrow morning at eleven. It was only an hour's flight. That would give him plenty of time to rent a car, find a hotel, locate the Munch Museum, and stake it out.

As for the driver of the black truck, Snorre Uflaks, he stayed in place until seven-thirty. Then he drove back to the Hotel Bristol and parked in the nearby garage where he had slept the night before. He would do the same tonight after grabbing a meal, and early tomorrow morning would find him on the job again in the lobby of the Hotel Bristol. This time he would be successful and Myrtl Kildahl would be immensely gratified by the results. This time Uflaks would defy the meaning of his surname: bad luck.

75

Pål Enger's copy—sent by UPS—of Strindberg's painting of the distant skyline of Stockholm under the battering of a violent storm of brush and thumb strokes was fabulous. "Fabulous," Axel Blomqvist had told Enger on the phone. He already loved the portrait Enger had personally delivered to him in which he stood beside Munch's portrayal of Strindberg. And now he had one of Strindberg's "paintings" as well. What treasures he had been able to assemble for his attic temple to his illustrious grandfather.

Enger had really done three remarkable jobs for him. For a brief moment he felt inclined to commission more Strindberg "paintings," but on second thought decided he should sever his relationship with the infamous former Munch thief turned popular painter of portraits à la Munch with glimpses of *The Scream* in every background. His success with the Oslo public had been phenomenal. Axel did not want him to repeat this triumph in Stockholm.

It was already enough that Enger seemed taken by his newly acquired ability to simulate Strindberg landscapes with his palette knife and thumb scrapes. Heaven forbid that he should start doing so as yet another activity. Flood the market with "newly discovered" Strindbergs. No. It was better not to encourage him to do anything more associated with Strindberg. It was sufficient that he had masterminded the theft of Munch's portrait of his grandfather from the Swedish Museum of Modern Art. But the less Enger was in Sweden, the better. He was one of only a few people who even knew for certain of Axel Blomqvist's relationship to Strindberg. The only persons to whom he had ever confirmed his kinship were the members of the Stockholm city council And they had promised to keep his secret. Axel intended to keep it that way.

Although, he was tempted to show off a bit for the American scholar who was to visit him shortly. He had finally heard from her and quickly responded, agreeing happily to her proposed meeting date. A late afternoon visit would be ideal. Say four o'clock? He sent along specific directions as to how to find his home in Östermalm by taxi. After all, given that Stockholm was comprised of fourteen self-contained islands, it was always important to give visitors very clear driving instructions as to how to get from the Old Town center to his elegant neighborhood.

"Are you sure you don't want to go with me to Trondheim?" Megan asked Lili over dinner that evening in the comfortable Bristol Grill.

"I am absolutely sure. All my energy seems to be taken up in trying to breathe without causing too much pain. And I keep remembering how the doctor told me not to take shallow breaths but to keep on breathing normally. I'm really just too tired to do any traveling right now."

"I do sympathize, Lili. And I am just so sorry you were hurt while Button and I escaped with only minor injuries." Megan was thinking about the fact that she still had to apply baby powder to her facial bruises every morning.

"Anyway. Don't you need to put together the PowerPoint images for your lecture tomorrow evening?"

"You bet I do. It shouldn't take me over an hour considering the images I already have and I'll start when we go back upstairs."

"Any idea how you're going to handle your theme? Munch's impact on Vienna?"

"Oh, yes. And I know exactly how I am going to start and finish the lecture."

"How?" Lili was used to the dramatic openings and closings of her friend's engaging lecture style.

"I'll begin and end with *The Scream* on the left and Egon Schiele's *Self-Portrait Screaming* of nineteen-ten on the right."

"That should grip them!"

"Well, I hope so. It really is amazing how Munch's message of angst translated into Viennese Expressionism. And for the writers as well. You know, that terrorizer of Vienna Karl Kraus, the one who published the satirist magazine *Die Fackel—The Torch*—once described the imperial city of Vienna as 'an isolation cell in which one is allowed to scream.'"

"No, I didn't know that. Makes my skin crawl. Perfect description for what the stifling metropolis of Vienna was at that time. With society's hypocritical emphasis on the façade of correctness and its widespread conspiratorial indulgence in every form of sex. I can see why Schiele would have wanted to scream."

"Right. And from Schiele I'll go on to show the up-close facial studies and despairing grimaces of Richard Gerstl, who ran off with Schönberg's wife. And Oskar Kokoschka, whose early *Murderer, Hope of Women* poster shows a screaming woman flaying a shrieking man. Is your skin still tingling?"

"Yes, thank you very much."

"Well, now I feel inspired just talking about it, so let's go back to the room and I'll begin to line up images. *Love* doing that."

Skipping dessert, they went up to their room and Lili volunteered to take Button for a short walk while Megan prepared her lecture material.

As Lili and Button were walking along the street in front of the hotel, she was surprised when a short man with graying hair and short moustache coming toward them suddenly bent down and took a smartphone photograph of Button.

"You must be a fan of Malteses," she said pleasantly to the man.

"Yes, that I am," he said, straightening up and taking a shot of her as well before walking briskly on without any explanation.

What a crazy tourist, Lili thought, pulling Button back in the direction of the hotel.

An hour and a half later Megan had finished lining up her images along with some wonderful details and photographs of the artists concerned. She addressed the question of how Munch's *Scream* could have been known about in the Vienna of 1910 by including an image of the artist's 1895 black and white lithographic version of the work, one that was reproduced in various art magazines around Europe. Then she wrote out the major points she wished to make. Contrary to her usual habit of speaking dramatically from a written text with image cues, she would ad lib this presentation in the hope of drawing the audience in. Even if English was the second language of the audience, Megan knew that direct communication would be best for the situation.

Lili was the willing audience of one, two if Button were counted, who then listened to Megan's trial run. All went well and they turned in for the night. Megan's flight up to Trondheim was scheduled for the civilized hour of eleven in the morning, giving her plenty of time to have breakfast, walk the dog, and not fret about getting to the airport on time—one of her perennial fears. Better to arrive an hour early than two minutes too late. Since the introduction of smartphones, waiting at an airport was never boring. She packed the warmest clothes she had with her, including her red parka and a "sensible" beige jacket, suitable for wearing at lectures. Tomorrow she was northward bound!

76

Earlier that day Gunnar Tufte had just okayed his Oslo staff's plans for updating advertisements for Kontakt. As he looked at the accompanying images the team had suggested, he realized they all featured women and men who were blond and blue-eyed. The stereotypical Norwegian. He could not help but recall the ubiquitous Myrtl Cosmetics ads that showcased seductive women who, almost uniformly, had dark hair and green eyes. Why did Kildahl emphasize only this type of woman? Wasn't the Norseliga all about the superiority of the Nordic race? Wasn't the Nordic race almost entirely composed of blond-haired individuals whose eyes were usually blue? Why this apparent racial denigration in Kildahl's ads?

On an impulse he phoned her. Sophia Grimm, realizing it was a Norseliga member who was calling, put him straight through to Myrtl. It was a mistake. Myrtl had not had a good day. The British lawsuit against her firm might be successful.

"Hallo, Myrtl/Hel, queen of Helheim. This is Gunnar/Tyr."

"Yes, what can I do for you, Gunnar?" Why would this Norseliga member with a passion for collecting dull Bjørnstjerne Bjørnson memorabilia be calling her at work?

"Well, first of all, I wondered if you saw the television show ASK last night. And if so what did you think?"

"What did I think? Well, if you really want to know, I think Norseliga has a real problem on its hands. Frankly, I feel taken in by Olaf. Based on what the panel was saying, what he showed us was a copy and not the real thing. Now the question is: did he know it or not?"

"Oh, surely he did *not* know!"

"He'll have to tell us that himself."

"But you know how committed he is to the cause. He would never try to mislead Norseliga members."

"Well, he will have to explain things when we have our next meeting, that's all I can say."

"I am distressed to hear you say this. But on another matter concerning Norseliga business, I wanted to talk to you about Myrtl Cosmetics."

"Oh?" Myrtl glanced at her calendar. So many things still to take care of today.

"First, I wonder why you haven't given a Norwegian name to your company: say, like 'Myrtl Kosmetikk.' Why have you used the English word 'Cosmetics'?"

Myrtl was completely taken aback.

"You are asking me about why I have named my company as I have? Why do you think? I wanted it to have international appeal, and English is the best for that. Myrtl Cosmetics is extraordinarily successful, and to no small part because of its name."

Gunnar's strategy was working.

"Secondly, and I have to ask this straight out, why are most of the women in your ads not Norwegian looking? Not blonde and blue-eyed?"

"You've got to be kidding! There are plenty of dark-haired, dark-eyed Norwegians. Especially along the western coast, and in Bergen. It is to them, the dark *Nordmenn* minority, that I have made a tremendous effort to attract, since the stereotype is always the blonde, blue-eyed person."

"Yes, but the majority of Norwegians are what you call the stereotype. I think, and I believe I can speak on behalf of the other Norseliga members, that you should include more blonde women."

"*Are you telling me how to run my business?* This conversation is over!" Enraged, Myrtl slammed down the receiver.

It took her a full five minutes to recover and when she did, her master plan for the Norseliga had crystalized.

77

It was the green hour again. Sven had, as usual, served Olaf Petersen his bottle of Vieux Pontarlier absinthe in the den. Olaf was sipping slowly and pondering exactly when he would make his next move. Now that he possessed the Munch Museum's uncontested original, very likely the first version of *The Scream*, he was eager to call a special meeting of the Norseliga. They deserved to see the treasure Haakon Sando had brought to Norsehjem. They needed to know about his selfless bravery. And he wanted them all to have a chance to examine the so-called "copy" he had shown them at the previous meeting. A meeting which, before the bewildering poster prank, had been such a joyous event, then so tainted with the crazy ravings of a disgraced museum director and his machinating restorer. Details! Ravings over whether a tiny church steeple did or did not exist in *The Scream*'s background.

Well, at least he had fixed that! Last night, after he had quizzed his restorer without giving away why he was asking the question he put to him, he had "corrected" the picture in question. Working with his large magnifying glass, a tube of titanium white, and a two-inch nylon brush, he had dabbed in a miniscule white steeple in the exact same background location as the other *Scream*'s indication of Oslo cathedral's spire. Then he had aged it with a touch of light brown paint and an oil-based varnish.

And it was all so unnecessary! If he had to kidnap every Munch expert in the country to attest to the painting's authenticity, he would. But with Megan Crespi, he would have a nonpartisan, international authority to vouch in writing for the work, for both works. He should be hearing from Christian Drapsmann anytime now.

Yes. Unlike that incompetent woman Isabell, what's her name, Farlig, Drapsmann was a true professional. His work had come recommended by one of the country's top crime lords. And now he would be bringing the American art historian to Norsehjem. The woman who had said to him that the loss of a Munch painting might not be as "catastrophic" as people might think. What the hell had she meant by that? She must have been referring to what she had been told was a copy. That was the mantra. It was only a copy that had been stolen. Norway can rest easy now. Oh, yes? Now Norway had lost a second Munch. Where were the naysayers now? Perhaps it was good for Norway, for the Norwegians, to suffer national losses. Where was their pride in Munch? The greatest painter the country had ever produced. Perhaps now Norwegians would be more open to Norseliga's message of racial superiority. Yes, there had to be a reason for the cartwheeling events of the past two weeks.

Olaf's sprawling thoughts, mellowed by the absinthe, were interrupted by the sound of his cellphone playing the first eleven notes of Grieg's famous love song *Jeg elsker Dig—I Love You*. A welcome text popped up.

"Target under surveillance in Oslo."

78

The next morning at nine, unusually cloudy for June in Oslo, saw Megan, Lili, and Button taking a short walk in front of the Hotel Bristol before Megan alone entered a taxi. She waved a long, energetic goodbye to her two companions as the vehicle pulled out.

On the job in the hotel lobby since seven that morning, Snorre Uflaks had seen Crespi, pulling a small Prima Classe roller bag, walk out of the hotel with her ubiquitous female companion and damn dog. He slipped out, broke into a limping run for his truck, which was parked almost opposite the hotel, and was ready to follow when Crespi got into a taxi. With that suitcase, she must be going either to the train station, or the ferry dock, or the airport. Snorre decided it must be Gardermoen airport since the taxi was traveling in a northeast direction out of the city. He allowed two cars to get in front of him and had no problem keeping the taxi in sight for the thirty some miles to reach the airport.

Crespi's taxi pulled up at Norwegian Airlines. Seeing that, Snorre hastened to park his truck, then entered where Crespi had entered, and walked over to the Norwegian Airlines ticket counter. He spotted Crespi in a line and he could see that she was going to be the next person to be served. As soon as she had been checked in she walked with her roller bag over to security. Snorre rushed up to the agent who had checked her in, cutting ahead of the next person in line.

"*Excuse me, please*! Which flight is the woman you just helped taking? She dropped her wallet." He waved his own in the air.

"Oh, dear! The eleven o'clock flight to Trondheim. I hope you catch her in time."

"I do too," Snorre tossed back as he turned to follow in Crespi's direction. Instead, as soon as he was out of the helpful clerk's sight, he returned to Norwegian Airlines and stood in line at a different check-in counter. He put a large pair of very dark sunglasses on. When he reached the clerk he bought a ticket for Trondheim on the eleven o'clock flight. After getting though security he scouted around the waiting area and saw Crespi seated in the lounge near the gate for Norwegian Flight A33 to Trondheim. He found a seat far away from her but with a good view of the gate. It took another half hour before the flight was called and he watched Crespi board. He would probably have to walk by her seat when he boarded but he hoped his sunglasses would help make him anonymous. He also tried not to limp.

Things worked out as he hoped. Crespi had an aisle seat in the fifth row on the right; his aisle seat was on the opposite side in the seventh row. Holding a newspaper up to the right side of his face, he passed by Crespi. She had her laptop open and did not even glance up. Snorre was pleased with his success so far and he would use the flight time to plan what to do next. He had no tools with him. Because of airport security he had had to leave the brand new black pearl Taser C2 he had just acquired in his truck at the Oslo airport. Bummer.

There was another passenger on the eleven o'clock flight from Oslo to Trondheim. A short, muscular man with graying hair and a trim gray moustache sat in the eighth row of the plane. His long-sleeved, white shirt hid the swastikas tattooed on both of his upper arms. In his carryon bag, placed in the luggage rack above his head, were a uniform, a badge, and a white wig. Halfway through the flight Drapsmann took his wallet from his back pocket and drew out two photographs. He studied them carefully and replaced them carefully. Then he examined his police ID card. It was an excellent forgery.

As the airplane made its descent over Trondheim, Megan looked out her window at the picturesque view of the Trondheimsjford. She could see the Nid River as it circled around the city and ancient gothic cathedral with its great spire. Would she be able to spot the new Munch Museum from above? She knew it was right at the juncture of the river and the fjord and that it had been built to project out over the river. Sure enough, she soon spotted the long rectangular building with glass sides and gleaming metallic roof. What a venue for Munch's *Frieze of Life* panels! And right next to it and the Bakke Bridge she could see the Radisson Blu Hotel with its two glass towers alternating with three concrete ones. So that was where she was being put up tonight! So different from the student hostels she had stayed in the first time she had traveled around Norway decades ago. As the plane pulled up to its gate Megan pulled out her roller bag from underneath the seat in front of her, opened it, and slipped on the beige jacket that matched her beige blouse and slacks so nicely. It was going to be cooler out there than in Oslo.

A few minutes later Megan was walking through the airport. A few steps behind her, his eyes boring into her back, limped a thin, middle-aged man. And a few steps behind him, following in the same direction, was a short, muscular man with graying hair and trim moustache. He too was intent upon the figure of Megan Crespi in front of him.

Their prey came to a sudden halt. A smiling young man in a chauffeur's cap holding aloft a large white card with the words "Professor Crespi" on it was the cause. He escorted Megan to a black limousine, held a door open for her, then loaded her beige roller bag in the trunk. A minute later they were heading west on the twelve-mile drive from the airport to Trondheim.

Two taxis rolled up to the airport exit. Two men immediately hailed them and were on their way to Trondheim as well. In both instances, the cab drivers were instructed to keep a black limousine ahead of them in constant sight.

Megan's conveyance pulled up at the street entrance to the Radisson Blu Royal Garden Hotel. Two taxis stopped well behind her and two men got out. They witnessed a meeting between Crespi and an elderly bearded man with bald pate who was obviously her host. The two shook hands, chatted briefly, and then the man conducted his guest inside the hotel. Good, both men thought. Crespi's base in Trondheim is established.

"If you don't need to rest after your flight, I should be delighted to give you a tour of my two museums," Benno Landau was saying to Megan in the hotel lobby.

"I don't need to rest at all and I'd love to see your museums right away."

"Wonderful. Let's get you checked in and your bag upstairs and we'll be off. I'll wait for you down here."

"Perfect."

Megan took a glass-paneled elevator up to the fourth floor and was delighted to see that her room was in one of the glass towers overlooking the water. The room itself was cheerful and very modern. After a bathroom visit and a quick hot washcloth press to her face—ah, the soap smelled refreshingly of glycerin—she went back down to the lobby where Herr Landau stood waiting.

His limousine was lingering and a lively conversation ensued once they entered it.

"I thought it was going to be much cooler than it is here," Megan was saying, wishing she had left her parka in Oslo.

"Ah, everyone expects Trondheim to be cold since we are not far from the Arctic Circle, but we are warmed by the Gulf Stream here, so people are always surprised by our relatively mild climate—even in the winter." Landau looked amused. They were just passing the Trondheim cathedral with its "pedestrian only" square.

"I thought you might like to take a look at the Munchs in our city art museum before we go to the synagogue. They're not far from each other at all."

"Oh, what a treat. Yes!"

Minutes later they were in the museum, which, like Megan's hotel, also had a tall glass architectural component. She was pleased to see that, in addition to more modern artists, some of "her" nineteenth-century Norwegian and Danish painters were on display. Landau led her to a long corridor. It was well lit and lined on both sides with lithographs by Munch.

"This is where I got the idea for my museum building. I thought a long hallway where there are Munchs to the left and Munchs to the right of the viewer, not leading to any 'climax,' but simply showcasing each panel from *The Frieze of Life*, would be the most puissant way of experiencing the works."

"What an interesting idea!"

"And now, since it is nearby, let me take you over to our synagogue's Jewish Museum."

They walked just past the cathedral to the synagogue, almost hidden from view and painted blue, and down to its basement. The walls contained attractively arranged photographs forming various thematic groups, each set off from the other. Megan viewed the pictures in silence. The images were touching and she was very much moved, experiencing horror again at the fate of so many European Jews at the hands of Hitler and his henchmen.

"I hear that anti-Semitism is on the rise yet again in Norway," Megan murmured to her host.

"Oh, most unfortunately, yes. Perhaps you noticed that there are barriers outside the synagogue?"

"I did."

"Well, last year in October our small Jewish cemetery here in Trondheim was vandalized. Swastikas and the word 'Hitler' were spray-painted on its little chapel."

"Oh, no! That's terrible. I thought neo-Nazis were only in Germany."

"Quite the contrary. There are neo-Nazi organizations in Norway, Denmark, Sweden, and Finland. To say nothing of the Baltic countries."

"And what happened to Trondheim Jews during the war? Were they able to flee to Sweden?"

"Yes, about a hundred and seventy of them did so. The rest were sent to Auschwitz in October of nineteen-forty-two. Out of the one hundred and thirty-five individuals sent to Auschwitz, only five survived. The Nazis used our synagogue for military purposes and left it in shambles. We repaired it soon after the war ended and later I was allowed to create a museum in its basement—what you see here. In many respects it is a 'Lest We Forget' caveat museum."

"And rightly so, Herr Landau," Megan said quietly and sincerely.

"Shall we move to a first name basis?" Landau asked.

"I should love to."

"All right then, Megan—such a nice name—if you are not too tired, then let me take you now to the Munch Museum. You probably saw it from the air and realized that it is right next to your hotel."

"I did, and was fascinated to see how it extends out over the water."

"For me, and I think it would have been so in Munch's case as well, being poised over water symbolizes how fragile life is. How important we do something with it while we have it."

Megan nodded vigorously and said earnestly: "I've often thought that simply by striving to be the best person one can be is one of the ways we can be helpful to our particular place and time. I'm talking about generosity, love, and loyalty, but also—as a teacher all my professional life—about caring for and preserving our past and present history and showing how it relates to each and every one of us. The obligation has been to pass all that on to the next generations. I feel that, in my limited way, I have managed to do so."

"I like you, Megan," Benno pronounced, smiling.

"I like you too, Benno," declared Megan, smiling back at him.

"And now let's return to my car and go to the Munch Museum—the achievement of my life. Far beyond any of my successes at business."

When they pulled up to the museum some seven minutes later, a well-built man, short, with graying hair and moustache, was just exiting by way of the long pier that connected the glass-encased building to the street. Neither Megan nor Benno noticed that he had stopped to stare at her. On the other hand, neither had Drapsmann become aware of the fact that one of his fellow plane passengers had been in the museum casing the place just as he had done. Snorre Uflaks was still in the long hall of the museum when Megan and Benno entered. He scuttled out of sight immediately and left the building unobserved.

"What a novel way to exhibit the pictures," Megan complimented Benno after they entered the Munch Hall and she had taken her first sweeping look. Eleven open booths lined the left wall and were matched by eleven open booths on the right wall. Within each blond maple wood booth was one of *The Frieze of Life* panels. Facing them in each booth were four inviting chairs, very modern, very comfortable.

Slowly Megan followed the progression mandated by the placement of the individual panels: birth, childhood, innocence, family, forest, sea, companionship, solitariness, puberty, curiosity, and first confusing stirrings of the sexual impulse. She paused and sat down in front of *Puberty*, refreshing her memory of the naked young girl who sits facing the viewer, frozen on the edge of her bed, wide-eyed, arms protectively crossed over her tightly closed legs, and seemingly stunned by her first menstruation. Ominous harbinger of this perplexing new phenomenon in her life is the black humanoid shadow looming upward at her side. What an image!

Megan moved to the other side of the room taking long looks at the eleven panels. Now the paintings addressed lust, desire, phallic moon reflections, rejection, loneliness, panic, crowds, alienation, isolation, sickness, and death. Perhaps the most moving, at least for Megan, was Munch's heartfelt depiction of the all-embracing numbness of his own family members in the face of death. The artist, who wrote that disease, insanity, and death were the angels that attended his cradle, also wrote as an old man that these three black angels had followed him throughout his life. The pictorial starkness with which Munch depicted these forces resonated with anyone who took the time to look. No wonder Benno Landau had supplied chairs.

Benno derived the greatest of satisfaction from watching the American scholar unabashedly soaking up the energies emanated by Munch's compelling imagery. Finally he suggested that Megan take a look at the little auditorium where her evening lecture would be held. She came out of her trance and readily agreed. The room held about one hundred people and the podium at the front of the room accommodated her slight height and was already equipped with a glass and pitcher of water. She tried out the mike and handed over her thumb drive with the PowerPoint images to the pleasant technician who would be helping out that evening.

Benno pressed two copies of the museum's elegant, heavy Munch catalogue into Megan's hands and suggested that she return to the hotel and take a rest now.

"Thank you. I should like that. And you couldn't have booked me into a more convenient hotel. It's right next to your museum, after all," Megan acknowledged his offer gratefully. She had noticed that she was indeed becoming a little tired.

"And this evening after your lecture we'll go to my home and give you a nice smorgasbord dinner. My daughter and my two grandsons are coming to your lecture. The latter are a bit boisterous, but I want them to learn about Munch and his impact upon the world."

Megan smiled at her host and then carefully navigated the pier walk from the museum to the street. How did they ever get the Munch paintings into the place, she wondered, worrying about their safety and hers as well.

79

The first ten notes of Grieg's *Jeg elsker Dig* sounded on Olaf Petersen's cellphone in Bergen. Olaf was on his landline phone conducting business and hastened to end the conversation. He picked up his cellphone. There was another text bubble. This time it read *"Subject now in Trondheim."*

80

It had been standing room only at the local Munch Museum's seven o'clock lecture by the visiting art historian from America. Her presentation concerning Munch's impact on contemporary Viennese artists was compelling and set within the larger confines of literature, dance, architecture, music, and politics. There had been a long question and answer session afterward for which only two members of the audience, both male, did not stay. The shorter man walked over to the Radisson Blu, entered the men's room, quickly changed clothes, then sat in the lobby in a lounge chair that had a view of the street entrance. He would sit there no matter how late Crespi might return to the hotel.

The other man, thin and middle-aged, although he had left the building, did not actually leave the museum premises. Rather, he stood just next to the heavy glass doors that opened outward from the museum to the pier. He stood and waited, his plan only half formulated. This time he would really inflict damage on Crespi. Just how, he still wasn't sure. But this time he would not fail Myrtl Kildahl.

Inside the museum's auditorium a beaming Benno Landau was thanking the appreciative audience and trying to bring the evening to an end. His grand-sons were becoming impatient and needed to vent their energy. Benno did not see them slip out of the room and rush through the building to get outside. Snorre Uflaks did not see them either. When the two rowdy boys flung open the museum doors the one on the right hit Snorre full force, knocking him off the pier and into the restless water below. He sank without a sound. And no one noticed. Bad luck.

"And now we feed you," Benno said to Megan as he held the car door open for her. His daughter had collected the two noisy boys and they were already in the limousine. An hour later Megan felt she could not eat another bite of the delicious smorgasbord that had been spread out before her in the family home.

"I have learned from your website that you are a musician as well as an art historian," Benno said to her. "Let me show you my humble collection of musical instruments."

Megan followed him into a small room off the dining room with trepidation. She had learned in her long life that "humble" often meant overwhelming.

"This is my collection of instruments that are used to accompany the

Sami songs—yoiks—that they sing up in Hammerfest. Especially nowadays, when they chant yoiks, these are the instruments they use." He pointed toward a large round table covered with hand drums, both frame and bowl drums. Hanging on the wall above were some two dozen of what Benno identified as "fadnos"—flutes made from the reed-like tubes of Norwegian angelica. They were in different sizes and lengths.

"Please, try one, Megan. I noted on your website that you are a flutist."

Although she was tired now, Megan was game. She took one of the larger flutes off its hook, put her fingers over the two carved holes on the stem and blew tentatively. A high sound followed by two lower sounds was all she was able to get out of the instrument.

But now her interest in the Sami songs was reignited. She had first heard them up in Hammerfest, high above the Arctic Circle, when she visited there in the early nineteen-sixties. She had not been there since. And she said so to Benno.

"That is easily remedied," he replied instantly and seriously. "I fly there tomorrow with the whole family on my private Airbus for a noon concert of Sami yoiks in the new music pavilion there. I return here in the afternoon. What time is your flight back to Oslo?"

"You are kidding," laughed Megan.

"Oh, no, I am quite serious. Come fly with us to Hammerfest, *verdens nordligste by*, after all!"

"Yes, yes, that sign was everywhere even when I was there: 'the world's most northern city.'"

"And so it is. There may be villages that are farther north up there, but Hammerfest is the most northern town. It has over nine thousand regular in-habitants, after all. Now what do you say to my invitation? When do you have to be back in Oslo?"

"Wait, wait a minute! You're going too fast for me. I should really love retuning there, but I have to think a minute. My flight back to Oslo is at five in the afternoon." Megan paused, then hazarded: "Do you think you could return in sufficient time for me to catch that flight?"

"That is not a problem. On my Airbus three-twenty, the flight to and from Hammerfest only takes an hour and fifteen, twenty minutes at the most, and, after all, I use the same airport your Trondheim/Oslo flight does."

Megan was of two minds. Seeing that, Benno continued his persuasive talk.

"You thought it would be cooler here in Trondheim. Well, the standard temperature in Hammerfest this time of the year is around fifty-five degrees Fahrenheit. Now there's your cooler summer weather!" He was pulling out every stop on his persuasive organ of enticements.

"If I should come, and I'm saying *if*, what time would I have to be ready in the morning?"

"I, the family, and the limousine will pick you up at eight. Possible?"

Megan was defeated. Delightfully defeated.

"Yes. Let's do it."

"Wonderful. Now let me take you back to your hotel so you can get some sleep. Bring your suitcase with you tomorrow when we pick you up."

"All right. And you're correct. I'll be able to wear the warmest clothing I brought with me. My red parka."

Ten minutes later Megan was waving goodbye to the departing limousine and an elated Benno Landau. He had spent the travel time back to the hotel praising her lecture and its impact on the audience.

Megan walked to the front desk and asked the clerk to check her out this evening as she would be leaving early—for her, the lifelong night owl—the next morning. That accomplished, she took out her cardkey and headed toward the glass tower of the hotel where her room was. As she stood waiting in front of the elevators a uniformed officer strode up to her.

"Fru Megan Crespi?"

"Yes?" She wondered how a policeman would know her name.

"I am going to have to ask you to come with me. We need you to identify a man who was just injured in a car accident. He has been calling out for you." The officer flashed his ID card at her.

"Oh, my god! Yes of course." She hoped against hope that Benno Landau was not seriously injured.

The courteous officer walked ahead of her and led her to a black Volvo parked right by the hotel entrance on the Kjøpmannsgate.

"It's just a short distance to the police station," the man said reassuringly as he held the door open for Megan to get into the back seat.

She heard a clicking sound as the car started up. Looking toward the sound she saw that both back doors were now locked.

"Where did you say we are going?" Megan asked sharply, leaning forward.

"Actually, we're going to Bergen, and the quieter you stay the better it will be for you," answered Christian Drapsmann.

81

Browsing the neo-Nazi sites on his computer, an idle Max Linde came to a pause before the major one, *Deutschland Erst*. He had skipped the rolling website of Hitler saluting Olympian contestants and gone straight to the commentary page. The name Brunhilde stood out. She had posted an image along with the threatening comment: "Norseliga, Your Time Has Come." The riveting image showed a beautiful brunette with long hair and green eyes focused directly upon the viewer. A blood-red halo circled the top of her hair. Minimally clad except for shiny black boots, she had her right hand out in a Führerlike salute. In her left hand was what looked like a Glock pistol—the same weapon mass murderer Breivik had used in Norway in 2011.

Who in hell's name was this bold, in-your-face Brunhilde? Max's curiosity was aroused because of the word "Norseliga" used in the intimidating commentary. For the past week he had been hacking into the business and private e-mail of the six members he had identified as members of that fanatical group of super wealthy Norwegians who were engaged in trying to educate and incentivize naïve Norwegian children into thinking they were superior, as Norse descendants, to the Master Race.

This was too great a coincidence. Max went back to his file on Myrtl Kildahl, whose Myrtl Cosmetics advertising images looked a hell of a lot like the Brunhilde icon he had just come across. Could Kildahl and Brunhilde be one and the same? It certainly looked so. And if so, why was she threatening her very own organization, and on a neo-Nazi website?

Oh, what he could do with such a find! He could sell it to the person who seemed to be in charge of the Norseliga, Olaf Petersen. Or he could respond to Brunhilde's commentary and urge her on to bolder action. Down with Norwegian superiorism! Or he could simply alert the Norwegian police to the fact that an anonymous internet threat, signed by a "Brunhilde," was directed at an educational Norwegian entity called Norseliga.

Which should he choose?

82

It was eleven-thirty at night. Locked in the back of the speeding car of the man who had in an instant changed from concerned police officer to virtual kidnapper, Megan slipped her iPhone out of the outside pocket of her shoulder bag and turned off the volume. Then she quickly texted Erik Jensen in Oslo: "help kidnapped bergen."

Just as she finished sending the text the man driving the car suddenly turned into a side street, slammed on the brakes, and turned off the ignition. In a flash he had twisted around in his seat and extended his left hand toward Megan threateningly.

"Give me your bag," he commanded. "Now!"

"Why?" Megan asked boldly.

"Listen, lady. If you've got a smartphone in there I don't want you sending any messages. Now give it to me!"

Reluctantly Megan handed over her shoulder bag which did indeed have her phone back in its special pocket. Oh, why hadn't she had the wit to slip it down her blouse? But at least the message had been sent. That is if there was local Wi-Fi she hoped desperately. But of course, there just had to be in this hotel district. She had had no chance to see if the notation "delivered" had come up under her text message. She would simply have to hope for the best. In the meantime she would try to humor the tyrant in front of her.

"Could you tell me, please, why we are we going to Bergen?"

"Listen, woman. It's a ten-hour trip and I told you to be quiet. Now I'll make sure you are." Drapsmann turned in his seat again and thrust a stun gun directly into Megan's left cheek. Instantly she collapsed on the floor of the back seat, temporarily unconscious. She would be quiet now. Drapsmann opened the glove compartment and removed a white wig and a roll of duct tape. Then he stopped, got out of the car and opened the back door. He put a strip of tape over Crespi's mouth and bound her hands together in front of her with the tape. Then he pulled the wig down hard over her brown hair. The transformation was complete.

Drapsmann stood up, slammed the back door closed, and returned to the driver's seat. Using his own smartphone he texted Olaf Petersen in Bergen: "Subject on way to you. Estimated arrival time 9:30 am tomorrow." He started the car, drove back onto the Kjøpmannsgate, and drove southward out of town, picking up speed. Some twenty minutes later he was on the winding RV51 highway to Bergen by way of mountains, fjords, and glaciers. This was the fastest route as it did not require transferring to a ferry, as did the shortest route, RV55. Traveling by ferry with the Crespi woman was something Drapsmann certainly did not want to risk.

Although it was well after eleven in the evening Olaf Petersen was elated to be awakened by Grieg on his smartphone announcing an incoming text. Sleepily he reached for the phone. Yes, it was from Christian Drapsmann. And it contained superlative news. The Crespi woman would be delivered to Norsehjem in the morning!

This was an employee who delivered! Drapsmann had succeeded where what's her name had failed. Olaf would rise at six the next morning in order to have plenty of time to prepare for the woman's enforced visit. But right now, even though it was close to midnight, he would e-mail all Norseliga members and summon them to an emergency meeting early tomorrow evening.

83

Lili hoped the phone ringing in her Hotel Bristol bedroom so late in the evening meant that Megan was finally checking in with her. Odd that she didn't call her at her iPhone number. Button, who had been awakened by the noise, looked up at Lili questioningly.

But it was not Megan on the line.

"Fru Holm? This is Erik Jensen of the National Gallery."

"Yes, yes. I saw you with Megan on television."

"I am calling you, and sorry about the lateness of the hour, to ascertain whether or not Megan is there with you. Or if you know where she is."

"Oh, no, she's not in Oslo. She was giving a lecture at the Munch Museum in Trondheim earlier this evening. That's where she is, but she'll be flying back tomorrow."

"I don't want to worry you, but I have tried now repeatedly to reach her on her cellphone. She hasn't answered or returned my call. I've left her several messages."

"Oh, that's unusual. Megan is usually so prompt about returning calls."

"Can you tell me at what hotel she is staying?"

"Oh, yes. It's the Radisson Blu and Megan was very excited by the idea of overnighting there. She told me earlier today when she called that her room is in one of the glass towers and it overlooks the river and the Trondheim fjord."

"All right. I am going to see if I can reach her there. Is that the only time you have talked to her today?"

"Yes. But I've been expecting Megan to call and report on how her lecture went. Actually it's rather surprising that she hasn't."

"Now listen, Fru Holm. Something has come up, and I do not want to alarm you. I shall try to reach Megan at the Radisson, but if I am not successful I shall call you back. If you do *not* hear from me then everything is all right and I'll tell her you are waiting for a call from her. Good?"

"Fine," said Lili, surprised by the man's serious tone.

"Where's your Mama?" she asked Button who, excited by the repeated mentions of Megan's name, was wagging his tail expectantly.

A few minutes later the landline phone rang again. It was Erik and he sounded somber.

"I am very confused," he said. "The night clerk told me that Megan checked out of the hotel about an hour ago."

"But that's not possible," said Lili. She knew her friend was overnighting there.

"But the worst thing is that just about that same time I received a text from Megan. It's just three words: 'help kidnapped bergen.'"

"*What?*"

"That's what the text says. No punctuation, no caps. I think this is the real thing. That someone has kidnapped her and..."

"is taking her to Bergen," Lili finished his sentence. "We have to call the police! Immediately!"

"I shall do so right now. But I had first wanted to check with you and also her hotel. This text has to be taken seriously."

"Do you think it is the result of that television show you were both on?"

"I think that could very well be the case. Let me call the police now and I will get right back to you. Give me your cellphone number and I'll pass it on to them. They may want to talk to you."

Two minutes later Erik was talking to an Oslo police sergeant who scrupulously took down all the information he gave him, including Lili Holm's cellphone number.

"So you think the person who kidnapped Professor Crespi is driving her down from Trondheim to someplace in Bergen, correct?"

"Correct."

"I'll send a bulletin out to all officers on the three major routes from Trondheim to Bergen to be on the alert. You have no description of the car she might be in, do you?"

"No, unfortunately. Nor of the person or persons who have her."

Erik said goodbye so the officer could call Lili for possible insight and details.

Her cellphone had hardly begun to ring when Lili picked it up, sure that it was the police who were calling her now.

"Fru Holm?"

"Yes, yes, this is she." The officer was speaking in Norwegian and Lili was speaking in Danish but they understood each other.

"This is Police Sergeant Jonas Jacobsen. Dr. Erik Jensen has told me about the possible kidnapping in Trondheim of your travel companion, Professor Crespi. We are obtaining her photo from the Internet as well as from her recent television appearance here on ASK, and we will send it to all duty officers. But can you tell me perhaps what she was wearing, if you know, and any other details that might be helpful? "

"Oh, yes, I can. Exactly. She would have been wearing a beige jacket, beige blouse, and beige slacks, flat brown shoes. She is short, brunette, and wears her hair short. She also always carries a brown shoulder bag."

"And Professor Crespi is eighty, I'm told. Is she able to walk all right?"

"Absolutely," Lili confirmed indignantly. "She's in great shape. And she looks years younger than she actually is. Don't be looking for a fragile, white-haired old lady."

"All this is a great help. We will keep in touch and notify you of events as they unfold."

Erik called Lili again a few minutes later.

"Did the police tell you they are going to circulate photos of Megan and that they are setting up roadblocks on the three main highways from Trondheim to Bergen?"

"That's wonderful. I didn't know about the roadblocks."

"And tomorrow, just as soon as it is a civilized hour to call, I shall get in touch with Police Chief Inspector Finne Raske. He was on the ASK panel with us and you most likely know that Megan and I met with him the next day."

"Oh. Excellent. He would have a personal interest in helping us find Megan."

"Exactly what I thought. I suppose we should both get some sleep now, but, may I call you Lili? Lili, I will telephone you the moment I hear anything."

"Give me your cellphone number since you have mine."

Erik gave Lili both his cell number and his office number at the National Gallery.

Neither of them were able to sleep well that night, despite the late hour. Unanswered questions kept them both awake. *Who would want to kidnap Megan and why would they want to?*

83

Still fooling around on his laptop Max Linde had opted for his second choice concerning the Brunhilde/Kildahl conundrum. Were they really one and the same person? Perhaps the idea was just a figment of his bouncing brain. He could not be 100 percent sure that there was a connection between the two. He decided simply to urge Brunhilde on with her scary message to the Norseliga saying that its "time had come."

He logged into *Deutschland Erst* and pulled down to the comments section. By golly, there was another one from Brunhilde. This one said: "You want an emergency meeting? You will get one. An extreme one." Not being sure just what that was all about, Max simply added an encouraging comment: "You go, Hildechen, you go!" Using the endearing nickname for Brunhilde would demonstrate his loyalty to whatever the scary babe's cause really was.

The next morning at seven Erik Jensen tried calling his new police officer friend, Finne Raske. Surprisingly enough he was already in his office. Erik explained the situation to him.

"I was afraid our television ASK panel might have repercussions in the art world, but never did I think it would result in a kidnapping!"

"That is the word Megan used in her short text to me, "kidnapped.""

"And she also wrote 'Bergen?'"

"Yes. 'Help' and 'Bergen.'"

"I see here," Raske said, looking through the morning bulletins, "that roadblocks are being set up on the three main surface routes to Bergen from

Trondheim. But what if she was coerced into taking a plane flight? I'll have the airports at both ends covered too. Train stations also. Only makes sense. I doubt that she would be traveling by ship, but we can also post some men to cover Bergen Harbor arrivals from Trondheim. That should do it."

"I can't thank you enough for your help. Megan is a dear colleague and I would hate to think that our Munch mess could have endangered her in any way."

"Speaking of Munch messes," Raske said, "I've been doing some checking on that Bergen ship-building mogul Olaf Petersen. He comes out squeaky clean, but is known for extreme secrecy. Another thing he is known for is a big private collection that includes Munch and which he has allowed only a few persons to see. And as we learned from Crespi, she was one of them! Now you put two and two together and you get Petersen, if you see what I mean."

"Wow! Do I ever see what you mean. Megan did tell us that her visit to Petersen and his mysterious mansion was, didn't she use the word 'bizarre?'" Erik asked.

"Yes, that was the word, 'bizarre.' And remember she also told us about her dog chasing Petersen's dog around to the back of the manor and coming up against a bunker. Now I've checked if there are any bunker manufacturers in Norway and, surprisingly enough, there are two. One supplies bunkers and lubricants for ships; the other—*Beskyttelse Bunker*—actually installs factory-made underground bunkers on demand anywhere in Norway. And guess where it's based? Bergen."

"This is terrific! Do you have enough now to get a search warrant?"

"Working on it as we speak. My hope is that we get it by this afternoon so we can go out there and examine the house, the grounds, and, especially, the bunker Professor Crespi saw."

"May I tell her travel companion of your progress?"

"Yes of course, but don't hold out false hope. We may after all be climbing up the wrong tree."

"And you'll call me if and when you find something?"

"Absolutely. I have a feeling we are going to come up with something."

With great relief Erik called Lili and brought her up to date on his talk with Finne Raske. Afterward, he did once again what he had done many times in the past twenty-four hours. He called Megan's cellphone number. And once again Megan's recorded voice asked the caller to leave a message. Erik was not the only one to try and reach Megan on the off chance that she had access to her cellphone. Lili had been trying the same thing with no success.

In Trondheim at exactly eight that morning Benno Landau and family drove up to the Radisson Blu. He had hoped to see Professor Crespi standing at the entrance. She must be waiting in the lobby. Landau's chauffeur stayed with the limousine while he went inside. There was no sign of the American. He approached the front desk and asked the smiling clerk to please phone up to Professor Crespi's room and say the Landau party was waiting for her down in the main lobby. But there was no answer. The clerk tried again. Still no answer.

"She must be on her way down," Benno Landau concluded. He waited another five minutes.

"Would you try her room again, please?"

The clerk obliged. Still no answer. Eager to help, she studied last night's request list of wakeup calls. A frown crossed her forehead.

"I don't understand. She did an express checkout last night."

"Now I am worried. Could you possibly send someone up to her room? Perhaps she simply overslept."

"Well, we don't usually do such things. You say she was to meet you in the lobby this morning at eight?"

"Yes. We are flying to Hammerfest together this morning."

"Let me just check with my boss." The clerk picked up a phone, got through to the hotel manager and explained the situation. She was given the go-ahead and a porter was sent up to the room with a master key. When there was no answer to his series of knocks, he opened the door to the room. The room and bathroom were empty and the made up bed had obviously not been slept in. By the window was a beige Prima Classe roller bag. The porter immediately called down to the front desk and reported his findings.

"Professor Crespi's luggage is in her room but she is not," the clerk told Herr Landau.

"Here is my cellphone number. Would you kindly give me a call when she returns to pick up her luggage?"

"Glad to do so."

"We'll just have to take our flight without her."

Back at the limousine Benno reported the mysterious situation to his daughter.

"I guess she simply decided not to come. Rather rude of her not to leave a message for you."

"But if she checked out of the hotel, why didn't she take her luggage with her?"

84

"It is time Norseliga ceased to exist," Myrtl announced angrily to Sophia. As usual when at home they were speaking in German. They had stayed up late that evening watching a new German film, *Zeit der Kannibalen*—Age of Cannibals—that starred a feisty businesswoman.

"Why do you say that, Hildechen? What has upset you so terribly?"

"Look at the e-mail that imperious Olaf Petersen just sent me! All of a sudden he calls an 'emergency' meeting for tomorrow evening! As if we can all just drop everything we're doing and rush over to Bergen."

"Does he say what the emergency is, Hilde?"

"He doesn't, but I can damn well predict it has something to do with that television panel on the stolen Munchs we watched. They were such know-it-alls. And that honey-tongued Megan Crespi! We know how acid she can be. How she tried to tell us Munch had an affair with Eva Mudocci that produced children."

"Oh, yes, she was adamant on that, wasn't she? But why do you feel so strongly about its being time to break up Norseliga?"

"I've thought so for quite some time, *Liebling*. The education program for eliciting Norwegian pride is having too great a success. By god, those squirmy kids are starting to *believe* Norwegians are the superior race! Blond Vikings, and all."

"Well, I know you've been worried about the unexpected success of that twisted program for quite some time now."

"I tell you, if I didn't have *Deutschland Erst* to vent my feeling on, I think I'd go crazy with all the playacting I have to do in my life. Hell, we even have to pretend you're my secretary!"

"Hold on there," Sophia said hotly. "I *am* your secretary and a damn good one and you know it."

"Oh, honey, I didn't mean to denigrate what you do for me. It's just that we have to go along with this open secret business."

"I've never minded that."

"Honest to god, you have the patience of Job."

"Seriously, why do you think it is time to terminate Norseliga? Surely it's not just out of temporary pique?"

"Of course not. It's something I really have been considering for a long time. It's just that Olaf's 'acquisition' of Munch's *Scream* in the name of Norsehood has put it all in focus for me. Things have just gone too far. In Munch's *Madonna* I had found a comforting duplicate of myself when I was in the depths of self-doubt and suffering from a terrible inferiority complex. Munch showed me that women who looked like me could be beautiful."

"And sensual, Hilde, and sensual."

"Yes, that too, dear. But now Olaf is using Munch as the lodestar of Norseliga. He's even got it set up in his bunker as if it were an altarpiece. Doesn't have a clue that a miserable image depicting an insanely screaming man is hardly something to inspire exceptionalism in a nation. Or, if Norwegians do worship this artwork, then they are as neurotic as the creator of that artwork"

"When you put it that way, I have to shiver for the Norwegians."

"No, no, the Norseliga has outlived its purpose. I had thought association with it would help Myrtl Cosmetics, and for a while it did, but can you imagine that Gunnar Tufte gave me a bawling out for using primarily brunettes in our ads?"

"You hadn't told me that!"

"I was too angry. Hadn't processed it yet. The nerve of that man!"

"But featuring dark-haired women has helped so many Norwegian girls who aren't blonde achieve a sense of selfhood—that's what you always say."

"That's what I've told myself. And others, yes."

"You know you really have a love/hate relationship with Norway, don't you?"

"Ha! More hate than love. My business has flourished but my childhood here was absolute torture. You know that."

"Yes, yes, I know." Sophia took Myrtl's hand and pressed it sympathetically.

"Look, Sophia. You were born in Germany and your father was German. And after he died and your mother moved back with you to her native Norway, she made sure you never lost that heritage, in your case such a distinguished heritage—the Grimm brothers! So you have always felt you were a German in Norway. Isn't that so?"

"Yes."

"Well I too have always felt a German in Norway, but couldn't speak of it or acknowledge it. My mother was so proud of being a member of the Krupp family. She used to quote the Führer's enjoinder to the Hitler Youth to be '*hart wie Kruppstahl*— hard as Krupp steel.' And she would have been so proud of my business success in Germany."

"And now you think the Norseliga has become a threat to your business and your neo-Nazi colleagues here in Norway?"

"I am sure of it. Yes. The time has come to, shall I say, dissolve the association."

"But how will you *do* such a thing? These are five fanatical men, powerful members of society, who totally believe in Norwegian racial superiority."

"How will I do it? I have the means, don't you doubt that for an instant. I shall attend tomorrow evening's 'emergency' meeting, and after that, there will be no more Norseliga meetings."

"Now you're frightening me, Myrtl."

"Don't you fret about it, my love. Bergen is only an hour's flight time away. I shall fly there tomorrow, take care of business, and be back here with you by late tomorrow night. I promise."

Sophia felt a strange sense of misgiving but said nothing.

85

Megan had regained consciousness and was trying to yell through the duct tape that covered her mouth.

"Shut up or I'll give you another stun."

Megan fell silent and concentrated on trying to loosen her wrists. She made scant headway. At least her hands were in front of her and not bound behind. Managing to pull herself back up to the seat, she lay down thankfully. The car was gaining height and although it was dark outside she could see snow-capped mountains looming up on either side of the car.

Some half hour later Drapsmann suddenly pulled to a stop. In front of him was a sign: "ROAD CLOSED. CONSTRUCTION AHEAD. TAKE ALTERNATE RV55, CONNECT WITH RV15, CONNECT RV60 OR E39."

"God damn it to hell," he cursed out loud at the unwelcome and confusing sign. He was going to have to backtrack and get onto RV55. Yeah, it was the shortest route, but it included a ferry. Even though he wouldn't have to get out of the car after he'd driven onto the ferry, it was still going to be a touchy situation. He would have to make sure Crespi was unconscious again. That was no problem. But what if someone looked into the car and saw that her hands and mouth were taped? If only he had a blanket in the car.

A thought came to him. He could pull up the floor mats in the back seat and the one in the trunk and drape them over her. Okay, he'd do that while he was stopped. It was easy to throw them over her as she was lying prone on the back seat. He took the trouble to cover her face while he was at it, then turned the car around and drove back to where highway 51 and country road 55 merged. He was losing precious time. Should he text Petersen about the delay? Well, let's first see how much time we can make up. He pressed the accelerator pedal to the floor, taking the curves fast, but what the hell?

Two hours later he had passed over the Sognefjell mountain area, which took him through the highest pass in Northern Europe. Once at a lower elevation he took his eyes off the road for a moment and checked on an apparently dozing Crespi. When he looked back, there out of nowhere right in front of him on the road, was a mountain reindeer, frozen in the headlights. Drapsmann's car screeched to a stop and hit the huge animal full on its side, knocking it up in the air then down on the highway. The reindeer was killed instantly. Dazed, and trying to avoid the sight in front of him, Drapsmann stumbled out of his car and examined the crumpled front hood. It was covered with blood. Both front tires had been knocked out of alignment. He got back in the car and tried to move it, steering away from the carcass blocking the road. The wheels would not respond. He was stuck. Stuck at the base of a mountain.

It was six in the morning and still dark. Drapsmann tried his cellphone. There was no connection. Hell! What was there to do now? He couldn't even call for help, much less contact Petersen. He checked on Crespi. The floor pads had been knocked off her and she had been thrown to the floor again. He could hear her moaning. She was alive. But what good was that to him now?

Looking up the highway past the carcass that blocked the road, he thought he saw a pair of headlights in the distance. He kept looking and, yes, the headlights were getting larger. A vehicle was approaching. Talk about good luck! What if the driver looked in the car? He opened one of the back doors and cut the duct tape from off Crespi's mouth and hands, commanding her to lie still and not move. Then he zapped her lightly with the stun gun. She fell unconscious again as a moan escaped her throat. Leaving the car Drapsmann stepped out beyond the animal's cadaver and began waving his arms wildly at the approaching car.

Of all things it was an ambulance that pulled up. A young attendant jumped out and looked questioningly at the policeman standing in front of him.

"What's happened, officer?"

Drapsmann wondered for a split second why the fellow addressed him as "officer," then realized he was still wearing his police uniform."

"That reindeer out of nowhere ran smack into my car."

"Oh! Bad luck. It happens now and then. We can call a tow truck for you once we get out of this area and beyond the glacier. We're just on our way back from an emergency run up toward Stryn and when we return to Førde we can get you some help."

Just then there was a loud moan from the back of the stalled car.

"Sounds as if someone in there is hurt." The attendant ran to the car and looked in. He saw a white-haired woman lying on the back seat. She wasn't moving. Lucky I took those tapes off, Drapsmann thought, furious with the nosy kid.

"Yes! Yes! It's my mother!" he cried with feigned concern.

"Officer, you can't wait for a tow truck. She's unconscious! We'll transport her in to the hospital at Førde. We can take you both but we gotta move fast."

"Of course! What was I thinking of? It's a miracle that it was you on the road."

Drapsmann was grateful that he had thought of the wig idea. Something had told him to be prepared for the unexpected. And this certainly was. He knew that once they got to Førde it was only a three-hour trip down to Bergen. He would rent yet a second car and continue his ill-fated trip.

The ambulance took off with its two new passengers and its wailing siren filled the alpine valley with an unnatural echo.

It was allowed to pass right through a police barricade that had been set up on E39.

In the ER section of Førde's Central Hospital experienced nurse Inge Vik was checking Megan's vital signs. Her pulse was elevated and her blood pressure above normal. Vik had removed a tight wig the woman was wearing over her brown hair. That was a first, she thought. And now the patient was beginning to come to. But her breathing seemed to be impaired. Vik was waiting for the ER physician to come.

The man in a police uniform who had identified himself as the woman's son was watching them both with apprehension. He had a lame explanation concerning the white wig, something about his mother's wanting to look "older" than she really was. The nurse had looked at him with incomprehension and mild curiosity.

"Lili? Button? Where am I?" asked Megan groggily.

Nurse Vik took her hand and stroked it. "You are in a hospital, dear, and everything is going to be all right."

"You're in the ER," Drapsmann leaned over and whispered in Crespi's ear, hoping she would not recognize his voice. "There was a little accident."

"Ac...ci...dent?"

"Yes, but not to worry. As soon as they clear you to go we'll be on our way home."

"Home? Button? Lili? Where are you?"

Megan's voice trailed off and she fell asleep.

"We're worried about her respiration and need to keep her here for a few hours," the ER physician in charge told her "son" when he arrived on the scene.

"How many hours?" Drapsmann asked, his tight-lipped face a study in control.

"Probably until late afternoon."

"Late afternoon?"

"Yes, late afternoon at the earliest."

Damn! He still had a three hour drive to Bergen ahead of him. Drapsmann retired to the waiting room, looked around, then pulled out his cellphone. Well, I've got to tell Petersen sometime, he reasoned. A text would be far better than a phone call at this juncture. He got up his courage—an unusual circumstance for him—to send it. He used all caps.

"CAR ACCIDENT. UNAVOIDABLE DELAY. ESTIMATED ARRIVAL TIME NOW SEVEN PM."

Next he called the local Avis car rental. They had only a Mini Peugeot 107 available. Dark blue. All right, that would do. He'd have to put Crespi in the front seat, but if they met up with another roadblock on the way into Bergen, he would give her another light stun nudge. And the white wig did completely alter her appearance. His police uniform and ID should carry some weight as well if he were questioned.

Going online to www.taxibeat.no, he ordered a taxi to pick him up outside the ER entrance. Ten minutes later he was at the Avis on Rutebilstasjonen and signing a contract. He had yet to eat anything so he drove to one of Førde's fast food restaurants, Dolly Dimpels, and devoured two large pizzas. But he felt no better. What if Crespi were to come to again and realize what had happened to her? Blab it to the ER staff. He better get back to her side. He was beginning to play the role of concerned son very well.

At Norsehjem Olaf Petersen, who had been up since six, sat in stunned silence, holding his smartphone and staring at it blankly. Finally he found his voice and let out a scream. The butler Sven came running, fearing that his master had had another stroke. He found him sitting in his living- room armchair, his face ashen white.

"Are you all right, Herr Petersen?"

"No, I am not all right, Sven. But it isn't my health. It's my whole plan for tonight!"

"Yes, sir. Is there anything I can do to help?"

"No, but thank you. My guests are arriving at six. I am expecting another guest as well but now that person's arrival has been delayed and that messes up my agenda."

Sven discreetly left the room to lay out the master's breakfast. It was time he should eat something. He knew the master had been up and working in the bunker since early that morning.

Olaf Petersen ignored Sven's announcement that breakfast was served. A hundred scenarios were flashing through his head. The primary one was whether or not Crespi would be able to testify as to the authenticity of the two *Screams* in his bunker. How to compel her? In front of what would now be an audience of six persons? He had hoped merely to present her written opinion that both Munchs were genuine. Now she would have to be coerced into declaring them to be original. And Drapsmann had mentioned a car accident. Could Crespi have been involved? Hurt? Killed? Damn the shortness of the man's text. Petersen decided to text him back, and demand details. Breakfast was the last thing he wanted at such a time.

The abductor was back by the bedside of his "mother" who still lay sleeping. She had not awoken, confirmed nurse Vik, who had just rounded the corner, then taken off again. Drapsmann stared at the woman he had been charged to bring to his current employer. Who was she and why was it so important that she be brought to Petersen's home in Bergen?

As though she felt Drapsmann's piercing questions, Megan stirred, turned over on her side and opened her eyes. When she saw the uniformed officer in front of her she flinched in recognition, then opened her mouth to scream. Drapsmann immediately clamped his hand over her mouth.

"*Quiet!*" he hissed. Drawing out his wallet, he slipped out two photographs. One was of Lili, the other was of a dog. He showed them to a wide-eyed Crespi.

"If you say one word about how you got here, these two will be killed. They are in the hands of my associate and all I need do is send a text and they will be no more. *Do you understand?*"

Her eyes still wide open, Megan vigorously nodded assent. Then her head fell back and she slipped into unconsciousness.

Drapsmann replaced the photographs in his wallet. The hours passed by with excruciating slowness as the worried son sat by his mother's side.

During the hour's flight to Hammerfest Benno Landau continued to ponder the strange failure of Megan Crespi to join him and his family that morning. She had seemed so happy at the idea of attending a Sami song concert after he assured her they would get back in plenty of time for her to make her return flight to Oslo.

After they landed and while they were waiting for the Sami concert to begin, Benno Landau decided to report what he now considered Crespi's disappearance to the police. He had just checked with the Radisson Blu again and the news was the same: Professor Crespi had not returned to collect her luggage.

Benno placed a call to the Trondheim police and explained the situation. The officer in charge realized he was talking to one of the city's most distinguished citizens—the founder of two local museums—and promised immediate action. He would also get in touch with the Oslo police and have them check incoming flights. The police would locate the woman who had so recently been on national television, not to worry.

86

They had both gone to the Myrtl Cosmetics office earlier than usual and had taken the black poodle Magnus with them. For Myrtl, there was an overload of things to tend to before leaving Oslo. The British lawsuit against her company was in its final stages and her own lawyers had been slow in organizing a defense. The uncertainty was beginning to gnaw at her. If the Brits were successful Myrtl Cosmetics could lose millions. This was a worry she had kept to herself, but it accounted for her vacillations between unusually high spirits and deep depression. Sophia had several times urged her to see a psychiatrist. Her symptoms seemed to match those she had read about concerning bipolarity. Wouldn't it be good to know for sure and to have access to effective medication? Myrtl refused to talk about it. The friend who cared about her more than anyone else in the world got nowhere.

Sophia soon confirmed she had made a round trip reservation for Myrtl leaving at four in the afternoon and returning at ten in the evening. That would give her plenty of time to notify her standby chauffeur in Bergen to be at the airport for a five o'clock pickup.

After some six hours of mostly pedestrian but necessary work, Myrtl retired to her inner office, closed the door and sat at her desk for several minutes thinking things through. She turned to her computer and logged into *Deutschland Erst*. There, under the moniker Brunhilde, she announced the imminent end of a Norwegian anti-neo-Nazi group called Norseliga. She also tweeted and Facebooked the message to a vast cyber receivership.

Then she rose, walked over to the wall safe and opened it. Taking out five thick folders she returned to her desk and began looking through them. They contained business data for Norseliga's five other members. The thickest file was the one for Olaf Petersen. All the files contained information concerning questionable, and in many cases, illegal business practices. She fanned them out on her desk like a deck of playing cards, then typed out a directive, printed it, and laid it on top of them. The directive was addressed to Sophia and contained instructions to release the damaging data to the newspapers in the event of her not returning to Oslo that evening. A second note, in a sealed envelope addressed to Sophia, told her simply how much she loved her.

Myrtl returned to the safe, removed her Glock pistol, and placed it in her purse.

87

Off at last from a trying shift, nurse Inge Vik kicked up her feet in her small apartment near Førde's main hospital and turned on the television. The news cycle was just starting again. The opening bulletin caught her attention. It was titled "Missing in Norway" and showed the photograph of a brown-haired, older woman. The newscaster was saying: "a visiting American scholar, Megan Crespi, who lectured last night in Trondheim, was declared missing today under mysterious circumstances. Any persons having knowledge that might be helpful are requested to contact the police immediately."

Vik sat up straight. *She knew that face!* It was the face of the unconscious woman who had been brought into the ER early that morning. They had had to remove a wig she was wearing in order to examine her for injuries. The strange thing was that the wig was white whereas her hair was brown. Vik decided she should phone the police and give a description of the woman and her inexplicable disguise. She was traveling with her police officer son. A son that seemed more interested in what time the doctor would release the patient than how the patient was. Furthermore, when the patient revived, she spoke in English, not Norwegian. Inge Vik looked up the number and called the Førde police office.

▲ ▲ ▲

Someone else had seen the "Missing in Norway" news bulletin. Sitting in front of his television set in Stockholm, Axel Blomqvist had switched channels to the daily "Around Scandinavia" program and that was where he learned about the American Megan Crespi's mysterious disappearance.

What an inconvenience! He had so much been looking forward to their meeting. What could have happened to her? He hoped it wasn't related somehow to the recent Munch happenings in Norway. Might she somehow be involved? Had he perhaps been imprudent to invite her to view his unsurpassed collection of Munch graphics? Especially with his own recently acquired major Munch oil hanging upstairs in the attic? Had his invitation to Crespi been unwise? After all, it was she who had contacted him, not the other way around. He would follow the news closely. They were, after all, scheduled to meet in person in just a few days.

▲ ▲ ▲

Myrtl Kildahl had successfully gotten her Glock through Oslo airport security with the help of Magnus. The black poodle had to be released from his pet carrier so that Myrtl could carry him through the upright metal detector. When the metal tags on his collar were detected and the inspector saw what it was, he had smilingly waved Myrtl and the dog on. The compact pistol was safely tucked in her bra. When the carrier with her purse and brass key necklace came out of the scanner she ostentatiously put the S-shaped Viking symbol of exalted womanhood back around her neck.

A few minutes later she was comfortably installed in the airport lobby waiting for her four o'clock Norwegian Airlines flight to Bergen. She spotted fellow Norseliga members Petter Norgaard and Haakon Sando enter together. Myrtl acknowledged them unenthusiastically and they walked over to her, expressions of frustration on their faces.

"Can anyone tell me what this so-called emergency meeting is about?" Haakon asked, spreading his hands out before him in exasperation.

"I told Haakon that I tried calling Olaf several times but there was no answer on his private line. When I called Norsehjem and got the butler, he merely said that Petersen was 'not available.'" Petter imitated the butler's formal voice.

"Looks as if we're all going to be on the same plane," said a voice next to them. It was Gunnar Tufte. He expressed the same frustration as they had.

"It better really be an emergency," he continued. "I had to cancel a very important client dinner."

Their flight was called. Red-bearded Petter—for Myrtl the least irritating of the Norseliga males—sat down next to her. She would have preferred to be alone, collecting her thoughts, imagining the scenario to come. But instead she had to listen to his nonstop bragging about how well his hospital equipment company was doing. Yes, she thought ironically, ever since your hackers managed to infect German-made monitoring devices for cardiac pace readouts. That's when you swooped in and cornered the German market. An unforgiveable insult to Germany. And one that would soon be rectified if things went her way at the emergency meeting.

She thought about the illicit business practices of her other Norseliga members: the shady real estate deals Haakon Sando had made concerning his shopping malls and the bitterly competitive computer design company of the Tufte brothers with their shameless cyber siphoning of rival strategies around Europe. To say nothing of the grand master of it all, Olaf Petersen and his ship-building empire—an empire founded on one dirty deal after another, ranging from hijacking material and machinery to vandalizing competitors' factory sites. He was even secretly involved in the great warehouse fire that recently took down Hamburg's largest ship builder.

Yes, the whole group of Norseliga crooks deserved their just reward. And she was the one to give it to them. If she could only have some peace and quiet to plan her moves carefully. Magnus whined quietly and looked at her through the mesh of the pet carrier at her feet as though he understood her thoughts.

▲ ▲ ▲

It was half past five and Erik Jensen's voice was unusually high-pitched. He had reached Lili at the Hotel Bristol and there was exciting news. Inspector Finne Raske had just called him. Megan may have been spotted. A nurse working at a hospital in the small town of Førde had reported something suspicious to the local police. They in turn had contacted Oslo police and been put through to Raske. The nurse, one Inge Vik, had a strange story. She had been on ER duty when, at six that morning, an unconscious older woman had been brought in by ambulance. Accompanying her was a uniformed police officer who said he was her son. In caring for the patient, nurse Vik had had to slip off a white wig worn by the female patient, whose hair, it turned out, was brown. The son had given some odd explanation that she used the wig to make herself look older. Only the son had any identification with him: he was an Oslo police officer. His mother had nothing on her, not even a purse. While driving in the Sognefjell mountain area they had been smashed into by a wild reindeer and their car had been totaled. Fortunately for them an ambulance returning from Stryn had encountered them on the road and brought mother and son to the hospital in Førde.

"Førde?" Lili asked excitedly. "So that would mean, if it's Megan, that she was being driven down from Trondheim toward Bergen."

"Yes, and this is where the nurse's story gets really interesting. When the patient revived, she spoke in English, not Norwegian. And her son seemed far more interested in getting her out of the hospital than he did in her health."

"If that was the kidnapper, no wonder he wanted to get her out of the hospital!"

"Yes. And when nurse Vik heard the TV news bulletin and saw the missing woman's photograph, she was absolutely certain the missing American was the woman with brown hair who had been in her care this morning."

"Oh, yes, yes!" Lili was thrilled.

"Raske said local police had immediately gone to the hospital, but the patient and her son had just been checked out. One attendant had noticed that they drove off in a small Peugeot. What color? Black, maybe. Anyway, dark. Direction? Not noted. But enough info to update police roadblocks."

"So it was an accident that brought Crespi and her abductor into the limelight, thanks to that one observant nurse."

"Yes, that would fit into the brief text message Megan sent me: 'help kidnapped bergen,'" Erik said. "They must be headed for Bergen right now!"

Lili's head was spinning. But there was more.

"Listen, Lili. Raske is flying to Bergen immediately and he wants us to come with him on the police jet."

"Join him? Why, yes, of course, absolutely."

"Can you be ready for Raske and me to pick you up in ten minutes?"

"I can be ready now. Oh, dear! Just one thing, Erik."

"What?"

"I can't leave Button in the hotel for we don't know how long. We'll have to take him with us."

▲ ▲ ▲

"You will shut your mouth and keep it shut, or I will give you another stun tap," Drapsmann commanded Crespi, after brutally shoving her into the car.

Megan kept mum. In spite of feeling extremely weak, she studied her kidnapper on the sly as he put the car in gear and began driving. She could tell they were heading south, and that meant Bergen. Why were they in a different car now, she wondered. She was foggy on what happened those hours she'd spent in the hospital ER or why she was even there, but she remembered the gentle nurse who reassured her that everything would be all right. So different from the horrible bully who had forced her to wear a ridiculous white wig once they got into the new car.

If only she could talk to the man. Reason with him. Was he a policeman turned rogue? Their Bergen destination could only mean one thing: it had been engineered by that fanatic collector Olaf Petersen. All because she had turned down his urgent request that she return to see "something extraordinary." Now it looked as though she were going to be forced to see it, whether she wanted to or not. But what sort of off-duty policeman, even if in the employ of a ruthless Petersen, would use such rough physical measures to force her back to Bergen? Was he a policeman at all?

And, hope against hope, had her surreptitious text message to Erik Jensen been picked up? If so, had he contacted the police? What had the bully next to her done with her iPhone? With her shoulder bag? She swiveled to look back into the rear of the small car. Yes. there it was on the seat. Thank goodness. No shoulder bag, however. Heck! That meant no wallet, no cash. At least her passport was safe back at the Hotel Bristol. Wonder why the brute kept the iPhone.

"What the hell are you doing, woman? No moving around. Just sit still and keep your eyes front."

Megan absorbed the reprimand. All, perhaps, was not lost. And she was beginning to feel a bit stronger.

88

Their four o'clock flight from Oslo to Bergen landed precisely on time one hour later. Like faithful dogs the three Norseliga members followed Myrtl and her pet carrier past the airport lobby and outdoors to the pickup area. There, waiting at the curb, was her Bergen chauffeur and white limousine with the tinted windows and the Myrtl Cosmetics crest on the doors. Imperiously, Myrtl gestured to the men to get in. God, I have to do *everything* for them, she thought. But not much longer.

Battling commuter traffic, it took some time to cross the city and reach Norsehjem, but at five minutes to six they pulled up in front of the magnificent forest home. Sven came out to greet them.

"Take Magnus for a walk so he can do his business," Myrtle instructed her chauffeur. "Then wait for us over there." She pointed to the far part of the roundabout. Sven led them into the familiar living room with its overwhelming Nordic gods mural. Gustav Tufte was already there, having driven up from Skien. Petersen stood to greet them, a deadly serious expression on his face. He had given up his green hour in order to be in full possession of his senses. Both men already had applied the temporary tattoos of the Web of Wyrd to their cheeks.

"Thank you, thank all of you, for coming to this emergency meeting," Petersen said.

"As soon as you have prepared yourselves we shall proceed to the bunker."
He gestured to the watercolor sets, brushes, and water bowls set out on the large living- room table. Expertly, the four new arrivals applied the watercolors to form nine interlocking red and green bars on their cheeks. As before, Myrtl added the powerful female symbol of the black Valknut to her forehead. She presented a formidable persona.

While they were finishing their tattoos Sven set out six miniature metal goblets and placed a bottle of *akevitt* next to them.

"Let us drink to our Norseliga," said Petersen, pouring out the drink. Solemnly the members raised their goblets and drank to the Norseliga.

Sven held the front door open for the group as they walked single file to the bunker, Petersen leading the way. Myrtl Kildahl brought up the rear, her small, now unusually heavy purse tucked under her arm. The great bunker door was already open. The same chairs had been set out as before and the Norseliga took their places. In front of them, the curtains drawn apart, was the altarpiece they had seen before, Munch's *Scream*. The one characterized on television by a panel of experts as a copy. To the left stood a large easel with a spread draped over its load—obviously a painting. Other than Petersen, only Haakon Sando knew what that painting was. It had been Sando, after all, who had brought it to Norsehjem.

"My loyal members," Petersen began, standing in front of the group and interlacing his fingers in front of him, his one eye glinting. "There are two reasons I have bade you drop everything and come to Norsehjem. The first is the altarpiece we celebrated last time. Our illustrious countryman Edvard Munch's *The Scream*."

The Tufte brothers looked at each other in discomfort.

"You have all seen or heard about the ASK's panel of experts who con- nived on live television to say that it was only a copy that had left the walls of the National Gallery. That the original is still there in the museum."

The members looked around and nodded their heads knowingly.

"Well, if you remember, the pivot point of their argument was that, like the two versions in the Munch Museum, only the original showed the white steeple of Oslo Cathedral in the right background. Does everyone remember that?"

Again there was an energetic nodding of heads.

"Now I ask you to come forward, use this magnifying glass, look closely at that area of our painting, and tell me what you see."

Petter Norgaard was the first to come forward. He took the magnifying glass Petersen offered him and stepped up close to the painting. He scrutinized the area in question, then gasped.

"It's there! The steeple is there! This is the original."

One by one the other members stepped up and confirmed what Norgaard had seen. Haakon Sando looked at the thin white vertical line. He was mystified. If this was indeed the original, why then had Petersen congratulated him when he brought him the Munch Museum's version? Praised him for "redeeming" Norseliga? He looked at Petersen questioningly.

As if feeling his question, Petersen asked the members to take their seats again. He had a second important reason for calling them together. And this was it! He pulled the drape off the easel revealing the Munch Museum's 1893 version of *The Scream*.

Everyone gasped; Haakon Sando with pride.

"It is Haakon Sando who brought us this masterpiece. Now Norseliga has the *original* inspiration as well as the final realization of Munch's icon. What a double treasure!"

"Double treasure?" Myrtl Kildahl asked suddenly, standing up and walking briskly over to the first painting.

"I will have you all know that when I examined this so-called original with the magnifying glass just now, I smelled *fresh varnish*." She looked accusingly at Petersen.

"In other words, the steeple was not there the first time we saw this painting. Someone has added it."

"God damn you, woman! How dare you suggest such a thing?" Petersen demanded.

There were murmurs of support among the Norseliga males.

Myrtl whipped out the Glock from her purse and pointed it threateningly at Petersen.

"This is how much I believe you that the steeple was there all the time."

Turning to her left she leveled the pistol at the picture and shot a hole through the spot where the new steeple had been painted.

To a man, the Norseliga gasped in horror. They were too stunned to move.

"And this is how much I believe in your Norse superiority!"

In quick succession Myrtl shot each man in the heart as they sat in their chairs. Five bodies fell writhing to the ground. Then they were still. Quite still.

a bit unrealistic

89

Max Linde had just finished watching one of his favorite shows, "Around Scandinavia." When he saw an image of the woman his bro Christian Drapsmann had pursued to Trondheim, he thought he had better let him know that Crespi's face was being transmitted across Scandinavia. He dialed Drapsmann's smartphone number.

"Yeah?"

"Hey, bro, this is Max in Lübeck. Congrats on getting Crespi but did you know her face is plastered all over TV?"

"Damn! What are they saying?"

"That she has mysteriously disappeared after giving a lecture in Trondheim. There are probably roadblocks set up by now, so thought I better call you."

"Much appreciated. Thanks."

"Okay. Take care, bro."

A fulminating Drapsmann brought the Peugeot to a rough stop off the main highway to Bergen. It was getting close to seven o'clock, the time he had advised Petersen he would be bringing Crespi to him. He was already running late. A roadblock could really mess things up. Of course, the wig had greatly altered the woman's appearance, but what if she screamed for help when they were stopped and checked? He would have to zap her again before halting at any roadblock. He was counting on his police identity to get him through.

Okay, he had a backup plan. Reaching toward the back seat he grabbed Crespi's iPhone and brought it up front. Then he pulled out his wallet and held up one of the photos he had threatened Crespi with at the ER. He waved it in her face.

"Who is this woman?"

"I thought I wasn't supposed to talk," Megan couldn't help saying. That rated her a blow across the face.

"Don't be smart with me, bitch! What's her name?"

"Lili. Lili Holm."

"Let's see if you're telling the truth." Drapsmann opened up the phone directory. Yes, there was the name. He pressed the number given and waited.

Almost on the second ring his call was answered by a woman's anxious voice: "Megan? Megan!"

"No. Not Megan. But I have her. Right next to me. Now listen. I understand there are roadblocks out there waiting for us. I want you to call the police and tell them to back off. If I see one roadblock I will kill her immediately. Understand?"

"I don't believe you. Who are you?"

"Hold on." Drapsmann passed Megan's iPhone over to her.

"Say something to your friend," he commanded.

"Lili! Yes, it's me! He's got me!"

"Where are you?"

Drapsmann jerked the phone back.

"You heard her voice. Now do what I told you and I mean now!"

He hung up and glared at Crespi. Then he roared back onto the highway for the last forty miles to Bergen.

▲ ▲ ▲

Lili had received the flabbergasting call just as she, Button, Erik, and Finne Raske were piling into a waiting police car at Bergen's airport. It was at the head of a line of four police cars. Lili related the gist of the phone call to her companions.

"That's a threat we've got to take seriously," Raske said.

"Is there no way you can avoid pulling the roadblocks?" Erik wanted to know.

"Not in this situation. But at least we're pretty damn sure where Megan is being taken. Has to be Olaf Petersen's house. She herself told us about the demanding text he sent her to return there, the one she ignored."

"How long do you think it will take us to get there?" asked Lili anxiously.

"Forty minutes at the most. Airport's only twenty minutes from town, then we cross the city and head for Mount Fløyen." The other three police cars fell in behind them as they sped off toward Bergen.

▲ ▲ ▲

Around six thirty, getting bored, Myrtl's chauffeur decided to stretch his legs and take Magnus out again for a romp down the winding forest road leading to the highway where they had turned off. As they got to the highway six shots sounded. They seemed to be coming from the house. The man wheeled, pulled a reluctant Magnus to him, and began trotting back the way he had come. What was going on?

▲ ▲ ▲

Cleaning up inside Norsehjem's living room, Sven heard six shots. They seemed to come from the direction of the bunker. He picked up a fire poker, ran to the front door and headed cautiously toward the bunker. The limousine that had brought Norseliga members was still parked in the roundabout but the chauffeur was nowhere to be seen.

As Sven got within sight of the bunker he saw a woman running toward him. It was Fru Kildahl! He called out her name but she did not respond, just kept coming toward him. Then she came to a full stop in front of her limousine.

"What is it? What's happened?" Sven shouted, running toward her, the fire poker at his side.

"This!" Myrtl yelled. She aimed her pistol at the man and fired one shot. The butler fell to the ground.

"Where the hell is my driver?" Myrtl shouted to the air. There was no sign of him or Magnus. She ran to the house, pulled out her smartphone, and began frantically dialing the man in the light of the open front door.

She failed to see Sven get up slowly from where he had fallen and approach her, the poker raised in his right hand. Just as he struck at her, Myrtl moved. The chauffeur had answered her call. He was running back to the house right now, he told her. Myrtl did not take time to hang up or turn around and fire at the butler again. Instead she fled back toward the bunker. Sven was gaining on her. Hell! There was not enough time for her to get back in and close the bunker door. Hindered by her high heels, she lunged around to the back of the bunker, Sven right behind her. Suddenly she disappeared from sight.

She had plummeted into the open grave prepared for Megan Crespi. Myrtl's neck snapped, immediately disconnecting her brain from her vital organs. She died within a minute, the S-shaped brass key of her Viking necklace lodged decoratively in her throat.

As Myrtl's chauffeur ran back to his limo, four police cars roared past him up to the house called Norsehjem. Five people jumped out of the lead car: two armed policemen, Raske, Erik, and Lili.

"You take the house, we'll search the grounds," Raske commanded the two policemen.

"Look! Over there," Erik shouted. "There's a man running over to that limo. Don't let him get away!"

"He must be Megan's kidnapper!" Lili yelled, trying to keep up with Erik.

The man and a dog came to a panting stop by the limousine just as Raske reached it.

"Hands up!" he commanded, pointing his revolver at the man.

"*Is Megan in the car?*" Lili yelled desperately as she reached the men.

Erik looked inside the limousine. No one was there.

"She's not!" he answered.

"Oh, my god!" Lili breathed.

"Stay where you are and identify yourself," Raske ordered the man whose hands were raised above his head.

"I'm Fru Myrtl Kildahl's chauffeur."

"And where is she?"

"I don't know. She went straight into the house when I delivered her.

"When was that?"

"We got here at six. She's been in there ever since, I guess."

"Is this your dog?"

"No, it's Fru Kildahl's dog and I was taking him for a walk when I heard shots. Six shots."

"Six shots?"

"Yes, sir, six separate shots, very fast."

Just then the two policemen whom Raske had sent to search the house emerged from the front door.

"Nobody in the house," one of them shouted. "Just a big hound in the kitchen."

"Check again. Did you search the basement and attic?"

"Not the basement."

"Get back there then!" Raske shook his head. These Bergen police. Not at all like his well-trained Oslo police. He turned back to the frightened chauffeur.

"Okay, you can put your hands down. What direction do you think the shots came from?"

"Over there."

He pointed in the direction of the bunker. By then the police from the other three cars had joined Raske.

"Fan out," he instructed him.

Just then the figure of a man came running from around the back. It was Sven, still with the fire poker in his hand. When he saw the policemen coming toward him he began screaming.

"Help, help!"

Raske got to him first, pistol raised.

"Identify yourself! Who are you?"

"I'm Herr Petersen's butler! One of his guests took a shot at me. She grazed my shoulder and I took after her with this." Sven waved the poker at Raske.

"*Her?* You were chasing a woman?"

"Yes, sir, back around to the bunker where they had all retired. Then she suddenly disappeared." Sven was still panting for breath.

"Who is '*all?*'"

"Herr Petersen's guests. Five of them including the woman. They meet here once a month on business. Go through a ritual in the big house, painting their faces, and then they adjourn to Herr Petersen's bunker."

"And you don't know where the woman is now?"

"No, sir. It's dark there behind the bunker and I didn't want to take the chance she might shoot at me again."

"All right. Lead us to the bunker."

Three of the policemen fell in behind Raske, their guns drawn. Erik and Lili caught up with them and followed.

The bunker door was open. Warily the lead man looked in. Light streamed from the interior. What he saw within froze him.

Five men's contorted bodies lay on the floor. Each man had been shot in the heart. They were all dead.

"We've got a mass murder on our hands, Chief Inspector," the policeman finally said, standing aside to let Raske in.

"You stay here," he told Erik and Lili. I'll tell you if Megan is inside."

The wait seemed a lifetime. Lili and Erik looked at each other afraid to speak as they waited with dread for Raske's findings. Then they heard his voice.

"There is no sign of Megan. She's not here."

He appeared at the bunker door.

"You men stay in the bunker and preserve the crime scene. Get your photos taken. But I want you to close this door and remain down there until I come to get you. We are going to clear the scene temporarily."

Lili and Erik looked at Raske questioningly.

"Let's get back to the house. I want to alert the men there to stay inside and hide. I want to have the police cars moved from the driveway."

"Why?" Lili asked, perplexed.

"It is my belief that Megan's kidnapper will show up here to deliver her to Petersen. It could be any minute now. I want to clear the drive so he won't be spooked."

The four police cars were driven around to the back of the house. Lili, Erik, the chauffeur, and Kildahl's dog were in one of them. Only the limousine remained where it was. Raske and two other police men climbed inside. They could see out but nobody could see in through the tinted windows.

"Oh, my gosh, where is Button?" Lili asked suddenly. She looked at the other three police cars. She must have absent-mindedly left him in the one they arrived in.

Ten minutes went by. It was seven thirty.

Then it happened. A small, dark blue Peugeot pulled slowly up to the house. A short, muscular man with graying hair and a trim moustache got out. He was dressed in a police uniform, just as the ER nurse had described him.

He looked around then went to the far side of the car and opened the door. He reached in and yanked a white-haired woman out. She gave a loud cry of pain.

"Stop it! Just stop it!" she yelled.

Holding the captive's arms behind her, the man force-walked her to the front door of the house. He knocked loudly on the door. No answer.

"Herr Petersen?" he called. No answer.

Drapsmann tried the door knob. The door swung open. He started to push Crespi ahead of him into the house when suddenly he heard a series of high barks and growls.

"What the hell is that?" Drapsmann turned toward the sound. But not quickly enough. A small white Maltese leapt at him and bit him on the leg. He released his captive to hit the vicious little monster.

"Button!" Megan cried.

"Take that man down!" Raske yelled, turning on the car lights. He and his men ran from the limousine to the house. At the same time the police posted inside the house appeared at the door and pinned Megan's kidnapper to the ground. He broke free and began to run. The nearest policemen shot him twice. One of the bullets killed him and he fell on the ground in front of Megan.

It was all over in seconds.

But there was an unexpected sequel. In the flurry of activity, Petersen's Elkhound had gotten loose. When it saw Button it started to run back toward the bunker, just as before, and, also just as before, Button began a mad chase after it, yapping threateningly.

The police cars behind the bunker had turned on their lights at the sound of shots and began driving back to the big house. Seated in one of cars, Lili and

Erik heard the canine noise, then saw a large black and white huskie sort of dog racing toward them. A small white dog was in hot pursuit. They came to a stop in front of the bunker door, just as they had done once before.

"It's Button!" Lili yelled.

Then the dogs began the chase again and disappeared behind the bunker.

"Where are they going? We need to catch them," Erik urged. He asked the driver to stop the car, let them out, and lend them his flashlight.

When Erik and Lili rounded the bunker they saw both dogs sitting absolutely still at the head of a deep ditch, some six-feet long and six-feet deep. They had stopped barking and were staring down at something.

Erik turned the flashlight beam downward into the ditch. It lit up the crumpled body of a woman, her neck broken and her face turned upward toward them. Her mouth was open and in her throat a piece of polished brass reflected the flashlight's beam. At her feet lay a black poodle, whining quietly.

"*My god! That's Myrtl Kildahl!*" Lili gasped in recognition of the cosmetics queen who had been so eager to show her and Megan her private Munch *Madonna*.

▲ ▲ ▲

After Lili—Button in her arms—and Erik had been reunited with a still-shaken Megan, they decided to return on the police jet to Oslo that very evening. Finne Raske would remain in Bergen to oversee what he considered inept local law enforcement activities. One of the police car drivers would take them to the airport and the waiting jet. Raske had found and returned Megan's vital iPhone to her. By eleven o'clock an exhausted Megan and Lili were in their comfortable Hotel Bristol room. On the flight back to Oslo, realizing how exhausted the thwarted kidnapping had left them both, they decided to turn in their rental car and fly, rather than drive, to Stockholm the next day. That would make up for the days lost. Lili made the hotel and plane reservations while Megan repeatedly applied a very cold washcloth to the new bruises on her face. Then, finally, to bed. Button took his place at Megan's feet and the trio fell asleep instantly.

It was their last night in Norway and it could not come fast enough. Tomorrow, Sweden!

▲ ▲ ▲

While still at Norsehjem Raske had learned from the butler Sven that his murdered employer's monthly meetings concerned something called "Norse-liga." Sven showed him the miniature metal goblets they used, with the word inscribed on their stems.

Raske intended to research this Norseliga online later, but it turned out there was no need. The next morning's sizzling news headlines supplied a plethora of data leaked to them concerning the illicit business activities of five members of a harmless-sounding group referred to as Norseliga. They were the same men who had been found murdered in Bergen the evening before. And they were among the most prominent and wealthiest citizens of Norway! Olaf Petersen, the ship builder, Petter Norgaard, whose modern equipment had revolutionized hospital practice, Haakon Sando, the shopping-mall tycoon, and Gunnar and Gustav Tufte, of the giant Kontakt computer company. Their bodies had been found in a bunker on Petersen's property and all the murdered men had mysterious tattoos painted on their faces.

The only Norseliga member whose business practices were not discussed or even mentioned, was Myrtl Kildahl, founder of the famous cosmetics company that set the style for Norwegian women. This was explainable, as it was soon learned that Kildahl's office had released the damning files on her fellow Norseligans to the newspapers.

While Raske's investigation would continue to be ongoing, he had already established that it was Kildahl who had executed, for some unknown reason, all the male members of the Norseliga. When her body was found in the pit behind the bunker, Raske discovered that she had the same mysterious facial tattoos as did the men. The odd facial markings were apparently related to Viking gods of olden times.

Of interest to the art world was the discovery of two paintings in the bunker on Olaf Petersen's estate. Both appeared to be versions of Munch's *The Scream*, but one had a bullet hole through it and was identified by the National Gallery as the copy it had had on display for so many years. The other painting was authenticated by experts at the Munch Museum as being its stolen 1893 version. Why it had been stolen was now clear. When the thieves realized that they had only a copy the first time round, they carried out a second successful robbery.

But now all was well. The whole nation breathed a sigh of relief. One of the country's greatest artworks had been returned to its home, the Munch Museum, and another of its jewels had at last been put on proud display at the National Gallery. This great treasure was now guarded by the most ingenious security measures known to modern technology.

Norway had good reason to rejoice.

90

What a joy to be about to fly away from a Norway that had not been kind to them and on to Sweden! After a long night's rest and a lazy morning in Oslo, and even a lazier early afternoon, pecking away at a Mount Everest of accumulated e-mail, Megan and Lili returned their—third—Volvo to Herz. They took a taxi to the airport for their four o'clock flight to Stockholm.

"Where only *one* Munch painting has been stolen," Megan joked tiredly.

"Are you still going to go through with your appointment to visit Axel Blomqvist day after tomorrow?"

"Of course. But I also intend first to visit with Finne Raske's counterpart on the Stockholm police force, Berndt Hammar. Maybe I can help 'hammer' the missing Munch case closed."

"Excuse me while I throw up," Lili protested, only too used to Megan's usually dreadful puns. "Well, at least we have one day of just plain rest ahead of us," she sighed, impressed as she always was by her friend's resolve and persistence once she decided to pursue something.

In his pet carrier underneath the seat in front of Megan, Button gave out one tired yowl of agreement.

"It's strange that you didn't receive any confirmation of the reservations you made for us at Bentleys Hotel last night," Megan worried.

"Perhaps their e-mail will be waiting for us once we get to Stockholm. I surely hope so."

Bentleys Hotel, at Drottninggatan 77, was their favorite hotel in the city. It was wonderfully near the Strindberg Museum, which was No. 85 on the same street. They loved the hot and cold breakfast buffet that was served every morning in the hotel's glassed-in courtyard. And Stockholm's Old Town was only a walk of some fifteen minutes away. Although at the moment neither of them felt like walking for that long. Being eighty had a few drawbacks. Lili liked to say that eighty was the new eighty-one.

The SAS flight from Oslo to Stockholm took only fifty-five minutes and soon they were looking down at the busy city spread out majestically over fourteen islands. In no time, it seemed, Megan and Lili had picked up their suitcases at the baggage claim—one of them an inexpensive substitute for the Prima Classe bag languishing in Trondheim—and they were ready to take a taxi. Megan let a tail-wagging Button out of his carrier. As they waited in line Lili checked her iPhone.

"Ah! Here is something from Bentleys Hotel. Let's see. Yes, they confirm our reservation but, oh, dear, only for three nights. They say they are fully booked for the next two days after that. But then they could take us again for as much as a week, if we like."

"Oh, bummer."

"Well, let's stay there for our first three nights and maybe we can talk them into letting us stay on after all. There could always be a cancellation. You never know."

"Boy, I hope so. Hate having to move from one place to another." Megan frowned. She was feeling discouraged. Things were becoming too complicated. And her face still hurt where Drapsmann had hit her.

"Gosh, I wouldn't mind turning right around and going to Skagen as we had originally planned," Lili said, picturing the atmospheric coastline at the tip of her native Denmark.

"Yes. It's such a pity your condo is fully booked for the next weeks. I'm really sorry about that."

When they got to Bentleys on Drottninggatan and checked in, the receptionist looked doubtfully at Button who had trotted in on the blue leash that matched his blue collar.

"Åh , men vi inte tar hundar här," she said, frowning.

"Did she just say what I think she said?" asked Megan, who had recognized the negative "inte" and the word "hundar." Otherwise the Swedish sounded to her like the continuous rise and fall of a mother emphatically chiding her child.

"No, you heard right. They don't take dogs here."

"I am so sorry," the receptionist said in English, turning to Megan. When she saw the bruises on Megan's face and how exhausted both women looked, however, she said softly. "But if you take hound to room *snabbt* we do not notice for tonight." Neither Lili nor Megan knew the Swedish word, but they had no trouble in guessing what it meant.

With grateful thanks they put Button back in his carrier and climbed down to their requested basement room, a room they had had before and liked very much. They plopped down on the two beds and Button joined them, choosing Lili this time. She was looking at her iPhone screen.

After a moment she said: "Oh! No wonder I didn't recognize the word 'snabbt.' In Danish it's 'hurtigt.'"

"Same in Norwegian, I bet," contributed Megan.

"Nope. In Norwegian it's 'raskt.'"

Megan sighed. "I'll never be able to speak any Scandinavian language."

"Not to worry," Lili soothed. "None of us can understand Finnish."

"Small consolation."

"Now you've got me wondering how to say 'quickly' in Finnish."

"You're kidding, Lili."

"No." Lili addressed her iPhone again and returned to Google Translate. "Ah here it is: '*nopeasti*.'"

"Just as I thought, "Megan grinned. "I do know that almost all Finnish words are accented on the first syllable, like HEL-sinki, for example. Listen. I know it's only six-thirty but what would you say to our not doing anything special tonight and just eating at the restaurant across the street?"

"Great idea, and let's do it *nopeasti*!"

Dinner at the Drottninghof by candlelight was quiet and relaxing. Lili ordered a '*Plankstek*'—beef on a piece of wood—and Megan had trout. They ended up with green tea and slices of almond cake. Soothing.

But back at the hotel when they stretched out on their beds neither one was able truly to relax. They could sigh and stretch, but not relax and fall asleep.

"Okay, Lili, let me tell you one of my favorite language jokes." Lili groaned.

"Must you?"

"Here's the situation. The scene is a ladies restroom at an international airport. One woman is hurrying in, another is leaving, and the third is doing her business in one of the stalls."

"Yes?"

"What are their nationalities?"

"What?"

"What are their nationalities?"

"I give up."

"The one hurrying in is Russian, the one leaving is Finnish, and the third one, well she's just European."

"Help! Button, save me from this."

"Come on now. You tell *me* one."

"All right. It's an international flight and suddenly one of the plane motors goes out. The pilot needs to get the passengers to parachute jump. To the Germans he says 'Jump! It's an order.' The Germans jump. To the Italians he says 'Jump! It's against the law.' The Italians jump. To the Frenchmen he says 'Jump! It's for love. The...'"

[handwritten margin note: are the dumb jokes vital to the story?]

"Stop! I get it," said Megan. "I suppose he says to the Brits, 'Jump! It's for the Queen.'"

"Right. And to the Americans he says 'Jump! You can take it off your income tax.'"

"Very good. Here's another one for you, Lili. An international contest is held for the best encyclopedia entry on the topic of elephant. The Italian writes 'The Love Life of the Elephant.' The Englishman writes 'The Elephant and How to Hunt Him.' The Frenchman writes 'The Elephant and How to Cook Him,' and the Polish entry is titled 'The Elephant and the Polish Question.'"

"Wonderful reflection of Poland's kaleidoscopic history," Lili acknowledged, laughing.

The mirthful women relaxed and finally fell asleep. When they awoke early the next morning they felt refreshed and ready to take on the day. Megan sneaked Button past the front desk and up the street and across to a small park she remembered being nearby. Yes, there it was, dominated by a large writhing statue on a very high pedestal. It was by Carl Eldh and showed a muscular male nude with a head of Strindberg hair—possibly the only similarity to the author, Megan had always thought. Button was more impressed by the green grass and quickly did his business. Megan opened up a small container of Cesar beef strips and put them on the ground. They disappeared almost immediately. She initiated a brisk walk around the rectangular park before they returned to the hotel room. Luckily they were not noticed as they passed by the front desk.

After sampling this and that from the huge breakfast buffet offered in the courtyard Megan and Lili returned to their cozy basement room and Megan began making her business calls.

The first one was to the Stockholm police contact that Raske had given her, Berndt Hammar. The officer answered immediately. Yes, Officer Raske had advised him of her arrival. And yes, tomorrow at ten would be excellent. Did she know where the central police station was? No, but she could Google it. Fine, go to the one at Kungsholmsgatan 43. He would be waiting for her and he had several things to discuss.

The next contact Megan wanted to get in touch with was Erik's curator friend at the Museum of Modern Art, Ingrid Konstrom. Megan was put on hold, then heard a lovely cantilena: "*Detta är Ingrid Konstrom talande.*"

"Yes, hello, this is Megan Crespi. Our mutual friend Erik Jensen gave me your name."

Konstrom switched languages effortlessly. "Ah, good. Erik e-mailed me you might call. And that you are going to visit Axel Blomqvist. I should love to meet you and get your thoughts about him and our robbery here at the museum."

"And I should very much like to meet you as well.

"Would you like to meet before or after you see Herr Blomqvist?"

"How about both?"

Ingrid Konstrom gave a low, delighted laugh.

"When do you meet with him?"

"Tomorrow at four in the afternoon."

"Could you come by the museum today? Perhaps have lunch here?"

"That sounds ideal. What time?"

"Would one o'clock be convenient?"

"That's just fine."

"Just ask for me at the entry and I'll come and get you."

"Wonderful. I am looking forward to it."

Lili smiled at her friend's success and was privately happy that she did not have to go along. She would prefer to study the holdings of a nearby antiquarian bookstore.

Megan's final bit of business was to e-mail Axel Blomqvist, confirming their four o'clock meeting for the next day. She received a telegraphic answer immediately.

"Great relief to hear from you! Was worried by television reports you were missing. Looking forward to hearing true story."

"Okay, Lili, my business is done. Shall we go to the Strindberg Museum this morning? Button trotted over to them eagerly. He had heard the word "go." Megan used her regular explanation for why he wasn't going to accompany them. Sadly she said: "Button, we have to go to the vet."

The Maltese immediately turned around and lay down, his head between his front paws. You go. I stay.

Emerging from the hotel onto Drottninggatan, they walked up to the corner building at No. 85.

"*Blå Tornet*," Megan said reverently. "Now there's some Swedish I can understand." She walked across the street from it and photographed, as she had twice before, the building with its blue-roofed apartment tower rising two stories above the rest of the floors.

Since they had been there last, the little museum shop had expanded and now carried interesting DVDs of performances of Strindberg plays as well as books by and about the author. Lots of tourists, speaking many languages, filled the three rooms but Megan slithered through the crowd and into the room that contained the upright piano. She was eager to see the Beethoven life mask that had been labeled incorrectly as his death mask. The last time she was there she had photographed the label then later enclosed it in a letter of correction to the museum, referencing several Beethoven books, including, modestly, her own. She looked at the label. It was new and it identified the mask as Beethoven's life mask. One small step for correcting errors, one giant step for historical correctness. She photographed the new label with her iPhone. Then she looked more closely at the mask. It was slightly askew, as though someone had removed it, then put it back hastily. She asked Lili to look and she had the same impression. Odd.

"You know, there are just too many people here right now for a good visit," Lili said.

"Boy, do I agree. Shall we go upstairs to his library and poke around?"

"Good idea."

Shouldering their way back to the entrance, they climbed the flights of stairs to the attic story and flashed their tickets at the library attendant. But the room was equally crowded so they gave up and went back down to the street.

"What a pity!" Lili said resignedly.

"Well, it is the height of the tourist season after all. What time is it?"

"Eleven o'clock."

"I have an idea, Lili. Why don't you come with me to the Museum of Modern Art now and we'll see which Munchs are on exhibit after the Strindberg portrait was stolen."

"Well, all right, yes. There is so much to see there. I could just disappear when it's time for your lunch appointment."

"Oh, good, do come with me. It'll be interesting to see what new security precautions the museum has taken now."

"And that was the only theft the museum's ever had, right?"

"No, actually. In nineteen ninety-three, some burglars made off with six Picassos and two Braques. And the fascinating thing about *that* robbery is that they copied a heist glamorized in a nineteen-fifty-five French film *Du rififi chez les hommes*. Cut right through the roof."

"Come on. You're kidding."

"No, I'm not. The paintings were valued at well over sixty-five million dollars. And three of the Picassos have never been recovered. Probably somewhere in Russia."

"What about Stockholm's Nationalmuseum?"

"Oh, yes, it too has been burglarized. Back in two thousand. In that case three armed men, one of them with a submachine gun, invaded and snatched two small Renoirs and an early Rembrandt self-portrait. Now imagine this. You know the museum is right on the water, right? Well the men actually used a motor boat to escape! And just before the heist they'd set several cars near the museum on fire so the police were distracted trying to put out the flames."

"Unbelievable! Were the paintings ever recovered?"

"Yes, within five years' time they had all been found, two of them during a police raid. It was thought that the artworks were stolen to sell in Eastern Europe where so many newly wealthy businessmen are ready and eager to invest in art."

"Oh, dear. And art is supposed to be about inspiration and beauty."

After taking a bus over to Skeppsholmen, the island across from the Old Town where the Museum of Modern Art held sway, Megan and Lili stopped before entering the museum to admire a multipiece sculpture. They remembered it from their last visit. It was a humorous ensemble of bobbing figures by Niki de Saint Phalle and Jean Tinguely called *The Fantastic Paradise.*

"At least *one* woman artist is out here," Lili sniffed.

"Yeah, but hey, wait a sec! Look over there in front of the museum entrance. That has to be a Lila Katzen. It's monumental. Wonderful metal curves and crevices. Like her piece at Lincoln Center. Good for the museum and for her. We were staunch friends during the early feminist days of our annual professional conventions."

Lili walked around admiring the work. Then they entered the museum and walked through the lantern-lit galleries that housed the museum's permanent collection. They went up to the fourth floor where the Early Modernism section was. But, disappointingly, there were only graphic works by Munch. Opposite them were several paintings by Kandinsky and the next room held works by Matisse and Picasso. They looked carefully at the images displayed. Only two were new to them.

"How about going back downstairs and on through to the architecture museum building?" Lili suggested. "We've never done that."

"Great idea."

From the museum there was a direct connection into what had once been a former naval drill hall. Displayed in a long room the permanent exhibition presented an impressive history of Swedish architecture from its very beginnings. It concluded with small models of the work of Mia Hägg and her master plan for the Djugården IF football stadium in southern Stockholm.

"Now here's a woman architect!" Lili said excitedly. They studied the Hägg models with keen interest, so much so that time slipped away and when Megan checked her watch it was almost one o'clock.

"Oh, dear, it's about time I went back. Will you be okay here, Lili?"

"Of course. I'll be in that café in the courtyard."

"All right. I'll come back when I'm finished and pick you up there."

Megan walked back through to the other museum. Now she was five minutes early. She stepped outside, casting a glance at the wonderful view the island had of Stockholm's Old Town—the *Gamla Stan*. She had to admit to herself that of the Scandinavian languages, she thought Swedish was the most beautiful. Sometimes it almost sounded Italian to her. Same lilt.

Back in the museum she asked for Ingrid Konstrom and waited while the volunteer at the front desk dialed her number.

"She'll be right down," the woman assured her with a look of earnestness.

While she waited Megan glanced into the museum shop and was amused to see that there were more reproductions of *The Scream* than there were of Munch's portrait of Strindberg. Nothing beats that *Scream* she thought with renewed admiration for the pulsating emblem of angst. And now, in the twenty-first century, it was again cause for anxiety.

"Professor Crespi?"

Megan turned to see a smiling, plump, red-haired woman in her mid-forties. She was dressed in a blue pantsuit and wore sensible shoes. Her hand was extended. They shook hands heartily and Megan liked her instantly.

"Let me take you to the scene of the crime first and then after lunch we can talk in my office."

Instead of taking an elevator to the fourth floor, Konstrom led the way toward a gallery on the ground floor.

"One of the reasons the thieves got away with Munch's Strindberg portrait was that it was not on the fourth floor as usual but down here in this very accessible gallery. We had put together a small exhibition featuring Munch and Gauguin—they met, you know—and the Frenchman's influence on Munch. There was a tour going on in Serbo-Croatian—it was a little after ten in the morning and the museum had just opened—and suddenly three Albanian nationalists appeared waving revolvers at the terrified group. They were told to lie down on the floor. The guard was viciously knocked down."

"Is he all right now?"

"Oh, yes. He's recovering nicely. Anyway, suddenly uniformed police rushed into the gallery and arrested the Albanians. They warned the tour group to continue lying on the floor, and then they cut the hang wires and grabbed the Munch portrait right off the wall. Shouting loudly for people to stay still, they took the Albanians and the Munch outdoors to a waiting 'police' van and disappeared before the real police could arrive. Few people involved in the incident even realized that they had also taken a painting. An incredibly valuable painting."

"Wow, what a story!"

"Well, I wanted you to see the actual site of the theft before we went to lunch. Shall we go now?"

"Yes, but after hearing such a scary art story I'm not sure I can keep anything down," Megan smiled sympathetically.

They entered the museum restaurant and Konstrom led the way to a corner table that commanded a marvelous view of Stockholm's *Gamla Stan*.

"Would you like to go up to the buffet or order what I consider the best offering?"

"What's that?"

"Home-baked, vegetable-stuffed baguettes."

"Yum! How can I resist that? Yes!"

The order was given and minutes later the two women munched on their delicious food while exchanging bits and pieces of their life stories.

Ingrid Konstrom had come to the museum world circuitously, she explained, by way of an uncle who was a professor of microelectronics at Stockholm's Royal Institute of Technology. With his help she enrolled there and became interested in chemistry, specifically surface and corrosion science.

When not at the Institute she spent her free time in the city's National Gallery. There she was enthralled not by Rembrandt's famous, candle-lit *Conspiracy of Claudius Civilis*, but with another equally impressive group picture. Entitled *Midwinter Sacrifice*, the 1915 work by Sweden's beloved artist, Carl Larsson, adorned the National Gallery's upper staircase vestibule. It showed the mythical Swedish king Dolmade being sacrificed in order to save his people from famine.

But the gigantic oil stretched on two canvases showed something else to Ingrid's penetrating gaze. It was a small spidery text inscribed in creamy light green on a green garment in the extreme left foreground. It read: "I, Fredde Olsson, participated in the rolling up and storage of this great work."

Ingrid knew that the Larsson had recently, with tremendous group effort, been taken down and then put back in place after renovations to the museum were completed. Apparently this workman wanted to immortalize his participation.

"So I photographed the green drapery and sent it to the museum's director along with an explanatory note," Ingrid continued. "The very next day I was contacted and offered a job on the curatorial staff. They trained me on the spot and I've been with the museum ever since."

"What a charming story. Do you know what happened to Fredde Olsson?"

"Oh, yes. He was just a young kid and he was fired immediately. Banned from the museum permanently."

They walked over to the buffet and got coffee. Both women used lots of cream and sugar.

"Now tell me how you came to art history," Ingrid urged.

"It's a long saga, so I'll just say that when I first saw the work of Egon Schiele in an exhibition at the University of California in Berkeley, it was an epiphany. I went to Vienna determined to find out as much as I could about him. And perhaps just because I was from America and naively inquisitive, I did something no Austrian art historian had bothered to do. Went to the little town of Neulengbach searching for the basement prison cell where Schiele was incarcerated in 1912. He had drawn its interior meticulously, including the initials a previous prisoner had carved into the wooden door: 'M H.' I found what could be the only building with a cellar in town, went down into it and saw six cells. The very second door I opened had the 'M H' initials carved in it."

"*Herregud*! How very exciting," Ingrid said, looking appreciatively at the sprightly scholar across the table from her.

"Oh, yes. It was the most exciting day of my life. I could hardly hold my camera still to photograph it."

"Shall we go up to my office and continue this wonderful conversation?"

"By all means. And thank you for this delicious lunch, Ingrid."

They were by now on a first name basis, something that usually happened when Megan visited museum personnel.

Ingrid's office workplace contained all the implements of the trade. Bottles, brushes, and tools were all lined up meticulously. Closing the door behind them, she indicated a chair to Megan, and sat down opposite her.

"First let's address the Axel Blomqvist situation. Erik Jensen has told me that you will be visiting him while you're here in Stockholm."

"Yes. Tomorrow at four o'clock."

"How much do you know about the man?"

"Almost nothing except that he has the largest private collection of Munch graphics in the world. And that he is rumored to be the grandson of Strindberg."

"Rumored? No, it is definitely true. The curious thing is that he has never publically acknowledged the relationship. In fact, emphatically denied it. Once during a television show concerning his collection the interviewer suddenly held up a photograph of Strindberg to the camera and asked him directly if Strindberg wasn't his grandfather—'You look just like him,' he said. The startled man answered something to the effect that his surname was Blomqvist, not Strindberg, and walked off the set. Of course the crazy thing is that with that wavy blond hair and wiry blond moustache he does look the very image of Strindberg."

"But why do you think he avoids acknowledging he's Strindberg's grandson?"

"Probably because he doesn't want to be importuned by a bevy of Strindberg scholars with hundreds of questions. Also his wife has been suffering from Alzheimer's for years and recently he had to place her in an institution. He was always a solitary man, despite steering a home appliance manufacturing business that dominates the market. But now he is even more so. At least as far as the public is concerned. To us here at the museum he has been most cooperative concerning loans to shows."

"Well, that's one good thing at least."

Ingrid looked at Megan mischievously.

"Do you know what Blomqvist's *other* great collection is?"

"No. I didn't know he collected other artists."

"It's not artists. He has the world's largest collection of..." Ingrid broke off and affected great seriousness.

"Of what?"

"Hoverflies."

"*Hoverflies?*"

"Hoverflies." Ingrid giggled.

"All right, what are hoverflies?"

" Well, I'm not really clear about that, but they are some sort of flying insect. I'm sure Blomqvist will tell you more if you show the slightest interest."

"In other words you are subtly telling me that if I show interest in his 'other collection,' he might be more apt to open up."

"Exactly."

The two women talked about the possibilities of finding the Strindberg portrait, now that the two missing Munchs in Norway had been retrieved. The news had been all over Swedish television and the papers. The big question, of course, was whether the strange Norseliga association that had been uncovered in Norway was also responsible for the Swedish snatch. In that case Axel Blomqvist would no longer be a suspect.

"We all hope the Norwegian police come up with something that will link the robberies in Oslo with our missing Munch here," Ingrid said in parting.

The two women promised to keep in cyber contact, especially right after Megan had visited Blomqvist. Axel Blomqvist and his hoverflies!

91

After picking up his two oversize suitcases at the baggage claim that afternoon Pål Enger rented an Opel Astra Caravan, loaded the bags in the back, and headed straight from the Stockholm Arlanda airport to Axel Blomqvist's mansion in Östermalm. The wealthy suburb was, ironically, the home of Sweden's Police Museum. Enger had decided not to alert Blomqvist of his visit, just drop in announced. He had the funny feeling that his patron had been eager to part ways with him. But how could that be so? After all, Blomqvist had praised the picture Enger had painted of him standing next to his grandfather's portrait, and he had congratulated him on the Strindberg "landscape" he had created at his request. But after that there had been no further contact between the two men. It was as if his patron wanted no more of him.

That would be remedied this afternoon when Enger showed Blomqvist what he had brought with him from Oslo. He pulled into the horseshoe-shaped driveway, took one of the suitcases out, went up the stairs to the front door, and rang the door bell. A butler answered and his long face expressed surprise.

Yes, the master was at home but who was he and what was his business?

"Just announce me. He'll know what my business is."

A minute later Blomqvist himself appeared at the front door. He frowned when he saw the infamous Norwegian and the Opel station wagon parked in his driveway.

"Why are you here?" he asked, without any greeting.

"To show you eight more 'Strindberg' landscapes you're not going to be able to resist."

"I told you I wanted only one. The view from the water of Stockholm you sent me."

"Yeah, but you were so pleased with it that I thought you could use a few more."

Blomqvist stared at his unwelcome visitor without speaking

"Just wait till I show you what I've got. There are four in this suitcase and I have one more bag in the truck. You are going be amazed." *trunk?*

"Now you listen to me, Pål Enger. You and I have no more business together. It is dangerous for both of us that you have even come to Stockholm, much less to my own home!"

"But aren't you even going to take a look at what I've brought?" Enger sounded like a petulant child.

"Not on your life! Now leave. Leave my house at once. We have no more business to conduct."

Pål Enger drew himself up to his full height. In a low voice he hissed: "You forget that I am in possession of information that could set the police on you and ruin your life."

"I have not forgotten. But you have forgotten that your crime and imprisonment record precede you and that I have an impeccable reputation. I am one of the most respected citizens in Sweden."

Enger was nonplussed. And the man didn't even want to see what he had so arduously created?

"But wait here a minute. I do have something for you," said the Swede.

Blomqvist slammed the door in the importuning man's face and ran to his study. Shouting a command, he sent the butler upstairs on a specious errand to find a certain suitcase, and strode quickly back to the front door. A pistol was in his hand. He opened the door and pointed the weapon at waist level.

Only there was no one to point the pistol at. The man and his suitcase were gone. The car had vanished.

"God damn it to hell!"

▲ ▲ ▲

In Oslo, Finne Raske placed a call to Erik Jensen.

"*Hei*, Erik. Finne here. Did you tell me Professor Crespi was going on to Stockholm?"

"Yes. In fact she's there now."

"And didn't you mention that she'd be visiting with the Munch man there, Axel Blomqvist?"

"Yes. Why?"

"We've just received a tip that Pål Enger—you know, the jerk who went to prison for snatching Munch's *Vampire*— anyway, he took a flight to Stockholm earlier today."

"Yes?"

"Well, I was just putting two and two together and came up with a scenario that maybe Enger is also visiting Blomqvist. Catch my drift?"

"Oh, yes. Hm. Do you think he is capable of violence?"

"Yep, we do."

"So I should warn both Megan and Herr Blomqvist that he is in the city? I do know him slightly in conjunction with museum business."

"I think that wouldn't be a bad idea. With all that's been going on about Munch lately, it's best to be alert. Also, we've checked back on Enger's movements and it turns out he was also in Stockholm earlier this month."

"Ah! I'll get right on it. Oh, while I have you, Finne, is there any new information on what the Norseliga is or was?"

"I think it's a 'was.' We haven't been able to find any other members. Looks as if the organization was hell-bent on beefing up what they called 'Nordic pride.' What they've been sending out to our school system is full of propaganda as to how 'superior' Norwegians are to Germans. Must be feelings left over from World War II, you know. Most of those guys were in their late fifties, or sixties or seventies. The lady too, although I think she was the youngest. By the way, her secretary committed suicide the day those Norseliga folders were leaked to the press." tying up loose ends

"Oh, that's terrible! Well, will you let me know if you learn anything more, Finne?"

"You bet."

As soon as they hung up Erik dialed Megan's iPhone number. He caught her just as she and Lili were about to leave their hotel to let Button have some exercise.

"Hi, Megan. I got a call from Finne Raske just now and he wants me to let you know that a notorious gangster associated with a Munch robbery in the past has just arrived in Stockholm."

"Whew! That is very interesting. What's his name?"

"Pål Enger."

"Yikes! I know that name. And here I am about to visit a Munch collector tomorrow. Do you think there is any connection?"

"That's what Finne is worried about. Worried enough to want me to contact both you and Blomqvist. It does seem odd that he would go to Stockholm at the same time you have. Especially after what happened to you in Trondheim. And then the Bergen mess."

"Now you've got me frightened, Erik. We thought my kidnapping was solved when that crazy man Drapsmann was killed."

"And so it was, partially. We still don't know why you were kidnapped, why you were being brought to Petersen's house. Have any ideas about that crystallized for you?"

"Only that it might have been in regard to the weird text Petersen sent me, asking me to return, remember?

"Yes. That he wanted to show you something."

"His exact words were that he wanted to show me 'something extraordinary' and 'in all confidence.' Then when I turned him down, remember, he texted that bizarre message 'UNACCEPTABLE. Call.'"

"What do you think it could have been that he wanted to show you?"

"Considering what was found in the bunker it was either the first Munch stolen—the copy—or the other one of the original four versions."

"My bet is that he learned about the first one being a copy from our TV show and somehow managed to steal another one."

"So what would he have wanted to show me? Both of them? That would just be admitting he'd stolen the paintings."

"Too bad we can't ask Drapsmann why Petersen wanted you so badly."

"He may not have known."

"Megan, I'm worried on your behalf."

"Me too now. Good thing I'll be seeing Officer Hammar tomorrow morning. I'll tell him everything you've told me."

"Oh, I'm sure Raske has contacted him and done that, but go ahead anyway. And keep your eyes open, promise?"

"I promise."

As she and Lili walked Button in the park near their hotel they discussed Erik's phone call.

"You know what, Megan? I'm going to make a suggestion and I don't want you to reject it."

"What's that?"

"That I come with you tomorrow. To both your appointments, the one with Hammar and the one with Blomqvist."

"You'll get no resistance from me. I think it's a good idea. We can even take Button to the afternoon one."

"I almost believe you'd do it."

"I'm going to."

That afternoon both friends visited the antiquarian bookstore that interested Lili and came out with an old book of Carl Larsson's charming country garden and home illustrations. They had once driven to the artist's enchanting little house and garden in the village of Sundborn. They had also visited, in the same province of Dalarna, Anders Zorn's far more prepossessing house. Both homes exuded the character of their owners.

"Gosh, I'd like to be back there in Dalarna," Lili sighed, "with those red cottages, deep forests, and glimmering lakes. I'm tired of being in big cities on this so-called vacation." Her two broken ribs were still slowing her down.

"Yes, I'd like to get out of here as well," Megan admitted. She wanted to have the peace of mind to get back to her Grieg essay. In Texas she would have been writing it in the peace and calm of her tree-surrounded lake house. Button loved it and so did she. Jean Sibelius had had a lake view from his forest study at Järvenpää and so did Megan at humble Lake Bonham.

"Well, maybe we could drive up to Dalarna after tomorrow's visits," she suggested, hoping to take her disappointed friend's mind off the canceled visit to Skagen.

"I would love simply just to rest in beautiful surroundings while we're still here in Scandinavia."

Button looked up at his two humans. He had heard the word "drive."

92

Megan and Lili were at the Kungsholmsgatan police station right on the dot of ten the next morning. Lili waited in the outer office while Megan was ushered into Officer Hammar's inner sanctum. The tall, thin man with blond hair rose to shake her hand and beckoned her to sit down in the chair opposite his desk.

"Erik Jensen has reached you?" Megan asked.

"Yes. Officer Finne Raske as well. And I appreciate being alerted to the fact of Pål Enger's being here in Stockholm. Now we don't want you to worry. The man is being followed as we speak. And I know you are visiting Herr Blomqvist this afternoon. We will be nearby."

Hammar told his American visitor that Enger had already been to Blomqvist's home the day before. He had been sighted and followed from the airport and the rented Opel station wagon he drove was parked in front of Blomqvist's place for only some five minutes. Apparently he never entered the house. At the moment, Enger's car was parked near a fast food restaurant near the city center.

"Oh, good. That is very consoling."

"After we tracked Enger to Blomqvist's home yesterday we contacted Blomqvist and he told us that the man, whom he did not know, had come to his door offering him some paintings he had in a suitcase. Blomqvist said he was not interested and asked him to leave immediately and he did."

"Pretty audacious, peddling paintings in a suitcase like that to a respected Munch collector."

"Yes. Well, Blomqvist was very surprised when I told him who the man at his door was. He said of course he knew about that criminal. Thought he might still be in jail. I disabused him of that notion and asked him to telephone us immediately if Enger came back. He promised to do so."

"Is there anything special you'd like me to do or be on the watch for when I visit Herr Blomqvist this afternoon?"

"Yes, there is, but it is a very delicate matter." Hammar frowned.

"Would I be right to think that what you want to discuss with me could be about the possibility that, as the grandson of Strindberg, he might have been involved in the theft of Munch's portrait of the author?"

"There you have it in a nutshell," Hammar said in relief. He had not really known how to bring up the delicate subject concerning one of Sweden's most well-known and wealthy citizens.

"We would ask simply that you give keen attention to everything he says or shows you. And if anything strikes you as odd, or slightly off, then tell us. I don't mean to put you under any pressure. It is very likely that nothing you see or hear is going to different from what would be expected in an art historian's visiting any private collector."

"I've certainly done a lot of that," Megan laughed, remembering some of the odd situations she'd found herself in.

"Very good. And just so we know, where are you staying?"

"At Bentleys Hotel."

"And might I ask that you enter my direct number into your smartphone?"

"Gladly," said Megan, tapping in the number Hammar dictated to her.

They stood up at the same time and shook hands firmly. As they reentered the outer office Megan introduced Lili and said she would be accompanying her to Herr Blomqvist's.

"All the better."

"How about having lunch at the new Vasa Museum, Megan?"

"Wonderful idea."

They took a bus out to the Djurgården island and the maritime museum that housed the seventeenth-century 64-gun Swedish warship Vasa that sank on her maiden voyage. Salvaged in 1961, a museum was built for it in 1990. When Megan and Lili had seen the ship back in the 1960s it was still housed in a temporary structure. It would be a treat to see it in its new showcase setting.

And so it was, especially being able to get closer to the ship than before. But they did not linger long after eating at the restaurant there because they wanted to pick up Button before the four o'clock visit to Blomqvist.

At the hotel they found the Uber taxi they had booked to arrive at twenty to four. When Megan informed Button that he was coming along, his joy was something to behold. Twenty minutes later, at exactly four o'clock, their Uber pulled up to the handsome house on a high lawn. From his window Axel Blomqvist, his short-haired Persian kitten Maya cuddled against his chest, stood watching as a trio emerged from the taxi: two women in slacks and a small white dog.

Putting Maya down, he opened the front door himself, looking quickly up and down the street to make sure the vehicle that had been parked in front of his house earlier was not there.

"*Välkommen*, welcome," he smiled at the two women coming up the steps, wondering which of the two was Professor Crespi.

Megan and Lili both came to a startled stop. Their host, with his wavy blond hair and wiry blond moustache, looked the very image of August Strindberg.

"I'm Megan Crespi," said a recovered Megan, "and this is my dear friend Lili Holm. I hope you don't mind that I asked her to come with me."

"Not at all! Lili Holm? *Är ni danska eller norska?*" Blomqvist asked Lili in Swedish.

"*Jeg er dansk,*" affirmed Lili in Danish.

Megan loved such linguistic exchanges and hopped into the arena using the Danish she had learned from Lili with a touch of Swedish/Italian at the end: "*Og jeg er amerikanska.*" She giggled as she said it.

"And what is your little Maltese's name?" Blomqvist had switched to English and was smiling at Button who was standing at attention next to Megan.

"Button," Lili and Megan answered simultaneously.

"Come in, come in," invited Blomqvist. "All of you," he said, looking at Button with amusement.

He escorted them into a cozy living room where he had laid out some aquavit and two tulip-shaped glasses. Pressing a button on the wall that summoned his butler, he asked for a third glass.

While he was doing this Megan and Lili stood riveted before the fireplace on the far side of the room. Above it hung a large picture showing their host standing with his hand on top of the frame of an image that was immediately recognizable. It was Munch's portrait of Strindberg!

"Yes, ladies, I can see your surprise," Blomqvist said. "It's this way. Since so many people have remarked on my supposed 'uncanny' likeness to our great national writer August Strindberg over the years, I decided to commission an artist to paint me holding the Norwegian artist's portrait of him. A portrait that was, until very recently as you may know, in our city's Museum of Modern Art."

Good lord, Megan thought to herself. If Blomqvist is the one who stole Munch's painting, what unbelievable brazenness! But could anyone be *that* brash?

"Well, it is certainly true that many people do claim you are related; especially my Norwegian friends." Megan hoped it wasn't too obvious that she was fishing.

'Ah, well, if that were so, then it would be a family secret, I'm not privy to, ha ha!" Blomqvist smiled broadly as he poured and held out aquavit to them both.

"To family secrets and forever may they be kept," he toasted.

Rather reluctantly Megan and Lili clinked glasses with their host.

"Oooooh! What is this?" Blomqvist looked down at the floor behind them. They turned to see. Maya, the ginger kitten, had gone up to a frozen Button and was eagerly licking his face. Button was allowing it and obviously was beginning to enjoy it.

"That's the first time I've seen something like that," Lili purred.

They all three stood watching the unusual scene. Then they gasped. Button began licking Maya back. The spectacle and the aquavit were beginning to connect the three human witnesses.

"Let's sit down," Blomqvist invited his guests. "I want to hear a bit about you," he said, turning to Lili. He added a bit sadly: "My wife was, is Danish. From Aarhus."

"Oh, but that's where I'm from!"

Megan looked at Lili fondly. She had many happy memories of staying with her friend's parents in Aarhus on previous trips to Scandinavia.

Lili told Blomqvist briefly how she had come to America as a young girl and made her way up in the business world until she became a corporate officer in a maritime firm. She had retired early and was now enjoying traveling the world, although it meant leaving her cat Smokey behind.

The two looked at each other sympathetically. Blomqvist permitted himself to see a faint resemblance between her and his wife.

"And you, Professor Crespi? Won't you tell me a bit about yourself?"

Megan obliged, slanting her history toward Scandinavian things—her extensive travels by car with Lili over the years and her scholarship on Scandinavian painters, especially the Swedes Anders Zorn, Carl Larsson and his artist wife Karin Larsson.

"Ah. So you were able to write about a woman artist. My wife Mimmi was, is also an artist. A graphic artist. That is one reason we became so interested in collecting graphic works by Munch."

Megan was hoping Blomqvist was getting around to showing them some of the gems in his collection.

"Tell me, Professor Crespi, I know you are a respected scholar on Egon Schiele, but have you also *collected* art?"

"Why, yes I have, actually, although I don't think of myself as a collector." She had been unprepared for such a question.

"What have you collected in particular," Blomqvist pressed.

"I had a wonderful, very wise professor at Barnard College in New York, Julius Held. He advised me, when I went to Vienna for the first time, back in nineteen fifty-six, to *collect*. To go to galleries and collect what appealed to me, what I could afford. To collect periodical runs from the turn of the last century. Which I did. And to go to Vienna's great auction house, the Dorotheum..."

"*Ja*, I know it well," Blomqvist interrupted eagerly. "I've done business with them a number of times."

"Well, I did buy or bid on what I could afford and ended up with a small graphic collection of works by German Expressionists."

"Who in particular?"

Megan was becoming exasperated. She had wanted the conversation to be about him not her.

"One print each by Emil Nolde—a rare blue background one—Kirchner, Heckel, Schmidt-Rotluff, and the like, also some, again one each, by Félicien

Rops, Kandinsky, Segantini, and the Austrian Alfred Kubin. And then a few drawings Egon Schiele's sister Melanie gave me during our long friendship."

"Lucky you!" Blomqvist seemed keenly interested in the collecting activity of the scholar in front of him.

"What else?"

"Well, and then later on, when I became interested in furthering the work of women artists, I managed to acquire a nineteenth-century, life-size marble statue of Lady Godiva by Anne Whitney. It was in my house in Dallas until just recently, when I gave it to the Dallas Museum of Art in memory of my colleague Eleanor Tufts."

Megan hoped that was enough about her collection. They had come to see and discuss his Munch collection. But Blomqvist persevered.

"Tell me what else you have collected in your lifetime," he commanded, a twinkle in his eye.

Ah ha, Megan realized. He's dying to tell me about his hoverfly collection! Okay, I'll play along. Let's see what I can do in the insect category.

"Well, as a child I used to sit on the front lawn of our house in Dallas at twilight time with my brother Paolo and we would catch fireflies. Then we would put them in a bottle and light our way around the lawn. Does that qualify as a 'collection' for you?"

Blomqvist nodded encouragingly.

Megan became inspired. "And then I began collecting butterflies. Monarchs, Skippers, Queens, Buckeyes, Swallowtails..." She had run out of real names.

"And on the wall in my study at home I have a very large butterfly with beautiful, iridescent blue wings." She was telling the truth, except that the butterfly was in her breakfast room. But she wanted to sound scholarly.

"Ah! That is most likely a Blue Morpho butterfly," her host informed her enthusiastically.

Now Megan turned the tables, just as her host had hoped she would.

"And do you have anything else that you collect apart from Munch works?"

"*Ja, ja*, indeed I do." Blomqvist's eyes lit up. He leaned forward to the coffee table and pulled a large leather box toward him. He opened it dramatically and turned it toward Megan and Lili. It contained multiple small, square compartments covered by glass.

"*I collect hoverflies.*"

The two women stared at a display of what looked like very dead wasps and bees on pins. It was repulsive. They tried with all their might not to react.

"Ah! I can see your confusion. These, my ladies, are not what you think. Hoverflies are syrphidae, they have adapted to look like biting or stinging insects, but they are actually harmless. On Runmarö, the island where I have my summer house, I have a collection of over sixty thousand."

"Oh, how very interesting," Megan said lamely. "Many times then, the size of your *Munch* collection." Could she now bring this frustrating man back to the artist?

But again her host veered off track.

"And now you must tell me, if you will, about your mysterious 'disappearance.' It certainly gave you a bit of overnight television fame."

Megan frowned and looked at Lili. Should she tell him the whole story about Petersen and that dreadful Drapsmann? What if Blomqvist were in fact a member of the Norseliga? Knew them both? Wasn't this the sort of thing Norwegian and Swedish police were trying to find out about him? If the Norseliga had been responsible for stealing two Munch works in Oslo—one of them of course the now famous copy—might they not also have been responsible for the Stockholm heist? Perhaps if she told Blomqvist a few of the details but not everything, he might be more forthcoming.

"I truly do not know why, but shortly after I visited the Norwegian collector Olaf Petersen in his Bergen home, I received a text message from him urging me to come back and see something he termed 'extraordinary.' But I had commitments elsewhere and forgot to answer his text. The next thing I knew, as I was returning to my hotel after an evening lecture in Trondheim, a 'police officer' approached me saying my host had been in an accident and that I should come with him. And so I did. Once in his car I found myself his captive, had to give him my iPhone, and he zapped me with a stun gun. I was out. Later I found myself at a hospital ER but he was by my side and I could not say to the nurses or doctor that I was being kidnapped."

"*Himmel*! Why ever not?"

"Because," Megan began to tear up, "he showed me photos he had taken of Lili and Button, told me they were in the hands of an associate, and they would be killed if I said a word to anyone."

"But this is terrible!" Blomqvist's reaction seemed to be genuine. "You poor woman. But how did the situation end?"

"When we drove up to Petersen's home the police were hidden there and after my kidnapper led me to the front door he was shot dead."

"So you never learned why you were kidnapped?"

"No," Megan lied.

Just then Lili leaned over to photograph with her iPhone the touching ensemble of Maya and Button licking each other. But she leaned too far and her broken ribs pinched.

"*Av for Søren!*" she screamed.

"What happened?" Blomqvist and Megan asked at the same time.

"Oh, it's just my ribs. They suddenly hurt me. Just took me by surprise. I'm all right now."

"Oh, you poor woman!" exclaimed Blomqvist. How she reminded him of Mimmi, with her gold and white hair.

"We were in a car accident a few days ago," Megan explained.

"Ah, *that* is why your face is bruised," Blomqvist said, looking at Megan sympathetically.

There was a long silence. Only the sound of licking continued from the floor.

"You know what?" Blomqvist suddenly asked.

The two women looked at him quizzically.

"Fuck art! Let's forget Munch! Now look here. Today is Thursday. Tomorrow I'm going to take you two wonderful ladies to my island for a weekend of rest."

The two wonderful ladies looked at each other nonplussed.

"Yes, rest, that is what you need. Rest. How much longer do you two stay in Sweden?"

"Uh, through this weekend and probably a few days beyond."

"And do you have commitments?"

"No, not yet." Megan admitted.

"Then you come with me to Runmarö. I will pick you up at your hotel tomorrow morning at nine. Runmarö is only a two-hour drive and a couple of ferries from here."

"Oh, I really don't think..." Lili was cut off.

"We stay as long or as short as you like. I have a guest house with two bedrooms. And plenty of places for your Button to explore."

There was no saying no to the insistent Herr Blomqvist. He ushered his three guests out to their waiting Uber taxi.

"Until tomorrow!"

Neither Megan nor Lili heard him murmur under his breath, "Until tomorrow, my darling Mimmi."

93

The Stockholm police car parked down the street from Axel Blomqvist's house, quietly started up and followed the Uber taxi containing Megan, Lili, and Button across the city to Bentleys Hotel. The officer then reported in that all had proceeded normally; nothing of special interest.

Another vehicle had pulled away from Blomqvist's quiet street after his two lady guests had entered their taxi. It was an Opel station wagon and its occupant was Pål Enger, who had been parked far down the block. He was swearing out loud as he drove back to his hotel on Sturegatan.

So that god-damned, stuck-up bastard Blomqvist doesn't want any of my marvelous Strindberg landscapes! Yet he is the one who commissioned one from me. He told me how pleased he was with both items I painted for him. How conceited he is, wanting a portrait of himself holding Munch's portrait of his grandfather! And my city-across-the- water view a la Strindberg is a fabulous creation! Where does he get off turning me down? And he didn't even ask to see my new Strindbergs! It's clear that he looks down on Norwegians. How dare he? That stuck-up Swede.

Enger's fulminations continued. Finally he calmed down. A plan began to jell in his mind. Blomqvist simply did not deserve the two stunning works of art he had created for him.

Why, he, Pål Enger, had taken an extreme risk in procuring Munch's Strindberg portrait for him from Stockholm's Nationalmuseum. His cloaking the theft under the guise of an Albanian nationalist attack on a tour group of Serbo-Croatians right in the museum had been nothing short of genius!

But this great wrong of nonappreciation could be righted. The smug, haughty Swede who was no longer interested in what he had to offer needed to be put down. He did not deserve to live. Enger would continue to keep watch on his movements until the right moment came. Tomorrow morning at seven he would be back at his post on Östermalm.

"I can't believe we said yes!" Lili exclaimed to Megan back at Bentleys Hotel.

"Well, one benefit is that we have to get out of this hotel for the weekend anyway, until they can take us again Monday night. And we can cancel the reservation we made for two days at the Lydmar. I'll do that right now." She opened up her laptop and went to work. Lili was silent, stroking Button.

Well, I guess there's no harm in spending our weekend on a Swedish island," she said, surrendering.

"An *idyllic* Swedish island," Megan emphasized with growing enthusiasm. Having cancelled their hotel reservation she was already looking at Internet entries on the island of Runmarö.

"Listen to this. 'You may also see the unusual and beautiful Apollo butterfly on Runmarö.' Oh, that's really neat. They're the white ones with black spots on their front wings and red ones on their back wings. I've read that they are an endangered species. Wonder if Blomqvist collects them too. He only spoke of those repulsive hoverflies. Yikes! Sixty thousand of them."

"Let's hope he does also collect butterflies. What else does it say about the island?"

"Here's a photo. Look. It's taken from the island and shows hundreds of skerries around it in the archipelago. Perhaps we could buy one for ourselves?"

"No thank you. A bit far from California. I'd rather we kept on meeting at Lake Tahoe."

Megan continued reading aloud. "It says there are twenty-seven orchid species plus some 'unusual carnivorous' plants at Runmarö's freshwater Lake Silverträsk."

"Oh, scary. But wait a minute. The name Silverträsk rings a bell."

"Oh? What does the word mean?"

"Simple. It means silver swamp."

"Yeah, simple for you, Lili."

"No, not simple for me, Megan. Swamp in Danish is '*sump*,' not *träsk*. No, no, I know the name *Silverträsk* from something I've read."

"Well this Internet entry goes on to say that, oh! Guess who went pike fishing there three different summers in the eighteen-eighties?"

"That's it! *Strindberg* is the connection! He wrote a short story by that name, '*Silverträsk*.' It's about the legend that a trove of silver was hidden by the Runmarö islanders from ravaging Russians on their way to attack Stockholm. The silver has never been found and the myth is that bad luck will follow anyone who looks for it. Hm, perhaps Blomqvist found it?"

"Oh, sure. We'll ask him first thing tomorrow."

"Well, it's not completely out of the question."

"Three different summers in the eighteen-eighties," Megan mused. "Now I remember. That's when Strindberg's marriage to Siri von Essen was breaking up. It was at Runmarö. Remember the fight with Siri's friend Marie David and how Strindberg was sued for physical assault and had to pay a fine? Well it was at Runmarö. Duh. I should have recalled the Silverträsk connection with him."

"But, Megan, on the plus side, you can now say that two factors attracted Axel Blomqvist to Runmarö: hoverflies *and* his grandfather's connection to the island. That is, the grandfather he denies ever having."

"Excellent points. Now all we have to do is uncover the depth of his passion for Munch. After becoming the world's greatest private collector of Munch graphics, did he yearn for something more. Like, obviously, the portrait of his grandfather?"

"Perhaps we will make headway during our weekend at Runmarö."

"I certainly intend to try." Megan had the twinkle in her eye she always had when met with a challenge.

93

At five minutes to nine the next morning, after breakfast in the hotel courtyard and walking Button in the park, Megan and Lili were checked out and waiting for Blomqvist to appear. Megan had her dark blue pantsuit on and Lili was wearing a light beige one. Button's tail was wagging. He knew something big was coming up.

"I wonder what sort of car Blomqvist drives," Lili pondered

"Let's make a bet. I bet he drives a Mercedes-Benz."

"Okay, I bet he drives a Porsche."

The two friends grinned at each other then burst out laughing when a white Audi station wagon pulled up at the hotel curb, one of the sections of the mostly pedestrian Drottninggatan that allowed cars.

"I bet that cost him a fortune," murmured Lili.

"Perhaps something like sixty thousand?"

Like his car, Blomqvist was dressed in white down to his shoes. Smiling widely, he hurried around the front of the elegant car to his guests and loaded their small suitcases in the back.

"Button might like to sit with Maya," he suggested as Lili opted for the rear seat. A small, soft-sided cat carrier was already in place on the far side, and Lili began patting Maya. But her hand was pushed aside by Button who jumped up onto the seat. He began licking the kitten's face through the mesh and Maya started purring loudly.

Megan took the front passenger seat and they were off. At each ferry crossing Button was allowed to reconnoiter and relieve himself and at the final ferry landing he began yowling excitedly at the new odors around him. The large island was located just on the border of Stockholm's outer archipelago. It was still a fifteen minute drive through forests and past small lakes before they saw Blomqvist's two red cottages, one quite large and on a small rise of ground, the other much smaller and on the same level as the garage. It too was painted red.

"I'll let you two ladies get settled in and then why don't you come over to the main house for some lunch," suggested their host. Blomqvist carried their suitcases to the guest cottage door, then began walking to the big house.

As soon as he got out of earshot, an exasperated Megan said: "I cannot believe that in two hours' time I was not able to direct the conversation to Munch!"

"Well, you made a noble try," Lili consoled her.

"And he was incredibly adept at avoiding all my openings. You'd think that at the very least he would want to discuss his collection."

"Look at it this way. Now we are on a first-name basis. That's the beginning of trust, I should think."

"And he talked to you more than he talked to me."

"He was probably trying to make up for the fact that I was in the back with the animals."

"I don't know about that. I think he has a thing for you, Lili. Remember, his wife is Danish."

They had cleared up why Axel referred to his wife Mimmi so frequently as "was/is" She was still living but had had to be institutionalized, a victim of Alzheimer's in the worst possible way. Axel's detailed description of her slow, steady decline and his efforts to deal with it were quite touching. They were both beginning to like the lonely man. Perhaps, despite his strange insistence that he was not related to Strindberg, he was *not* connected in any way to the Munch theft. It was entirely plausible that his denial of kinship was merely meant to fend off visitors and scholars. He did appear to live the life of a hermit from what they had gathered.

"And yet," Megan protested after they had discussed the matter for the umpteenth time, "why does the man wear a moustache exactly like Strindberg's?"

"We may yet solve the mystery. Shall we go on over to the big house now?"

"Yes. Let's hope he doesn't serve us hoverflies."

They walked up the rise to the wooden house, knocked, and entered.

"Ah! There you are. Lunch is ready, ladies." They walked through the entry hall and into a quaint old kitchen with multipaneled windows. Axel waved them to a wooden table that was surrounded on two sides by a wall bench. They slid into place and looked down with pleasant surprise at the attractive lunch that had been laid out. Smoked salmon, cream cheese, capers, lemon slices, and brown bread.

"Do you like beer, Lili, Megan?"

Both answered yes. A cold beer seemed just right.

Dessert was strawberries smothered by thick white cream, and espresso coffee.

"What a satisfying meal," Lili pronounced contentedly.

Before Megan could add her praise Axel turned toward Lili and, taking her hand, said: "I am delighted to be able to serve you." His blue eyes met Lili's blue eyes and held them for several long seconds.

"And now let me take you into the living room. There is a treat in store for you there."

Megan and Lili followed Axel obediently into the living room—obviously the only room in the house other than the kitchen and the bedroom—and were surprised to see only an upright piano and bench. No chairs or coffee table. On the far side of the room where the windows were, stood a barstool. It was pulled up to a high, narrow table. On it were a small but powerful lamp, a stand magnifier, some tweezers, a bottle, small pins, and dozens of what looked like miniature match boxes but without covers.

"This is my workroom," Axel said proudly, pointing to the long table and barstool. "This is where I preserve my hoverflies. I have one-hundred-and-ninety-seven species. All found on Runmarö, all hoverflies."

Megan and Lili were silent, taking in the worktable and its contents. Finally Megan spoke.

"And where is your collection?"

Axel's eyes sparkled.

"Look around you," he commanded, waving his hand in a wide circle.

Lili looked up at the ceiling, then at the walls. At the same moment as Megan, she saw them. What she had thought was wood paneling was actually a floor to ceiling mosaic of miniscule glass-topped specimen boxes. They were all the same size: one inch wide and deep, two inches high. Once Megan and Lili realized what they were looking at it seemed as though the walls were heaving, breathing. They both fought a frantic instinct to run out of the house.

"Are they all dead?" Lili asked timorously.

"Oh yes, definitely. I kill them with cyanide once I've caught them. Then I pin them down."

To Megan's ears this sounded very much like a potential Munch robber.

"Would you like to see how I trap them?"

The women were stone silent. Their host took their silence for assent.

"This is how." Axel walked over to his worktable and picked up a large fiberglass straw covered with a mesh filter and a net. He pretended to catch a hoverfly in his net, then clapped the straw over it, sucked in quickly, then gently blew into a specimen box, as though depositing an insect.

"So this is where and how you keep your collection of over sixty thousand hoverflies," Megan finally thought to comment. She had been too stupefied to speak before.

"Yes. And there are many more in the bedroom."

Repulsed by the idea, Lili attempted to change the subject: "Will you be showing us around this marvelous island?"

"That would be my pleasure. I presume you would like to take a little nap before we go?"

"Yes!" Megan almost shouted, eager to get out of Axel's presence so they could both give vent to the hysterical laughter they were suppressing with all their might.

"Then I shall meet you by the car at three o'clock, if that meets with your approval."

As soon as they got back to their cottage they dissolved in hoots and howls of laughter. Button looked at them puzzled but pleased that his humans were happy.

▲ ▲ ▲

Before going off duty that Friday, Berndt Hammar had given his colleague in Oslo, Finne Raske, a report on Megan's movements in Stockholm.

"Things are looking good. She and her friend and dog were picked up this morning at their hotel by Blomqvist. He was driving a white Audi station wagon. Our officer followed them all the way to the ferry for Runmarö. Looks as though they are his guests out there. Probably for the weekend."

"That's great news. Seems as if she's in really good with that man."

"Yes. So we'll keep an eye out for their return to Stockholm. We've got video cameras at every ferry landing and unmarked police cars nearby. I'll have a man on it day and night."

After the conversation was over Finne Raske decided to call Erik Jensen and fill him in on his friend's latest movements.

Erik did not like what he heard. He was absolutely convinced that Blomqvist had engineered the Munch theft and he did not like at all Megan's being on a remote island over the weekend. What if the man were planning something harmful for Megan and Lili? He decided to fly to Stockholm on Sunday and be on hand for whatever might develop. Finne agreed with him. It was probably a good idea. By then Megan should have divined whether or not Blomqvist was involved in any shady business.

Watching the house since seven that morning, Pål Enger had followed Blomqvist when he left his house and drove to Bentleys Hotel. From his position on Drottninggatan he could see him drive off with three passengers—two women, and some mutt of a dog.

He certainly hadn't expected what happened next. Highway, ferries, and Runmarö! No use following them over to the big island; it would be too conspicuous to shadow them there. Much easier just to drive back to Stockholm and continue his watch on Blomqvist's house. Why, he could even call his home, pretending to be an acquaintance wanting to know if Herr Blomqvist were in town that weekend, and if not, when was he expected back? Sure. Much easier than trailing around an island that was full of flying insects and snakes. He turned his Opel Caravan around and headed back to Stockholm, whistling as he drove. That stuck-up Swede was going to get what was coming to him.

94

That first evening at Runmarö had been an evening of music. Remarking on the strange combination of piano and insects in the living room, Megan asked if Axel played. He went to the piano immediately and gave forth, slowly and carefully, with Brahms' Sonata No. 3 in F minor.

"Do either of you play?"

"I do somewhat," answered Megan. "And Lili sings."

Megan took a seat on the piano bench and Lili stood beside her, facing Axel. The two women looked at each other.

"Shall we do the H. C.?" Lili asked.

Megan nodded and played the introductory notes to Grieg's great love song set to Hans Christian Andersen's heartfelt words, *Jeg Elsker Dig—I Love You.*

Lili sang the short Danish text:

Min Tankes Tanke ene Du er vorden.
Du er mit Hjertes første Kærlighed.
Jeg elsker Dig, som Ingen her på
Jorden.
Jeg elsker Dig, jeg elsker Dig.
Jeg elsker Dig i Tid og Evighed!
Jeg elsker Dig i Tid og Evighed!

The thought of my thoughts only you
have become.
You are my heart's first love.
I love you as no one here on earth.
I love you, I love you.
I love you for time and eternity!
I love you for time and eternity!

Axel Blomqvist was overwhelmed. Not so much by the song, which was known to every Scandinavian, but by the spectacle the two women presented. Performing there in his cottage: Megan, in profile seated at the black upright in her dark blue pantsuit, and Lili, in light colored garb, facing him. Why they were exactly like Munch's lithograph of the violinist Eva Mudocci and her pianist partner Bella Edwards. Axel could not believe his eyes. Or the sudden revelation that overwhelmed him.

Lili, Eva, and Mimmi were one and the same!

The weekend passed quickly after that. Driving tours of the island during the day with stops at handicraft cottages and modest restaurants for lunch, then stops at the little grocery store near Axel's cottages, dinner and music-making back at the big cottage in the evening.

Megan and Lili had relaxed completely and were even sorry that they had to leave. They had already agreed to their host's urgent invitation to stay over Sunday night. But their Bentleys Hotel reservation had been confirmed for

Monday evening and it was time to return to Stockholm. Only in the very late afternoon, Axel had pleaded. They should enjoy the languid island pace as long as possible.

From Axel's point of view, arriving back in Stockholm in the evening was ideal for the extraordinary plan simmering in his mind. Monday evenings were the nights he was allowed full access to Strindberg's apartment. He would stop by his house upon returning to the city, grab a few nails, bring the actual Munch portrait of his grandfather down from the attic, encase it in the bubble wrap he had used on his last visit, load it in the car, then drive his wonderful guests to the Strindberg Museum. They would see it as no one except he had ever seen it. He would have them wait up in the library until he had hung the portrait, then take them down for the unique spectacle. Mimmi would be so thrilled!

At six that evening the video cameras on the ferry dock opposite the island of Runmarö recorded a white Audi station wagon driving off the ferry and heading in the direction of Stockholm. Word was immediately passed on to Stockholm's main police station and soon Berndt Hammar was advised of sudden movement in the ongoing Blomqvist case. He in turn contacted Erik Jensen, who had arrived in Stockholm the previous day and was anxiously awaiting any news concerning Megan.

"I'll pick you up at your hotel and we'll join in the surveillance once the car reaches the city," said Hammar.

Another person keenly interested in Blomqvist's movements was Pål Enger. He had telephoned Blomqvist's home on both Saturday and Sunday. His second call elicited information from the butler that Herr Blomqvist would not be coming home until Monday, probably in the early evening. Enger stationed himself on Blomqvist's street late that same morning. He was taking no chances.

An unmarked police car had picked up Blomqvist's trail right after the ferry from Runmarö landed and it followed the white Audi back to Stockholm and to the owner's house. In his Opel parked up the street, Enger watched as Blomqvist pulled into his driveway, got out with a cat carrier in his hand, spoke to someone inside the car, and then went into his house. One of the car occupants, a woman, stepped outside briefly. She lowered a small dog onto the lawn's lush grass for a pee, then lifted it up in her arms and climbed back into the car.

A few more minutes passed, then Herr Blomqvist reappeared holding a large flat object encased in bubble wrap which he gingerly loaded into the back of the station wagon. After that he drove off, heading toward the city center. Two cars discreetly followed him, Enger's and an unmarked police car. Neither was aware of the other.

A second unmarked police car joined in the surveillance as Blomqvist drove through the *Gamla Stan* and on to Drottninggatan. He stopped in front of No. 85. The Strindberg Museum. Enger's Opel and the two police cars came to a halt. The occupants watched as three people—a man and two women—plus a dog climbed out of the Audi and walked to the apartment house entrance.

Enger, Hammar, and Jensen watched as the man punched a code into the wall panel and the group entered the building. Hammar decided to call for support, specifying that a police van be parked on the nearside of the adjacent park, ready to move in at a moment's notice. He stressed that no siren was to be sounded.

Inside the apartment building Blomqvist rang for the elevator. Then he turned with a blissful smile on his face.

"Mimmi, Megan, Please enter the elevator with me. I am going to show you something magnificent."

Lili and Megan exchanged stupefied glances. The man in front of them had actually metamorphosed Lili into his wife! Blomqvist turned to them. A serious expression was on his face.

"I have previously avoided speaking to you about my Munch collection. Now I wish to. You have earned the right to see my most recent, most glorious acquisition. An acquisition I have deserved to possess for years."

The elevator stopped at the attic floor. The floor where Strindberg had kept his library and which was now part of the museum, the numerous volumes arranged just as he had left them.

Blomqvist punched a code into the panel by the locked door and opened it. He beckoned the women inside and Button followed.

"I ask that you stay here for a few minutes while I prepare things downstairs. It will be worth the wait for... *For I am indeed the grandson of August Strindberg.*"

Leaving his astonished guests, he turned on his heel, quickly descended the staircase, and hurried out to his car.

The watchers outside saw Blomqvist emerge from the building and run to the back of his station wagon. He lifted the lid and took out a bubble-wrapped object. Then he ran into the building again, neglecting to close the front door.

"Damn it! I could have shot him when he came back to his car alone," Pål Enger raged to himself out loud. He decided to wait ten more minutes. If Blomqvist did not appear again he would go after him. It was obvious to Enger what he was up to. Carrying the Munch portrait he had stolen for him right into the Strindberg Museum. The nerve!

In the lead police car Berndt Hammar had come to the same decision. Wait ten minutes, then storm the place. The women's lives could be in danger.

Out of breath from his exertions, Blomqvist took the elevator to the third floor and let himself into his grandfather's apartment. He went directly to the upright piano in the dining room and removed the bronze busts of Goethe and Schiller from the piano top. Then he took the Beethoven mask down, laying it carefully on the dining table next to the two busts. He pulled off the bubble wrap and held the canvas in front of him. Munch's fabulous portrait of Strindberg!

He reached into his pocket and produced two nails. Then he took the Goethe bust and hammered them into the wall at just the right distance from the piano top. He lifted up the canvas, held it a few inches above the two nails and then lowered it. A perfect fit. Now to get Mimmi and her friend Megan.

Leaving the apartment unlocked, he raced back up the stairs to the library. Lili was looking at a 1912 volume of the popular turn-of-the-last century German art periodical, *Die Kunst*, one of Strindberg's favorite publications. Megan was munching on a peanut butter energy bar, as they had had nothing to eat since leaving Runmarö.

Blomqvist came storming into the room, shouting, "It's ready, it's ready! Come down quickly to the apartment!"

Lili almost let the heavy volume fall out of her hands she was so astonished by the man's sudden appearance and Megan dropped her energy bar on the floor in surprise. They quickly followed their excited host down the stairs to the third floor. Button elected to stay in the library. Not that he was a bibliophile. No, he had detected the scent of his favorite treat, peanut butter.

Strindberg's grandson eagerly led the two women past the study and bedroom of the apartment and into the large dining room. He pointed to the piano wall. Megan and Lili gasped. There, hanging before them, was Munch's portrait of Strindberg! The one stolen from Stockholm's Museum of Modern Art. Open mouthed, they stared at it in silence while Blomqvist gazed proudly at them.

Ten minutes had gone by. Pål Enger could wait no longer. He wanted to get to Blomqvist indoors, not outside on the street. He ran from his car on the other side of Drottninggatan past two other parked cars and up to the Blue Tower. He pushed against the entry door. It swung open. He glanced at the sign in the small lobby. It read: *"Strindberg Museet, Våningen* 3." He started running up the stairs to the third floor.

Berndt Hammar and Erik Jensen had seen the man rush past them and enter the Blue Tower. They waited no longer. Hammar gave a terse command into his shoulder mic, then bolted toward the building, Erik close behind him. Four policemen from the other car ran after them. They stormed up the stairs to the third floor.

Pål Enger was pointing his revolver directly at Blomqvist's head. The two stunned women were ignored.

"Now, you Swedish son of a bitch, you die. You who do not appreciate my work."

He pulled the trigger and fired. But the bullet missed its mark as Officer Hammar tackled him to the ground. Within seconds Enger was in handcuffs and in the custody of the policemen.

"Oh, thank god! Just in time. Erik? How did you know?" Megan gasped out her words. Lili was too shaken to speak.

Erik answered: "Police have been following you ever since you left Runmarö. We joined in when you got to Stockholm."

"Take Enger down to the police van," Hammar commanded two of his officers. He turned to Blomqvist who stood motionless, his arms crossed protectively in front of his body, paralyzed by the events.

"And you are Axel Blomqvist," Erik identified the man. "Why have you brought these women here?"

Blomqvist gave no answer. His head drooped. He could not bring himself to speak.

Suddenly a piercing series of yelps was heard. They came from outside the apartment and they were the sound of a dog in distress.

"Oh, no! It's Button! We left him in the library." Megan ran out of the apartment and bounded up the stairs as quickly as she could. The others followed suit, even Blomqvist.

When they reached the library they saw why the dog was yelping. In his effort to reach the peanut butter bar Megan had dropped on the floor, his right front paw had been caught in a swinging panel. The peanut butter bar was caught underneath and in his efforts to reach it, Button had somehow hit a lever that released one section of the floor-to-ceiling bookcases. The panel had opened to reveal a small closet.

Megan worked gently to release Button's paw as he howled in pain. Erik strained to lift the bookcase panel up from the floor and the extra space afforded by this made it possible to extract Button's bloody paw. Megan took him in her arms and tried to soothe him.

"What's in this closet?" asked Erik after Button stopped whimpering. He borrowed a flashlight from one of the policemen and directed its beam inside the small rectangular closet. He flashed the light around the walls, then gasped.

"*Herregud*! This is incredible!"

"What, what?" they all asked.

"*There are six Munch paintings in here!*"

Silence briefly filled the room. Blomqvist had grown pale. He looked as if he might faint.

"Let's get them out and into the light," Hammar finally commanded.

The two policemen began carrying small, unframed canvasses out. They all measured, Megan judged, some fifteen-inches high and twenty-inches wide. The men began laying the painted canvasses out on the library desk, then on the floor. There were six of them.

The group devoured them in silence. Finally Megan spoke up.

"Do you realize what we have here? This is a frieze painted by Munch specifically for Strindberg. *But this is not a frieze of life, like his other ones.*"

She stooped and rearranged the paintings on the floor then did the same with the ones on the desk. Strindberg figured in each of the six artworks.

"*This is a frieze of death.*"

Erik looked at Megan's new arrangement and saw that it progressed chronologically through Strindberg's unhappy childhood and into his Bohemian years in Berlin and Paris, those turbulent years spent with Munch. The first painting showed him as a child being caned by his father while his mother looked on unmoved. The next pictured a ferocious large dog with long fangs running after him—telling reference to the author's famous fear of canines. The two paintings that followed showed him as victim in the company of seductive young girls in one, paralyzed in front of an older, authoritative woman in the other. A pair of ladies boots held his stare. The fifth painting reiterated Munch's mocking cartoon of him in the company of doctors in a hospital ward for syphilitics—brought there because of his alchemical experiments. The final image showed him in a death slump over the crowded table of a dark café. The unmistakable tulip glass of absinthe faced him on the table: at once enticing and accusatory. Deadly in its consequences.

"Oh, god, Mimmi! and this is what we could have had," moaned Blomqvist suddenly.

His outburst brought the group back to reality.

Hammar commanded his men to take the deranged man down to the van to join his would-be assassin, Enger. He called up more men and put them at Erik's disposal to help the museum director and Megan carry the paintings downstairs and load them in the lead police car.

"Which museum do you think this "frieze of death," as you so rightly put it, will end up with this treasure" Erik asked Megan worriedly as they descended the staircase. "Norway's Munch Museum or Sweden's Museum of Modern Art?"

Megan, despite her emotional and physical exhaustion, looked at her friend and smiled mischievously.

"You and Ingrid Konstrom will just have to fight it out between the two of you."

Button had heard the firmness of Megan's answer. He too could be firm. "It's time to go home," he barked. "Time to leave Scandinavia."

A very tired Megan and Lili looked at each other and smiled. They could not have agreed more.

In concert they voiced a farewell in Swedish, then Norwegian, then Danish, "till next time!"

Farväl Skandinavia tills nästa gång!
Farvel Skandinavia til neste gang!
Farvel Skandinavien til næste gang!

The story has to end somehow

Readers Guide

1. After the electricity suddenly fails, a night guard at Oslo's National Gallery cries out when she discovers that Edvard Munch's iconic painting *The Scream* is missing. What did the police find when they searched the museum?

2. Megan Crespi, retired art history professor and Munch expert, is on vacation in Scandinavia with her little Maltese dog Button and her old friend Lili Holm. She receives an urgent e-mail message to contact Erik Jensen. Who is he and what does he want? What city is Megan in when he contacts her?

3. We meet Axel Blomqvist, Sweden's greatest private collector of Munch graphics. We also meet the shady Norwegian criminal, Pål Enger. What assignment does Blomqvist have for Enger and what is the relationship of Blomqvist to Sweden's greatest author, August Strindberg?

4. Megan agrees to fly to Oslo. What is it that the police and the public do not know about the stolen Munch *The Scream*?

5. Among the heroes of Norwegian ship-building tycoon Olaf Petersen, are Edvard Munch, Edvard Grieg, and Henrik Ibsen. With whom does Petersen share these idols and what is the Norseliga?

6. What stunning fact does Megan learn about the Munch robbery when she meets with the director of Oslo's National Gallery? Megan is told about three Munch collectors who might be suspects: Olaf Petersen of Bergen, Myrtl Kildahl, fabled founder of Myrtl Cosmetics, of Oslo, and the Swede we have met before, Axel Blomqvist. What is Megan's "assignment" concerning them?

7. We learn more about the beautiful, dark-haired, mysterious Myrtl Kildahl. With which woman in Munch's work does she identify and why? What happens when Megan visits Myrtl at her home?

8. Olaf Petersen finds poignant similarities between his life and that of Munch's. What are they and what might he show the visiting American professor Crespi when she arrives in Bergen to visit him?

9. We meet Max Linde of Lübeck, cyber-savvy great-grandson of Maximilian Linde, whose four sons were portrayed by Munch in 1903. He is a neo-Nazi. What is his Internet passion? How does the Norseliga fit into his cyber plans?

10. Why does Axel Blomqvist want Pål Enger to postpone the job he had commissioned him to do? What bold plan has Enger concocted?

11. The trio—Megan, Lili, and little Button—make the seven-hour drive to Bergen. What happens on the way?

12. Max Linde's cyber snooping brings up the question of whether Myrtl Cosmetics' riveting advertisements reflect the persona of Myrtl Kildahl herself. What do the images show and how is beauty conveyed?

13. In his bunker before meeting with Megan at ten that morning, Olaf Petersen contemplates his stolen version of Munch's *The Scream* and we learn some of its history and physical vantage point. What is the back story to this iconic painting? And what links Olaf to Munch biographically?

14. In Stockholm, Axel Blomqvist communes with the Munch portrait of his grandfather. Where is the picture kept? Can it be shared?

15. After Megan's prolonged visit with the strange collector Olaf Petersen in his Bergen mansion Norsehjem, Lili and Button arrive to pick up Megan. What happens when Button gets out of the car? What important thing do they find out about Petersen's back yard?

16. Max Linde's cyber search reveals much about the individual Norseliga members and their meetings. What does he learn and what did the Norwegian neo-Nazi Anders Behring Breivik do?

17. The Crespi trio visit Grieg's home, *Troldhaugen*. What happens when Megan goes to see his composing hut?

18. In Lübeck, Max Linde has broken into the Norseliga members private e-mail. What does he do and what decision does he make concerning Petersen's home in Bergen?

19. In that home Petersen is enjoying the "green hour," sipping his absinthe. Megan's throwaway comment that "the Munch loss may not be as big a catastrophe as might be thought" irritates him beyond measure. Why? What does he decide to do about it?

20. In Oslo, Erik Jensen makes a major decision that will impact the theft of his museum's *The Scream*. Why is the decision so startling?

21. In Stockholm, Blomqvist comes to a financial agreement with the city council. What does this allow him to do?

22. Because she wants to visit the newly reopened Munch Museum in Bergen, Megan decides not to comply with Petersen's urgent request that she return to his house. What does he furiously text her and how does she treat it?

23. We meet Isabell Farlig, hired by Petersen for a special mission concerning Megan. What is it and what does "Farlig" mean in Norwegian?

24. Snorre Uflak and Megan are both in the Bergen Munch Museum. What happens when he lunges at her? Who is in the crowd that gathers afterward?

25. Olaf Petersen's gardener has been given the task of digging a six-by-six by two-foot ditch behind the bunker. Why?

26. How does Button and Lili's entering the Bergen Munch Museum result in saving Megan's life?

27. Axel Blomqvist brings Munch's Strindberg portrait to the Blue Tower on the first Monday night he has access to the building. After looking at the foyer, the study, and the bedroom, he decides upon the perfect place. This is where it belongs, this is where it has belonged for over a century! Where is the perfect place?

28. Max Linde flies into Bergen. What is his vicious plan and is he successful?

29. Megan, Lili, and Button drive to Åsgårdstrand. Why have they decided to go there and what happens on the way?

30. Axel Blomqvist in Stockholm reads about his henchman Pål Enger's new and successful profession as an artist, exhibiting fourteen of his own works—portraits in the style of Munch with sly quotations of *The Scream*—at an Oslo gallery. What intriguing idea is sparked in Blomqvist's mind?

31. After the Norseliga members have seen and reverently reacted to Munch's *The Scream* in Petersen's possession they begin to leave. But the first to leave, the Tufte brothers, run back to announce that they had all been "exposed." What is this exposure? Who is responsible?

32. Myrtl Kildahl calls Olaf Petersen after hearing Erik Jensen's surprising announcement on Norwegian TV. What has she heard and what happens to Petersen after he hears what Kildahl has to say?

33. In Åsgårdstrand, Snorre Uflaks follows the woman he believes to be Crespi into the crowd celebrating the summer solstice. What happens next?

34. Petersen calls the Norseliga members and assures them that it was not he who had sent an upsetting e-mail to them. He also tells them that it is Erik Jensen of the National Gallery who is lying. Lying about what?

35. By sheer accident Norseliga member Gustav Tufte of Skien meets the Crespi trio in front of a Munch site Megan was photographing in Åsgårdstrand. What does he invite them to do, how do they respond, and how does he feel about it later?

36. Megan pulls out from the Hotel Thon, but when she tries to back up, the brakes fail. Airbags are instantly deployed as the car hits the single tree lining the

street. Who is responsible for this apparent accident? Are Megan and Lili hurt? Is Button all right?

37. Max Linde, looking at a neo-Nazi site online, comes across the pseudonym "Brunhilde." Do you think this will play a role later in the book, and can you imagine who Brunhilde might be?

38. Pål Enger is in Stockholm at Axel Blomqvist's request. Axel commissions Pål to paint his portrait holding the stolen Munch portrait of Strindberg. What are Blomqvist's conditions and what is their agreement?

39. After a pub dinner in Åsgårdstrand the Crespi trio retire early. But Megan's iPhone rings. It is Erik Jensen. "Turn on your television," he says. "The Munch Museum's *Scream* has been stolen!" The following chapter tells us how the picture was taken. Is it similar to the method used to steal the National Gallery's version of *The Scream*? What does the theft have in common with the Louvre's Mona Lisa robbery in 1911?

40. Olaf Petersen's underworld contact has come up with a man to replace Isabell Farlig. His name is Christian Drapsmann. What does Drapsmann mean in Norwegian? What does Norseliga member Haakon Sando propose to bring to Petersen and why is it so important?

41. Back in Oslo Megan appears as one of the panelists on a television show broadcast in English to all of Scandinavia. It is a Q & A session about Norway's two Munch thefts. The National Gallery's senior curator Katarina Kopi affirms she made an exact copy of *The Scream* but intentionally left out the miniscule spire of Oslo Cathedral present in all four versions of *The Scream*. Olaf Petersen, watching in Bergen, goes crazy, rushes to the bunker and scrutinizes his *Scream* with a magnifying glass. What doers he discover?

42. The national television show Megan was on has been watched by over thirteen million viewers in Scandinavia and Germany. Six of these viewers had particular interest in the show. In addition to Olaf Petersen in Bergen, they are: Snorre Uflaks and Myrtl Kildahl in Oslo, Max Linde in Lübeck, Axel Blomqvist in Stockholm, and Benno Landau in northern Norway's harbor city of Trondheim. Why are they so affected?

43. We learn more about Myrtl Kildahl and Sophia Grimm's ancestry and why so many of Myrtl Cosmetics advertisements feature dark-haired women. What is the real reason for these advertisements?

44. Megan does research for her essay on Edvard Grieg's "lost lady loves" at the Oslo National Library. Both Snorre Uflaks and Christian Drapsmann follow her there. What happens then?

45. Gunnar Tufte, irritated by Myrtl Cosmetics' dark poster girls, decides to call her and complain. She gets furious and hangs up on him thus crystallizing her master plan for the Norseliga. Can we guess what it is?

46. Megan flies to Trondheim while Lili and Button stay in Oslo. At the end of Megan's lecture two people leave during the Q & A period: Drapsmann goes to her hotel and awaits her return; Uflaks waits behind the museum's heavy glass entry door. Do we have any premonition as to what will happen next? Who is the uniformed policeman who comes up to Megan at her hotel and how does he persuade her to get into his waiting car?

47. In the car, the "policeman" knocks Megan unconscious with a stun gun after taking her shoulder bag and cellphone from her. But not before she manages to send a text to Peter Jensen in Oslo: "help kidnapped bergen." What happens during the car trip to Bergen? Do they make it there?

48. At the office, Myrtl takes damaging evidence files concerning the other five Norseliga members' shady business practice and lays them out on her desk with instructions to Sophia to release them to the newspapers if she does not return from Bergen that evening. She leaves a second note, sealed in an envelope addressed to Sophia, simply telling her how much she loves her. What does she then remove from her safe? What does that tell us about her ominous plans?

49. After a sudden encounter with a mountain reindeer causes their car to crash, an ambulance takes Megan and Drapsmann to the ER in Førde where the attending physician wants to keep the slowly recovering Megan until late afternoon. Why doesn't Megan tell the ER staff that she has been kidnapped?

50. In Bergen, Myrtl's chauffeur picks up four Norseliga members at the Bergen airport and delivers them to Petersen's Norsehjem home. After painting their faces with the customary temporary Viking tattoos, they all go to the bunker where Petersen has them look for the steeple in the "original" Munch's *Scream*. What unthinkable event happens next?

51. Lili, Button, Erik Jensen, and police detective Finne Raske arrive at the Bergen airport and head for Petersen's home. There, Myrtl's chauffeur, on a walk with her dog Magnus, hears shots. He runs back to the house. Sven the butler hears them too and running toward the bunker encounters Myrtl, who shoots him down. She flees toward the back of the bunker and suddenly disappears. How? Raske has the police cars taken round behind the house as he is sure Megan's kidnapper will be delivering her to Norsehjem any minute. Is he right? What role does Button play in this unexpected denouement? And why does Norway have good reason to rejoice?

52. Megan, Lili, and Button arrive at Bentleys Hotel on Drottninggatan in Stockholm. The next morning they visit the Strindberg Museum just doors away and Megan notices that the Beethoven mask over the author's upright piano is crooked. We know why but she does not. Will this figure later in the plot?

53. At Stockholm's Museum of Modern Art, Megan has a delightful conference with the curator Ingrid Konstrom, who shows her the room where Munch's portrait of Strindberg was stolen. She also mischievously tells Megan what Axel

Blomqvist's "other" great collecting passion is. What is it? Does it have anything to do with Munch?

54. Megan visits Stockholm police officer Berndt Hammar who tells her about Pål Enger's having been spotted at the front door of Axel Blomqvist's home. He asks that when Megan meets Blomqvist that afternoon she be on the watch for any hint that he might be involved in the Strindberg heist. What happens when she, Lili, and Button arrive for their four o'clock appointment with Blomqvist? Whom does he think Lili looks like and why is that so meaningful for him? And what is the sudden proposal he makes to them? What makes them accept?

55. Late Monday afternoon, after a relaxing stay on the island of Runmarö, Blomqvist drives the Crespi trio back to Stockholm. Once there he takes them, by way of a short stop at his home to pick up a large flat package protected by bubble wrap, to the Strindberg Museum. His hefty financial deal with the city council allows him entry with a private key code on Monday evenings after the museum is closed to the public. He takes the Crespi trio up to Strindberg's library on the top floor and leaves them there while he goes down to the writer's apartment and hangs Munch's portrait of Strindberg. Where exactly does he hang it?. Blomqvist then returns to his guests and brings them down and into the apartment. Megan and Lili behold the portrait in place and are speechless. A series of sudden events then takes place that results in the arrest of both Pål Enger and Axel Blomqvist. What are these events? And how does Button play a role in the startling discovery that is made? A discovery that no one could have imagined and which will make either Sweden or Norway—they will have to fight it out—very happy?